"Carmen Peone offers a un contemporary romance."
—Shanna Hatfield, *USA Today* bestselling author

"Carmen Peone has penned another winner in *Captured Secrets*. She captures a sweet romance inside a fast-paced story that twists and turns like a young colt enjoying a spring meadow. It's a page-turner! Best of all, *Captured Secrets* is the first in a trilogy, so there'll be more of Sydney and Trey's efforts to uncover the secrets of the guest ranch they are trying to save and discover how love conquers the unknown."
—Jane Kirkpatrick, award-winning author of *Beneath the Bending Skies*

"Sydney Moomaw is a tough cookie. She's internalized past trauma so she can be strong for everyone else. Life keeps tossing her obstacles, but Sydney is surrounded by faith, friends, and family."
—Linda Ulleseit, award-winning author of *The Aloha Spirit*

"Peone portrays the complications of abuse with a deft hand. She's crafted a strong, triumphant heroine and a hero who will capture your heart. Readers will cheer every mile of their difficult journey to love."
—Pam Nowak, award-winning historical romance author

"Brimming with suspense and adventure, *Captured Secrets* is a love story I'll not soon forget. An engrossing tale with all the twists and turns that make a contemporary Western so hard to put down."
—Debra Whiting Alexander, award-winning author of *Zetty*

"*Captured Secrets* is a walk on fragile ground. Its depiction of love, pain, and vulnerability is what happens when the outside world calls into question the thing closest to our hearts: family. This incredible story of 'for better or worse' will leave you breathless by the end!"
—K. S. Jones, award-winning author of *Change of Fortune*

"In the midst of family tragedy and sorrow, Sydney finds help from an unexpected source and learns, with God, love heals all. Carmen Peone has written a Western love story that will touch the heart."
—Linda Wommack, award-winning author and historian

"A wonderful read from Carmen Peone again. Horses, love, lessons in trust, and great characters make this a hard-to-put-down story!"
—Deanna Dickinson McCall, award-winning writer and poet

"Carmen Peone writes the West with grit, grace, and an authentic voice."
—Dalyn Weller, author of
The Rancher's Surprise Second Chance

"Carmen Peone is a master at creating characters so real, lovable, and witty, you think of them long after the last page. This book is a roller coaster ride of emotions, heartbreak, bravery, and laughter. A well-written, entertaining story full of surprises and triumph that feels like 'coming home.'"
—B. K. Froman, award-winning author of Hope and Hometown series, *Hardly Any Shooting Stars Left*

"Sydney Moomaw battles demons from her past, unable to accept the love that is in her presence. A devastating loss creates more stress as she strives to keep her family's ranch intact while helping the daughter she gave up. Only with God's guidance can she realize there is always hope and a way forward. A story of self-acceptance and second chances, and finding an internal strength Sydney never knew she had."
—Natalie Bright, author of the Wild Cow Ranch series

"A dramatic story of loss and violence, but also a journey about tender love and a woman's strength and independent spirit. I thoroughly enjoyed this story, expertly woven by Carmen Peone, and look forward to more of this series."
—Denise F. McAllister, coauthor of the Wild Cow Ranch series and freelance editor

"Weaving the best elements of contemporary fiction, including a tender love story and one woman's recovery from profound loss and abuse, Carmen Peone writes with a sure sense of time and place. She brings us into a life she knows and understands with remarkable detail, but even more, into the darkest and brightest corners of the human heart. A powerful read that boils into an unstoppable page-turner."

—Corinne Joy Brown, award-winning author of *Hidden Star*

"*Captured Secrets* by Carmen Peone is a very well-written novel. The author's vast personal knowledge of Native Americans, reservation life, horses, and ranching are spot on in this story. It is a wonderful story of doubt, abuse, sacrifice, loss, and love and coming out on the other side better for it. The author brings a brand-new twist to the familiar genre of a woman in trouble saved by a man, which I found most educational and entertaining. The story moves along smoothly from start to finish. A page-turner that was easy to get immersed in."

—Roni McFadden, award-winning author of
The Longest Trail

"True to her family's Native American heritage, Peone draws on personal tragedy to create an award-worthy novel. Filled with raw emotion, *Captured Secrets* is one woman's story of healing and coming to terms with a past filled with physical and emotional pain. With the help of family and friends, she learns to trust in one man who has captured her heart and find *real* love and complete faith in Creator."

—Deborah Swenson, award-winning author of
Till My Last Breath

"Carmen Peone writes about reservation life and the blessings of community and family life. She writes about abuse, death, and trust. Her writing keeps the reader engaged and wanting to continue reading until the end yet wanting more and hoping for a series from this first book. I will be recommending this book to all mystery, contemporary romance, and inspirational romance readers."

—Judi Wutzke, owner/manager ...and BOOKS, too!

"*Captured Secrets* entertains, inspires, and challenges its readers through a well-crafted tale of tragedy and triumph wrapped in suspense, hope, and Western gumption. Carmen Peone's debut Western romance has it all."

—P. J. Gover, award-winning writer and author of
Desert Mountain Conspiracy

CAPTURED SECRETS

A Novel

Book 1 of the Seven Tine Ranch series

CARMEN PEONE

BIRMINGHAM, ALABAMA

Captured Secrets

Iron Stream Fiction
An imprint of Iron Stream Media
100 Missionary Ridge
Birmingham, AL 35242
IronStreamMedia.com

Library of Congress Control Number: 2022942123

Cover design by For the Muse Designs
Author photo by Laura Sigmund Photography

ISBN: 978-1-64526-361-6 (paperback)
ISBN: 978-1-64526-360-9 (eBook)
1 2 3 4 5—27 26 25 24 23

To Collette Jo, may you find peace in heaven.

God is our refuge and strength, an ever-present help in trouble.
—Psalm 46:1

CHAPTER 1

Nespelem, Washington, Colville Confederated Reservation
Tuesday, June 13

Cooper Payne's words clawed at Sydney Moomaw. *Leave me and I'll kill you.* His seductive smile in the photo she held made her shudder. Her hands trembled as she put a match to the snapshot, let it burn a few seconds, and flicked it into the Seven Tine Guest Ranch's rustic stone fireplace. "Worthless pig!"

His curly blond hair and indigo eyes had tricked her once. Never again. She'd left his hide at the courthouse years ago—makeup covered her bruises while handcuffs bound his wrists.

"Who are you talking about?" Glenda Williams, Sydney's older sister, asked.

"Cooper. I found a photo of him last night stuck to the pages of my old college marketing binder." Sydney placed the lighter on the wooden mantel, then peered absently out the bay windows of the lodge's great room. When he got out of jail, would Cooper try to find her? Come after her again?

"It's about time you tell Mom and Dad. Besides, I'm tired of keeping your secrets."

The Moomaws were about to leave for an Alaska cruise. "They don't need to know." The marriage had only lasted about six months. The first month seemed great at the time, partying with her friend Jaycee and his rodeo buddies. Until Cooper hooked up with the wrong crowd and started using drugs. Hard drugs. The kind that led to fiery outbursts and broken ribs.

"If you don't say something when they come back, I will."

"It's my life. My business—"

"Oh, sheesh. It's time to grow up and tell the truth. We're not little girls anymore. Would you rather them hear about your past from someone else?" Glenda headed for the ranch office, weaving through a handful of guests lingering in the dining area.

The heels of Glenda's western boots clicking on the wooden floorboards grated on Sydney's nerves. She hated her sister's constant harping. Always telling her what to do and how. Besides, her parents didn't need the added strain. Running the guest ranch was stressful enough.

"We're ready, Syd," her mother, Jennie Moomaw, called from the massive, wooden entryway. "Can you check in the new guests? They'll be here anytime. And Glenda, did you find my favorite sweater?"

Sydney wiped her hands on her jeans and went to help her mom, passing through the foyer lined with weathered boots in various colors and sizes, a few coiled ropes hanging from hooks, and a rectangular information table.

"I'll get this for you." She rolled her mom's suitcase to the brown three-quarter-ton pickup and hefted it onto the bed. With light Monday traffic, her folks were expected to make good timing to the Spokane airport. "Don't worry, Mom, I'll take care of everything while you and Daddy are sipping drinks from the ship's deck."

Glenda caught up to them at the truck, a light green sweater and cell phone in hand. "How about a family photo?"

"That would be lovely, dear," Jennie said before Sydney could stop her. She gathered her husband and two daughters in front of the ranch steps like a hen collecting her chicks, then glanced around. "Where's Robert?"

"He's catching horses for my riding lessons this morning," Sydney answered. Robert Elliot was Sydney and Glenda's half brother and ranch foreman. They shared the same father but didn't know it until recently. "He told me he'd said goodbye last night."

"Darn. I wanted him in the photo." Jennie let out a heavy sigh.

"Next time. We need to get you guys on the road." Sydney placed an arm around her mother's waist.

Glenda attached a selfie stick to her phone and snapped a couple of photos. "This should do." She hugged her folks. "Safe travels, and for once, let loose and have a little fun."

Jennie laughed, hugged Sydney, and climbed into the pickup. "We'll be back before you know it."

"Get some rest, Mom." Sydney covered her mother's icy hand with hers. "And don't let Dad stuff himself," she teased as she shut the door.

For months now, she'd noticed something wrong with her mom but couldn't pinpoint it. Based on the way Jennie had been raised, she kept most personal matters to herself. Sydney prayed this trip would revive her. Get her back on her feet.

Jennie nodded, her weathered face etched in deep creases. "Wish me luck!"

Standing outside the pickup, Lester Moomaw stared at the weathered horse barn—a Ponderosa pine–covered knoll its backdrop. A tricolored Australian shepherd with reddish-brown eyebrows sat beside him. Caliber's shaggy tail stirred the dirt.

Sydney joined her bow-legged father and hugged him from behind. He always wore the same thing, dusty black cowboy boots and faded blue jeans with long shirtsleeves buttoned at the wrists. Cropped hair told he was a veteran. A faded gold ring circled his left finger. He carried a multi-tool in a holster on his hip.

"The colt's going to make it, ya know." She stood on her tiptoes and kissed his balding head. "Remember to leave your tools in the truck. Airport security might cuff ya." She winked at him.

He gave her a small smile and nodded, patted his dog for a long moment, and slipped behind the wheel.

"We'll take care of Caliber too. Don't worry, Daddy, we got this."

"I know you do." Lester rubbed her hand as it rested on the door.

Excited for her parents' long-earned vacation, she waved goodbye, watching the dust swirl as the truck bounced down their half-mile driveway. She was thankful so many people had pitched in to help pay for the anniversary gift.

Sydney rubbed the back of her neck as a sharp pain inched its way up her head, settling on her forehead. She shuffled to the office, pinching the bridge of her nose, and fished in her floral Western-tooled purse for migraine medication. Her fingers found a plastic box. She set a tiny tablet on her tongue, then went to the lodge's coffee bar and poured a strong cup of joe to wash away the residual, bitter taste. Her head spun for several minutes, which was normal for her.

Once she caught her balance, she settled her sunglasses on her nose and plucked her Stetson off the rack. The thermometer on the covered porch read sixty-five degrees, and it was only ten. Awesome. Another scorcher in the forecast, which was unusual for this time of year. With an oncoming migraine, morning riding lessons would be brutal, but the smiles on the young guests' faces would help her endure the pain.

"Robert says he's got the horses saddled and tied to the hitching post for you," Glenda said as she leaned against the doorjamb. After studying her for a moment, she added, "Maybe you need to cancel your riding lessons."

Good grief. Enough already. "I'm fine." Sydney waved her sister's offer away.

"He said one little girl has to change into jeans. She came in a frilly skirt." Glenda folded her arms over her chest. "You sure you don't want me to have him take over the lesson for you? I can holler at him on my way out."

"No. I got it." *If only she'd go back to work.* "Shoot, I need to check on the foal first."

"Oh, he also said there's a busted pipe in the north field that's flooding the place." Glenda patted the door frame. "Well, then, I better get back to council chambers." She disappeared around a corner.

Good grief. Busted pipes, vet bills, feed bills—what next?

Sydney slinked to the barn, praying her head would stop pounding. Once at the colt's stall, she gripped the handle to steady herself, then slid the door open. The vet had assured the family the blue roan would survive. Twister lay in the straw, eyes closed, his plume of a tail swatting at a pesky fly. Dropping to the fresh-smelling straw, she held gentle pressure to his soft side. "You have to make it," she whispered. Heat from his bony ribs penetrated the skin on her palm and shot right to her heart.

She backed into the aisle and shut the door, grimacing with every squeak. She called the vet and left a message on his voice mail, hoping he could come by later in the day and check on the foal again. The ranch didn't need more vet bills, but with an exceptional line like Blue Valentine, she could not afford a death as he could potentially be a huge moneymaker. God knew the ranch needed the added income. There were too many bills and not enough cash coming in. Cattle prices had been inflated for too long. Plus, her heart would crack in two if anything happened to the little guy.

"Ready?" Robert held his charcoal eyes on her, his brows furrowed. They matched his clean-cut hair. "You OK?"

Sydney nodded. "My meds will kick in soon." Robert held out reins attached to her mare, Cyan, a blue roan. She sighed and took hold of the leather straps. "We have to keep track of his temperature and keep the stall clean. We also need to watch for dehydration and make sure he's eating."

"I'll let the others know so we can all keep an eye on him." He wiped his hands on his ragged jeans.

"Let's make sure we initial when the stall is cleaned and his temp is checked." She tapped a clipboard hanging from a nail on the wall outside his stall. "There's a spot on his chart to jot things down."

"Don't worry, he's a fighter."

"Hope so." She gave him a small smile, holding back hot tears, and patted Cyan on the neck. Robert's coming to live with them when he was nine—after his mother had passed from cancer—had been a huge gift from Creator. He'd always pulled his weight. "Good luck with the pipes."

"I'll need it," he said over his shoulder. He jumped into his Toyota Tacoma and sped off, dirt spraying from behind the tires.

As she led her mare from the barn, Sydney squinted and pulled her hat down to shade the sun, but she pasted on a smile. "You guys ready?"

With squeals of delight, five elementary-aged children surrounded her. She winced. "Let's keep our voices low today, all right?"

Their eager faces made her wonder what the daughter she'd given up at birth looked like. She'd be sixteen by now. Would she be a mix of her and Cooper? Or would she resemble Sydney? Where did she live? Was she safe? Sydney could only hope. She considered what her interests might be: sports, music, horses.

She vowed to make sure Cooper never found out about her.

During the next hour, she taught the kids how to ride with balance and control, using their legs, seat, and reins. How wonderful it would have been to have taught her daughter.

She shoved the thoughts away and concentrated on the students in the arena. When their lesson was finished, she tied the horses to hitching posts for a rest between rides, then faced the little ones again. "Who wants ice cream?"

"I do! I do!"

Without a backward look, they ran to the lodge, shouting what flavors they wanted.

Laughing, Sydney stopped to cool off at a spigot circled by grass and colorful flowers. The migraine pill made her mouth dry as sagebrush. Sweat poured down her back. Weak-kneed, she flipped up the spigot handle and sipped cool water, then rinsed her head and neck.

The clock on her phone indicated she'd have time to work on her new marketing plan before the vet arrived to check on Twister. The new ad proofs of the horses she'd been working on for the last few weeks made her smile.

Sydney visited with a few guests on the covered porch before grabbing a cup of vanilla-flavored coffee and going to the office. The other guests were either fishing, on a guided trail ride, or sightseeing. The area was rich in history, including the Grand Coulee Dam, which was south of Nespelem.

She settled in the leather chair, excited to start a fresh marketing project she'd planned to surprise her folks with upon their return. Suffocating heat would soon hover in the lodge office. She added a note on a lengthy list of repairs to fix the air conditioner. Her headache lingering to the point of annoyance, she tried to concentrate on her ad proofs.

When satisfied with her selections, she inserted the winning proofs into a folder. "These should prove I can handle things myself." A tattered manila envelope from Stockton Life Insurance captured her interest. She'd opened it and tugged the contents partway out when a Tribal Police SUV caught her attention from outside the window. Sydney slipped the papers back inside their envelope and tossed them on the desk.

The vehicle parked in front of the lodge, and Chuck Williams, her brother-in-law, got out. The look on his face made Sydney's chest tighten. She went to meet him outside, stopping on the porch's landing. He strode toward her, shoulders drooping. Holding on to the railing, she crept down a couple of steps, shading the sun from her eyes with her hand. "Why the long face?"

"Syd," he said, a hitch in his voice. He met her on the steps. "Your parents have been killed in an accident."

CHAPTER 2

W hat?" Sydney covered her mouth with a shaky hand.
"They should be in the air. Are you sure?" She
studied the sky as if she could see the plane flying overhead.
"Where's Glenda?"

"She's headed to the hospital. She wanted me to come
get you and meet her there."

"I can't go. Can't see them like that." Sydney shook her
head. "What happened?"

"A car sped out of Spring Canyon and struck their truck."
He wiped a tear from his eye with his husky hand and cleared
his throat. "An EMT unit happened to be coming back
from another accident and was on the scene right after it
happened. There was nothing they could do. The truck was so
old, it had no airbags. It was . . ." He pressed his lips together
as though in deep thought. "I'm so sorry, Syd."

She eased down onto the porch steps, her knees weak.
Caliber trotted over from the barn and rested next to her,
then nosed her hand. She bent over and cradled his head in
her arms. "I'm glad you're here." The words squeaked from
her mouth. She let go of the dog and wrapped her arms
around herself. "Was it a teen driver? They always scare me,
roaring out of there . . ."

He nodded. "Yeah. The female driver's in critical condition.
Two others are banged up pretty bad, but they'll live."

Sydney's chest tightened as she looked at the empty
driveway. "Always figured someone would get hurt . . ." A

wave of dizziness came over her. "I never imagined them both going at the same time. This soon. I didn't even give my dad a proper hug before they left. You know—a short vacation—back home before long." Her body shook. She gripped herself tighter and buried her face in her hands, allowing tears to flow.

How could this have happened? A sob escaped as she exhaled. "I should have never pressured them to go. They resisted from the start. It's like they knew something bad would happen."

"It's not your fault," Chuck said. "We all urged them to go. They needed time off. They wore themselves down running this place. You know they needed the trip, Syd."

She sniffed and wiped her face with her shirt. "Yeah, they may have needed the trip, but look where persistence landed them." She wrung her hands. "I'll never forgive myself."

Chuck knelt in front of her. "Let me take you to the hospital. You and Glenda need to put your differences aside. C'mon, you two need each other." He offered her his handkerchief.

Sydney blew her nose and stood, legs quivering. She pressed the back of a hand against her mouth. Like she told him, there was no way she could see her folks in that condition. She definitely couldn't handle Glenda's snarkiness right now.

"There's too much to do here. We have guests coming. It's a full house. I'll let you deal with her." She swallowed her fear and grief down her tight throat. "We have horses to saddle, the vet's coming, rooms need to be changed, dinner cooked."

"Syd, you don't have to do this alone," Chuck said. "You have Mandie to cook and help clean—"

"Yeah, but she's eight-months pregnant. She needs help herself. And, my blasted housekeeper's a no-show."

"I'll call Pam. She's your best friend. You know she'll come."

"Maybe. I think she mentioned something about company showing up." Her lungs strained to draw in ample oxygen, tears blurring her dusty boots. "I need to get things done. Have Glenda call me later." Sydney clambered to the office, Caliber following close behind. She texted Robert to come meet her there.

Between sobs, she sorted through a notebook of guests leaving by noon and new arrivals coming at four. Her parents refused to use the internet, making Sydney angrier as she thumbed through worn pages. With a pregnant cook and diminished crew, she did need Pam's help. Her mind unwilling to concentrate, she pushed back from her desk and picked up a framed photo of her parents. "Why now . . . ?" She hugged the frame and wept.

The sound of Chuck's tribal rig faded, and minutes later a vehicle roared up and stopped within view of the office window. Sydney wiped her face with a tissue and went outside, covering her eyes with sunglasses. Dust from a familiar black Jeep swirled in the dry air. She waved it from her face. How could Pam have gotten here so quickly?

Sydney smiled, telling herself she could make it through the day.

Pam Gibbs, a leggy brunette with golden highlights, got out of the rig and raced toward the porch, leaving her husband, Jim, and a man Sydney didn't know lingering at the Jeep. "Oh, Syd . . ."

"Pam!" They met at the bottom of the stairs and embraced. "How'd you get here so fast?"

"We just saw Chuck. He told us. I'm so sorry to hear about your folks."

For a long moment, Sydney held on to Pam and cried, feeling her friend's tears dampen her own shoulder.

"I know the timing is terrible, but Jim has a buddy who wants to stay here." Pam rubbed Sydney's back. "What can I do to help?"

Sydney let go and sniffed. "I don't know. Guests are on their way. My housekeeper didn't show up. The vet should be here shortly. . . . There's so much to do."

"Put us to work." Pam turned to Jim, who looked Special Forces—medium height, bulging muscles, crew cut. Behind him stood another guy with a camera bag in hand, dressed in creased jeans, tennis shoes, and a ball cap. "Let's get inside and figure this out. We'll help you through this, sweetie."

Sydney's eyes burned.

Jim gave her a hug and gestured to his friend. "This is my college buddy, Trey Hardy. He's here for a little R and R."

"Sorry for your loss." Trey stood about six foot two, his deep-set hazel-green eyes showering her with compassion.

Sydney pursed her lips to keep from crying. "Thanks." She wanted to give him a proper welcome but couldn't seem to get the right words out of her mouth. So she changed the subject instead. "I'm assuming by your camera bag you plan on taking photos?"

"Yeah, he's a world-famous photographer. *On vacation.*" Pam arched a brow at Trey, then crooked her finger to get the men to follow her. She linked arms with Sydney and escorted her up the lodge steps under the triangular portico. "You'll like this guy, Syd. He's a true gentleman. Jim met him at a Bible study group in college. They've been good friends ever since. Now, what room do you want Trey in? Do I need to clean it? What do you want me to do?"

Trey put his camera bag on a round dinner table. "Listen, you don't have to worry about me. I can stay somewhere else or—"

"No. You're fine," Sydney said. Guest bookings were a huge chunk of the ranch's income. She couldn't afford cancellations. Not now. She swallowed the emotions creeping up her tight throat. To break down in front of a guest? Never. Her parents had drilled professionalism into her, no matter the circumstances. "If you and Jim want to scope out different places for photoshoots go ahead. I'll get Pam lined out."

Jim nodded and set Trey's luggage aside, then the men went outside, Trey carrying his camera case. Thank goodness Jim knew her well enough to let her and Pam have a few minutes alone.

Pam watched them leave. "That one's a workaholic who doesn't know how to rest. He's a fancy photographer from Arizona. It took years for Jim to talk him into coming." She studied Sydney. "Are you all right?"

"I'm fighting a headache. I better find my meds and see what rooms are open. You want to check on Mandie?" A very pregnant Mandie Louie cooked for the ranch guests. "But don't say anything about my parents. Let me tell her."

"I won't."

After taking more medication, Sydney made her way to the modest office, pulled the shades, put on a Luther Vandross CD, and sank onto her desk chair in front of a wall-to-wall bookcase. Although Pam would be a huge help, Sydney would rather be a turtle in a shell. Robert should have been here by now. Had he gotten her text? She picked up her cell and checked for a reply. There wasn't one.

She started to call Glenda, her finger hovering over the green phone icon, but tossed her cell on the desk instead. Picked it back up and punched in her mom's number. As her mother's sweet voice greeted the call, she hunched over and sobbed, shoulders shaking.

Once every tear squeezed from her eyes, she leaned back. An insurance envelope peeking from a pile of mail snagged her curiosity. She slid out the letter and gasped. "Canceled due to nonpayment."

"This can't be right!" How could they have allowed the life insurance policy to lapse? She slammed the letter on the desk. Was the ranch in that much debt they couldn't pay the bill? She fished out a stack of invoices from the desk drawer, wishing her mother had agreed to use accounting software, and organized them into piles: feed bills, vet bills, fencing supplies . . . the stacks expanding.

Pam poked her head into the office. "How's it going in here?"

"Not good. At all." The paper in her hand shook.

Pam joined her by the desk. "What's going on?"

"Check this out." Sydney handed her the insurance letter. "And look at these stacks of bills. I had no idea they were so behind."

"This isn't like them. What do you think's going on?"

"I don't have a clue."

"Does Glenda know?"

"I doubt it. She has no interest in the ranch."

Pam gave the notice back to her. "What are you going to do?"

"Other than pray, I have no idea."

"You know you're going to have to tell her. Have you even talked to her yet?"

"Not about this mess. I'm not ready to. I need to figure it out first. I have a feeling she's going to push to sell." Sydney nabbed a tissue and blew her nose. "I can't let her take this away from me, Pam. It's my life. It's all I've got."

"Is that why you stayed here? To avoid your sister?"

"It's not the only reason." She picked up a framed photo of her parents and stroked the image of her mother's face with her finger. "I can't see them like . . ." She pressed the frame to her chest. "I want to remember them walking out this morning. Smiles on their faces."

"I understand." Pam offered a sympathetic smile. "How about you tell me what needs to be done—who's coming in today, how Trey can help—and we'll get things ready? Jim has family showing up soon and needs to leave, but he can come back tomorrow."

She handed Pam a folder. "Here are today's arrivals. If you can take care of those, I'll check on the wranglers and let everyone know what's going on. And Trey is a guest. He doesn't need to help."

"He'll help, trust me. I'll take care of incoming guests, see what he can do, and clean rooms." Pam perused the guest list. "How about I stay with you tonight? Looks like you're booked solid."

"Yes, please." Having her longtime friend around to take charge lightened her heavy load. Especially if Glenda showed up, which no doubt would happen. Sydney would need a voice of reason to keep her calm.

She kissed the glass covering her parents' image, a seal on a promise. "I don't know how, but I'll do whatever it takes to keep Glenda's hands off the ranch. I'll fight for this place no matter what."

"I know your sister can be hardheaded," Pam said, "but she's not a monster. Sweetie, I'm confident you two will work this out."

And they would. Just not today. Sydney replaced the photo. "Now what?"

"We can figure out more tonight." Pam reached across the desk and took Sydney's hand. "Are you going to be OK?"

"As long as I stay busy. There'll be plenty of time to grieve after we bury them." So far this year, there'd been ten deaths on the rez, and she felt numb. She'd never get used to losing loved ones. Exhaustion from the two-to-three-day funeral services consumed her. The suicides, alcohol- and drug-related deaths, elder deaths—each one had taken its toll.

Clutching the file folder, Pam gave her a hug then left her alone.

Out the window, Chad and Rich, the other two ranch hands, seemed to be in deep conversation. Besides regular ranch duties, Rich, tall and wispy, stood as head wrangler and led most of the trail rides, while Chad, shorter and stocky with trademark sideburns, started colts. She rose to gather her crew. Maybe they'd know where Robert went.

CHAPTER 3

Trey leaned against the horse corral, admiring the cottonwood trees edging the back fence of the mare and foal pen. To his left, a paddock of horses held a draft cross. Did she raise bucking horses too?

"I don't think I should stay." He couldn't think of one reason why. Not even for the photoshoot for hire from one of the top cowboy magazines in the nation. There had to be other ranches he could visit.

"I think you should," Jim answered. "You need the vacation, man. You're always on the go. Besides, Sydney's tougher than most women. Heck, the women around here are tougher than most men. She'll be fine. But she does need our support and prayers."

"Prayer is right." God would be the only one who could pull her through the deaths of both of her parents while she ran a guest ranch. Hopefully, she had siblings to help.

"Folks around here amaze me." Jim set a foot on the bottom fence pole. "They're hardy people who have survived generations of persecution. In the middle of the Termination Era, 1956, Senator Henry Jackson tried to get rid of this rez. Tribal leader Lucy Covington waged war against it. She even created a newspaper called *Our Heritage* to get members involved to help preserve it. Syd has Lucy's drive and determination. I'm not saying she'll bounce right back. But I will say she's one tough gal who'll not only survive this but will come out tougher."

"'What doesn't kill us makes us stronger,' huh?" What would losing both of his parents at the same time be like? His chest tightened. If he decided to stay, he'd get his photos and get out.

"You're about to get a crash course on how folks around here deal with life," Jim told him. "It's a lot different on the rez. They're tough around here because they've had to be. The first thing you'll learn is Syd doesn't like to show emotion. She prefers to work through her circumstances by tending to ranch chores and working horses. It's just her way."

A filly spun around, reared, and bolted off toward another youngster. Is that how Sydney felt inside but didn't know how to express it? He had a sister who acted the same way and didn't understand her either.

Trey took out his camera and snapped a few photos of the horses. "You think I should stick around, huh?" He didn't want to. But this place, tucked in a nest of its own surrounded by hills and trees and water, would be a nice place to investigate. On horseback would be even better.

He missed ranch life. Growing up, he'd looked forward to riding horses and chasing cows every day but hated the long hours with the pressure of school. And yeah, a thread of resentment laced through him because his dad had refused to let him play sports. "Work hard and long," his pop's motto. His thoughts shifted back to the horses. This place seemed perfect for the magazine he freelanced for.

Jim shifted his feet on the fence rung. "Yeah, you'll be a good distraction for her. And knowing you, you won't be able to keep away from the livestock. Ranching's in your blood, brother, whether you want to admit it or not."

"I suppose you're right." A curious mare plodded close enough for Trey to take in her fresh, earthy scent. He snapped a close-up of her eye, then stroked her gritty, gray hair.

Jim pushed away from the fence. "Let's head inside and get you squared away. Pam and I can't stay much longer. My aunt and uncle are on their way to the house. They're coming in from Wyoming. I haven't seen 'em in twenty years."

"I bet you're excited." Trey secured his camera back in its padded bag.

"I am. But they're only staying overnight. They're hooking up with coastal friends to check out the San Juan Islands. You'd love it over there."

"I'll keep that in mind." Trey followed him to the lodge. Going to the islands with Jim's family sounded a lot more relaxing.

A well-maintained flower garden lined the base of the sixteen-thousand-square-foot log lodge towering over them. Its rock column bases held up the triangular portico. On a porch sat a rocker and a wooden bench with carved horse heads on either end.

Inside the spacious lodge, Pendleton blankets draped the backs of leather furniture by the bay windows and wagon-wheel lights hung over pine tables in the dining area. A mounted elk head hung above the stone hearth. On the other walls, a handful of stuffed deer and moose heads stared down at everyone through glassy eyes. Wafting aromas of fried chicken and chocolate floated through the great room. An elderly couple manipulated a puzzle on one of the tables.

Pam met them at the door. "There you are." She glanced at her watch and regarded Jim. "You better get going, honey. I'm staying the night here. Can you come back tomorrow? Bring me clean clothes and help out?"

"You know I can." He kissed his wife and said his goodbyes before leaving.

Pam turned to Sydney and Trey. "I'm going to find Mandie and see what's next on her list. Trey, you're in the trout room." The heels of her sandals clicked on the floor as she scurried to the kitchen, calling over her shoulder, "Hey Syd, don't hesitate to put him to work."

Sydney turned a deep shade of red, her gaze dropping to the rustic wooden floor. "Best show you to your room."

Yep. She'd mastered stuffing her emotions. Most women would have been a blubbering mess.

Trey grabbed his bags and followed her up the curved staircase leading to the southwest wing of the lodge.

"How long you plan to stay?"

"I'm not sure. If Jim has it his way, a week. But I'm thinking a night. Two at the most." After recently returning from covering the aftermath of a hurricane in Haiti, the last thing he wanted to be around was more sorrow.

CHAPTER 4

A *night? Two at the most?* How could Sydney convince him to stay longer? His remaining a week would cover today's vet bill and help with employee wages.

They stopped in front of the room with a sign over the door that read, "Schoolthum."

"And what does *school . . . lth . . . um* mean?"

Sydney repeated it correctly. The word rolled off her tongue like a fragrant poem. She forced herself to smile. "It's Arrow Lakes, or Sinixt, and means "bull trout." My mom is—was—Nimi'ipuu, or Nez Perce, and my father was Arrow Lakes." She choked out the words, turned away, and wiped her eyes.

"I assume you speak the language then?"

"Yeah. Both Sinixt and Nimi'ipuu, which means the 'real people' or 'we the people.'"

Trey stepped into the trout-themed room and set his bags on the bed. "Let me know how I can help."

"Thanks, but you're a guest. And what I gather, one who needs a vacation." She tried to sound upbeat. "How 'bout you settle in, and I'll catch up with you later. Feel free to roam around and take as many photos as you need."

"Will do." He lowered his gaze, then looked into her eyes. "And again, I'm so sorry for your loss."

Sydney nodded briefly. She hated pity. And that's what filled his tone.

As she closed the door, she could hear his voice drifting from the other side. Was he praying? For her? *Oh, wow. How . . . thoughtful.* Guilt over her pity-hating attitude scolded her.

She made her way down the steps to Caliber, trotting toward her with his bushy tail wagging. Poor guy must be looking for her dad as they'd never been separated before. Wherever Lester went, Caliber trailed by his side.

The smell of baked beans and greasy hamburgers made her stomach roil. After grabbing an ice pack from the freezer, she gathered Chad, Rich, and Mandie in the office and broke the news of her parents' deaths.

Tears streaked down Mandie's round face. "When's the funeral?" She plucked a tissue from a box on the desk and blew her nose.

"Not sure yet."

Wiping his eyes with the palm of his hand, Chad went to the window and stared outside as though he didn't believe her. "Does Robert know?"

"I've been looking for him. He won't answer my calls. Have any of you seen him lately?"

"Not since this morning," Rich said.

"Shoot. If you find him, send him here. He needs to hear this from me." Sydney wept with them, and they shared memories. By the time the crew went back to work, she felt worn out with no tears left to shed.

For the rest of the afternoon, she planned to hide in her office and tackle the debt. And try to figure out why the insurance hadn't been paid. Caliber curled up on the floor beside her and whined. "Don't worry, buddy. We'll get through this." She scratched his neck, then pressed the ice pack to the top of her head. The mound of bills remained piled on the desk.

About to exchange ice packs, the rattle of a truck snagged her attention. Out the window stood Glenda's dusty, red

Toyota Tacoma. Sydney groaned as her sister got out and scanned the lodge as though pricing it for sale.

A door creaked open. Boot heels clicked a staccato rhythm. And the office door swung wide open. "Why didn't you meet me at the hospital? How could you make me go through that by myself?"

Sydney tossed the ice pack on the cluttered desk. "You weren't alone. Chuck was with you. Besides, someone had to stay here and run the place."

"Where's Robert?"

"Doing his job." Or so she hoped. A twinge of guilt for not going to the hospital with Chuck settled in her gut. "Did you see them?"

"I had to identify them." Glenda plopped down on the wooden rocking chair their mother used to spend hours in when needing to tackle tough ranch problems. "Why didn't you come?"

Wrinkling her nose at her sister's pungent perfume, Sydney moved to the worn couch covered by a tattered green blanket. She picked at a frayed edge. "I couldn't see them like that."

"You never could stomach blood."

"Don't talk about them as if they're roadkill."

"I wasn't." Glenda stopped rocking. "Suppose we better plan the funerals. I'll call Pastor Jake."

Sydney shuddered. "What about the kids who hit them? What will happen to them?"

"Chuck said they arrested one of the teens. He'd messed with the steering wheel while a girl was driving, trying to be funny or something, and caused the accident. There were three of them, one drunk, the other two had no alcohol on their breath."

Sydney pressed a hand to her throat. "Holy . . ."

"Good news is he'll get jail time."

"How can you be so flippant?"

Glenda's jaw dropped. "About what? Wanting justice for our parents? Good Lord, Syd. Don't be so judgmental. I'm the one who showed up. Saw their mangled bodies." She pursed her lips and shook her head, fire in her eyes. "You know, we're going to have to sell this place—"

"Over my dead body!" Sydney flinched at her choice of words. She shot out of her seat and paced the worn, Southwestern rug, her fingers curling into fists. "Just because you've never cared about the ranch doesn't mean the rest of us don't."

"I don't have time to run this place, and you can't do it by yourself. Selling's the only option."

"The only option? Between me and Bobby—"

Glenda waved a hand in the air. "How? What's your plan, little sister?"

"I'll figure it out." Sydney wasn't about to fuel her sister's fire by telling her the insurance policy had been canceled. She didn't have a clue how she'd protect the Seven Tine from changing hands—not yet anyhow—but there had to be a way.

"You don't get it. They could hardly keep up with our help. How are you planning to keep this going with just you?"

"*Our* help? You do nothing around here. Sheesh, Glenda, even growing up you did the bare minimum." Sydney winced as a bolt of pain shot through her head. If she didn't find a way to calm herself, the migraine would only keep pecking her head. "Yeah, you call the preacher, and I'll contact family."

She picked up the phone and dialed a number. When the call went to voice mail, she slammed the handset into the cradle.

Glenda leaned forward. "Look, I'm as upset about Mom and Dad as you are but can't afford to lose it now. I have kids to think about. Besides, after all the funerals around here, I'm all dried up."

"Yeah, me too."

She rose. "We'll get through this. I'll go make the calls before the kids get home from school."

"Sounds good. I'll call our aunties and have them help notify family." Sydney stood and gave her sister a light hug.

Seconds after Glenda left, Pam poked her head in the office. "Syd? We . . . uh . . . ." She glanced over her shoulder.

"What's up?"

"There's a problem."

Sydney closed her eyes and sighed. *Oh great.* She didn't have the strength to deal with anything else.

"Follow me."

Pam led her to the main floor's sunflower-themed bathroom. "Look." She pointed to a puddle covering three-quarters of the barnwood floor. The planks had been salvaged from her great-grandfather's barn that used to be two miles up the road on the original homestead.

Sydney bit her lip till it bled and wiped the blood on her pants. "I'll go get help."

"I'll throw towels on the floor." Pam opened the cupboards and pulled out a stack.

Sydney marched to the barn, the sun burning her eyes. She hadn't felt this burdened since the day she'd let go of her baby girl. She stopped, allowing her eyes to adjust, then stepped deeper into the eight-stall structure.

Trey jumped off a bale of hay across from the tack room, camera in hand. "How's it going?"

"Not so well." She passed him, keeping her focus toward the east barn door. Light spilled through, exposing dancing dust motes. "Where's Chad?"

"Who's Chad?"

"One of my ranch hands. About five-ten, stocky, sideburns."

"Oh, him. He went to get another truckload of hay from the field."

"Shoot. Which field?"

"Not sure."

"Great." She pressed her hands on her hips, wishing she had the ice pack. "What about a guy with wavy, dark hair? Kinda like a smaller, darker version of Blake Shelton?"

"Nope. Haven't seen him either. How can I help?"

Rich was missing too? Good grief. She regarded Trey for a minute, then said, "Come with me." This was the first time a guest had been asked to help. And it would be the last. She headed back to the lodge.

He caught up with her. "What's the problem?"

"There's a leak in one of the bathrooms." She struggled to keep tears in the back of her eyelids. Her dad had taken care of things like broken pipes and faulty wiring. What did she know about household repair? Let alone water damage.

Trey opened the lodge door for her, and she led him to the bathroom. Yellow-, green-, and orange-soaked bath towels littered the floor.

"I'll check it out," Trey said. "Can you get more dry towels?" He tossed the wet ones into the shower stall.

"Yep." She rushed to the laundry room, gathered an armload of warm towels off the top of the dryer, and went back, arranging them across the soggy boards. In front of the sink, she doubled up a set for him to kneel on.

Her phone chirped. She pulled it from her back pocket and found she'd missed a call from her housekeeper. She called back and got a voice mail. "Hey, it's Syd. Sorry I missed you. *Please* call me back."

"You've got a busted pipe under the sink," Trey told her. "I turned the water off but will need tools to fix it."

"I'll get 'em."

He caught her wrist. "I'm sure you have plenty to do. Tell me where, and I'll get them."

Her jaw clenched from his tight hold. He seemed to notice her annoyance and released his grip. "In the shop."

"And where's that?"

"I'll go." She fled the bathroom and stormed through the kitchen door, allowing the dam of tears to burst.

CHAPTER 5

Trey found Sydney crumpled in a heap on the cold cement floor in the shop, pipe wrench clutched in her fist. The sight of her looking so defeated crushed him. He settled beside her and gathered her into his arms. "It's going to be all right."

She rested her head against his chest. "I can't believe they're gone."

He stroked her soft, shoulder-length hair and inhaled its floral scent, glad to see her let loose. "Tell me about them."

When she didn't answer, he prodded her with his gaze, then said, "I'd really like to know."

"My mom was incredibly strong and determined. One time the flu ran through the ranch. Mom wasn't as bad as the rest of us. She needed to get a large round bale of hay into the back of the flatbed truck. She rigged up a pulley system and got the job done."

"She sounds like a true ranchwoman." And as stubborn as her daughter. Did the Moomaw women have to be so tough though? His mom sure wasn't. As a real estate socialite, she hired out most everything. She simply checked off her list and instructed the accountant to pay the bills.

"She was a hardy gal. As was her mother."

"And your dad?"

She sighed. A mournful smile tipped her lips. "He was the most amazing man in the world. Kind. Had a sense of humor. He could fix anything, and he worked from dawn till dusk. We never did have to hire out for repairs." She caught a sob. "How am I going to run this place without them?"

"One day at a time. Maybe even moment by moment." He took the wrench from her. "My grandma always told me time doesn't necessarily mend wounds. Instead, we have to learn to live with new realities. Take each day as it comes. Let ourselves grieve."

"Our pastor says God cares, even in times like these. I'm not so sure He does. At least not about me."

Her doubt made his chest clench. What could have caused her cynicism? "Why wouldn't He? Do you really think God never stops caring?" When she fell silent, he asked, "Do you have any siblings to help you out?"

"My brother will. My sister . . . not so much."

Her stiff upper lip suggested he back off. "Should we go fix the pipe?"

"We?"

"Me." If he cradled her much longer it would be hard to let her go. His affection for her caught him off guard. Was it because he felt sorry for her?

He stood and offered his hand. She took it, and he lifted her off the concrete floor. As she dusted off the seat of her jeans, she looked at the time on the shop's wall clock. "How about you fix the pipes while I head to the barn? The vet should be here any minute."

Trey guided her outside with a hand on the small of her back. He wanted to keep it there the rest of the way, to comfort her broken heart, but she might take it the wrong way. Once inside, he fixed the pipe and cleaned the bathroom, then straightened the sunflower-embroidered towels before putting the tools away.

A handful of guests lingered in the great room, visiting as they waited for their lunches. The rest were on a trail ride and picnic.

Trey found the coffee bar and poured himself a cup. Was the vet still around? He took a quick drink of the bitter brew and set the cup down. His curiosity led him to the barn. A blast of heat brought him back to Arizona, way different from the Nespelem valley. Yes, patches of sagebrush surrounded them. So did trees, streams, and lush green grass.

When Trey reached the horse barn's birthing stall, the graying vet had his stethoscope to the foal's belly. Sydney sat cross-legged with the foal's head in her lap, stroking his neck. A clipboard lay by her in the straw, as did a fresh, ripe pile of manure. Trey remained in the aisle, giving them as much privacy as his investigative tendencies would allow.

"How's he doing, Saul?" The space between Sydney's brows pinched.

"Heart sounds strong. How's his appetite?" The vet moved the scope to another location.

"Good."

"His diarrhea gone?" Saul seemed to study the ground as he listened.

"Yep." Sydney kept vigil over the foal as though the realization of death swarmed her. And he didn't blame her. Her head lifted enough to expose the moisture lingering in her red-rimmed eyes.

Trey prayed the colt would make it. She didn't need to lose something else close to her heart.

"His temp's back to normal." Sydney handed him the foal's chart.

"He's going to be fine. His gut sounds healthy. Antibiotics are doing their job. If he's nursing, he'll pull through."

Sydney blew out a heavy breath, and her eyes brightened. "Good news."

Saul placed a hand on her shoulder. "Sure sorry about your folks. Let me know if there's anything I can do." He packed his bag and nodded at Trey, then offered Sydney a compassionate smile. "Today's on me."

The foal struggled to all fours and turned to his mother. He wobbled over and suckled. Sydney joined Trey in the aisle and hung the colt's clipboard on the outside of the stall wall.

"What's his name?"

"Twister."

"He's a dandy. What's wrong with him?"

She crossed her arms on the stall door and watched as the foal nudged his mother. "He's recovering from a bacterial infection called clostridium—a toxin which causes fluid secretion and leads to intestinal inflammation, which gives the foals bad diarrhea. It's common in newborns."

"Wow." No wonder Twister seemed so thin. "How do you treat something like that?"

"He's had IVs, ulcer meds, antibiotics four times a day, and low doses of Banamine. He wasn't allowed to eat for the first forty-eight hours, and we have to keep his stall spotless. It's been a rough road."

"I'll say." He turned to her, leaning against the stall post. "What are your plans for him?"

"My dad wanted to geld him, but I think he'll produce winning foals, so I talked him into keeping Twister as a stud." She gave the foal one more wistful glance. "He'd bring in a hefty profit."

A slender guy with short dark hair and a straw cowboy hat entered the barn and stopped by Sydney's side. Judging by his muscular arms, dirt-smudged face, and mud-covered jeans, Trey assumed him to be one of the ranch hands she'd been looking for earlier. "There are enough stallions on this place."

The color drained from her face. "I've been looking for you all day. We need to talk." Her chin quivered as she darted her eyes toward Trey. "Privately."

"Sorry," the ranch hand said. "My phone went dead, and I forgot my charger. Who's this?"

"Trey Hardy, this is my brother, Robert Elliot. Trey is Jim and Pam's friend and will be staying here for several days."

Several days? What happened to one or two nights?

Robert shook Trey's hand. "Nice to meet you. Where ya from?"

By the look on Sydney's face, she needed a moment to gather her wits, so Trey kept talking. "Tucson. Nice place y'all got here."

"Thanks." Robert leaned against Twister's stall. "With only fifteen guest rooms, we like to keep it small. One big happy family." He winked at Sydney.

She burst into tears.

"Oh, crap, Syd. What's wrong?"

"I've been trying to call you." She managed to choke out the words. "Dad . . . my mom . . . they've been in an accident."

Robert's face paled. "Are they OK?"

She shook her head. "They didn't make it."

"Where? What happened?"

Trey crept out of the barn. Their family needed time to grieve. Alone. He called Jim to come and get him. Darn if he didn't get his voice mail.

CHAPTER 6

Sydney had never seen her brother cry before, and it almost made her crack. But as ranch boss, she couldn't allow that to happen. What would guests think if they found her crumpled in the dirt of the barn floor blubbering? She rubbed the back of her neck. "You going to be OK?"

Robert wiped his eyes with his knuckles and nodded. "Yeah. It's . . . well . . . after all these years of not being able to call him *dad*, and now . . ." He shrugged, disappointment in his eyes.

"I know. It's not fair."

"What's going to happen to the ranch?"

"I'll find a way to keep it."

He looked at her with his dark, wet eyes and nodded. "I'll help in whatever way I can. It's all I got. I don't need anything else."

Was he talking about inheritance? Or their father's possessions? "It's all *we've* got. Glenda's pushing to sell, but I'm going to fight her. I need you to focus on the day-to-day things and ride herd on the boys."

"You got it. Let me know what you need done for the funeral."

She squeezed her eyes shut against the sharp prickles behind her lids. "I will. Look, I gotta go take something for this headache. I'll catch up to you later." She hugged him and slipped away to her simple, tidy cabin tucked among pine trees and minty-smelling wildflowers about one hundred yards northwest of the lodge.

After taking another nasty-tasting migraine pill, she ate a few bites of buttered toast and sipped milk to settle her tummy. She went to her stuffy room, closed the black-out curtains, and lay down, sagging against the headboard and rubbing her temples. The family photo above her dresser caused a fresh set of tears to flow.

The urge to look at more photos overcame her. She'd need them for the funeral, but she would have to wait until the pain subsided.

About an hour later, when the pain began to dwindle, she went to her closet and dug out a photo album. She flipped through the pages and smiled at photos of them fishing or riding horses. Traced one of her grandfathers holding a seven-point elk antler shed over his head. Cried at those of her, Glenda, and their mother in the garden in the back of the main house, surrounded by sunflowers and daisies.

Near the back of the album were pictures of her grandparents in various stages of building the guest ranch. It had taken years of hard work and sweat to construct the place she was now responsible for. The realization of her new charge formed a deep pit in her gut.

She hugged the album, curled into a ball on her side, and covered her eyes with a pillow. If she didn't get rid of her migraine soon, she wouldn't be good for anyone. Especially Twister. His vitals needed to be recorded before lights out, and it was her turn. They'd all worked hard to get him healthy. She wished she could call her dad and let him know the treatments were working and the foal would live.

Missing her parents, Sydney punched in her dad's cell number. Seconds later, his matter-of-fact voice-mail greeting rang through her room. She hung up and called her mom's cell. Jennie's gentle voice lingered well after ending the call. "I can't do this without you guys," she whispered.

She made herself get up, shuffle to the bathroom, and wash her face. Grandma Moomaw had always said, "Self-pity dwells in the heart of the lazy."

A knock sounded. "Syd?"

She went to the living room. Mandie stood on the other side of a screen door with a covered plate settled on her swollen belly. She wore a floral apron over her five-foot frame, her long hair pulled into a ponytail. "Pam and I think you need to eat. I brought you fruit, celery sticks, and cheese. How are you doing?"

"I'm fine, thanks." Unsteady on her feet, Sydney opened the door, squinting from the sting of the sun, and took the plate. "Don't know what I'd do without you guys."

"So you know, Bobby took off. He looked pretty upset. You think he's going to be all right?"

"Yeah. He's got things to process." As did she. Would Robert fight her and Glenda for a portion of the ranch as his inheritance? Would he stay on and help or be deadweight? Would he fight for control, being a man?

"OK, just wanted to let you know." Mandie hugged her and waddled away.

Sydney eased down on her hunter-green sofa and uncovered the plate. She took a bite of cheese. After eating a few juicy grapes, she set the plate on her wooden coffee table. Why did her body feel so weak? And why wouldn't her headache go away? She padded back to bed.

She tossed and turned for what seemed like hours before settling into one spot, her mind drifting to the day she'd learned Robert was her half-sibling. It'd been a few short months ago. And when the idea of having a brother—not a ranch hand—was settling in, their parents' deaths slapped her in the face. By the sound of it, Robert's too.

She held her head and groaned from the vice-like pain. Then jumped out of bed and ran to the bathroom, crashing her shoulder against the doorjamb and biting back a curse word. She retched, rinsed out her mouth with cold water, and got an ice pack from the freezer on her way back to bed.

Her mind wouldn't let up. *No wonder Bobby's such a mess.* All those years their father had denied him a sonship. She couldn't imagine. And him never saying why he'd hid the relationship—refusing to explain his past. She'd been tired of hearing, "That's the way it is." She needed answers.

Creator nudged her. Hadn't she done the same? Hid her child? Her explosive marriage? But it had been for different reasons. Robert had lived under their roof. Ate their food. Worked the ranch. No one had known about her baby. She'd hidden her circumstances out of fear and humiliation. Her father's decision seemed out of convenience. But, who stood to get hurt the most? Robert.

Should she find out what he expected to get from the estate? Search for a will? Not say anything and hope he doesn't bring it up? Her head hurt too much to think about it.

She prayed her brother wouldn't do something stupid and hoped his rodeos would help him focus. She needed everyone to pull their weight to keep the ranch afloat.

But would he try to take over? Turning on her other side and hugging a pillow, she vowed to hold her ground as ranch owner, even if she had to sell cattle to buy out her siblings.

She winced and cried, exhaustion and frustration encasing her.

Between her dad's dishonesty and Cooper's beatings, she could trust no one. Not even God. He'd never protected her. She'd have to save the ranch by herself.

Sydney felt so wound up, she put on a CD of soft Native flute music, and laid back down. After the first song, the medication kicked in, and it made her feel like she'd taken a shot or two of whisky. While her body relaxed, her mind drifted to that morning. Her father's hesitation. Her mother's anticipation.

If only she could turn back time.

A tear trickled down her face as she closed her eyes. She'd allow a short nap. Anticipate waking up refreshed. Then find that blasted will.

CHAPTER 7

Wednesday, June 14

Sydney woke with a start. What time was it? The clock read six in the morning. "Shoot!" She jumped to her feet and dressed in jeans and a T-shirt, then pulled on her boots and sprinted to the barn. According to Twister's chart, his meds had been given and his vitals recorded. Chad's initials had been scribbled on the sheet.

She sighed, her pulse racing. She drew in a few deep breaths. Pam entered the barn and strode to her, handing her a cup of warm, tan coffee. The vanilla aroma settled her nerves.

Pam leaned against the stall beside Twister's. She gestured to the colt. "He looks good this morning."

"Yeah, he does."

"I bet you're hungry."

"Kinda." She still felt sick to her stomach. "I know they're gone, but I'm not ready to let them go. I miss them so much."

"It's a shock, Syd. Let yourself grieve."

"I did yesterday. Now it's time to get back to work. This ranch isn't gonna run itself."

"How about we get breakfast and line things out for the next few days?"

"Sounds good." She started for the lodge. "I need to find a new housekeeper. Got any ideas?"

Pam let out a quiet chuckle. "Take a minute to be still, Syd. Let God work out the details."

If only it would do any good.

A rig came toward them as it rambled down the mile-long dirt driveway, dust twirling behind. "Is that Jim?"

"Sure looks like it."

They went inside and settled at a dining table near the stone fireplace. There were only two other people in the room, an older couple who were sipping coffee and talking on the opposite side. Their presence reminded her to check on the other reservations.

About the time Jim wandered in with a duffle bag, Trey trotted down the stairs wearing creased jeans, cowboy boots, a red T-shirt, and a scowl. The men exchanged hardened glances. Was he headed back to Tucson? Darn. Maybe he'll change his mind and stay on for a week or so.

Jim dropped the bag and kissed his wife. "How's it going?"

"Good." She scooted the chair out beside her. "You're here early."

"My aunt and uncle decided I needed to be here with you guys and took off. We had a great visit last night, and they promised to stop by on their way back." He took Pam's hand in his.

Trey filled two cups at the coffee bar and strode to the table. Sydney fought the draw to his scruffy, handsome face, athletic build, and laid-back demeanor. From the stairs to the table his expression had softened. After yesterday in the barn and the heaviness on the ranch, she wouldn't blame him for wanting to leave. He gave one cup to Jim and took a seat next to her.

Jim thanked Trey and took a sip. "What's the plan?"

Sydney inhaled, catching a whiff of the dark brew. "Well, I need to figure out who's checking out and in, update the books, deal with Twister, line up my riding lessons—"

Pam lifted her finger. "Syd."

"Find a new housekeeper—"

"Sydney!" Pam tipped her head, her finger waving in the air.

She pinched her brows together. "What?"

"I have an idea." Pam lowered her hand to the table. "I'll check the guests in and out, the books can wait, and your lessons can be rescheduled. Chad has agreed to keep tabs on the colt, and for now, I'm your housekeeper and receptionist. So, why don't you take the morning off to relax, refresh, and recharge? Find your balance."

Sydney laughed. "Take the morning off? Are you crazy? If anything, I need to ramp things up—"

"No, sweetie, you don't." Pam tapped the table as though to capture Sydney's attention. "I know you were taught to work until you drop, but if you don't slow down, you're going to crack. You won't be good to nobody. Is that what you want?"

Sydney crossed her arms. "What do you have in mind?"

"Why don't you saddle a couple of horses and take Trey on a ride. Show him why we've been hounding him for years to come to the Seven Tine."

Trey's brows shot up, and he scowled at Pam.

"Great idea, darlin'." Jim nodded at both women. "Pam and I can cover things here for a few hours."

"A few hours?"

Pam turned around. "Hey, Mandie?"

The kitchen door opened and the cook appeared, her hand resting on her baby bump. She wasn't due for another seven weeks. "Whatcha need?"

"Can you fix a picnic lunch for two?"

Mandie's lips spread into a wide smile. "On it."

Oh, great. Now they have the official ranch's busybody conspiring against her. Jeez. "No, I don't want a picnic. It'll be easier to eat here."

Knowing Pam would not let up until she got her way, Sydney closed her eyes and nodded. "Fine. I'll take the morning off. Relax and do the other two Rs. Then come back and get to work. There's too much to do."

"I can live with that." A look of victory crossed over her face.

"Breakfast is ready," Mandie hollered as she swept through the kitchen door.

After a quick bite to eat, Sydney grabbed her straw cowboy hat and sunglasses and went outside to saddle up. She found Caliber lying in a shady spot under the overhang by Daisy's pen—a mama Jersey with a spunky calf the guests adored and at times helped feed. Sydney tossed the pair an extra flake of hay, then ran her fingers over the cow's smooth, mulberry coat, admiring her long lashes.

The young calf kicked up her heels and ran in circles, seeming to enjoy the morning sunshine. Caliber rose, his sights pinned on the cow-calf pair. "Down," Sydney commanded.

After making sure all the equine mamas and babies had water, she checked the foal's medical chart, took his temperature, and recorded her findings. Why had she agreed to Pam's scheme? Trey hadn't looked one bit interested in a horseback ride. She saddled Cyan and Robert's bay gelding and waited for him outside.

Minutes later, he strode toward her, the same baseball cap he'd come with on his head. Sydney motioned to the letter on the front of the cap. "What's the A for?"

He flashed her a pleasing grin. "Arizona Diamondbacks."

"Um. Isn't that a snake?"

"And a major league baseball team in Arizona."

"You're from Tucson, right?" She handed him the bay's reins.

"Sure am." He took the leather straps and positioned his camera behind his back.

She could never live in a sweltering place inundated by cacti and snakes. "What kind of settings are you looking for?"

"Not sure until I see the place. But we don't have to worry about that right now. I've decided to stay the full week. I've got time and this country is exactly what the magazine's looking for. But—um—as you've probably noticed, Pam and Jim are bent on keeping me here. Jim's been hounding me for years to come. I, uh, can't imagine what you're going through and don't want to be a burden. Guess I want to make sure you're fine with me staying."

"Yeah, Pam's a little over the top sometimes, but they both mean well. And I'm fine with you staying." Her chest fluttered, and her body released tight muscles. The money would go to good use. "Alrighty then. Let's see what you got, Tucson." She mounted Cyan and headed north, Caliber trailing behind.

CHAPTER 8

"This is gorgeous country." Trey shot multiple photos of two bald eagles circling an enormous Ponderosa pine tree. One of the bird's wings spanned a good six feet. He searched for a nest but couldn't find one. As he twisted in the saddle, brush to his right rustled and a young calf poked its head out. Trey focused the camera, took a few shots, and studied them in the LCD panel, then took a couple more as the calf crept closer to them.

Sydney stilled, her horse's ears pinned on the curious youngster. She commanded Caliber to lie down, and he did. "Snap much wildlife?"

"Here and there. Lately, I've been focusing on those caught in horrific situations." The mother cow emerged into the meadow and gave her calf a low call. "I recently covered a hurricane aftermath in Haiti. The floods were severe. Kids crying—cold and hungry. They had nothing left." He swallowed the lump clogging his throat.

"I can't imagine," she said. "We deal with devastating wildfires around here. Over the past few years, we've had several huge ones. Most of the damage was contained in the mountains. A few houses and outbuildings burned. But, thankfully, most of our communities have gone untouched."

Sydney led him up the valley for a couple of miles before circling down along Nespelem Creek. He marveled at her knowledge about the reservation and surrounding area and wouldn't be surprised if she had a history degree. He found himself drinking in every word she spoke, even her stories of alleged secret dances up the valley that had included moonshine and murder in the old days.

She reminded him of Southwestern women storytellers surrounded by gaping children cocooned in a shawl. Teacher. It had to be one of her God-given gifts.

"Have you ever thought of having local children come to the ranch for story time? You'd be great at it." He liked the way she smiled under her cowboy hat at the compliment.

"All the time. Unfortunately, there's too much work to be done."

"What about in the winter when things slow down?"

"Life doesn't 'slow down' in the winter. We have guests, snow removal, frozen water pipes and tanks, livestock to feed. My chore list gets longer when snow and freezing temperatures are involved and cattle are no longer out to pasture."

"Too bad. Like I said, you'd be good at it." Trey shifted in the saddle, his backside aching. She rode like she'd been in the saddle since birth. He could imagine it—bottle clutched in one hand and reins in the other. But something about her troubled him. Like a familiar sense of self-protection hovering over her like a storm cloud. He wanted to ask but reminded himself it was not his business.

Her eyes narrowed. "I think we have a problem." She pointed to a small, dark form partially hidden in tan grass. She kicked her horse and sped to its side. "Caliber, down!" The dog stopped his quest and dropped.

Trey caught up and dismounted. Blood stained the ground beside a motionless calf. A chunk of its hindquarters was missing. "Cougar?"

"That or wolves." A mama cow bawled behind Sydney. She searched the rocky hillsides, turning in a circle. "Don't see anything."

Trey snapped a few photos of the calf in case she'd need evidence for Fish and Wildlife. "Can you set a trap?"

"I don't have one." She put a rope around its neck. "We'll bury her at the ranch." She dallied the rope around the saddle horn and waved her heels against the mare's sides, dragging the carcass and trying to keep Caliber in check.

Trey shot several more pictures of her, the Australian shepherd, the dead calf, and its distressed mother trailing behind before catching up to them. Sydney's determination was worth capturing, even if only for himself.

It seemed to take forever before they reached the ranch. As Sydney approached with the half-eaten calf, the horses ran around their pens, ears perked forward. The calf's mother let out mournful wails. Trey dismounted and took hold of Sydney's reins.

"What's this?" A stocky guy with sideburns said as he watched Sydney coil her rope.

Sydney introduced him as Chad, then gestured north with her head. "Found her a couple miles out. I think it may be our *Incheechun*."

"Another wolf?" Hardness in his eyes, Chad strode into the barn and came back with a rifle and two shovels. He handed the shovels to Sydney and swiped the reins from Trey. "I'll be back."

Sydney yanked the reins away from him. "He's not around. I checked. Call Fish and Wildlife."

Trey held up his camera to mention he'd taken photos but got cut off.

"I'm not waiting for them. I'll take care of it." Chad took the reins back and pulled himself into the saddle. He tugged his Stetson over his eyes and urged the horse into a lope.

Trey turned to Sydney. "Why won't he call them?"

"He knows my dad and the director go . . . went head-to-head when it comes to wolves." She gave him a shovel.

"Let's bury this little one, then I'll show you stock you can take pictures of."

He nodded. What he wanted to do was tag along with Chad. If he could get shots of a wolf or two, that would be a bonus. Magazine editors were hungry for such images. The cowboy and his rifle disappeared into the trees. Trey sighed.

"We'll bury the calf, then take care of the cow." Sydney tapped his shoulder with the coiled rope. "Coming?"

"Yeah." He helped haul the carcass several yards behind the barn to the base of a rocky knoll. The longer he worked, the more shriveled his tongue became, but he kept digging dirt, forming a large hole. She dug beside him, keeping a strong pace. After a while he said, "Got any water?"

"We're almost done. Then you can have all you want."

He pulled his shirt off and shoveled faster as sweat dribbled down his back. When the hole was deep enough, he helped place the animal in it, and they packed it with dirt. Spitting out dust, he snatched his shirt off the ground and mopped his face. "How often does this happen?"

"This is the second one since March."

"Only two?"

"Two too many." Sydney bent over and wiped her face with the hem of her shirt. "We can't afford to lose stock. No one can."

She grabbed the rope, snuck close to the cow, and swung. She tossed it, aiming for the head. Once over, she pulled, and the rope tightened around the cow's neck. The cow bucked and tried to break free, dragging Sydney along. Trey jumped in and helped wrangle her into an empty pen.

"We'll keep her here for a few days," Sydney said. "When she settles down, we can turn her back out with the others."

Trey started for a spigot. "I've got to get a drink," he said over his shoulder. *Two too many*, she'd said. Were they in financial trouble? If so, it would explain why she tried to talk him into staying a week.

"Me too." After they'd both taken long drinks, she asked, "Want ice cream?"

"Huckleberry?" Trey recalled the stand of huckleberry soap, syrup, and candy at a gas station in Grand Coulee. But where would they pick them in rocky ground, thick with sagebrush and dirt? Sage brought him back to Tucson, minus the saguaros, and his miserable childhood.

"How about vanilla topped with huckleberries?"

"I'm in." They must pick them in the forested mountain ranges bookending the Seven Tine. He'd make sure Jim took him fishing in the smaller lakes in those areas as promised. He could sell quality photos to *Fishing America* or *Bait and Tackle*.

She smiled, but her dull eyes suggested she was stuffing loose anger and frustration and sorrow down deep in her gut. Perhaps for his sake because he was a guest. He tried to read her but struggled. Her strong demeanor irritated him. And thrilled him at the same time.

Once inside and settled on the overstuffed chairs by the bay window with their dessert, she took a small bite and acted like her stomach was queasy. "When we finish here, I need to check on the colt. You can tag along if you want."

"Take more photos?"

"Sure, why not."

Pam entered the dining area from the kitchen and took a seat by Sydney. "You look more haggard than before you left."

"We found a dead calf. I'm sure the pesky wolf is back."

The corner of Pam's mouth tugged downward. "I hate to stack burdens, but Mandie went to the doctor. She's having mild contractions—"

"What? When?"

"She went to get checked," Pam said in a reassuring tone. "Sounds like a mild case of Braxton-Hicks. I told her to take the night off. She has already prepped dinner, so I'll finish it for her. Don't worry. She'll be fine."

Sydney sank back, her bowl of ice cream on her lap. What else would the poor woman have to endure? Jim was right, she was one tough lady.

"By the way, Glenda's on her way over." Pam bumped Sydney's shoulder with hers.

The look on Sydney's face suggested things might get a little tense. His cue to get out of there. He caught Pam's attention. "Where's Jim?"

"He's around here somewhere."

Good. He'd skip whatever contention was brewing and find his buddy.

CHAPTER 9

After Trey left, Sydney turned to Pam. "Why is my sister coming over?"

"To help pick out photos for the funeral."

She sighed. "Guess we need to set the date."

"Honey, she—uh—she already did. It's happening on Friday."

"In three days. Of course she did." She jumped to her feet, her bowl of ice cream splattering on the floor, and paced the hardwood boards of the great room's floor, her boots clunking harder against the wood with each step. "Why would she think to include me? Ever? This is how she is. Such a control freak. I can't stand it when she acts like the queen of—of—everything!"

Pam scooped the ice cream into the bowl and cleaned up the remaining mess with tissue from the box on a side table. "You have a lot on your plate here. Don't you think she's trying to help?"

"Help? I doubt it." Sydney leaned against the back of an overstuffed chair and inhaled a few deep breaths. "Glenda doesn't help. She takes over. Will she ever get over herself? Being on council has her thinking she can rule over everyone, especially me." She went back to pacing, jabbing her finger in the air. "Not this time."

She started for the bathroom to wash up and over her shoulder said, "I'll be right back." She stalked across the room, her hands fisted at her sides, and stormed into the bathroom. After slamming the door shut, she turned on the faucet and splashed cold water on her face. She stood a minute, staring at the sunflower soap decanter. Oh, how she missed her mom. After shedding a few tears, she patted her face dry with a yellow hand towel and went back to Pam.

"Mandie called," Pam told her.

"How is she?"

"Doctor said she's fine. Baby's in good health."

"Thank God."

"Doctor wants her to rest the remainder of the day. She'll be here in the morning." Pam waved her toward a chair. "You sit for a minute. I'll get us lemonade. It might cool you off."

She grunted. "None for me. I need to check on Twister."

"Chad says he's taking this shift." Pam covered Sydney's hand with hers. "Listen, I know you're worried about him, but it would be nice if you'd let your ranch hands do their job. They feel horrible and, like you, may need to work through their grief. Can you let him handle it for the rest of the day? You can check on him before you go to bed."

"Hmm. I see your point."

"Oh, and Robert put the mail on your desk. What time do the guests get back from their trail ride?"

She conferred the time on the mantel clock. "In about half an hour or so."

"Perfect. I'll work on dinner." Pam gathered the ice cream bowls and went to the kitchen.

Sydney headed to the office and went through the mail, finding one particular envelope addressed to her. She opened it and tugged out a piece of paper with a cheap Spokane motel logo on it. The familiar handwriting made her chest clench. She read the note, pressed a hand to her throat. "God, no. Cooper can't be out . . ." She searched the envelope for a return address. There wasn't one. She unzipped the concealed-weapon pocket of her purse and made sure her pistol was loaded.

The sound of a rig grew louder. Sydney stiffened, her palms sweating. After hiding the gun in her purse, she inserted the paper into the envelope and tucked it under several folders before rushing outside.

Glenda came racing up the drive.

"Ohhh . . ." Sydney was not looking forward to the drama that normally tagged along with her sister. She'd have to be the mature one. All she needed to do was shut her mouth and get the pictures. Show Glenda she was able to keep the place running smoothly. She plopped down onto the rocker, leaned her head back, and closed her eyes. *Keep your mouth shut.*

The engine cut off, and a door opened and closed. Sharp footsteps clambered up the steps and stopped. The rocker creaked.

"Got time to gather pictures?"

Sydney opened her eyes. "Hear you took care of the arrangements." So much for self-control. Her mind hopped between the funeral preparations and Cooper's letter. When had he gotten released? What made her sister pick the date without her input? Where was Cooper now? She folded her arms across her chest. How had Cooper found out about the deaths so quickly? She scanned the perimeter.

Glenda took a seat on the horse head bench. "You have enough to think about, don't you?"

"So I've been told."

"Pastor Jake's going on vacation. I needed to act quickly."

"You could have called." She focused on hilly terrain heavily ladened with trees behind the barn. Cooper could hide anywhere, plan his next move, and come after her at any time.

"We needed to make decisions."

"*We* being key."

Glenda frowned. "OK. I should have called."

"I've got five families coming anytime. Once I get them signed in, we can dig through pictures."

"Sounds good." Glenda wiped her sweat-covered brow. "Let's go inside and talk. It's flippin' hot out here."

Sydney surveyed the ranch before following her sister into the office. She flipped on a room fan as Pam entered and handed them glasses of lemonade.

"How's dad's colt?" Glenda settled on the couch and held the glass to her cheek.

Dad's colt? Good grief. Was Glenda identifying the foal as their dad's so it would be easier to sell him with no attachments? "Twister's fine." To keep peace, Sydney decided to pick her battles. And Twister's ownership was not worth the argument. Not at this instance, anyhow.

Glenda studied her. "He's going to make it then?"

"Sure is." Sydney took a sip. Her sister looked like she was trying to figure out what hefty price he'd bring in. Glenda's greed raked on her nerves. "So what's the plan concerning the funeral?"

"I sent Jim and Trey to get more tables and chairs," Pam said.

"Good idea." Glenda took a long swallow of her drink. "When's family coming in?"

"Not sure. I've been pretty busy. Frankly, too busy to check in with our aunties." Sydney fingered her glass. "I suppose a handful tonight, most tomorrow. Robert's going to take care of parking." Good thing Pam was with them. With her there, Glenda wouldn't bring up selling the ranch.

"Jodie and Lacey will gather cooks." Glenda regarded Pam, then addressed Sydney. "Sooner or later we will have to talk about this place."

"Ugh. I'm not selling."

"How 'bout you guys get through the funeral first." Pam's eyes shifted between the sisters.

"Great idea."

Glenda agreed. "Shall we tackle the pictures?"

"Sure." The sooner they finished, the quicker she could slip away and check on Twister.

They went through the kitchen to the main house behind the lodge. Jennie had fixed a pathway between the two buildings with boulders, cedar chips, flowering shrubs, and a garden pond stocked with yellow and orange koi.

They spent the next two hours selecting photos from Jennie's albums while shedding tears and sharing memories at the kitchen table. Sydney let Glenda do most of the choosing so she could get out of her folks' house. She couldn't handle being in there without them in it.

Glenda tapped her watch. "I'll be back later tonight. I can run to the Dam after the kids get back from school and pick up trifolds. Let me know if you need anything else."

"How are the kids?" Sydney twisted a lock of hair.

"Franky and Junie are hanging in there, but Kimberly's having a hard time of it. You know how she loved helping her Tima Jennie."

"She sure did. Well, if you hang on a minute, I'll make a list." Sydney fetched a pad of paper and a pen from her father's home office and sat back down. She scribbled the items she needed on the paper and handed it to Glenda. "That should do."

Glenda stood. "Good to see you, Pam."

"You too." When the door creaked shut, Pam said, "That went well."

"Yep." Sydney closed and stacked the albums. "I'm going to che—, um, back to the lodge to tackle paperwork. Holler when the guests arrive. Hopefully, none of the new arrivals will come until after dinner." She wasn't in the mood for Pam to try to keep her from Twister.

After Pam left, Sydney raced to the barn and was relieved to find he'd gotten a trace of his spunk back. She opened the stall run so he could wander outside for fresh air.

When satisfied with his progress, she went to the ranch office and picked up her folks' photo off the desktop and traced their smiling faces with her sweaty finger. How would she ever deal with their belongings? After the funeral? Next week? Next month? Maybe she'd wake up tomorrow and find it was all a bad dream. If only she were that lucky. She put the photo back and went to the closet.

She dug around for a will and came up empty but did find a box marked *2017 Taxes*. She set it on the floor and riffled through old bills. Finding the Stockton Life Insurance receipts, she organized them into piles. January through December had been paid. So had February and March. Then nothing.

"What the heck?"

She opened a desk drawer and pulled out the Stockton file, then picked up the notice of cancellation. It couldn't have been the first. Where were the others?

After finding a notepad, she made a list of whom to call: Stockton Life Insurance, accountant, lawyer. She tossed the pen on the desk, not able to do a thing without organizing the clutter first. Fear and rage motivated her to create files and organize the bills. She couldn't let Glenda know how bad things were. No one could know.

CHAPTER 10

Everyone stood to the jarring beat of a large, powwow-style drum signaling the start of the funeral. The sound echoed off the walls of the Nespelem Community Center's gymnasium.

Sydney rubbed her arms like she used to rub the bruises. People packed the center like hatchlings in a nest. The human overflow lined the ramp descending into the gym. Ranchers slid hats from graying or bald heads. Women dabbed their eyes. Kids wiggled beside extended family.

A row of Pendleton blankets hung from wire behind twin caskets. To the south side of the gym, tables lined part of a wall holding photographic memories of the Moomaws. Reflections of their past. A past she wasn't ready to release.

Traditional singers wailed their mournful tribute as Marcie Louie, Jennie Moomaw's fraternal twin, clung to Sydney's hand, tears cascading down her face. Three days earlier, Sydney had waved goodbye as her folks drove down the dusty lane. Why God? She patted her eyes with a tissue.

Robert sat in the front row on the opposite aisle with the other pallbearers. All six of them wore black, yellow, and red ribbon shirts. Did the space between them make him feel like more of an outsider? Or was he used to it?

Sydney's seven-year-old niece, Kimberly, hugged her waist. She stroked the girl's back. An elder used smoking cedar and an eagle feather to smudge the mourners. Sydney's nostrils filled with the woodsy aroma, and she sent Creator a prayer of healing for her family.

When the singers finished, the crowd sat back down. Kimberly crawled onto her lap, clutching her doll. Glenda's three kids no longer had *tupas*—maternal grandparents—to teach them life and cultural skills. She sniffed and blew her nose, recognizing that her future kids would never know how wonderful her parents had been.

Pastor Jake Owens shared what life on the ranch had been like with the Moomaws leading the herd. He talked about their dedication to family and community. Would Sydney ever be that dedicated? Could she greet guests as sweetly as her mother had? Work as hard as her father? She had big shoes to fill, and to be honest, it scared her.

She'd have to fight for the guest ranch if only to honor her parents' memory. They'd worked hard to build the place up. Log by log, beam by beam, nail by nail. No outsider could take care of it as well as they had.

The Gibbses and Trey sat four rows back and off to the side. She caught a glimpse of Trey staring at her, a soft, concerned look on his face. She turned back around to the sprays of yellow and orange flowers spilling over the closed bottom half of the caskets.

She pulled in a deep breath and focused on the Seven Tine brands burned into each of the pine boxes. If only her folks would rise from the dead. Then together, they could retain the ranch. Preserve the past. Transform her future. How on earth would she pull it off? Tears slid down her face.

"They're in heaven, right, Auntie?" Kimberly looked at Sydney, tears pooling in her almond-colored eyes.

Sydney nodded and pressed a finger to her lips. "They sure are, sweetie bug." She squeezed her niece, planting a kiss on the top of her head and inhaling her fruity aroma.

"How much longer?" Kimberly whispered.

"It's almost over. We'll finish here, go to the gravesite, then head back to the ranch and eat. You hungry?"

She nodded.

Sydney stroked her niece's cropped hair and whispered, "It will all be over soon."

At the Seven Tine lodge, Sydney stirred her potato salad with a fork. On the other side of the dining room, Trey seemed comfortable visiting with one of her male cousins and an uncle. They'd borrowed extra tables and chairs from Nespelem's long house, and their family and closest friends filled each spot.

"How you doing?" Pam took a bite of salmon.

"Not too bad, actually." Sydney gave her a small smile. "The crowd shows how much they were loved."

"It does." Pam leaned back in her chair. "Jim and I plan to head home so your family can have our room. Your Oregon uncle wants to stay for a couple extra days. He's already paid." She fingered her spoon for an instant. "Trey's staying longer too."

"Sounds good." She'd gladly take his money. "He probably needs more photos anyway, huh? It's been crazy since he got here."

"Sure has. But trust me, he'll get them. He's a complete workaholic."

"I bet he will." As long as she didn't have to entertain him. She'd be busy trying to find the will and plan her next step.

"And don't worry about thinking you have to entertain him because he's our friend. Jim took time off work and plans on taking him sightseeing and fishing. Think in terms of marketing. *True Cowboy* is the hottest magazine for ranchers, cowboys, and the rich. It could be good for business."

She hadn't thought of that. "Think he'd take horse photos?"

"I'm sure he would. I bet he won't charge you either."

"That would be even better."

Pam smiled. "And who wouldn't want to work with someone as good looking as Trey Hardy?"

Huh? Was Pam trying to set her up? Surely not at her folks' funeral. Truth be told, yes, he was one of the most handsome men she'd laid eyes on. But the last thing on her mind was romance. Besides, she didn't get romantically involved with guests. Ever.

CHAPTER 11

I'll take you places Sydney doesn't know about for great wildlife pictures," Walt Moomaw, Sydney's Oregon uncle, told Trey.

"That'd be great." Trey grinned at Sydney, and she gave him a bashful smile and looked away. Though her black dress suggested mourning, her red beaded earrings and matching lip gloss reeled him in. "We'll talk more tonight." He clapped Walt on the back and zigzagged through the crowd to her table. "Can I get you ladies anything?"

Sydney gave him a small grin. "I'm fine, thanks."

"I'll see if the kitchen needs help." Pam excused herself, a twinkle in her eye.

Trey slid into her warm chair. "How you holding up?"

"Better than I thought I would."

"That's good." Even her fingernails were that delicious red. It was the first time he'd seen her dressed up.

She blushed and looked away. "So Pam tells me you're staying on for a few days."

"If that's fine with you." He didn't want to try to find another ranch, losing valuable time in the process. Already here, he'd make the best of it.

Sydney tapped a finger on the table. "Would you be willing to take pictures I can use for marketing?"

"I would love to. What's your angle?"

"I'm thinking photos with horses, cows, streams, and mountains. There are so many wonderful options, I don't know where to begin. But I'll make a list of ideas tonight before I turn in, and we can get started in the morning."

Trey tipped his head. "Isn't that too soon?" *She's either tough or crazy scared and wanting to avoid her feelings.*

"Not for me."

Her spunk hooked him every time. He reached a hand toward hers, wanting to feel her soft skin like he had in the shop when he'd found her sprawled on the floor, grieving and in shock, but knowing it wasn't appropriate.

Glenda waltzed over, clinked her glass of iced tea on the table, and plopped down beside Sydney. "We need to talk."

"About?"

"This place."

Sydney rolled her eyes. "This is hardly the time."

Glenda leaned closer. "It's never a good time, is it?" she said in a low tone, glancing around the room. "Don't make a scene. Let's talk in the office."

"Like I said, this is not the time." Her voice rose a bit. "Besides, by now you should have figured out I'm not selling."

"I've already secured a Realtor. She's coming in the morning."

"You don't waste time, do you?" Sydney stood, the screech of the chair causing stares. "Besides, it's not your call."

"I know what's best. You can't run this place alone, and I won't let you run it into the ground. Mom and Dad worked too hard to have it go under. As did our grandparents."

"And how would you know? You don't work the land or the cattle. Or the horses for that matter. You don't even own one." Sydney took a step toward her sister. "I'm a fourth-generation ranchwoman and, trust me, it won't go under. I've had plans to expand this place for years. Plans I never told you about because you've never had a lick of interest in the ranch."

A hush fell over the room, the guests' eyes plastered on the sisters. Trey stood, held up a hand, and suggested they speak in the morning after they'd both had a good night's rest. Where was Chuck? And the kids? Had he taken them home already?

Glenda narrowed her eyes. "See you tomorrow."

"The gate'll be locked."

Trey took hold of Sydney's hand and led her through the kitchen, her heels clacking on the wooden floor, and outside to the path between the lodge and the main house. "You have a gate?"

"I will by nightfall."

"Think that'll make this all go away?"

"It'll stop the Realtor."

"Will it?"

Sydney shrugged. "What do you suggest? And what do you know about running a place like this?"

He softened his tone. "I think you're running scared. And maybe searching for something you can't find."

"What makes you think that?"

"I saw you madly digging through a box."

Sydney's eye muscle twitched. "You were spying on me?"

"I was looking for you." He raked his fingers through his coarse hair. Her anger made him hesitate. "I wanted to talk to you about staying for several weeks."

"Sorry to interrupt," Robert said to Sydney. "I'm headed to Princeton."

"You're still going?"

"Is there a problem?"

"I got it." Trey shifted his weight. "I'll help out until you get back. I'll be here anyhow."

"Thanks for offering," Sydney said to him, "but it's not your job."

"You said I had the time off." Robert clenched his teeth. "I'll be back Sunday night."

"Fine. Then go." She rubbed the back of her neck as he trotted into the lodge. "He's got the sense of a thirteen-year-old."

She turned to Trey. "Tell me again, why are you here?"

"To take pictures and go fishing."

"Good. Stick to that." She marched off, shouldering past Pam as she came out of the lodge.

"It's obvious she doesn't want me around," Trey said to Pam.

Pam touched his arm. "You know she's under a lot of pressure right now. Her folks' death is pretty fresh. It probably feels like everything around her is falling apart, but she's too proud to ask for help. And I'm sure believes no one thinks she can make a go of it."

"Yep. That about covers it."

"Oh, c'mon, Trey." Pam placed a hand on his chest. "She needs our support. Be patient with her, will you?"

Trey shook his head, understanding why Jim succumbs to his wife's wishes. Her heart always seemed to be in the right place. "I'll do my best."

CHAPTER 12

"Forgive me for snapping at Trey," Sydney told Creator. "I know he means well." She punched number six on the CD player, cranked the volume, and lit a vanilla candle. After kicking off her boots, she ran a bubble bath and scrubbed off the dust, sweat, and death. While soaking in the hot water, Mercy Me sang about *beautiful* and *loneliness*.

There was nothing beautiful about being alone—her new life without her folks.

And why did Robert insist on going to the rodeo? So what if his goal was to make it to the Indian National Finals Rodeo in Las Vegas? So what if he needed to ride every bronc he could cinch a saddle to? She wanted her brother's help. Not Trey's.

Most of the family had left, but she couldn't succumb to the quiet. Not tonight. She planned to mingle with family for a bit, then tackle the ranch books. She was determined to get to the bottom of the financial decline. Why hadn't her parents mentioned anything? What had they been thinking to let their insurance lapse? Why hadn't they paid their bills? There had to be a reason.

And then there was Glenda. Sydney needed to find a will. If there was one. And what about probate? Good grief. What made Glenda think she could go rogue and call a Realtor without talking to her first?

She scooped up a handful of mango-scented bubbles and blew them into the stifling air, hoping they'd take her anxiety with them.

"Syd?"

She recognized Pam's voice and sighed, wanting to be left alone.

"Honey . . . ?" The door cracked open. "Jim and I have to go. My sister's rig broke down."

"Give me a minute." Sydney dried off, slipped into her robe, and moved into the living room. She gasped when finding Trey and Jim sitting on the couch and clutched the top of her robe closed below her chin. "I thought it was only you," she told Pam.

Trey smiled, then adverted his eyes, blushing. She twirled around and fled to her room.

She picked out a green T-shirt and tugged it over her head. Then found a clean pair of shorts and pulled them on. *Good grief. She could have warned me.* Then there was the matter of apologizing to Trey. She'd wait until morning when they were alone. She ran a brush through her hair and joined them in the living room.

"Martin's here," Jim told Sydney, then muttered to Trey. "This guy could have been a Navy SEAL. Half the time he appears under everyone's radar. We'll be at a campfire, telling stories, next thing he's sitting by us, no one even notices when he showed up. It's creepy."

"And enlightening. He keeps people on their toes." Sydney smiled and strode to Martin. "Hey, Uncle!" She gave the wiry man a hug, holding on for a long moment. His firm grip transferred needed strength. The top of her head came up to the middle of his chest.

"They're related?" Trey whispered to Jim.

"No. They sometimes call those who are close family friends auntie and uncle."

Martin held her at arm's length, his eyes weary. "I miss them too." Thin, gray braids fell down his front. He wore a long-sleeved plaid shirt tucked into his Wranglers, making his rodeo buckle glint. "How you holding up?"

"I'm fine."

"You can't fool me." He studied her face, concern in his eyes. "You need to come to the barn. Something's wrong with your colt."

After hugging Pam and Jim goodbye, Sydney pulled on her barn boots, grabbed her cell, and went with Martin. She'd been sure Twister would pull through. She found him sprawled in the straw, lying in his watery feces, eyes thin slits. She placed a hand on his side. His breaths came as if he'd galloped a quarter mile.

She punched in the vet's number on her cell phone and got his voice mail. "Twister's down. Doesn't look good. Call me as soon as you get this." Then, she grabbed the pitchfork and cleaned his stall.

Returning to his side, she ran her hand down his slender neck.

"How's he doing?" Trey knelt beside her.

"Not so good. I thought he was out of the woods." She called the vet again, and this time he answered.

"Saul, he's in bad shape." Her voice cracked. "Hurry."

She rushed to the tack room and examined his meds. Pills from a half-empty bottle of metronidazole with Twister's name on it lay scattered over a *Tribal Tribune*. According to his chart, Chad had missed giving him two doses. She slammed the palm of her hand on the counter.

"What's wrong?" Martin stood in the doorway.

She handed him the container. "Chad, that's what." She leaned against the counter. "Even though he normally remembers, I should have done this myself. There's too much going on. It was easy to miss. I should have at least double-checked." She chided herself for allowing Pam to talk her into letting him handle everything and not following her gut.

"Is Saul on his way?"

"Yeah." Sydney waved her cell. "He'll be here in five."

Martin handed the antibiotics back to her. "Remember, life is not separate from death. It only looks that way."

"It is separate. They aren't here."

"Are they not in your heart?"

Sydney chewed on her lower lip. It wasn't the same. She couldn't ask her dad for advice. He couldn't answer her questions as to why they were broke. "They are."

"Then you know there is no death, only a change of worlds." He handed her a small necklace pouch filled with herbs used by traditional elders for protection.

Yes, they were in heaven, but she wanted—no, needed—them now. Why had God taken them so soon? Why couldn't they have enjoyed their vacation? Why had He taken it from them? She put the medicine bag around her neck.

The crunch of gravel sounded outside the barn. Sydney shouldered past Martin and met the vet outside the stall door. "I think Twister missed a couple doses."

"Was someone covering for you?"

"Yeah, Chad."

"Get ahold of him and find out for sure."

While Saul went to the stall, Sydney tapped in Chad's number. Trey strode past and into the colt's stall. When Chad answered, she said, "Hey, Twister's down. Come to the barn." She hung up and found Trey in the straw, stroking the colt's neck with a cool rag, and the vet checking the colt's pulse.

"He's severely dehydrated," Saul said.

Sydney knelt beside the colt. "Is he gonna make it?"

"It's too early to tell." Saul pulled out an IV and inserted the catheter into the foal's neck. Sydney held the fluid bag head-high as he flushed the antibiotic through the IV. "How much was left in the bottle?"

"More than half."

Saul capped the empty syringe. "That's not like Chad. He's always been responsible. Do you think there was a miscommunication between the hands?"

Heavy footfalls rushed into the barn, and Chad appeared in the doorway. "How is he? What's wrong?"

"According to his chart, you missed two doses."

"Robert told me he'd take care of it and sent me to fix the fence."

Sydney groaned, walked to a more private spot in the barn, and called her brother. "Hey, did you tell Chad you'd give Twister his meds?"

"Oh, shoot."

"He's down, Bobby." She wiped her eyes with her knuckle. *Can't lose it now.*

"Sorry, Syd. We've all been busy setting up for the funeral—"

"I know." She pressed her lips together. "It's an honest mistake. Look, I gotta go. Saul's here."

"Keep me posted. I know how much he means to you."

What he didn't realize is that the colt was supposed to help carry the ranch into the future. She chewed on her bottom lip as she ended the call and strode back to the stall. "You're right. There was a miscommunication." She gave Chad a small smile and shrugged. "No one meant to hurt him. Go ahead and finish fixing the fence. I'll keep you posted."

He nodded and headed outside, his shoulders slumped. Martin followed him.

"It happens, Syd," Saul said. "Don't beat yourself up. Besides, this little guy's a fighter."

The foal's breaths slowed and his eyes opened, looking a bit brighter. The mare sniffed her baby and then Trey. He stroked her nose and spoke to her with a soft voice. For the first time Sydney saw him as a blessing and not another paying guest.

CHAPTER 13

Trey excused himself and rushed to get his camera. The dim light was enough to snap a few photos of the vet and Sydney working on the foal. The mare hadn't flinched with all the ruckus happening around her, so he figured all would be fine. He whisked his camera from the bag, switched lenses, and made his way back to the barn.

The stall door was open, so he went back in, stepping around a fresh pile of manure. With a balanced crouch, he snapped several photos using the soft glow of dusk light. Then, he moved backward and knelt outside the doorframe, zooming in on Sydney's delicate hands holding the nearly drained IV bag, and snapped several photos. He also shot the vet leaning close to the foal, listening through the stethoscope, the tired eyes of an ill and exhausted foal, and the quiet yet worried expression of his mother.

Since there wasn't much he could do, he went to the outdoor pens and took snapshots of the horses' curious eyes and various patterns on the Paints.

"What will you do with those pictures?"

Trey startled at Martin's voice. "Hey, thought you'd left."

"Not a chance." Martin looked at him as if he were trying to steal the ranch's finest stallion. He nodded at the camera. "What are you doing?"

"I intend to sell ranch pictures to a magazine called *True Cowboy*." It was obvious the old man didn't approve.

"Why did you choose this place?"

Trey looked over the images through the LED display. "Jim and I were college roommates. I was telling him I needed a cattle ranch surrounded by streams and mountains, not my usual desert scenes, for my next photo assignment. He suggested the Seven Tine. Said he knew the owner. I bought a plane ticket."

"You go to school for that?"

"Sure did. My degree's in photojournalism. I freelance for most major magazines." Trey held up his Nikon, a little miffed over the cross-examination. But for the sake of his relationship with Sydney, he held his tongue. "How 'bout I take a few of you?" He readied his camera.

Martin put a hand in front of his face. "No."

"I plan on helping Sydney market the ranch. You'd be the face of wisdom." He stopped himself from saying, *Now that her dad's gone.*

Martin turned red. "She doesn't need my face for that."

Trey lowered his camera. "Didn't mean to offend."

He grunted, then stalked away.

Trey had never known anyone to refuse a picture so adamantly but respected his choice. He'd come across one Native man in New Mexico who didn't care to have his photo taken. Said it'd steal his soul.

He finished photographing a few of the range horses and made his way back to the barn. Twister's stall door was closed. "You in there?"

A deep sigh floated into the aisle. "Come in."

He slid the door open. The colt's head rested in Sydney's lap. Soiled straw surrounded them, as did its stench. "How's he doing?"

"He's exhausted."

"So are you." Trey found a pitchfork and mucked the bedding, then replaced it with fresh flakes. When done, he eased to the golden straw bed and leaned against the wall.

"I owe you a huge apology." She gave him an embarrassed chuckle. "I normally don't treat guests so impetuously."

"Don't worry about it. You're under a lot of stress, and to be honest, I'm the one who should be apologizing to you. I overstepped my bounds." Her dull, charcoal-colored eyes pierced his chest. "I want to help, and I've got time on my hands. What can I do?"

"You're a city guy. What do you know about cows and horses?"

"I was actually raised on a ranch. My parents own a large spread about fifty miles south of Tucson. Dead center in rocks and cactus. Nothing like here." He paused. "I miss cows bawling. Feeding horses. Their scent. All ranch smells, for that matter."

"Well, aren't you full of surprises?" Sydney stroked the colt. "Why did you leave?"

"I hated it. Up at the crack of dawn, eating hot dust all day, no time for sports or friends. It was all about work with my dad. Hard work and little play. Didn't make teenage years fun. Or memorable."

"Sounds like you didn't get to be much of a kid."

"I couldn't wait to head to college."

"Bet you ran wild."

"For a couple years I did. Didn't know what I wanted. Until a *Nat Geo* photojournalist came to town. He spoke at the university. Listening to him talk about his adventures gave me all I needed to sign up and get as far away from my father as I could."

"U of A?"

"Yep."

"Why so close if you were trying to get away from your dad?"

"It was the only way he'd pay for it. I knew once I got my journalism degree, I was free."

"And you've been running ever since."

"I have a place in Tucson. Guess I want to keep an eye on my mom. Make sure Dad's not too hard on her."

"Hard?"

"He can be demanding. It's changed her. She used to be sweet and simple. Now she's somewhat of a diva." He twisted his mouth. She was easy to talk with, and he liked it. Yet at times it scared him, especially after his fiancée had left him for someone else. "What can I do for you? It's getting late."

"Well, it's time to feed." She stood and wiped straw off her pants. "Thanks for helping. I appreciate it."

"No problem." Trey brushed a piece of straw off her face. He was grateful she was willing to take the time to help him get the photos he needed, particularly after the trauma over the past few days, so he could be on his way.

CHAPTER 14

Monday, June 19

Wisps of a warm breeze pulsated through the office window screen. Mounds of bills covered the desk—her desk—and the Tribal Credit loan officer hadn't called back yet. But then, it had only been a couple of hours. Sydney tapped a pen on a credit card bill, the pile of debt crushing her chest.

Outside, the sound of tires crunching gravel resounded. Her sister's words rang in her ears. *I'm bringing the Realtor Monday morning.*

Mandie waddled into the office. "How's it going in here?"

"It's going."

She set a plate of cheese, almonds, and apples on Sydney's desk. "Thought you'd need a power snack."

"I do. Thanks." Sydney regarded her cook's ripe belly. "How's she doing?"

"Jumping on my bladder." Mandie rubbed the bump.

"Make sure you take time to get your feet up today. My place is open, if you need it."

"I'm almost done with lunch. I'll serve it, then take you up on the offer." She picked up a photo of the Moomaws. "Sure do miss them."

"Me too. They're in a better place, that's for sure."

Replacing the photo, Mandie nodded and then headed for the door.

Sydney's cell vibrated on the desk, and she answered it. "Hello?"

"Hey, it's Jade Reese at Tribal Credit. Can you come in? I have a meeting in an hour but can see you before then."

"I'll be right there." She scooped up the keys. Trey and Rich were moving cows to the east pasture. Mandie . . . well, she'd have to be by herself. Sydney found her in the dining room. "Got to run to the agency. Are you going to be OK?"

"Sure am." She patted a teenage girl on the shoulder. "This here's Kaylee. She didn't want to go horseback riding with her family and volunteered to stay and help."

Kaylee's short, curly hair, the color of fir bark, bounced when she nodded. Round-rimmed glasses topped her pointed nose. She gave Sydney a small wave and a big smile. "It's no problem. I want to be a chef when I grow up."

"Holy—put a tip jar out for that one!" Sydney winked at the girl. "Back soon." She took a few steps and turned. "Remind me to advertise for a new cleaning lady. I don't think Dani's coming back."

She blew through the front door to find her sister and the Realtor standing by a For Sale sign. Finding out if there was a will, which she feared there wasn't, was now at the top of her to-do list. Being the eldest didn't give Glenda the go-ahead to take charge.

Sydney stomped down the steps. "Take it down, Glenda. You don't have the right to do this." Her tone was low and firm, leaving Glenda and the Realtor's jaws slack.

Shoot. Glenda had brought in the big guns—one of her closest friends, Ellen Hayes. The ruthless woman would finagle anything for a buck. Who knew what the two of them were cooking up? What had Glenda told her? She'd made it clear long ago she had no interest in the ranch. It must be all about the money. Money they didn't have. Sydney snorted.

She must not have a clue about the ranch's financial state, and Sydney wasn't about to say a thing. Not yet anyhow.

"We talked about this." Glenda put a hand on her hip.

"I didn't agree to anything." Sydney dragged the sign from the grass, tossed it into the back of Ellen's truck, and turned to her. "Do you think we've had the time to meet with an attorney and go over the will?" She prayed there was one. Or would probate drag things out? Give her more time to come up with a plan to pay off Glenda?

"You told me that was in the works," Ellen said, "and Sydney had agreed to sell."

Ha! So it was all Glenda. "Sorry to have wasted your time." Not giving her a moment to respond, Sydney jumped into her pickup and peeled out of the driveway.

Fifteen minutes later, she pulled up to Tribal Credit, overshadowed by the new Lucy F. Covington Government Center, where council chambers sank its teeth into tribal affairs. The building that gave Glenda the impression she owned the tribe—and the ranch. "Not this time, sister."

Sydney parked in the Tribal Credit lot, marched to the front glass door, and flung it open. The building was empty of customers. A bank teller, wearing green beaded earrings and a gracious smile, regarded her.

"I'm looking for Jade Reese. She's expecting me."

"Over there." The woman pointed to a corner office, its door ajar.

Sydney went over and found Jade working her fingers over computer keys. She knocked on the doorjamb.

"Come on in. Sorry about your folks. The funeral was beautiful." Jade offered Sydney a chair. "Got your message."

"And?"

Jade sighed, regret in her eyes. "There's no way we can offer you a loan. Your parents are behind as it is." She scanned a file.

"They already borrowed money from you?"

She snapped her regard to Sydney. "You didn't know?"

Why hadn't she come across a bill? "How much?"

"They refinanced the guest lodge last year." Jade handed her a folder.

She opened it and read down the list of transactions, stopping on the balance owed, and closed the file. She let out a heavy sigh. "I had no idea things were this bad. How'd their spending get so out of control?"

"I don't know, Syd. But I'm sorry." Jade set the folder on the desk and handed her a business card. "Here's a name of a guy I trust. He might be able to help."

A liquidator? "Isn't that a bit extreme?"

"Just in case. I hope you don't have to use him. You can't file for bankruptcy because you own too much land."

"What about an auction? Cut the herd. Dad's got a bunch of old junk lying around—tractors, old rigs, tools."

"That might help, but I'm not sure it's enough to dig you out." Jade pulled open a desk drawer and browsed through it, then handed over another card. "Here's someone else. She's good."

"A financial planner. Not sure I can afford one."

"Can you afford to not get sound advice?"

On the drive home, Sydney weighed her options. She'd inventory anything that had value, find a list price, and call an auctioneer. That's a number she needed. She'd have to google the closest auction company. Cull the herd. Her stomach clenched.

She pulled into the town's only service station and reached for her purse. The seat next to her was empty and so was the back. "Good grief."

She found the cashier. "Can you put my diesel on the ranch tab? I was in such a rush when I left, I forgot to grab my wallet."

The employee went to the back room. The owner came out, grease in every crack of his wide hands. "Hey, Syd. How ya doing?"

"Good." She choked on the lump lodged in her throat.

His voice softened. "The tab's overdue. Hasn't been paid in a couple months. When can you make a payment?"

"I left my wallet at home. I can get money to you by the end of the week. Can you get me a current invoice?"

"I'll have Sandy mail you one today." He paused. "Everything OK, Syd?"

"Sure is." She gave him a forced smile, then went back outside and pumped fuel. Who else would ask for money owed? She'd have to make sure the bills were caught up before going into public again. Days of security that once bloomed in her mind were now fading and withering away.

Back at the ranch, she spent a few minutes mingling with guests, then got back to work googling the Farm Agency, Farm Bureau, and auctioneer companies. After making a few calls and finding out the ranch debt was too high for financial assistance, she tied a wet bandana around her neck, saddled her mare, and rode to the north pasture to change irrigation pipes. Her body numb, she moved a few pipes before collapsing on the ground in tears. Any trickle of hope seemed to flow downstream with a huge pile of watery cow dung.

CHAPTER 15

It was late afternoon when Rich selected a big bay for Trey to ride. The horse was an extra and wouldn't be needed until the evening guided trail ride, leaving Trey plenty of time for his photoshoot.

"You'll find cattle tucked inside a nice clearing surrounded by trees and shrubs. Nespelem Creek runs smack in the middle," Rich said. "It's a sweet spot for taking pictures."

Trey noticed the cloud cover and nodded. "I appreciate it. Thanks." His camera slung over his shoulder, he mounted and headed for the north pasture. Taking his time, he snapped photos of native birds and a squirrel scampering up a tree. Cows grazed in the distance, and a young bull kicked up, spun around, and slammed into his mother.

About thirty minutes later, Sydney's crumpled body by the irrigation pipe made Trey kick his horse into a gallop. She had worked herself to the ground, and now he'd found her lying in a patch of grass in the middle of the pasture. He'd never met such a bull-headed woman. Was never so attracted to one either.

He sprang from the bay gelding and crouched by her side. "What are you doing out here?"

Her eyes were tear-glistened and red-rimmed. "I'm done."

"What do you mean?"

"My parents left me with a mound of debt and no life insurance. Glenda's pushing to sell. She was even so brash as to hire a Realtor before we've located a will. Can you believe that? We hadn't agreed on anything."

Trey brushed damp hair from her cheek with his thumb. "How much?"

"Enough to sink us."

"Did they ever have life insurance? Or did it simply lapse?"

"It lapsed." She wiped her face with the bandana from her neck. "I think something was wrong with my mom. But I can't put my finger on it. Bills weren't paid, and that's not like her. There was only a hundred in the account the day they died. If we hadn't insisted they go, I wouldn't be in this mess."

"I'm sure they wanted to go, or they would have stayed home. Don't you think?"

"We thought so. My mom hadn't been feeling well but seemed excited. I assumed she was worn to a frazzle and needed the rest. Then again, my dad seemed to drag his feet. A bunch of us pitched in and paid for everything." Sydney took a sip from her water bottle. "I can't get a loan. There's not much left to do but liquidate and sell."

"How many cows do you have?"

"Three hundred."

Trey's eyes widened. "Horses?"

"Twenty head, counting foals."

It would be a stretch, but maybe the ranch could be saved after all. "Studs?"

"Two. One's a Blue Valentine grandson, the other is a grandson of The Boon."

"An Old Sorrel descendant." Trey blew out a low whistle. "You've got remarkable bloodlines on this place."

"You actually aren't a city boy, are you?"

He laughed. "Not in the least."

"Tell me the truth, do you think I can hold on to this place?"

"There's always a chance. I can help you run numbers later if you want."

"That'd be great."

"Now come on, let's move these pipes." He helped her up, noticing a flicker of hope in her eyes. Maybe he didn't need to be in such a hurry to leave. His next assignment wasn't for a few weeks. And he couldn't think of anything he'd rather do than be on an amazing ranch doing chores with a beautiful woman.

CHAPTER 16

Sydney dished up a plate of ribs smothered in barbecue sauce, garden salad, mashed potatoes and gravy, and peach cobbler, and took a seat on a leather chair by the big bay window. She was thankful her appetite was coming back. Trey set his heaping plate of food along with a glass of strawberry lemonade next to hers. "Hungry?"

"Starving." He bowed his head and closed his eyes for a short moment before picking up a rib and sinking his teeth into it like a famished dog.

She should have said grace, too, thanking Creator for Trey's help and for his taking photos to help her market the ranch, provided she's able to keep it. But until she was done being mad at God, her prayers would have to wait.

She took a bite of salad and enjoyed the tangy dressing. "What're your ideas?"

Trey wiped his mouth with a napkin. "You might be able to catch your breath if you sold half the herd of cows or more. You could have a dispersal sale."

"What's that?"

"Bidders come to you. Since you have purebred Angus, you'll bring in a better price. You'd sell cow/calf pairs and half the bulls. How many bulls do you have?"

"Twenty-five."

"You can sell ten bulls. What about horses?"

"Hang on, I'll grab a notebook." She rushed to the office. The answering machine light flashed, so she pushed the

Play button. Glenda wanted to talk about the ranch. Sydney cringed. If she had a plan before finding the will, she could hold Glenda off. She took a minute to google and print off information about probate to read later. She tugged a leather tooled notebook from her drawer, grabbed a mechanical pencil from a Seven Tine–logoed cup, and went back to the table.

"Got it." Trey tapped his cell and set it on the table.

She opened the book and made notes and columns. "A hundred fifty pairs, ten bulls, horses . . ." Trey had barbecue sauce around his lips. She reached for a napkin and dabbed his mouth. Their gazes locked for a few seconds before she sat back and focused on the notebook. "We list five colts for sure. If Twister pulls through, I want to keep him. He could potentially salvage this place."

"That's a big gamble. How's he doing?"

"It is, but he's much better. He was up and nursing this morning. Weak, but he's making remarkable improvements."

Trey studied her as though she'd stretched the truth, then gulped the last of his strawberry lemonade and clinked the glass on the table. "Good. You have a couple of reputable studs. Let's start listing stud fees online. I'll take their pictures tomorrow. You can work with Dr. Saul to freeze and ship semen. That will broaden the playing field."

"How do you know all this?"

"My dad raised more than cattle. He bred and trained high-end quarter horses too. When he had a good but middle-aged one that he wanted to cut and sell as a competition horse, he did the same thing."

"Nice." Sydney pushed potatoes around on her plate. "Why are you so intent on helping me?"

"To be honest, I care about you guys and would like to see you save this place. It's got a heartbeat to it that pumps a fruitful spirit through its veins. I've never known folks like you. This place has renewed me. It's filled with a sentimental grit and has sparked something in me that's been dead for a long time."

"Grit?" Sydney didn't feel an ounce of courage or security in herself or the ranch. Everything seemed to be crumbling around her. The dispersal sale would be a long shot depending on cattle prices.

"I know you can't see it right now, but I feel a huge sense of peace. I felt it the moment I stepped over the threshold—"

"That's because you're always on the go. This is new territory for you. The difference between parched desert and lush mountains."

Trey shook his head. "It's more than that. A kind of stability or bond or unity surrounds this place. It's strong. Like a gigantic magnet." He pointed to a framed photo of a young Lester and Jennie Moomaw on the wall. "You can see it in their eyes. You have that same determined look."

"The determination that used to exist? It's gone. I don't know where the money will come from to pay employee wages. I can't leave a single, pregnant mother in a lurch."

"We'll figure it out." He checked his phone. "I took pics of the ranch and stock. Looks like another magazine wants to buy them. I'll donate the check to you for a month's insurance premium."

"I can't take your money." But how she wanted to take him up on his offer. "I can't take on the additional debt."

"You don't have to pay me back."

"That's generous, but I can't do it." Besides, once he left, he'd be hard to catch up with. By the time she came up with the money, if she did, who knew where he'd be? She didn't want owing someone on her conscience.

"You can pay me back once the ranch gets in the black."

She steeled her spine and gave him a determined look. "Thank you, but no."

Hopefully, the dispersal sale would at least dig her partway out of the hole.

The will had to be in the lodge office. Sydney started at the file cabinets kept in the closet. She riffled through folders in the top drawer, which consisted of mostly horse pedigrees. The second drawer held ranch supply and stud fee receipts. Ranch history and photos filled the third drawer, and the bottom drawer consisted of past years' taxes.

"Where are you?" There had to be one.

Not finding the will, she turned to a three-foot safe next to the file cabinet. After punching in the code and snapping open the door, she fished through blank ranch checks, two loaded revolvers, boxes of spare bullets, copies of ranch vehicle and machinery registrations, birth certificates, and petty cash. Again, she came up empty. She went to the desk and searched the drawers but didn't see anything.

What would she do if there wasn't one? From what she'd read about probate, it could be a costly nightmare. She plopped down on the coffee table and chewed on her thumbnail.

Her other option was to search her dad's office in the main house. Was she ready to go back in? She'd have to be. It was late and she was bushed, so she plodded to her cabin and hit the hay. She'd look again in the morning with fresh eyes.

CHAPTER 17

Tuesday, June 20

The clock glowed four a.m. Sydney's mind would not stop trying to figure out where the blasted will was. She dressed in a long-sleeve T-shirt and jeans, grabbed her folks' house key, and headed that way. The twilight sky offered enough golden-amber illumination for her to make it without a flashlight.

Pots of wilted flowers covered the porch near the entrance. As she unlocked the door, she made a mental note to water the plants. Or see if her auntie Marcie could come and try to revive the ranch's flora.

She opened the door and stood at the threshold, for a moment expecting the familiar sounds of her parents' home. What she wouldn't give to hear their voices.

With a sigh and a heavy heart, she entered her dad's office and flicked on the light.

Photos of the Moomaw lineage and prize bulls lined all the white walls except the one covered by a floor-to-ceiling oak bookshelf. In the far corner of the room loomed a black five-foot gun safe. She settled at his desk and went through the drawers. They housed decades of cattle records, including stock inventory, individual animal identification, market dates, pregnancy and calving dates, pasture usage, and sire information. Her father had been a stickler for record keeping. Something she'd have to learn to pay more attention to.

She sank back in the roller chair. Out the window, trees, fading grass, and wildflowers edged a path leading to her cabin. She pushed the chair side to side. "Where are you?" Then swiveled around. *Could anything be in the gun safe?*

She rose and stood in front of the keypad. What was the combination? She punched in several groupings—family and bull birthdates, anniversaries, and names aligned with digits. If she only knew where the passcode had been hidden. After several frustrating attempts, she gave up and rummaged through the closet and bookshelves for both the will and the code.

After several hours of searching, all she could find was more information relating to her dad's cattle. Somewhat discouraged, she wandered to the living room, dropped to the couch, and studied the photos. Could there be a clue in them? After a short while, the silence was simply too much to bear. Locking the door behind her, she went back to her cabin to change into a cooler shirt, then headed out again to check on Twister.

She was halfway to the barn when Glenda drove up and parked in front of the lodge. Trey came out of the barn and headed toward them. Her throat tightened as she walked toward her sister. Once past the rig, she pursed her lips at the homemade For Sale sign. If she wasn't so irritated, it'd be funny.

"Don't trash it this time." Glenda set her hands on her hips.

"Kimberly make that for you?"

Glenda shot her a fiery glare.

"And what part of *we need to find a will or deal with probate* are you having a hard time with?"

"You know this place will take time to sell for the asking price—"

"Which is?" Sydney folded her arms over her chest.

"We need to discuss that."

She scoffed. "There's nothing to discuss."

"Come on, Syd. All I'm trying to do is get ahead of the game. Maybe one of the guests knows someone—"

"I doubt it."

Glenda grimaced. "There's one by the ranch entrance too. Leave 'em alone, *please*."

Trey came up beside her. Oh, good, she could use the moral support. After their ranch-saving session, she was convinced he was on her side.

They surrounded the sign as if it were a sick calf.

"No guarantees," Sydney said, her mouth dry and bitter as a waterless creek. "But I'll make you a deal."

"A deal? I don't have to make deals. I'm the oldest."

"You mean you're the tyrant." Sydney wished her sister wasn't such a schmuck. She'd turned high and mighty once she won a council seat. After five years, the big chief hat seemed to pinch her head. *Oh, Lord, if there's a will, help me find it.*

"What are you offering?" Glenda arched a brow.

"I take the insurance money and buy you out." Sydney prayed Trey wouldn't spill the beans. His eyes grew wide, and he looked away.

Glenda's poker face was solid. "When's the check coming? I assume you've contacted the insurance agency."

"It's in the mail."

Trey fiddled with the For Sale sign, a muscle in his jaw twitching.

"We need to have the place appraised," Glenda said. "Get halves worked out."

"You mean thirds." Why shouldn't Robert get part of the money? He was their brother, after all. And maybe, just maybe, he'd be willing to invest it back into the ranch. Because he had promised to do anything to help sustain it.

Glenda quirked a brow.

"I'm not leaving Bobby out." Besides, it was the right thing to do, and his portion would reduce Glenda's share. "I'll make the call."

"You figure everything up and let me know." Glenda spoke as if she knew the insurance money would come up short. "You have two weeks."

"You know getting an appraisal takes longer than that."

"Fine, call when you have the numbers." She jumped into her truck and left.

Trey leaned against her old Chevy. "Why'd you lie to her?"

"If she knew the truth, I wouldn't have a chance. It was the only way I could get her to back off."

"Won't lying dig you a bigger hole?"

Sydney shrugged.

"The truth allows a person to deal with problems head-on. Deception only complicates them, don't you think?"

"You talking from experience?" She felt God convicting her to admit it was true but wasn't brave enough to say it aloud.

"Make that plural."

"In this case, it's all I got."

"But if a person lays out the facts, they know where they stand. You yanked the pin out of a grenade."

Sydney opened her fist like fireworks. "It's coming either way." She started for the barn. "Gotta check on Twister," she said as she went past him.

Trey followed. "What's your next move then?"

"Marketing. It's all about how we reveal this place to the public."

A young girl about nine, wearing overalls, pink glasses, and a frayed straw cowboy hat, skipped up to Sydney. "Can I milk Daisy?"

"Sure can." Sydney waved to the girl's mom. "Remember where the bucket is?"

The nine-year-old nodded. "In the tack room under the sink."

"That's right." The girl and her family had been staying for a week. They resided in Seattle and had been coming for a few years. "Do you remember how I showed you to pull the teats without hurting her?"

"Like this." The girl made a milking motion with her hands.

"Good job! Have fun."

She bounced to the barn.

"That's what I'm talking about. The atmosphere here is so family-oriented," Trey said. "That's the fruitful spirit I was talking about. A welcoming place that's hard to leave."

A twinge of hope settled in her chest. "Are you thinking of staying on longer?"

"I can stay and help out until you get back on your feet." He wiped dirt from her nose. "I've got everything I need to work from here." He placed a hand on the small of her back and motioned for her to enter the barn ahead of him.

She wanted to melt in his arms. Instead, she stiffened at his tender touch. A response she prayed would someday disappear.

CHAPTER 18

W hy had Sydney gone rigid from Trey's touch? Was it him? Or did she recoil with every man? He'd have to take the pictures and remember to keep his hands to himself.

"What do you want to do first?" Standing at the open barn door, he watched the activity outside. Wranglers saddled horses. Kids sprayed each other with water guns. Hens clucked at their chicks, herding them out of the line of fire. "I could grab my camera and shoot more pictures."

"I'll check on Twister and the twin calves, and then we can take pictures of the stallions."

"Great. I'll be right back." He strode to the lodge to get his Nikon, a spring in his step, and found Mandie hunched over a chair, a hand on her stomach. "You all right?"

She shook her head. "Contractions," she said through gritted teeth.

"What should I do?" Trey reached for his cell.

"Take me to the doctor."

"Let me find Syd—"

"There's no time!" She held her breath, her teeth clenched.

He wrapped an arm around her waist and led her to the ranch's blue Chevy. He called a twig of a boy with saggy pants and earbuds to come over. "Hey, can you go find Sydney? Let her know I'm taking Mandie to the doctor."

"Who's Sydney?" The teenage guest shrugged and kept walking.

"Punk." Trey lifted Mandie into the truck, ran to the other side, and fumbled for the keys, finding them under the seat.

"Let's go!"

With shaky hands, he started the rig, then sped down the driveway.

Mandie groaned. "She's not due for another month or so!" She rubbed her belly, taking deep breaths.

"Can't they give you something to stop the contractions?"

"I hope so." She leaned back, beads of sweat covering her brow. "That was a bad one." She unrolled her window and turned her face to the wind.

"How far apart are they?"

"About five minutes."

Trey turned onto Highway 155 and stepped on the gas, the rear of the truck fishtailing.

"Holy! Slow down. I won't have the kid in the rig." She opened the wing window and grasped the dividing bar with one hand and her belly with the other.

White knuckled, Trey swallowed hard. "You having another one?"

She nodded, her face turning red.

He increased his speed. "Where do we turn?"

"Past the . . . Trading Post." She let out a moan. "Stay on . . . Lakes Avenue. It's on your . . . left."

Trey prayed the infant would stay in Mandie's belly. There was no way he was about to help deliver a baby. In a truck. He turned left at the Tribal Trading Post and parked in the clinic lot, then sprang from the truck and helped Mandie inside.

The receptionist took one look at her and escorted her to another room.

Trey's cell rang. He didn't recognize the number. "Hello?"

"Where'd you take her?" Sydney's voice blared through the line.

"The clinic."

"The *clinic?*"

Trey flinched and held the phone away from his ear for a few seconds. "That's where she told me to go."

"Why didn't you bring her to the hospital?"

"Um . . ." He did as he was told.

"Why didn't you come get me?"

He dropped to a chair. "She yelled and made me bring her to the doctor."

Sydney sighed. "I'll be right there."

The receptionist handed Trey a clipboard. "You the father?"

"What? No!" He shoved it away. "I'm her ride. Someone will be here to fill that out shortly."

The receptionist went back to the front desk.

Trey picked up a magazine and thumbed through its pages. Beauty products and gossip didn't interest him, so he tossed it back on the table. A text flashed on the screen. It was from one of his sisters. He groaned and ignored it. Called Jim. Got his voice mail. Hung up.

He paced the waiting room. *So this is what dads go through?* A shriek came from behind the door Mandie had disappeared through. He strode to it and reached for the knob. Then dropped his hand. *Relax!* He was never this uptight when his sister had given birth. *It's not even my baby.*

He turned to go outside when Sydney rushed through the door and slammed into him. He caught her, the mixture of horse and vanilla tickling his senses, and set her upright.

"Where is she?" Sydney took one look at him and turned toward the front desk.

"Hey, Syd. You must be here for Mandie," a different receptionist said. "Is the father on his way?"

She snorted. "The deadbeat left her last week. Where is she?"

Another shriek pierced the room from behind closed doors. Sydney didn't wait for the receptionist to invite her back. "You can head back to the ranch now," she said to Trey before bursting through the door. "Mandie?"

Trey's mouth dropped. "Wow. *Thanks for your help, man!*" He stomped to the truck, got in, and held on to the steering wheel. "Maybe I want to see if she has the baby, Miss Bossy Pants." He clenched his teeth and turned over the motor. Why couldn't he wait and find out if the baby would be born anytime soon? Who was she to stop him?

He killed the engine and strode to the front desk. "How is she?"

The receptionist Sydney had talked with blinked at him, then scanned him with curious eyes. "You a new boyfriend?"

Heat rose up his neck. "I'm the guy who drove her here."

"Then sorry, I can't tell you anything." She picked up the phone and punched in a number.

He took a seat and grabbed a magazine, wondering how long it would take for an update. When no one came out after thirty minutes, he drove back to the ranch, pondering what it would be like to be a dad. Would he be better than his?

CHAPTER 19

It was late afternoon when Sydney burst through the lodge door. "It's a girl!"

The few guests lingering in the cool room broke out in cheers. And Trey was at a table with two women, gobbling what looked like huckleberry cheesecake like there was gold at the bottom of the bowl. She started for him, wanting to ask if she could talk to him privately, but went to her office instead. She'd give him a minute.

After dropping her purse on the desk, she picked up a flyer for the Nespelem Fourth of July Rodeo. She had a few weeks to come up with a plan that would reel in interest—hook, line, and sinker.

Trey knocked on the doorjamb. "Got a minute?"

She was surprised to see the concern on his face. "What's on your mind?"

"I . . . Um, how's Mandie and the baby?"

"Good. They're both healthy." She leaned back. "Listen. I'm sorry I snapped at you. You didn't deserve it. I was feeling sorry for myself because she didn't wait for me."

"You're right, I didn't deserve it." He leaned against the doorframe and crossed his arms over his chest. "Everything went well, then?"

"Yeah."

"Is there a name?"

She grinned. "Nona. Isn't it beautiful?"

"Nona?" He nodded. "Sure is. What does it mean?"

"It means ninth. Normally given to the ninth live child. In this case, it refers to nine tries for a live baby." She understood how heartrending it felt to lose a child.

His eyes grew wide. "She's lost eight babies? How?"

"She's had eight miscarriages. The doctor told her to quit trying. But she was convinced God would give her a live baby. Guess she was right." Sydney moved to the stuffed chair across from him and rested her feet on the coffee table. "Do you think the dispersal sale will help?"

Trey plunked down on the sofa across from her. "I sure do." He watched her for a moment, then stretched his legs parallel to hers.

Robert burst into the office and held out a bag of venison jerky. Sydney was sure he was on a high from winning the Princeton Rodeo after riding two rank broncs. "You have to try this!" He handed them each a piece.

"I love this stuff." Sydney ripped off a slice and popped it into her mouth.

Trey tore off a chunk with his teeth. He examined the rest of the dried meat while he chewed as if it were made of sugar. "What's in it?"

"She won't say," Robert said with a sarcastic tone.

"Who won't say?"

Robert pointed at Sydney and laughed as he left.

"Does he always do that?"

"What?" She tore off a slice.

"Burst into here, pass out food, then leave?" Trey took a bite.

"I think he's just being nosy." And probably wanted to see if there's anything going on between her and Trey, the little snoop.

He held up his sliver. "Here's the answer to your financial problems."

"How so?" Sydney said. "It's only meat. Everyone has it around here."

"I bet not this good. You can sell this stuff like crazy. People would pay big money. You could even sell it online. What's in it?"

Sydney chuckled. "Nice try."

"No. Seriously. You could try different flavors. How much of this do you have?"

"Ten big boxes in the deep freeze."

He held up his piece. "Bag 'em up and stick a label on 'em."

"We'll see. I'm sure Glenda will find a barrier even to that."

"Quit using her as an excuse," he said, then recoiled. "Sorry. That was out of line."

She grunted. "You're right."

He leaned forward, a wide grin on his face, his eyes sparkling. "I'm sorry. Did I hear you right? I'm what?"

Laughing, she wadded up a paper from the coffee table and threw it at him. "You're right."

He ducked, then sobered. "What about putting in a gift shop?"

"Yeah, I mentioned that to my dad last winter. He said it was a waste of time. We have a skeleton crew as it is. 'Who'd run it?' he'd ask. I offered. He declined. Said my time was better used with the horses and kids." She plucked a decorative Western pillow off the floor and hugged it.

"You're good with kids. And horses."

How nice of him to say so. "I do enjoy giving them lessons. Love how they connect with the horses. One time we had a family come who had an autistic boy. He shrieked and ripped around the place. I took him to the barn, and he instantly calmed down. Once he touched my mare, he seemed like a totally different kid. He was a sweet boy. About ten. Yeah, I'd love to settle down someday and have a batch of my own."

Would the jerky be as big a hit as Trey claimed? Or was he being polite, trying to encourage her? Online sales piqued her interest. But having the time to dry it would be another item on her already busy schedule.

CHAPTER 20

A batch of her own?

Trey gulped and began to rethink his own aspirations about becoming a father. The way he'd handled Mandie's labor made him realize he might not be cut out to be a dad. His mind skipped back to his childhood. Long, hard days on the ranch since he was a bump in the saddle was not the ideal upbringing. Ranching conventions made the worst family vacations. In college, he vowed to never subject a child to a militant, shallow upbringing but wasn't sure he knew any other way.

He fingered the jerky. That's what he'd focus on. Helping Sydney and getting back to photojournalism. He took a bite, never having tasted venison so sweet and spicy before. Not the kind that burns the hide off a tongue but dried meat that tingles a person's senses. It melted in his mouth, making him want more. "You design the labels, and I'll help package these. Trust me, they'll sell."

Sydney rolled her eyes. "I suppose it won't hurt to try."

"That a girl."

She still looked skeptical. "But where will I sell them? We don't have enough guests to turn a sustaining profit."

"Isn't there a carnival or summer event coming up?"

"The Fourth of July rodeo and powwow actually starts on the seventh. We have less than two weeks."

"The seventh?"

"The fourth is on a Tuesday so the events are pushed up to the following weekend."

"Got it. Why not call some friends? I bet for a small bag of this they'd gladly help. I know this is bad timing, but . . ." He smiled as her eyes twinkled. "You have any empty space to start a gift shop?" He hoped she wouldn't use her dad's past rejection as an excuse.

"Come with me."

She led him to a dark, empty space behind the office and flipped on a light. Boxes lined the walls, as did extra tables and folding chairs.

Trey straddled a saddle secured to a wooden stand. The doorless space was dark but open and inviting. Down the road a window could be added to brighten the room. "This is a perfect spot. You can install can lights or chandeliers, build glass cases and shelves, make it look appealing." He pointed to a closet in the corner of the room. "What's in there?"

"Old pictures and knickknacks. Things my mom insisted on keeping." She opened the door and pulled a chain. A light glowed.

Trey brushed the warm skin of her arm with his as he stepped inside. She was close enough he felt her breath on the lump in his throat. He wet his lips, wanting to kiss her soft skin, but reminded himself to be a gentleman.

She stood on her tiptoes, reaching toward his neck, closing the space between their lips. "What's this?"

He jerked back, fumbling for words. He turned around and lifted the box off the shelf labeled "beads." What he wanted to do was grab his belongings and run for the hills before he made a move he'd regret. Being close to her made his insides throb. He dragged his focus back to the cartons. "This looks interesting."

"I've never paid attention to what was in there. Let's check it out." Sydney moved aside so he could get around her. "Here's another one." She grabbed it and followed him to the dining area. "Did you see all those boxes?"

He nodded, lifted out a fabric pouch heavier than expected, and peeked inside. Slipping out a turquoise-, purple-, and black-seed beaded necklace, he held it up to the light. "This is incredible. Did your mom make it?"

"Not sure. I've never seen it before." She took the necklace from him and examined the deft intricacies. "Mom used to talk about my grandma making necklaces like this from a wooden loom my grandpa fashioned for her." She peered inside her box. "She said she'd done a little beading before she married Dad. As the ranch and her ties to it grew, she had to quit and ended up helping with the paperwork and animals." She set several fabric pouches on the table and opened them.

"Look at this." He showed her an AM stitched into the right-hand corner with red thread.

"Abigail Moomaw. My grandmother."

Trey went to grab another pouch from his box and noticed the label. "Same 'AM.'"

Sydney turned to her box. JM had been stitched into the various color and patterned fabric pouches. "This was my mom's—Jennie Moomaw." She lifted a pouch off the table and pulled out its contents. Draped over her hand was a loom-beaded rose necklace, its buds in hues of red, orange, and yellow, backed with white and blue, and outlined in black. Attached to either end was a round chevron using the same fire colors. Black and white fringe hung from the chevron.

Sydney lay all the jewelry on top of the pouches they'd been nestled in, saving the largest one in a buckskin pouch for last. She slipped it out and smiled at a child's buckskin handbag. Colorful, running horses graced the front. Beaded in black lettering was *Esperanza*. "I wonder what this means."

Trey stood beside her. "It means *hope*."

"How do you know?" She handed him the bag.

He fingered the letters. "It's a shrub that blooms yellow flowers. My mom has them all over their ranch. With y'all being Native, why would there be a Spanish word on this bag?"

"There's a large Hispanic population around here. Many of them pick apples in the orchards. Heck, some of my relatives are married to them. Maybe it was a gift from a Hispanic friend. I honestly don't know."

"Could be."

She placed the bag on the table and retrieved another box.

Trey stepped in behind her. This time, he kept his distance.

She strained to gather another box with JM on it. "Can you get it?"

His body hugged hers as he reached behind her. He lingered for a moment, enjoying the scent of her herbal shampoo. Tempted to kiss the back of her neck, he grabbed the box and backed out of the closet, one slow step at a time as if luring a filly to a sweet treat. Sydney's cheeks glowed, her stare clinging to his until he turned and bumped into a table.

Moments later, Sydney joined him, two boxes stacked in her arms. "We should get them all out and take inventory."

He fetched the remaining boxes while she laid the unopened pouches on tables by size. Guests were either out on a trail ride or fishing nearby at Buffalo Lake, giving them time to spread out before the dinner rush.

After retrieving his camera, he laid out a box of jewelry.

Sydney's face lit up with each piece pulled out. Trey picked up his camera and took a close up of her admiring pastel beaded earrings. Her long nose and sculpted jaw drew his attention. He snapped a few more pictures, admitting to himself she'd captured his curiosity from the moment they met.

"What do you think of this one?" She held up a loomed necklace with cactus lined down the sides. "Think your mom would fancy it?"

He laughed. "Probably. Although she's more into squash blossoms." He snapped her photo. "What are you going to do with all of this?"

She studied the pieces. "Sell 'em."

These should help convince her to open up a gift shop.

CHAPTER 21

Sunday, June 25

After church, Sydney scoured the internet, trying to locate comparative values of her family's beadwork. She thought about the Esperanza bag. *It means hope.* Was there hope for the ranch? Only God knew the answer to that question.

She'd spent bits of time during the week trying to learn what she could about each piece. Auntie Marcie had recorded short descriptions on cards for most of them after Trey and Sandra, the temporary cook covering for Mandie, had helped her record the inventory. Thankfully, Sandra had been available to fill in until Mandie returned. Word of mouth had connected her with the reserved forty-five-year-old single woman who was in need of earning extra money to help care for her four children.

When the tedious task was complete, Sydney had locked them in the five-foot gun safe. Guilt clenched her chest, but it had to be done. Thousands of dollars were invested—she'd need every cent.

Upon finding ballpark prices for most of the items, she jotted them in a notebook. It was hard for her to concentrate with thoughts of Trey hugging her back like he had the day they'd discovered the boxes of merchandise.

Most of the week, he'd been fishing with Jim. A few times, Uncle Walt had taken him around the reservation and surrounding towns for photoshoots. Oh, my. Was she missing him? *Good grief, Sydney, you barely know each other. Come on, focus!*

But minutes later, her mind meandered back to when they'd have time to uncover any further treasures buried in the closet. Maybe later that night? She groaned, needing her mom for advice. She'd go it alone, figuring it best to keep him at bay.

Trey entered the office and leaned against the corner of her desk, camera in hand. "Wanna get shots for a flyer? From what I've learned, the Nespelem Celebration is the best place to get coverage. Did you find any friends to help?"

Her neck warmed. "Not yet. Let's get the photos, line out the brochure, and then I'll make the calls."

They spent the rest of the afternoon capturing the right images for the brochure. Trey taste-tested several dried venison samples and wrote a description for each. As guests came in and out, a handful were pulled aside, given samples, and asked for their feedback. They seemed to enjoy being part of the fun, so Sydney rounded up a few clipboards and asked for input concerning the gift shop.

"This one's quite tasty, hey?" a lady from British Columbia asked her friend. She then offered advice on how to arrange and organize a ranch-style boutique. "This would be a top seller."

According to additional feedback, local woodworkers would be a good resource to build glass display cases, and card games, squirt guns, and other small toys would be in high demand. Around four, Sydney printed a proof of the brochure and handed it to Trey.

"It's perfect! You're great at this. The venison alone will pull in traffic, especially if you have samples at the booth. They'll love the teriyaki one for sure."

"You think so?"

"Absolutely."

His encouragement gave her courage and reassurance. But she'd have to be careful. Needing comfort so soon after her folks' deaths would be an emotional trap to avoid. She'd never met a man so willing. So kind. So striking.

"Can we get more photos in the north pasture?" he asked. "One more shoot, and I should have all I need. For a least two magazines. I picked up another one this morning."

"That's great!" Sydney checked her cell. "We've got time." It was Sunday, after all, and was supposed to be a day of rest.

He escorted her to the barn, and they saddled up.

When ready, Sydney said, "Follow me. I've got the perfect place." They rode for several miles and stopped at a cozy spot beside a secluded pond. "Isn't this beautiful?"

"I've never seen anything like it." He shot pictures of the water, cottonwood and aspen trees, and Sydney.

She chuckled and covered her eyes with her hand. "Not me!"

He photographed a few cows before riding up beside her. "This beauty makes me want to move up here."

Oh, how she'd like that. "But your roots are tied to Arizona. I get that." She could never leave the rez.

Trey dismounted. "In a few months, I'll be headed to South America on assignment. I can hang around until then."

"That sounds interesting." Her disappointment surprised her. She got off Cyan and dropped the reins, then settled on a bed of grass closer to the pond.

He settled beside her. "I'm following a mission team to the Amazon. I use the money from the photos to help them with clean water, medical needs, and food."

"How long have you been going? Isn't it dangerous?"

"A few years now. It is. But getting the gospel to nations who don't know God and providing for their needs is worth it."

"So it's about being a martyr?"

Trey laughed. "No. It's about giving people hope."

"I was asked to go on a mission trip in high school to build houses in Mexico. But my folks needed me at the ranch. I feel like I missed a big opportunity."

Trey leaned back on his elbows. "There will be other chances. Maybe you can go once things settle down and the ranch gets back in the black."

"That's a hard pass. Look what happened to my parents."

He crossed his ankles and studied her. "I don't know. I've found it's better to trust God, in good times and bad."

"Maybe." When she'd finally found someone she felt safe enough to open up her fractured heart to, he announced his Amazon plans. Just her luck. On the other hand, perhaps Creator was saving her from another heartache.

"Over the years I've learned that God goes before me, breaking the trail, and promises to be with me every step of the way. Knowing God's with me is what gives me the courage to keep going." He gave her a concerned grin.

She wanted to trust Creator more but felt blocked.

"How are you holding up?"

"I can't get rid of the nightmares." Sydney rubbed her temples. "Every morning I wake up to a mock crash. Me screaming, chasing after the girl's car, finding my folks bloody and mangled."

Trey leaned over and brushed her hair to the side, then gently massaged her neck. "I wish I could take them away."

She lifted her chin to him. "I wish you could too." If only Trey could be the one to fill her void. He made her feel safe. Protected. Could they make a relationship work? Her pulse sped up.

"Find any strays?"

Sydney startled and jumped to her feet. "Darn you!" She hated when Martin snuck up on people like the Cheyenne Dog Soldiers in *The Last of the Dogmen*. His palomino munched grass about fifty yards behind them.

Martin glared at Trey, then regarded Sydney. "Those that lie down with a dog, get up with fleas."

"Martin!" Why did he have to be so rude? "Mind your manners."

Trey rose and stood beside her. "No strays around here."

"I see one right in front of me." He speared Trey with a stony stare.

She wedged her hands in her front pockets. "What's gotten into you? And what are you doing here anyway?"

"Looking for wolf tracks." He turned to Trey. "I've seen guys like you come in like a whirlwind, wreak havoc, and disappear. What do you want with Syd?"

"I want to help. Nothing's going on between us—"

"It didn't look like nothing to me." Martin stepped closer to Sydney. "Certain things catch your eye, but pursue only those that capture your heart. Watch out for Coyote. He'll bite you in the tail." He turned and ambled back to his horse.

"He about gave me a heart attack." Trey reached for her. "What about you?"

Sydney moved away. "I'll never get used to him sneaking around." She started for Cyan. "We better head back."

Amazon. That would be her prompt to keep him at bay. She'd need something, because he was way too tempting.

CHAPTER 22

Friday, July 7

Stifling heat inside the canopy tent covered Sydney like prolonged time in a sweat lodge, so she positioned the table holding her bags of venison at the tent's edge. Under the table were boxes labeled teriyaki, garlic, cider, rosemary with lemon and honey, and, of course, her secret recipe.

She handed a squatty cowboy wearing a tan hat a sample of the jerky. "This is my new flavor. Whaddya think?"

The smile on his face gave her hope.

"This is great! What's in it?" He tore a second chunk off with his chew-stained teeth.

"A drip of amber ale and a dash of peppercorn." Sydney felt like the next Rachael Ray. "Doesn't it pop in your mouth?" She held a tray up to him. "Try another. And be sure to tell your friends."

"Heck, I'll take a bag of each. I've never tried jerky this savory before." He handed her a fifty. "Syd's Jazzy Jerky, huh? You bet I'll tell my partners, but I ain't sharing." He tipped his hat, gathered his sack of dried meat, and ambled to the next vendor.

Sydney slipped the bill into her beaded money pouch and served the next customer. She smiled at the human ribbon until Glenda stepped into view. Her hands shook, and a lump formed in her throat. How would she explain this to her sister? She sold three bags, then held up the sample tray to an elder.

"Ohhh, this has kick."

Sydney winked at the woman. "I wove in a little peppercorn."

She smiled, deep creases edging her green eyes. "I'll take two bags."

When it was her turn, Glenda stepped up to the table and examined a bag of rosemary-and-honey jerky. "What's going on here?"

"I'm being inventive. Here, try one." Sydney held up the sample tray.

"What aren't you telling me?" Glenda picked out a morsel. "I have yet to hear from you or receive an insurance check." She plopped it in her mouth. "Mm. This is good."

"This is hardly the place."

Glenda anchored her hands on her hips. "I want answers." Her voice rose. "What's the hold up?"

Sydney leaned forward and lowered her voice. "Don't make a scene."

Chuck strolled up and eyeballed the tray. "Is this your famous jerky?" He grabbed a sample and popped it in his mouth.

"Sure is." Sydney wasn't about to let Glenda intimidate her.

"How's it going in here?" Trey approached the booth from behind. He lifted his chin to Chuck. "Good, huh?"

Chuck took another sample. "Syd's the best."

Glenda smacked her husband's arm.

He jerked to the side. "Only at jerky, babe." His remark didn't seem to put out any fires. "Let's go, I want to introduce you to a friend before he takes off." He turned to Sydney. "I'll be back." He waved at her and escorted his wife down the lane of tents.

"At some point, you have to come clean." Trey snuck another sample.

Sydney ignored his comment and helped the next person in line.

After three hours, the five boxes she'd brought were empty. She fingered through her swollen money pouch. "We made a killing, and it's only Friday."

Trey took a peek. "Nice work."

"I've got friends willing to hang around the rest of the day and pass out brochures. If things keep going like they did this morning, we're in business."

Trey motioned to the pouch. "How much do you think you made?"

"At least a few grand."

"Whoa! Congrats. Got anymore stashed in a hidden freezer?"

"As a matter of fact." Sydney flashed him a sassy look. "Come with me." She reached for his hand.

"Hey Syd, you takin' off?" A spunky woman with a bone-bead choker around her neck eyed Trey from head to toe. "This is him, huh?"

"Yeah." Sydney frowned, giving her a signal to keep quiet. She cleared her throat. "This is Trey Hardy."

"Hey, handsome. I'm Keyonna." She extended long fingers with blue-painted nails.

Trey probed Sydney with his eyes before shaking her hand. "It's a pleasure."

"Indeed it is." Keyonna gave him a playful grin.

Sydney thrust a handful of brochures at her. "Pass these out, will ya?"

"That's why I'm here." Keyonna examined the booth. "Hey, where's the jerky? I've been licking my lips all morning."

"We sold out."

"No way."

Trey jingled a set of keys.

"We have more. I'll save you a package." Sydney hugged her. "Later." She grabbed Trey's hand again and escorted him toward the parking lot. "Thank you!" she called over her shoulder, not wanting to subject him to a flirt like Keyonna. Being longtime friends, she knew her antics all too well.

"She's a handful." Trey shook his head.

"You have no idea."

He squeezed her hand. "This is a nice touch."

Sydney wanted to return the pressure, but wiggled her hand free instead. "Amazon, remember?" She tried to hide her displeasure and focused on her fruitful sales.

CHAPTER 23

Back at the ranch, Sydney made flyers and handed them out to the guests, placing leftovers on the dining tables and the foyer's welcome table. Then she and Trey went to the shop, pulled out the remaining five boxes of jerky from a long chest freezer, and set them on the shop's wooden counter.

She opened the box labeled "cider" and pulled out a gallon baggie. "If I sell all of this, I'll have to find someone to get me a young buck." She handed Trey the clear packet.

He unzipped the pouch and took a sniff. "I can shoot one for you."

"I wish, but you can't." She took the bag from him and closed it. "You can't eat all the merchandise, silly."

"I'm a good shot."

"I don't doubt that. You can't hunt because you're non-Native."

"Even on private land?"

"Those are the rules." She put the baggie back in the box. "We can't hunt year-round anymore either unless for a ceremony, which is usually a funeral, on fee or trust land. At least they aren't supposed to."

"Huh. I figured reservations might be laxer when it comes to private property."

"Nope. Not this one anyway."

"Who can hunt for you? Robert?"

"Yep. Or Chad and Rich. They're tribal members too."

"Who shot these?" Trey tapped a box.

"My dad." Thinking of him tugged her heartstrings, but she wouldn't give in to the sadness. The morning had been too successful. He'd be proud of her. "Let's get these down to the booth. They'll sell in no time. And thaw as quick in this heat."

He clutched her arm. "Wait." Then let go when she scowled at him. "Can I ride along with them when they hunt?"

"No. Trust me, you don't want to be thrust into that kind of rumor mill."

"Why not? The only weapon I'll have is my Nikon." His expression turned playful. "I promise to get you a shot or two of pretty little does. One pretty as you." He took a step closer to her.

She stiffened. Cooper used to make the same types of comments when he was drunk. And when she didn't respond in the way he thought she should have, he'd thump her a good one. "That's lame." She picked up a box and trekked to the door.

Trey grabbed another box. "What? The pictures or the comment?"

"The comment." She had to find a way to get past the triggers and not take things so seriously. A counselor once told her implementing humor was an effective way to heal.

"It kills you to take a compliment, doesn't it?"

She stopped and turned around. "That was a compliment? *This jerky's the best I've ever tasted. Your horse-training skills are stellar. This ranch is well run.* Those are compliments. What you said was nothing short of shallow manipulation women have had to endure for way too long." She swiveled and strode to the truck.

"Please, don't hold back." Trey followed her and lifted the box into the back of the truck. "I was trying to be playful. Didn't mean anything by it."

"Didn't mean anything?"

He threw his head back and groaned. "You're impossible!"

She reached for a water gun in the back of the truck and shot him in the chest. "That was playful!" At his shocked expression, she took the gun and ran. Over her shoulder, she said, "I'm not impossible!"

Trey searched for another gun, then chased her empty-handed and caught her behind her cabin.

Sydney shot at him again, this time the stream splattered his head. She giggled, threatening to do it again. Maybe this was the first step to breaking those nasty triggers and finding a little fun.

Trey took hold of her wrist and tossed the gun aside. "You'll pay for that." He grinned and gave her a gentle kiss.

She pushed away. "I can't . . ." She wasn't used to a man's tender touch. She didn't trust it. She longed for his affection but knew it wouldn't last. How could a long-distance romance survive?

"There has to be a way we can make this work." He ran his fingers through his hair. "We can stay here in the summer and go to Tucson in the winter. You can stay with one of my sisters."

She flicked her finger toward the barn. "And who would take care of the place? Feed the animals? We have guests year-round."

"So you've said. But what do they do in the winter? There's nothing here."

"Sledding and snowmobiling. Ice fishing and bonfires. I have a few women who hold writing retreats, and companies reserve weekend bonuses for their employees. There's money in Seattle and Portland and even in BC, and we get a hefty piece of it."

A shocked look crossed Trey's face. "Then why are you broke?"

Good question. "I haven't figured that out yet."

"Want me to take a look at your books?"

"I've got it." The thought of him perusing her finances made her feel exposed. It also gave her the urge to check them out and now. "I'm hot and sticky. I'm going to go cool off."

"What about the jerky? I thought we were going back."

"It's getting pretty hot. We can sell it tomorrow. Would you mind putting the meat in coolers?" The look on his face clenched her chest as she said over her shoulder, "I'll catch up with you later." She headed for her cabin. "Why are we broke? Good question."

After a tepid shower, she found an unmarked box of receipts in the lodge office, brought them back to her cabin, and organized them on the kitchen table. What was she missing? Could her parents have gotten in trouble and not told her and Glenda?

Digging into the box, she found several receipts for meals at the Twelve Tribes Casino south of Omak. Good Lord, could they have had a gambling problem? She dug deeper, finding several feed-and-tack invoices.

Trey knocked on the screen door.

"What's up?" Sydney set the statements on her lap.

"Are we going to the powwow tonight? I've not seen one from this area before."

"Can we talk later?"

"I'd like to learn how to play stick games." He grinned, but his eyes told her he was worried.

"How'd you hear about the stick games?"

"This." He pressed a flyer to the screen.

"Yes, we're going."

"See you later then?"

"Yep, later. Thanks." She picked up another invoice.

After a sigh floated through the wire netting of the screen door, heavy footsteps fell on the split-log steps.

Although she admired his persistence and wanted to taste more of his sweet lips, she needed to follow her head and not her emotions. Besides, he was right, they were buried in debt, and she was determined to find out why.

She put the receipts back in the box, took it to the lodge office, and spent the next several hours matching invoices to receipts and recorded every dime spent in a ledger. Fuel and feed seemed normal. Vet bills were up, but then again, there were more boys to castrate this year—both bovine and equine.

The need to find the will drove her crazy. Frustrated, she swirled the chair around and faced the bookshelf. Her mother was a history buff and had numerous books written by Native Americans and local historians. She squinted at the pink spine of a hardbound book and pulled it off the shelf. *With God All Things Are Possible* graced the cover. It was her mom's favorite verse.

Inside the cover was a series of six numbers followed by a pound sign. She flipped through the pages, stopping on May 21.

I don't know how to tell the girls I have breast cancer. They'll be so upset I didn't tell them sooner. But I don't want them to worry. Especially because the tumor is shrinking, thanks to Dr. Gordon's treatments and supplements.

Cancer? Her belly churned. Who was Dr. Gordon? Where was he located? Her chest clenched. Had Glenda known? Had her aunties? She continued reading.

Things have been so stressful with the ranch in such financial disarray. I pray we can save it. Losing the Seven Tine would break Sydney's heart. Lester's too. Oh, Lord, I need wisdom, direction, and strength to get through all of this. Give me the words when I'm ready to tell the girls. Hopefully, I'll have the courage when we get back.

116

Sydney wiped her eyes and flipped back to the six digits. Was this the combination to her dad's safe? Surely, they'd drawn up a will knowing her mother had cancer. She jotted the numbers on a sticky note and rushed to the main house. Inside her dad's office, she held out the note and punched in the code. The safe clicked, and she opened the door.

Three hunting rifles lined the safe's right side and four shelves ran down the left. On the first shelf were a blue folder and a thick manila envelope with Dr. Gordon's name on it. She settled at her father's desk with the blue folder.

"There you are." Her pulse raced as she read through her folks' Last Will and Testament. She sighed, noting she'd been listed as executor. *Thank you.*

The envelope held receipts adding up to thousands of dollars for treatments and supplements. Treatments she assumed Indian Health hadn't covered. She googled Dr. Gordon on her phone. A website popped up for the Omak Naturopathic Clinic. According to the dates on the receipts, her mom had been going for several months. Almost a year.

"Thank goodness they hadn't been gambling."

What kind of supplements had she been taking? Sydney went to the kitchen but didn't find any, so she checked her mom's bathroom. The medicine cabinet held various bottles and a green box of tea labeled Essiac. She unscrewed the cap of a sixteen-ounce vial of Hoxey and sniffed the pungent brown tonic. "Eww."

Four other glass vials labeled UNDA 10, 21, 48, and 243 all smelled like alcohol. All of this to treat cancer? Another bottle labeled Indole 3 Carbonol contained sixty veggie caps.

"Fractionated Pectin Powder? What the heck?" She shook the jar. Almost empty.

Carrying the meds, she went back to her dad's office and called Glenda.

"What's up?" Glenda sounded annoyed. "I'm headed to council chambers."

"Did you know Mom had cancer?" She jotted the names of the medicines on a sticky note as they talked.

"What makes you think she did?"

"I found her journal and a ton of receipts for Dr. Gordon from the Omak Naturopathic Clinic in dad's gun safe. Then found a handful of Mom's supplements and weird herbal tea in her medicine cabinet."

"Dad's gun safe?"

"Did you know?"

"No! Listen, I'll be done in an hour and will head to the ranch." Glenda paused, rushed footsteps thumped through the phone line. "Sounds like we have a lot to discuss."

"I'm taking Trey to the powwow soon, but I'll leave Mom's journal on the desk. Let's meet in the morning after you've had time to check it out." Sydney needed more time. She'd have to come clean and divulge the financial state of the ranch and lack of insurance.

A throaty groan sizzled through the phone. "Fine. See you first thing."

Sydney put the will back in the gun safe. She could only handle one crisis at a time and wanted to meet with the attorney first. She took the medical receipts to the lodge office and locked them in the minisafe, then decided to enter more bills into the accounting software before finding Trey.

She needed the distraction of the Fourth of July Celebration but also worried about being with Trey. Her heart was rapidly softening for him. And it terrified her. It was way too soon.

CHAPTER 24

Thirty minutes later, Glenda blew into the office. "I couldn't wait."

Oh no. "I don't blame you." Hiding her disappointment, Sydney saved her accounting entries and got the envelope and journal out of the minisafe. They settled on the couch. "Check these out. Look on May 21."

Glenda put the manila envelope on her lap and opened the journal, finding the date. As she read, her jaw dropped. "We need to call Dr. Gordon and find out more."

"I agree. You want to call him and see what you can find out?" That would give Sydney time to concentrate on the will.

"I can do that."

"There you are." Trey ambled into the office wearing polished boots, a Western shirt that matched his emerald eyes, and a delicious grin. "Ready?"

"I'll take these and let you know what I find out. You two have fun." Glenda acknowledged Trey and left.

"Yep." She jumped to her feet, a starry blackness blocking her vision. She swayed, her knees wanting to buckle.

"Whoa . . ." Strong arms held her steady. "You stand up too fast?"

"Must have." She inhaled and closed her eyes. His light, spicy cologne floated to her, making her head swim. When her eyes opened, her hands were resting on his arms and her mouth went dry. "I'll go get ready."

"Are you sure you're up to going?"

"I am, thanks." The sense of refuge she felt in his arms pulled at her like a hummingbird to nectar. She kissed his smooth cheek and hurried to the exit. "Be right back."

"I'll wait on the porch."

She dashed to her cabin, chiding herself for kissing him. *Amazon.* What had gotten into her? She was acting like a mare in heat. She'd have to keep her distance. Find her niece and have her tag along.

She prayed for strength to resist his charms as she changed into jeans, boots, and a flowery blouse. After combing her hair, she glided pink gloss across her lips and pressed them together. "What am I doing?"

"What *are* you doing?"

Sydney screamed and spun around to face Trey. "How'd you get in here?"

He glanced behind him. "The door was open. I knocked." He shrugged. "You look beautiful." He took a step closer. "I fed the horses for you so we don't have to rush back, and Chad gave Twister his meds."

She dropped her gloss into her purse. "How thoughtful. I appreciate that."

He held out a hand and escorted her to the truck, then went to the driver's door and got in. Sydney followed him, put a hand on her hip, and tapped a foot.

"I take it you're driving."

"Yep." She thumbed him out. "You're the guest."

He chuckled and shifted over to the passenger's side.

She slid under the steering wheel. The scent of his cologne filled the cab, making it hard for her to concentrate on anything but him. If she couldn't find her niece, she'd have to round up a couple of friends to close the gap. "Where did you put the jerky?"

"In the cooler."

She arched a brow.

"Relax. I put it on the shop counter so Caliber will leave it alone." He smiled, a twinkle in his eyes.

"You're the best." She started the truck and shoved it into drive. "So you want to learn how to play stick games, huh?"

"I sure do." Trey rolled down the window and hung his arm out. "What're we going to see first, dancing or rodeo?"

With her luck, once their feet touched the powwow grounds, the owl dance would begin. She'd have to ask him to participate in the couple's dance, and he'd have to accept her offer. If she didn't ask, she was certain he'd badger her until she agreed, making a spectacle of themselves. Or simply not care who was supposed to ask whom and drag her onto the green outdoor-carpet-covered floor. "Rodeo. I don't want to miss Robert's ride. The stick games go on practically all night. You can learn after that, sound good?"

"I can live with that," Trey said. "I saw a sign for a powwow burger. Gotta try one. They any good?"

"Have you ever had frybread?"

"Not yet."

Sydney imagined this was how he'd been in college—fun and adventurous—not the stuffy workaholic Pam had described. She liked this version. If only timing were different. She drove past the community center and found a parking spot near the rodeo arena. They grabbed their camping chairs from the back and found a spot to sit.

"Have you ever photographed rodeos?"

"Yep." He held her chair while she sat down on top of the hill overlooking the arena. "I shot a lot of sports pictures in college for the *Daily Wildcat* and worked for the *Arizona Daily Star* fresh out of college, built my portfolio, then began freelancing. I was lucky enough to land a few lucrative assignments with a couple of top magazines. It took off from there."

"You love your job, don't you?"

"I do." He settled beside her. "It's taken me all over the world. It's been one big adventure."

"A gift I suppose." A gift she could never interfere with. She could never ask him to plant roots on their land. He was obviously made for a thrilling life.

After watching Robert win the saddle bronc event, Trey bought them both a powwow burger—a bacon cheeseburger with desired toppings between two large pieces of frybread—and they relaxed under the arbor near the community center.

"Why don't you serve these at the ranch?" His regard darted from one dancer wearing colorful regalia to another as if seeing a powwow for the first time.

"We do once in a while. Mom made the best frybread . . ." Her voice caught.

Trey elbowed her. "Look, your jerky." He pointed to an elder in a buckskin dress and a traditional basket hat. The labeled package laid on top of her bag.

"We need to sell more tomorrow." She waved at Martin and her auntie Marcie as they strode past.

Sydney was about to ask Trey if he could help Chad cut hay in the pasture closest to the Columbia River the following morning when the announcer called for the owl dance. *Oh no.* She wiped her mouth and stood. "Well, we better go. We've got a big day tomorrow."

Trey furrowed his brows and sipped his soda. Women took hold of men and led them onto the covered dance floor inside railings, finding spots around the center pole of the arbor. American, Canadian, Colville Tribal pole flags, and a staff with eagle feathers flared from the center pole. "What is this dance, the Owl?"

"C'mon." She motioned for him to rise, pretending she hadn't heard him.

"This is like the Sadie Hawkins, isn't it?" He sprang out of his chair, took her hand, and started for the dance floor.

Sydney groaned. "I meant let's go *home*." She dropped her food in her chair and begrudgingly went with him to a spot by a young, smitten couple. The guy was dressed for the grass dance in blue, orange, and green ribbon and yarn dangling off his shirt and leggings, and the girl wore a women's fancy dress of red, turquoise, and white with a matching shawl and moccasins.

"What do we do?" Trey leaned close, brushing stray hair from her face.

Dressed in men's traditional regalia complete with a feathery bustle and roach, Martin glared at him from the dance floor. Marcie stood next to him in a quill-adorned buckskin dress with a running horse basket hat snug on her head and a beaded rose bag hanging from the crook of her arm. She was talking to him, but his snarly focus was pinned on Trey.

Tingles shimmied up Sydney's arms when Trey put one arm around her back and took her free hand in his.

"It's easy." Realizing there was no way off the dance floor, she gave him directions. "Two steps forward with your left foot and one step back with your right." She loosely pressed an arm against his back. "Don't mind Martin. He's a little protective."

"A little?" Trey followed her steps. He pulled her close, staring down at her with an affectionate look.

"Wait for the beat." She swallowed the boulder in her throat and struggled to concentrate on what she was supposed to be doing.

Trey nodded. "I think I'm going to like this."

She moved their hands in a push-pull motion. His grip was firm and damp. Claiming. Six drummers sitting in a circle around a large drum, their sticks beating the stiff buckskin surface, sent their voices, a sweet falsetto tone, swirling through the dancers.

She led Trey around the circle, clunky at first. His steps smoothed as he relaxed, seeming to study other men's movements from time to time. Her steps swayed with each beat. Once he focused on her and seemed to forget about everyone else, their bodies moved in one fluid glide. When the drummers quit, he clung to her hand. He leaned in, his breath on her lips.

Her heart pounded. "I can't do this," she whispered, then fled the dance floor.

Saturday, July 8
Trey packed coolers into the truck bed for Sydney, stewing over being left on the dance floor. He had enjoyed the evening as they took in the local traditions and culture and thought she had too. Then, as if a switch flipped, Sydney bolted. What had he done wrong?

She was a master at evading her feelings and avoiding affection. Too many times she'd stiffened at his touch. Was it him, or had an ex crushed her heart? He knew how that felt. And it seemed like a breakup—if indeed that was the case—was fresh. Which would explain her irregular moods. As would the death of her parents. So maybe he needed to cut her some slack.

He cleaned his lens and snapped on the cap. "You sure Robert has time to take me to Owhi?"

"Yeah. It's good fishing. Lots of birds, too, that might make for good photos." Sydney handed him a cooler. "There's not much to do. My guests will be at the powwow grounds. And if things go as they did yesterday, I'll sell out quickly, giving me more quiet time to work on the business end of the ranch. Besides, you've done a lot around here. You'll have more fun with Robert. He's a kick."

"Sure you don't need help?" Or did she not want him to go with her? Which bothered him because he found himself wanting to spend every minute with her.

"Keyonna's meeting me this morning."

He nodded. "Will you tell me what set you off last night?"

She sighed. "You and I both know long-distance relationships fail. You're a great guy, but . . ." She inched up a shoulder, then dropped it. "Besides, we hardly know each other. This is moving too quickly. I'm trying to deal with the deaths."

"Are you coming off a breakup by any chance?" The look on her face made him regret asking.

She scanned the ground as her face flushed, and in a soft tone, said, "I need you to stay out of my personal life." She lifted her sad-looking eyes to meet his. "I'm sorry. There can never be anything between us." She got in her truck and drove off.

He waved the dust out of his face. She was right. A long-distance relationship would be hard. But he was willing to try. Why wasn't she? He'd thought she was attracted to him. Had he mistaken her intentions?

The fishing trip would at least get his mind off things. And maybe Robert would have a little insight into her guarded heart. And how he could get her to lower the wall a little so she'd give him a chance.

CHAPTER 25

Sydney's computer clock glowed 4:00 p.m. "Can't it wait?"
Glenda insisted on coming over. It sounded like she had another bee in her bonnet over the sale of the ranch. Sydney hid the checkbook and all receipts leading to a possible foreclosure in the bottom drawer.

She rubbed her head, irritated with the intrusion on her short break to read some of her mom's highlighted Bible verses. After hours of entering finances into the accounting software, she longed for a little inspiration and a connection with her mom. With Glenda coming over, she needed the tie even more.

Though it was Saturday late afternoon, it felt more like a super-bad Monday. Creator had taken her parents, and the ranch seemed to be slipping through her fingers.

The stress tempted her to tip the bottle like she had with Cooper in her college days. She could give in and let the alcohol release the pressure like so many of her friends and family did. Let it numb the fear of her future.

Where would she go if she lost the ranch? What would she do? Her degree was half-finished. Who'd hire her?

She drummed the fragile pages of the Bible. How could she trust God now? He didn't seem to notice everything crumbling around her. She closed the book and tossed it on a shelf behind the desk. Then shoved the craving for a nice cold beer out of her mind. Staying sober meant she'd have a fighting chance.

Sydney thumbed through the growing pile of mail before her sister was due to arrive. Most of the stack was unpaid bills. She opened an envelope and pulled out a photo of her and Trey dancing at the powwow. A note accompanied the print.

You look cozy in his arms. I've missed you. Remember, you're mine.

Her belly clenched. The envelope offered no return address, but the postmark was from Spokane. She swallowed. Could Cooper be out? It's too soon. He had to be toying with her, having someone else send the notes.

With trembling hands, she stuffed the print and note back in the envelope and hid them in the top drawer as Glenda pulled up. She'd have to decide later if it was wise to share the picture and notes with Trey or not. He was in the photo, after all.

She felt helpless. No way would she get a restraining order against Cooper. They were useless. Besides, there was no proof he was the one sending the notes.

She smoothed her hair with shaky hands and prepared for the next dilemma, watching out the window as her sister exited her car. Glenda's pursed lips and sharp heel-clicks on wood confirmed Sydney would have a fight on her hands.

Glenda blew through the office door and plopped Mom's journal on the desk. "How much of this did you read?"

Whew. There would be no fight about the ranch. "Only that day. Why?"

Glenda grasped the glasses hanging from the front of her shirt and read a few lines about the malignancy. "I had no idea her cancer was so bad. Why didn't she get chemo? Stick with the oncologist?"

"You know she prefers traditional medicine. Tima Louise did too." Louise was Jennie's mother. She had spent hours in the woods harvesting plant medicines and making sure her family and friends were always well stocked.

"We need to give the oncologist a visit, don't you think?"

"Why? Was it terminal?"

"Not that I could see, but . . ." Glenda searched through the pages.

"Then what's the point? She didn't really see him."

"He could tell us how bad it was."

"Did you get a hold of Dr. Gordon?"

"He said because of HIPAA, he can't tell us anything. If we had a medical power of attorney or if Mom had signed a release, he could have."

"The same applies for the oncologist, so why call?" Sydney hated the privacy law at times like these. "Let's check out the supplements I found." She woke up her computer and googled the medication, bringing up separate pages for each item. "Wow. This explains the elevated medical costs."

"That bad, huh?" Glenda leaned over her shoulder, her musky perfume overbearing.

She clicked through the pages. "Check these out. The UNDAs are about twenty-three each, the Fractionated Pectin Powder is sixty-eight, and the Indole 3 Carbonol is . . . sheesh, ninety-seven bucks." She clicked to another page. "The Essiac tea is forty and sixteen ounces of the Hoxey is two-hundred!"

"Holy. That's crazy expensive."

"I know, right?"

"What are they used for?"

Sydney again went through the pages, taking a minute to study how each natural medicine worked. "It looks like the UNDAs might be deep cleaners, ridding the body of toxins, and the others fight the cancer. Oh, look here, Indole 3 reduces estrogen." She then clicked on the page describing the pectin powder. "This appears to bind metastasized cells so they can't spread."

Glenda gasped. "That's gotta mean Mom's cancer had advanced."

"Yeah, probably to the lymph nodes."

"This can't get any worse."

Sydney paused, her palms clammy. "It actually can."

"What do you mean?" Glenda hovered over the desk.

"There's no life insurance." Shoot. She slipped. Not all bad because the longing for alcohol dissipated with her confession, making her feel as unbound as the children playing in the water sprinkler outside. *And you will know the truth, and the truth will set you free.* Ah, one of her father's favorites. And one highlighted in her mom's Bible.

Glenda's face reddened. "What?"

"Maybe due to the mound of doctor's bills, those spendy supplements, and every other bill this ranch seems to collect, the insurance hadn't been paid and therefore canceled." Sydney leaned back. "They must have been pretty worried to have kept something like this to themselves."

"You know all about keeping secrets." Glenda plopped down on the couch. "How long have you known?"

Tired of fighting and picking her battles, Sydney ignored the snide remark and chuckled. "A while."

"You find this humorous?"

"Not at all. It feels good to be free from hiding it from you."

"You're not free of anything. I'm going to force the sale."

It was time to show her the will. "Come with me." Sydney led Glenda into their dad's office in the main house, opened the gun safe, and handed her their folks' Last Will and Testament. "According to this, you won't be selling anything anytime soon."

"What are you talking about?" Glenda opened the folder.

"They made me the executor. They must have known I'd do whatever it took to keep air in the Seven Tine's lungs." She pointed to her name on the document. "Says right here."

"I'll take you to court!" Glenda slammed the will on the desk and stormed out the door.

Sydney smiled and thanked God. Maybe He had been listening and was on her side after all.

CHAPTER 26

Trey darted out to scoop up a four-year-old from the treacherous path of Glenda's roaring truck. He set the boy down near his frantic mother, then went to find Sydney. "What's with your sister? She almost ran over a little guy out there."

Holding a manilla folder in her hands, she patted the sofa beside her. "Look at this."

He took a seat on the couch, careful not to get too close and set her off again. He'd hoped Robert would have shed a little light on her mood swings, but that was a bust. Her brother had been just as clueless. He took the folder and opened it. "Your parents' will?"

"Read the first paragraph." She crossed her leg and bounced a foot. "See it?"

Trey smiled. "Unbelievable." He thumbed through the pages. "It's not signed."

"What?" Two white spaces with arrowed sticky tabs beside her parents' names knotted her belly. "Is this a draft?"

"Could be. Here's an attorney's card."

"Jones and Hopkins, PLLC. I'll give them a ring." She took the card to her desk, picked up her cell, and tapped in the number. "Hey, I'm Sydney Moomaw, is Krystal Hopkins available?"

She seemed so anxious lately. So edgy. More than when they'd met. Like it had shifted from grief to fear. And apprehension. There had to be a way he could help her. But how? He'd give anything to ease her load. Share the burden. Anything to release the tension lines between her brow. The strain in her shoulders.

She hung up and scribbled something on her day planner. "They've been expecting me."

"Do you think they have the signed copy?"

"Let's hope!"

Hope. It beamed on her face. Made the sparkle in her eyes ignite. Like when they were selling jerky at the powwow. Together. Yeah, they did make a good pair.

Monday, July 10

Midmorning traffic over the tree-lined Desautel Pass to Omak was minimal, save a handful of rigs pulling boats or camp trailers, giving Sydney time to relax and think.

Would the will stick even if it had not been signed? Better yet, if the office had a final copy, would she have total control? If indeed she was still named executor. If the document was legal, Sydney could find a way to keep the ranch. Like Trey had suggested, a dispersal sale might be her only way to retain generations of grit and sweat.

To escape from her reflections, she popped in a country CD and cranked the volume.

Fifty minutes later, she drove across the bridge over the Okanogan River and turned left on Ash. In front of a wooden sign reading Jones and Hopkins, PLLC was an open parking space. She nabbed it. Behind the stylish board stood an old tan house converted into an office. Orange daylilies lined the walkway. Inside, cool air revived her hot skin, but the pungent aroma of pine in a wax warmer on a side table churned her tummy.

"Can I help you?" A woman with a braided updo gave her a warm smile.

"I'm Sydney Moomaw. I have an appointment with Krystal Hopkins."

"She'll be right with you. Go ahead and have a seat." The woman motioned to a thick leather chair in the cramped waiting room.

Sweat formed on Sydney's hands. What if the will wasn't legal? What then? All the years of hard work for nothing. Her throat dry, she pulled out a bottle of water from her purse and took a sip, rinsing her parched mouth. Then took a second gulp.

She thumbed through a *Country Living* magazine.

"You must be Sydney." A woman in a purple floral summer dress gave her a bright smile. "I'm Krystal Hopkins. It's a pleasure to meet you." She motioned for Sydney to follow her.

Sydney sat in an office chair opposite the attorney in a large conference room and gave her the unattested will. "That's not signed." A long, cherrywood-stained table separated them. Stacked in front of Krystal were three blue folders. "I'm hoping you have an official copy."

Krystal scanned the document. "You're right, this isn't valid." She looked up and smiled. "The good news is I do have a signed copy of your folks' updated will. Did your sister come with you?" She set the document aside.

Sydney blew a rush of air through her mouth. "No. I'm here on my own, hoping to . . ." She bit her bottom lip, stopping herself from divulging unnecessary information. "I came by myself."

"First off, I am sorry for your loss. I do have to say, the will you brought and this copy are nearly the same. Before Lester and Jennie left for their cruise, they came in and changed one stipulation." Krystal spread apart the top folder, flipped to the desired page, and slid it to Sydney, then opened a copy for herself. "Your parents had concerns about you girls' intentions for the ranch. They knew you would want to keep it in operation and Glenda wanted nothing to do with the ranch, horses, or livestock. The reason the will was changed was to protect you."

"That's a relief." She couldn't wait to tell Trey.

Krystal paused. "You know about your mother's cancer?"

"Only after I came across her journal while searching for the will." She shook her head. "Here she survives breast cancer and dies from a car wreck."

"Well, they had hoped the ranch would have been solely in your name prior to death, but unfortunately that didn't happen."

Why put the Seven Tine in her name? Was her mom terminal after all? Sydney's pulse raced. "So they were going to sign it over to me?"

"Yes, after returning from vacation."

"Glenda's already had a Realtor out. She's determined to sell."

"She can't. That's more good news."

"Really?" Oh no, there's bad news.

"That's your copy, and clearly, you're the executor. But your folks didn't want an all-out war between you girls." She chuckled. "Their words, not mine. I've never seen this before, but they insisted you two either find an amicable solution both of you can live with, or I take over and sell the ranch and all proceeds go to charity."

She felt her authority dissolve. "No way. What charity?"

"Melody's House of Hope. A home in Spokane that lodges cancer patients for free while they go through treatment."

Sydney tapped the will. "I'm sure Glenda and I can come to an agreement, and once I'm in the black, I'd like to donate funds to this place. Can you get me more information?"

"Oh, is the ranch in financial trouble?"

She slouched. "Yeah. I never knew how much until after the funeral. Their life insurance lapsed, and they didn't bother to tell either of us."

"Sorry to hear that."

"I'm sure they believed they'd have more time to untangle the knots."

"I agree." Krystal pulled a business card out of her briefcase. "This is a good friend of mine. She may be able to help. In the meantime, talk with Glenda and come up with a financial arrangement and business plan. There's no time limit, but I wouldn't drag it out either." She studied Sydney. "Do you have any ideas?"

"I'll have to sell cows and horses." She took the card and the file folder holding the executed will. "Along with anything that's not nailed down and absolutely necessary to run the ranch. I plan on opening a gift shop in the lodge. My jerky is a huge hit. I may have to begin from bare bones, but since the ranch was successful once, it can be built strong twice." Or so she hoped.

"I think that's a great start. Let me know if you need anything. And send jerky my way. I'll help advertise." Krystal walked Sydney to the door and opened it for her. "Call my friend."

Sydney waved the card in the air and strolled to her car. She couldn't wait to show Glenda.

Trey came out of the barn as Sydney parked by the flower garden between the barn and the lodge, cutting him off. She got out and met him by the hood, her back to the lodge.

"How'd it go?"

"It was interesting, that's for sure. More like sickening. I dread the conversation I'm about to have with Glenda."

"Oh yeah? What's going on?"

Sydney told him about her being executor and about the stipulation. "Glenda's going to flip. She's dead set on selling. I have no idea how we'll work this out. How long has she been here?"

"I'm not sure. I've been out walking around." He leaned against her truck, a pit and a plan forming in his gut. "What do you have in mind?"

"I'm not sure. I know I have to come up with a business plan. The good news is, she always keeps her word. If we can come to an agreement, she'll stick with it." She looked away and blew out a heavy breath.

He hated how hopeless she looked. What if he asked her to marry him? Would she accept? After all, he was honest and dependable. Committed. Hardworking. Everything she seemed to need. But how would she react?

Would Glenda back off with this kind of arrangement? *The good news is she always keeps her word.*

He had to do something. And with his ranching and business skills, he could make sure she kept the Seven Tine going. Because it seemed like it was all she had left of her parents.

But could they make a marriage work? Good grief, they hardly knew each other. Yet, she'd snagged him with those mournful, brown eyes the moment they'd met, and when she'd dragged a cow several miles so she could be buried at home, and when she'd fought for her place like a mother wolf protecting her pups. Yep, she was the woman for him.

He wiped his sweaty palms on his jeans. "Hey. I have a wild idea if you're interested."

She rested against her pickup, her elbow on the hood. "Oh, yeah? At this point, I'm open to anything."

He placed his hand on her arm. She stiffened but didn't ask to remove it. Which was all the encouragement he needed to blurt out, "Marry me."

She hugged herself as though he'd asked her to rob a bank. "Are you kidding me?"

He lifted his shoulder. "Maybe."

She burst out laughing. "Good one. I love your sense of humor."

Trey laughed too. Though to him, it was no joke. "How do you think your sister'd react to us taking the vows?"

"She'd freak. I told her awhile back I wouldn't marry for anything other than love. But hey, it'd be worth telling her we were getting hitched just to see her reaction. But you'd have to move here, ya know."

"Whatever. We could split our time between here and Arizona. Or you could travel with me. We could see some amazing places." He'd love to take her to Australia. Whatever it'd take to convince her.

"A true adventure." She cleared her throat. "Well, I better get this over with. Here goes nothing."

CHAPTER 27

Sydney found the maverick at her desk, perusing through the ranch's financial books. Her glass of iced tea sat on a coaster beside a stack of folders.

"What are you doing?" Sydney dropped her purse on the sofa, her heart thumping her chest.

"Hello to you too." Glenda's brows rose as Sydney stalked to the desk and handed her a blue folder.

"What's this?"

"The official will."

Glenda opened the file and started reading. When her eyes grew round, Sydney figured she'd reached the section talking about the charity and stifled a laugh. Oh, the feeling of sweet revenge.

"I see Robert's not listed in here. I wonder why?"

Sheesh. She'd forgotten to ask Krystal about how to add him to the will and handle his portion. "Maybe they planned on talking to us first. The news of him being our brother is pretty fresh, so maybe they planned on adding him when they got back."

"Probably."

"Thankfully, Mom and Dad trusted me with the ranch. So I'll come up with a business plan, and you can let me know the amount you can live with."

"We'll need to get the ranch appraised." Glenda laid the will on the desk. "How far in debt are they?"

"The appraisal's in the works. And they were in debt pretty far, but not so bad the ranch can't pull through." Sydney leaned against the bookcase. "Why are you so against me taking over? You know this is my life—my choice. It might not be yours, which is fine, but seriously, why are you resisting me keeping the ranch?"

"You're right, you have the option. But in this instance, your choice does affect me and my family. Did you know Mom and Dad forced me out?"

"That's a bit extreme, don't you think? Good grief, you never had an interest in the place. Let's be honest." *What hogwash.*

"I had ideas to expand and make it the talk of the state."

Sydney snorted. "No one wanted to be the talk of anything. They kept the small-family feel for a reason." Now she understood why their father would not let her sister get her grubby hands on the ranch. He always knew smaller was better. Intimate. Manageable. Less debt created less worry. And she agreed. Sydney took a drink of Glenda's iced tea.

"Guess I'm worried this place'll run you down like it did Mom and Dad." Glenda picked up a photo of their parents. "I suppose if you had a husband, I wouldn't be as concerned. That way you would have a lifelong partner in the endeavor and not everything would be on your shoulders."

Sydney choked on the tea. "Are you serious? All I have to do is get married, and you'll retract your claws?" *Marry me.* His offer didn't seem so ridiculous now. Until her heart plunged to her feet as an image of her ex exploded into her mind. She set the glass on the desk and broke out into a sweat.

OK. Cooper was a drug addict and a woman-beater. A man from the pit of hell. Trey was gentle. Caring. Sober. An angel from heaven. Cooper was a selfish psychopath. Trey was warm. Loving. Dependable. Maybe being married to him wouldn't be so bad.

And the spark in his green eyes when he'd mentioned getting married made her chest flutter. Yeah, he was a hunk with a capital H. But really, was this a simple solution for a single woman? Maybe it was the only way.

Then there was the issue of deception. Would God bless or curse such an arrangement?

"And pay me my portion."

"Which I'll know once we get the appraisal."

"And then we'll make a deal."

"Done." What she agreed to was nothing short of ludicrous. But she simply didn't know any other way. The Seven Tine was her *heritage. Her life.* Good Lord. And now she'd have to tell Trey she'd accept. Would he take her seriously?

"*Done?* It's that simple? This'll be interesting. Who do you have in mind? Your third-grade crush, Johnny Simpson? Or are you going to run a lottery? Oh, hey. I know, you can go on TV. I hear *The Rancherette* has an opening." Glenda rolled her eyes. "Get real, Syd. The only reasonable option is to sell and divide the cash, and you know it."

"Aww, you sound a little peeved because I've got the power. Or is it because I want to make sure Bobby gets his cut?" No way was she going to tell her about Trey's jesting offer. She'd talk to him first. Then if he agreed, she'd find the right time to tell Glenda.

"No, I can live with him having a third. And selling the equipment and livestock will simply jack up all our portions." Glenda flashed her a sarcastic grin. "Let me know when you find Mr. Right." She stormed out of the office.

"You bet I will!" Yep. She'd catch her off guard and get the last laugh.

CHAPTER 28

Sydney found Trey resting under the shade of a ponderosa pine tree near the mare and foal pen. She rode one horse and led a second. "Wanna take a ride?" She leaned back and padded her bulging saddle bags. "I have a picnic."

"Your talk with Glenda must have gone well."

"Something like that."

"Where we going?"

Trying to keep her composure, she said, "Somewhere special."

Trey took the reins that were attached to a blue roan with the Seven Tine brand on its rump and mounted. Shade and cool air from towering trees and valleys, wildflower's sweet aromas, streams trickling over rock beds surrounded them on the north pasture, and he became more enamored with the setting the longer they rode.

Sydney led him to a cool spot in a copse of aspen by a creek. She dismounted, then pulled out two sacks and a thermos from the worn saddlebags. After finding a nice patch of green grass, she arranged cheese, crackers, and apple slices on the bags and poured two tin cups of iced tea, handing him one of them.

"Trying to butter me up for something?" He winked at her, then took a drink.

"No." Her face warmed as she gave him a sassy sideways glance. "Maybe a little."

"Maybe?"

"This is one of my favorite spots. I come here to think." She gestured to the food. "Dig in."

Trey put a slice of cheese on a cracker. "I'd like to bring the stud colts here, a couple at a time, and take photos for the website."

She looked around and pointed to a backdrop of aspen and rock bluffs. "Over there'd be a nice spot."

"It sure would." He ate the cracker and took a sip of tea. "Why did you bring me here?"

Oh. *Why?* She held her hands in her lap so he couldn't see them shaking. "Um." *Do I tell him straight out, or should I ease him into it?* "I thought you'd like this spot for taking pictures."

He set his cup on the grass. "This isn't about horses, is it?"

Of course it wasn't. *Here goes nothing.* "I've considered your offer."

"I've offered a few things. Which one are you talking about?"

Really? She gave him a nervous laugh. After considering all her other options, Trey was the only one she'd be willing to spend her life with. Because he was hardworking and committed, among all his other amazing qualities. "The one when you asked me to marry you."

"Oh." He looked away and tugged at the neck of his T-shirt. "What changed your mind?"

"It's kind of . . . Well, Glenda said if I had a husband, she'd be inclined to make a deal. Back off from selling the ranch because I wouldn't be running it alone. She doesn't know we talked—

He snorted. "The woman who won't marry for anything less than love caves for a deal? What'd you two do, roll the dice?"

She hugged her knees. "I know it sounds bad."

"I take it you gambled and lost." He stood. "You've been right all along. I think it's best if you did this on your own." He mounted, spun the horse around, and sped off.

Trey put the blue roan in the stall and closed the door. *Glenda said if I had a husband, she'd be inclined to make a deal.*

So what if she'd laughed at him when he suggested marriage in the first place? Like his dad used to when he was a boy learning to rope. He needed to let it go. After all, he wasn't seven anymore. But it hurt. Because he'd meant it. He'd marry her in a heartbeat to help her save the ranch.

And it didn't help when she showed up in the cute, little Stetson with twisted stampede strings hanging loose and a purple tank top that enhanced her curves. Her dense lashes had weakened his stiff armor. Until she mentioned the deal.

He gulped, fear curling his toes. Seriously. Could a marriage based on a sham survive? But he didn't see any other way to help her. To shoulder the load. He couldn't watch her lose everything she'd worked so hard to hold on to. And there was no way he would divorce her if things didn't work out. He didn't believe in it. Neither did God.

And really. She was amazing. Diligent, loyal, generous. Yeah, he could spend the rest of his life with her. Build the ranch back up. Together. From bare bones. He needed to go back. Tell her how stupid he'd been. Tell her, *yes, I'll marry you.*

He opened the gate, saddled the horse, and headed back. Back for the woman he was ready to commit too. And was falling in love with.

CHAPTER 29

Sydney buried her face in her knees. How on earth was she going to convince Trey to marry her? She couldn't lose the ranch. She'd worked too hard to hang on to it. Rescue it from Glenda's coldhearted talons.

The sound of horse hooves pounding the ground caught her attention. Trey? She stood. Took a few steps toward him, a giggle bubbling up her throat. Could he have changed his mind? She couldn't tell by the intense look on his face.

He reined the blue roan to a stop and jumped off. "I accept." His tone sounded soft and caring.

She ran into his arms. Yes. She'd save the ranch. No. They'd do it together. Side by side.

"I'm sorry for running out on you like I did. And for my accusations. I was wrong. About a lot of things."

"What changed your mind?"

He held both of her hands. "You're the heartbeat of this ranch. I'd hate to see you lose it. What changed my mind? My need to help you. The look on your face when I left. The fact that I'm falling for you."

Falling for me? "What about the Amazon? How is this going to work?" *What if it doesn't work?* She pulled away from him and folded her hands over her chest. No, they had to make it work. She'd already been divorced. Didn't want to go through it twice. Even if domestic violence wasn't an issue.

"We'll have to come up with a plan. Take things a step at a time."

She nodded. "Saying it out loud is kind of scary, isn't it?" Especially with Cooper stalking her mind. She'd have to trust Creator. After all, the union was meant for good and not evil.

"Sure is." He glanced to the side.

Wait. "What's wrong?"

"Nothing. We'll be fine."

"No really. The look on your face when you tore out of here, it's the same one you just gave me. What's going on?"

He lifted a shoulder, then dropped it. "Talk of marriage brought back too many memories."

"Of?"

"Let's go sit by the creek, and I'll tell you everything." Once settled, he continued. "I was engaged once before. Six years ago. My ex-fiancée, Brenda, left me for another guy. It tore my heart open. I vowed to never get close to another woman again and plunged into work. But then I met you, and you're all I think about. You give me hope again. I can see myself making a life with you. Here." He pressed his lips against her trembling hands. "I'm glad you're going to fight for this place. I'll be right beside you. Every step of the way."

"I'm sorry about Brenda. And glad you're going to do this with me." She squeezed his hand.

He returned the pressure. "Let's get the Seven Tine back on its feet."

"Yeah. Let's do it."

He leaned closer, as if to kiss her, when Martin stepped out of the trees, fishing pole in hand and fire in his eyes. "Your father would never approve of this!"

Sydney jerked at his voice. "How long have you been eavesdropping?"

Martin glared at Trey. "Long enough. There are better ways to hold on to the ranch."

Sydney sprang to her feet. "You don't know what all's involved."

"The debt? Insurance lapse? Jennie's cancer? The will?" Martin said. "I know more than you think."

"Why would they tell you and not me and Glenda?"

"Your father and I go way back. There isn't much we didn't share with each other. He wanted to protect you girls." He slid his cowboy hat from his thick, gray hair.

Trey rose, locked his hand in hers. She pressed her shoulder against his, gleaning his strength.

"Protect us from what?"

"For a long time, they didn't know what would happen. Bills piled high. There was no money to continue with the insurance payments. When that lapsed, they looked into a couple more companies. And Jennie's treatments were working. They hadn't planned on leaving you with such a mess. After the cruise, they intended to downsize and get back on track. And had promised to tell you girls about everything. Harold Ives was planning a benefit." He was a family friend.

"And you think a benefit will fix this mess?" Sydney said. "Come on." Because she'd hid her pregnancy and baby, she couldn't fault them for keeping their matters private, but she didn't buy the idea that their debt could be so easily remedied.

"No—"

"Then what do you think is better than our plan?"

"I agree with Lester," Martin said, his tone softer. "The only shot on the table is downsizing."

"Wish it was that simple. But the will states Glenda and I have to come up with a plan both of us can agree on, and she gets half. Actually, a third. It's only fair for Bobby to get in on the deal." Sydney let out a frustrated laugh. "The one portion to this nightmare you don't know is that they changed the will the day before they left."

"And Glenda suggested marriage," Martin said, "believing she'd win since you've banished all men from your life."

How'd he know? "Something like that."

"We plan to make this work." Trey held the elder's glare.

Martin turned to Sydney. "Hope you know what you're doing."

"Not sure I do. But I can't go down without a fight. I'm leaning on faith. Something I tossed aside a long time ago." Sydney grunted. "Big mistake."

"Faith, huh?" Martin left without saying goodbye.

CHAPTER 30

Friday, July 14

Sydney stood quaking outside the Hitching Post Lakeside Chapel in Coeur d'Alene, Idaho. July 14 would be a day she'd never forget.

Weak knees and a twisted stomach, memories of sleepless nights, midday beatings, and black, swollen eyes courtesy of Cooper Payne flooded her mind. She turned to run when Trey hooked her by the arm.

He leaned close to her ear. "We've got the True Love package in the Western Room."

She drew in his minty breath. "Splendid." It would go with the small, white country chapel tucked in the trees beside the enormous lake.

Feeling nauseated, Sydney looked for the nearest garbage can. She wanted to bolt from the constrictive building, rip off her turquoise dress in favor of her jeans, and dash back to the rez. Finishing college would have been the easier choice.

And would someone, please, turn off that annoying wedding music?

"It's going to be fine." Trey rubbed her back as they stepped into the cramped room filled with a few chairs, Western boots in a window, and a rifle hanging on the wall. He took her hands, holding her at arm's length, and scanned her from hair to sandals. "You look gorgeous."

Though the look of admiration in his eyes seemed genuine, they reminded her of what else usually happened on the day of the wedding. Her heart thudded against her chest. "Can I change my mind? I'm not ready."

"You're not?"

She drew her eyebrows together and smoothed the black embroidered vines that ran the length of her sleeveless, maxi dress on either side of twenty-two pearly buttons. *You look gorgeous.* She did love how it flattered her figure. Loved the flair from hips to hem. She felt feminine. And kind of sexy.

But, oh, man. No way she could consummate the marriage. They hardly knew each other. She couldn't let him see her ugly scars. Again, courtesy of Cooper Payne. Couldn't allow herself to offer the depth of intimacy a woman should give on her wedding night. It should be shared by lovers. "I-I can't . . . you know . . ."

"We don't have to sleep in the same bed or even live in the same house, if that's what you're worried about." He held up the marriage license. "I had the minister add a disclaimer." He winked, humor in his tone.

Though he tried to set her at ease, it wasn't working.

"You two ready?" A wispy man with a Bible and a big grin waved them to the podium.

"We are." Trey urged her forward with his hand on the small of her back.

She'd never seen him look so handsome in his tan hat and boots, freshly creased jeans bunching at the ankles, a cream-colored shirt. A turquoise vest and they'd be the perfect couple. But what caught her breath? His confidence. She had to admit, he made her feel safe. Even treasured. Something Cooper had never provided.

She stepped up and offered a small smile. Fought back tears as the minister spoke about love and commitment. Both of which she hoped to learn as time rolled on. Then she about passed out when he said, "I ask you each now, to repeat the marriage vows." She choked them out, somehow managing to keep her composure.

The preacher smiled at Trey, and said, "You may kiss your bride."

Oh, my. *Kiss the bride?* OK, yeah, she wanted to kiss him. More than ever. But a gut-wrenching angst made her want to put distance between them. Until his emerald eyes, sweet and pleasing, locked on hers. She composed herself enough to let in a trace of fearlessness as he leaned close, his breath caressing her mouth.

Trey gave her a tender kiss, the kind a man gives a woman when he adores her. The kind that made her soften in the warmth of his gentle, oh so gentle, embrace.

Trey brushed a thumb down her jawline. Inches from her lips, he whispered, "Forever."

She allowed a few tears to tumble down her cheeks. His eyes held promise. A promise he seemed to mean. She dreamed of forever, but never thought it'd stem from a bargain. She could only pray that forever would someday bloom love.

Following her newly acquired husband to the truck, Sydney thought about how different the ceremony would've been if her father had given her away. If her mother had made her dress. If their vows had been shared on the rez, in their home church. With Pam at her side and Glenda in the wedding party.

And why had Robert taken off to compete in an Indian sanctioned rodeo in Bear River, Oregon? OK, yeah, if he wins, he passes Go and heads directly to the Indian National Finals rodeo. Fine. But not only had he not been there to escort her down the aisle, he left her in a lurch with so much to do.

Yep. In the end, her sister won. She always had.

And what about Trey's family? How would they react to a marriage they weren't invited to? Would they accept her? "When will I meet your parents? What will they say? Do they even know about me?"

"It doesn't matter what they think." He helped her inside. "I'll tell them when the time is right."

"When will that be?" Butterflies swarmed her insides. "They probably think I married you for your money."

Trey recoiled. "What money?"

Sydney gave him a sheepish glance. "I googled them. I know about the Tucson ranch. Their estates. Trucks, house, condo. Top-of-the-line reining horses. Why hide it?"

He ambled around the truck and got in. "*They're* rich. Not me."

"How can that be? Don't you have a trust fund?"

"I refused anything from them years ago." He turned the key.

"Why? Because he was hard on you?"

He sighed. "Because I wanted to make a name for myself. I didn't want to be Beau Hardy's boy who got everything in life the easy way."

"Is he that bad?"

"They're that artificial." Trey slammed the truck in reverse and turned around. "I don't need anything from them, especially their money."

Trees sped past as they headed back to the Washington state line. She understood the need to make it on her own, not relying on others to coddle her. That's why he was her husband in name only. She'd run the Seven Tine.

Once back in Spokane Valley, he pulled in to Sophie's Jewelers off the corner of Sprague and Sullivan. "Let's make this proper, shall we?" He went around and opened her door.

"We don't have to . . ." Tired and queasy, she wanted to get home. They still needed to get provisions for the ranch. This stop would only delay her rest.

He leaned over and unbuckled her seat belt. "You're right. We don't have to do anything. However, I'd like you to have something nice." He held out his hand. "Besides, it will be more convincing. Especially for Glenda."

She took his hand, and they went inside where glass cases and bright lights filled the parameter and center of the sparkly space. Overwhelmed, she cringed.

"Pick one." Trey shoved his thumbs in his pockets and smiled.

Pick one? "Oh, um . . . all right." She spent several minutes perusing several rings. They were all big, expensive, and heart-shaped, tear-dropped, or square. Living and working on a ranch, she wanted something . . . well, plain. She moved to a case in the corner, out of center stage. On the upper edge of a black display tray, she spotted a silver band. On the top, a row of small diamonds wove its way around a ribbon of silver. Like two people entwined together. "I found one I like," she told Trey.

He strode to her, his gaze following her pointed finger, and leaned closer. Squinted. "You don't want something bigger?"

She shook her head. "No. I like simple. Besides, anything fancy would end up in a drawer. Ranch work would only ruin it."

"I see your point. If that's the one you want—"

"It is." She waved over a female jeweler wearing a pencil dress and stilettos.

The woman slipped the band on Sydney's finger. Oh, man. Did wearing the ring seal the deal or what? And it fit perfectly, making her pulse race. Trey must have seen her unsettling reaction because he draped an arm around her and squeezed.

"We'll take it." He picked one out for him too. A wide, platinum band with sharp edges.

As they walked back to the pickup, she asked, "Why buy the rings now and not before the ceremony?"

He opened the door for her. "I wanted to make sure you didn't run."

CHAPTER 31

Trey caught her glancing at the diamond ring as he drove, the corners of her mouth tugging upward. A platinum band hugged his ring finger like her dress embraced her curves. He wished this could be their wedding night, but he needed to keep his hands to himself.

A few hours later and as dusk settled in on them, he pulled up to the ranch. She took the ring off and buried it in her purse.

Trey scratched his neck. "Why'd you take it off?"

"How are we going to explain this to Bobby and the guys? Mandie? The guests? Jim and Pam? The community? The last thing I need is to be the talk of the town."

"Why do they need to know or even care? This is between us, and we don't need anyone's approval."

"People talk. They ask questions. I don't want to have to explain. Not more than I have to." She touched his hand. "For now, let's keep this to ourselves. At least until I tell Glenda. A few days is all. After that, everyone will know. Trust me."

He sighed. "Three days."

Her cell chirped, and she read the tiny screen. "Oh, no!"

"What?" Trey leaned over and read the message.

Robert broke his leg. Call me.

She called the number back. After hanging up, she scrunched her nose. "That was one of his bronc-riding buddies. He's in the Crook County Hospital with a broken leg and won't be here for a week or so because they have to put a pin in it. He'll be laid up for six weeks or longer."

"What happened?"

"His bronc flipped over in the chute, and his leg got hung up in the saddle. He's lucky he's alive and came out with only a broken leg. According to his friend, he's bruised and battered and mad as a rooster in a cock fight." She pounded a fist on her leg. "Darn him. I need all the hands I can get."

"You know I'll help."

"I do." She motioned to the window. "Best check on Twister."

"I'll come with you, babe." Good. She smiled at his slip of the tongue.

She got out and marched to the barn. Trey tailed behind. Sure enough, the hands were doing the final horse checks of the night. The scent of fresh pine chips filled the air.

"Have you heard how Robert did?" Chad thrust his pitchfork in the wheelbarrow of manure and shavings in front of Twister's stall.

Sydney waved her cell. "He's in the hospital."

"What happened?" Rich wiped his forehead with the back of his dirt-crusted hand, considering her attire under the dim barn lights. "And why are you all gussied up?"

Her cheeks tinged with pink as she wrapped her arms around her middle. Avoiding Rich's second question, she shared the details of Robert's accident with them.

"Oh, man, that sucks." He motioned to her. "And your outfit?"

"I, uh, we . . ." She raised her brows at Trey.

"She took me out to a fancy dinner and showed me around Spokane." He grinned at his bride, trying to sound convincing. She seemed to relax. "Besides, I needed a new lens." That part was true although they didn't stop at a camera store. "What needs to be done?"

"Nothing. We just finished up." Rich dipped into his snuff can and tucked a pinch of tobacco into his lower lip. After shoving the can in his back pocket, he took hold of the wheelbarrow and headed for the east door.

"When you're done, please help unload groceries," Sydney told her ranch hands, then rushed away.

Trey chased after her. "What's your hurry?"

"What was I thinking? Running into the barn in this dress." She opened the tailgate and grabbed a box.

Trey took it from her and headed for the lodge. She ran ahead and opened the door. "They believed us, so what's the problem?" He set the box on the kitchen island. "Where do you want this?"

"I'll take care of it." She went to lift it, but Trey blocked her.

"Listen, if I'm going to be your husband, you have to let me help."

"It's only a slip of paper."

"Not to me." He held a loose grip on her shoulders, afraid she'd reject the union and eventually agree to a divorce. No, they hadn't known each other long enough to fall in love, but his heart tugged him in that direction. "You realize we have to make this believable and act as though we're in love."

She took a step back, and he dropped his arms. "I have to get used to all this. Give me those three days and then . . ."

"Then what?"

"I'll try my best. For now, let's focus on the ranch."

"Try your—"

"Where do you want these?" Chad dropped an armload of boxes on the island. He took stock of Trey's left finger. "What's going on?" Then surveyed Sydney's ring finger. "What's the real reason you two are dressed up?"

Rich stood behind him. He gestured to Trey's ring. "What's that?"

Sydney pointed to the pantry. "Those boxes can go in there."

Chad and Rich exchanged glances, their feet planted on the wood flooring as though protecting her from a predator.

"What's going on, Syd?" Chad lifted her left hand in the air. "Did you get one too?"

"We got married today." Trey didn't understand why she insisted on secrecy. People would find out in a few days anyway. Why not get it over and done with?

She shot him a steely glare. "They didn't have to know."

"They aren't stupid." He crossed his arms over his chest.

Chad released her hand and leaned against the counter. "We're right here."

Sydney pressed her palms together and looked at her ranch hands. "Please, guys. This is complicated. Don't say anything until we announce it. It won't be but a few days. Promise?"

Chad narrowed his eyes. "Your father'd turn over in his grave."

"He'd turn over if I lost this place." Why couldn't they see that?

He raised a brow. "You in financial trouble? Is that why you married this city slicker?"

Trey stepped toward him. "Keep things quiet. That's the least you can do, if you care about her."

After the men finished unloading the boxes, Trey walked them out.

"Don't you hurt her." Chad's upper lip curled.

"I don't intend to," he responded and meant it.

CHAPTER 32

Saturday, July 15

Though a sense of peace came over her while sleeping in her folks' guest room, Sydney woke with a headache. After yesterday, she needed to be surrounded by their belongings. Clipping her hair up, she padded downstairs for coffee, then rested in a recliner with her mom's Bible.

The searing heat remained stagnant even at five in the morning. Opened windows and doors offered no relief, and they couldn't afford a small air-conditioning unit. She flipped the table fan on, pointing it so air propelled toward her face.

She thumbed through the pages, reading her mother's notes, and flipped to a bookmarked passage in Jeremiah about God offering a future and a hope. Her mother had highlighted it in pink. Although Sydney's future seemed uncertain, she held a twinge of hope.

With a boyish look, Trey knocked on the screen door. "I brought breakfast."

"Come on in."

He took off his boots and arranged a plate of huckleberry pancakes, bacon, and silverware on the coffee table. Kindness leaked from his eyes, making it hard to enforce her boundaries. "Can I warm your coffee?"

She nodded. "Please. Help yourself to a cup."

He sunk down onto the couch and propped his feet on the coffee table. "How's it going?"

"Other than my head pounding, I think I'm hanging in there." She tapped the Bible. "According to this, God promises us a hope and a future. Do you think that's true?"

He blew in his cup. "It's not always easy reaching our destination. But, yeah, I believe His promises are honorable."

She'd have to learn more about them. "We've got a lot to do today."

"Let me get you something for your headache." He stood.

"My purse is on the counter. My migraine pills are in it."

"There's nothing in there that will bite me, is there?"

She laughed and pressed a hand to her forehead. "Ohhh."

After he'd given her the tiny pill, he closed the shades and the door partway, blocking most of the sun. He eased onto the sofa as if the movement would make her head worse.

"You're so much more caring . . ."

"Than who?"

She winced. How could she have been so careless? She'd eventually have to tell him about Cooper, but not today. She closed her eyes, hoping someday the memories would fade. "The ranch hands."

"They helped us last night. And so far they've kept their word."

True. "Have you seen them this morning?"

"They're feeding. Said they'd load hay and rotate pipes in the northern pasture. They want to know if you can catch up with them later and check salt blocks. If you're not up to it, I can." He gestured to the Bible. "What else did you read?"

"That's as far as I got." She closed the book and placed it on the coffee table, then rubbed her forehead.

"You get some rest. I'll help the guys."

"Don't you have a photo shoot? A deadline? When do you leave for the Amazon?" With a groan, she pressed one hand to her brow and hugged her stomach with the other.

"I take it you should have eaten something first."

"Probably."

Trey forked a piece and held it to her mouth. "Take a bite of pancake."

He grabbed the migraine medication box out of her purse and read the directions, then handed her a glass of water. "I have a few more photos to take for other cowboy magazines, which I can get this week. And I've canceled the Amazon trip."

Sydney stopped chewing and held a hand to her mouth. "You what?"

"If you remember, we're married. My responsibilities are here now. With you."

"But that trip is important to you." She wouldn't let him use her as an excuse not to go.

"There's no need for me to act like a bachelor any longer and simply take off anytime I please. Jim's right. It's time to grow up. You're now the center of my world. We'll figure out details as we go. I can travel, just not as much. Or as far. Besides . . ."

Sydney swallowed, washing the pancake down with the water. "Besides?"

"There's enough money in my savings account. It'll get us by for several months." He gently kissed the side of her head as though she'd break. "I'll meet you in the office at noon. We can go over the ranch financials before the appraiser arrives."

"Today?"

"At two." He handed her the plate. "Eat and rest. I'll check on you later."

She closed her eyes. She wanted him to stay. Hold her in his strong embrace. Tell her again their future looked bright. Behind her lids, her murky fate prodded.

CHAPTER 33

I t's nice to meet you." Sydney shook the appraiser's hand. "We'll show you around."

They gave the clean-shaven man a tour of the lodge, barn, main house, her cabin, and land her parents owned. She didn't like him poking around her folks' house. It made her feel protective. As the appraiser took notes, she fought off the urge to crumble. At every turn, Lester and Jennie showed up. In family pictures. Beaded eagle feathers hanging from the wall. Their floral bedspread.

Trey rubbed her back and whispered, "Why don't you get something to drink? You look pale."

She nodded and strolled into the kitchen. Rummaging through her mother's cabinets, she selected a glass and got a cool drink. On the kitchen table by a wilted bouquet laid an envelope with her name on it. Hmm. Postmarked a week ago. How did it end up in her mother's kitchen? She pulled out the card.

I wish you'd given me the chance to meet them.

Meet who? Her folks? Had Cooper—or his freaking spy—sent this? Trembling, she shredded the card and tossed the bits in the trash. Slammed the garbage can lid shut. Would he ever leave her alone? Feeling faint, she stood at the window.

The garden. Had anyone been tending her mother's vegetables and flowers? Sydney had been so consumed with Trey, Glenda, and ranch finances, she hadn't considered their winter food supply. Through the window pane, she noticed her auntie Marcie pulling weeds in the half-acre garden.

Sydney grabbed an empty basket from the counter and joined her. She smiled and pulled carrots. "How you holding up?"

Marcie shrugged. "I miss her. Us two halves, we made a whole." A large-brimmed hat covered long, thick lashes. She knelt on a green gardening pad, her small, bare feet peeking from the hem of her ankle-length skirt. "Oh, I left a card on the table for you. Did you get it?"

"I did, thanks." Sydney stiffened and gave her a counterfeit smile. "Did you know about the cancer?"

Marcie stopped weeding. "Who had cancer?" She wiped dirt from her face with a bony finger.

"Mom had breast cancer. You sure you didn't know?"

"I had my suspicions something was wrong." She fingered carrot tops. "She normally told me everything."

"Why do you think they were so secretive?" Sydney squinted, closing her eyes for a moment, needing her sunglasses and hat. She shaded her eyes with her forearm. "Did you know about the ranch's financial troubles?"

"They never did like for us to worry. She was stubborn like that. Our mother was the same way. They both claimed any gossip added unnecessary stress." She plucked a pinky-sized weed from dark soil.

"She saw a naturopath in Omak."

"Ah, that's why. She and our mom preferred Indian medicine. She knew I'd try to talk her into seeing an oncologist. Your mom didn't like people telling her what to do."

"She saw one once, then switched to Dr. Gordon. It's all in her journal. I found it when looking for their will. I'll get it to you."

"I'd like that. What are you going to do about the ranch?"

Sydney shared her plans for a dispersal sale. "I can't lose my sanctuary, Auntie." She ran a finger across the basket three generations of women had cherished.

"It's a sanctuary for many." Marcie placed a hand on her shoulder. "You have help. Use us." She turned to the footsteps behind them and gestured with a raised brow at Trey, who stood on the wooden porch.

Sydney opened her mouth to share the marriage news, then snapped it shut. Not yet. "Pray for me, Auntie."

"I always do, dear." She patted Sydney's hand.

Sydney and Trey showed the rest of the property to the appraiser. He agreed to have an assessment within a few weeks and left.

Once inside the lodge office, Trey settled on the sofa. "What's next?"

"Since my head feels better and we seem to be on a roll, let's check out what horses we can cull. Some will sell as barrel horses, others for working cattle."

"And the stud colts?"

"We can drop a few. I have the names of several interested buyers."

Trey studied Sydney. "When are you going to tell Glenda?"

"Soon."

"The longer you wait . . ." He stretched out his long legs and crossed his ankles.

"I know. I'll do it today." She sighed. "She's coming over this afternoon." She also knew the longer she waited to tell him about the anonymous notes, the harder it would be.

"It's your life, Syd. Stop asking her permission to live it."

"I know. I'm working on it."

"It's never easy. But once you stand up to her, life will be better, and I think you'll be happier. Don't you?"

She cringed at the childhood memories when Glenda told her what doll to play with, how to dress her, and what horse to ride. "That would be nice."

"Glenda's not a bad person. She simply needs to learn boundaries and respect them."

"She knows the boundaries, it's the respect part she struggles with." Sydney grabbed a clipboard. "Let's go and take stock of the horses before she gets here." The distraction might settle her nerves.

On her way out, she chatted with guests, making sure they were having a good time. She asked if they needed anything and hugged a little girl who sat coloring. The guest part of the ranch seemed to be running smoothly for once. Needing her sunglasses, she went back to the office and reached for them. On the desk sat an envelope with her name on it. With the same handwriting as on the envelope in her mother's kitchen. She ripped it open and yanked out the card.

Congratulations on your nuptials. But remember, I never signed the papers.

What the heck? Who was keeping tabs on her? According to her internet research, Cooper wasn't supposed to be out for another year or more. She went rigid, her breaths escalating. Then grabbed her pistol and burst outside, scanning the grounds.

The note. What would happen if her auntie found the pieces of ripped up paper?

She rushed to the main house, fetched the scraps of card out of the garbage, and—

"Did you forget something, honey?"

Marcie's voice made her jump. She swung around, hiding the fragments behind her back. "I did. But I'm meeting Trey now, so I'll talk to you later." She kissed her on the cheek and fled her parents' house. *I forgot the envelope!* Marcie would no doubt snoop in the garbage. Shoot. No time to go back. Besides, the envelope would tell her nothing because it offered no return address.

In the office, she taped the pieces back together. Then along with the other notes and photos, stuffed them into a manila envelope and put them in the safe. The only way she felt secure. She typed in Cooper's name on the Washington State Department of Correction's website. Good. He's still in the slammer. *But if he's in jail, who on earth is sending the stinking notes?* Who on the outside is helping him?

Fighting to keep her composure, she put on her sunglasses, settled her straw cowboy hat on her head, and found Trey waiting for her beside the mare-and-foal pen. Foals darted in between their mamas, shaking their heads and rearing up. One spun around and kicked at another. Blue roans mingled with red and black and white Paints. A few sorrels and duns served as solid backsplashes. How could she cull the herd? Cows had always been her dad's passion whereas the horses were hers.

Inside the fence, Trey took photos of the foals, seeming to aim for the right angle. "Which ones do you want to sell? I'll try to get flattering shots."

A family strolled up and watched the horses. The dad leaned against the pole fence. "Rumor is you plan on selling. Is it true?"

Great. Let the gossip fly. In her sweetest voice, she replied, "We're downsizing is all. Getting rid of things we don't need. Cleaning up the place." She glanced around. Where would someone hide to spy on her? A shudder snaked through her. If only she had the funds for security cameras.

"Good," the wife said. "We plan on coming back next year." She smiled at her husband, and they walked toward the barn.

Feeling as though eyes were glued to her, Sydney opened the gate and strode through. A blue roan with a two-toned brown face ambled over to her. She stroked two white patches that followed the shape of the mare's eyes with each thumb. "You get to stay." She scratched the roan's neck.

Trey snapped photos of the two. "This would be a great picture for your website or brochures."

"She's given us quality foals." She took Trey through the youngsters she planned to sell. While he photographed, she recorded them on the clipboard. She pointed out which mare had to go and which she planned to keep.

When finished with the pairs, they went to the two- and three-year-olds that had already been started. Sydney jotted down their names and which discipline they might excel in: rodeo, mountain trail, showing, cattle work. With each name listed, she stuffed down her emotions, knowing full well she could no longer handle the large numbers on the ranch.

Nor much of anything else.

CHAPTER 34

Trey prided himself for his courage. He'd traveled to parts of the world where snake bites were common and lethal and hurricanes turned buildings into toothpicks. Where lions had chased him and frostbite threatened his fingers and toes. He'd lived in tents and motels, crashing at his sister's in Tucson when needed. But the fear of losing Sydney Moomaw turned him to mush.

Then again, was he ready to put down roots? Would the call of the wild be too strong after a few months or years?

He zoomed in on her hands as she stroked the mare's face. She turned to him and smiled before glancing down. No. He could spend the rest of his days by her side and not go anywhere. Ranching with her felt right.

"I'm keeping this one." She stroked the roan's neck.

He followed her around for the next hour, taking pictures and trying to figure out how to convince the woman he loved her. Telling her should have been easy, but it hadn't gone as planned.

"When do your pictures need to be turned in to the magazine?" Sydney asked, then pointed to a sorrel foal.

Trey snapped its photo. "Next week." He panned the colt with his lens and took a couple more. "Do you think there's enough interest around here for a guy to set up his own gallery?"

"No."

He recoiled from the speed of her answer. "There seems to be a lot of traffic from both the US and Canada along Highway 155."

She kept her back to him. "Most people stop in Omak and zip past here."

"Then how do you think your gift shop will pull people in?"

She wrote on her clipboard. "I don't. It's a gamble." She pointed to another foal.

Trey took the shots. "Are you saying I need to keep traveling?"

She sighed. "I'm saying I won't let the Seven Tine get in the way of your career—or the Amazon trip."

"I told you, I canceled the mission trip." He stepped closer to her. "What if it's not the ranch that holds me here?"

She studied him for a moment. "I won't get in your way. My work is here, not on the road."

Trey wished she would drop her hardheadedness and soften her heart a little. Heck, he'd be thankful for a crack to let him in. "I don't have to travel the world to be successful."

"We're done here." She marched out of the gate as though she'd not heard him talking. "Let's get the colts listed before my sister shows up."

If only he could get his wife to stop dashing away when he tried to talk with her about their relationship. He followed her to the outdoor colt stalls. She haltered a bay Paint and lunged him in circles in the round pen. After removing the halter, she stepped aside. Trey snapped a few photos on both sides. "Why are you pushing me away?"

"Why do you insist we act like a couple?"

"Because we are."

"I thought this was nothing more than an arrangement to please my sister." She haltered the colt again and put him away. "Even you said we could divorce down the road."

Her words stung worse than falling headfirst into cactus.

"And is that what you want?"

"I don't know what I want."

Would him moving into the main house acclimate her to the idea? He'd be willing to bunk in the guest room. Anything to help her think about keeping the marriage intact.

CHAPTER 35

Sunday, July 16

Pastor Jake's sermon on love and commitment that morning now niggled at the back of Sydney's mind. Divorce had never been an option in their home. She picked up a photo of her parents when they'd first took over the ranch from her grandparents. They were young, in their mid-twenties, faces lit with determination and hope and love.

"You'd understand, wouldn't you, Daddy?" She hated herself for keeping Trey at a distance. Especially when she needed him most. Would the scars Cooper left ever heal enough to let Trey in? The roar of an engine announced Glenda's arrival. Sydney put the photo back on the shelf and twisted her hair into a clip.

Glenda paraded into the office, her charcoal locks in a neat ponytail at the base of her neck. "Someone else is interested in the ranch."

Sydney strode to the window and studied the barn. "Man, they loved this place."

Glenda took a seat on the couch. "Love don't pay the bills."

Ha. Sydney couldn't wait to show Glenda the proof of her vows. She went back to the desk and dug through her purse. Oh no. She needed the ring to keep the ranch. *Where are you?* With trembling hands, she searched again, taking out her wallet, brush, and notebook. She didn't remember taking out her ring. She opened her wallet. Nothing. "It was here. I know it."

"What are you looking for?" Glenda tapped her watch. "I've got thirty minutes."

"My ring." Sydney turned her purse upside down and shook it. Keys and lip gloss clinked to the desk, and so did the diamond. She slipped it on her finger and held it up. "Trey and I got married."

Glenda leaned forward. "You what?"

"You heard me. Do I have to show you our license?"

"You went through with it? I had no idea how desperate you are to have this place." She let out a cackle. "Well, good for you. Where is the lucky groom?"

Sydney scowled. "He went to lend the boys a hand."

"When did this happen?"

She recalled Trey calling her a pushover and lifted her chin. "Friday."

"Wow. Sneaky, huh? You two run off to the Hitchin' Post? Who stood in for you?" Glenda's tone sharpened.

"No one."

"I'd say I'm happy for you, but . . ." She shook her head and grunted. "You think Daddy would approve?"

"He'd be happy I fought for the ranch his grandfather built and he sank his life into."

"Oh sheesh." Glenda rolled her eyes. "You always were the favorite."

"Hardly. I've worked my butt off. When the calves were sick, I helped the vet. When it was time to move cattle, I saddled up. When—"

"Ranching was never my thing." Her sister's face reddened. "I had other plans. Mom always told us to follow our heart. Mine led me in a different direction. I was never tied to this place like you."

"You mean the notoriety that comes from being a councilwoman?"

She shook her head. "I serve the membership."

Sydney burst into laughter. "You don't serve anyone but yourself." She grew serious. "You run around to all the meetings and trainings. Sure you're not sightseeing on the tribe's dime? How much money do you spend on travel each year?"

"This meeting isn't about me."

"This isn't a meeting."

"You know what I meant." Glenda sprang off the sofa and stalked to the window. After a long moment, she spun back around. "Since there's no money to pay me off, what's your plan?"

"The appraiser will get back to me in a couple weeks. I'm in the process of setting up a dispersal sale with my husband. Don't worry. You'll get your portion."

Glenda studied her for a long moment. "Trey in a room upstairs?"

Sydney's face heated. The less Glenda knew, the better. Once her sister got back to the agency, everyone would know Sydney Moomaw—Hardy—had eloped.

"I'll call off the Realtor." Glenda snorted and walked out, bumping into Robert and his crutches. "When did you get back?"

He caught his balance. "A few minutes ago. What's going on around here?"

"She can tell you." Glenda jerked her thumb toward Sydney, and before storming out, said, "Make sure she tells you everything."

"What's wrong with her?" Robert crutched into the office wearing a tee, shorts, and a walking boot.

Sydney sighed. "Take a seat and I'll catch you up."

He eased to the couch, and she sat across from him in the padded chair. "Not sure where to start."

"How 'bout at the beginning?"

She prayed he wouldn't contest the will but would stay on and work the ranch alongside of her. Especially since he'd be getting a third of everything.

When done listening, the space between his brows narrowed. "You know I'll stay on, Syd. And I'll invest my share back into the ranch. For you guys to include me when you didn't have to is pretty generous."

Thank goodness. Her belly unknotted.

"I wish you would have called me though. The heads-up about selling would have been nice. I could have helped you with Glenda and forming a plan so we don't lose anything."

"I know. I'm sorry. From here on out you'll be included in everything."

He nodded. "I'd like that. And congrats on taking the vows." He gave her a small smile.

The disappointment on his face made her stomach churn. She'd have to make it up to him somehow.

CHAPTER 36

Tuesday, July 18

Trey tossed and turned, wondering how his wife's soft skin would feel beside him. He wanted to be close to her. Acquire the intimate bond husband and wife should have. Share their plans and ideas. For him, their marriage certificate was more than dried ink. He rolled over and sighed. He should be in the main house, with her, even if in another room.

In the distance, a coyote howled. It sounded close and lonely. Trey identified with its desolate call.

Not able to sleep, he slipped on shorts and a T-shirt and tiptoed into the hall. A creak from the main-level floor made him freeze. Who could it be? A teen boy with saggy pants and long greasy hair from the city came to mind. Yesterday, his parents had to pry him away from his cell to go fishing. Was the kid casing the place for something to steal?

Trey crept down the southern staircase and padded into the dining room. The scrape of a chair made him stop. The moon offered enough light to show a small figure crouched over one of the tables across the room and nearest the office. The shadow seemed too small to be the scraggly teenager. He inched closer, feeling like a cougar stalking its prey.

A woman startled, her shriek piercing the air as a low, deep growl sounded beside her.

Sydney? "Sshhh. It's me." Trey held a hand out for the dog to smell, then rubbed its head. Relieved, he took a seat beside her. Caliber yawned and lay down between them and closed his eyes.

"What's up?" She leaned back.

"Couldn't sleep. Then I heard a noise and wanted to make sure no one was snooping around. I don't trust that city kid."

She waved off his concern. "He's harmless."

He watched her for a short moment. "You get Robert all caught up?"

"Yep."

"How'd he take everything?"

"He seemed upset I didn't call him. I feel awful for not including him in the wedding, but . . ." Not the wedding of her dreams. "He was happy about getting a third of everything. He wants to stay on and invest his money back into the ranch."

"That's good. How's his leg?"

"He may get a cast in a week or so. The doctor wants the swelling to go down before he makes the decision to keep him in the boot or cast him. I have a feeling keeping him down is going to be a problem."

"I'm sure we can all help give him small stuff to do to keep his mind occupied." He motioned to the papers spread across the table. "What's this?"

"My business plan."

"In the middle of the night?"

"Couldn't sleep." The clock on the wall read 12:42 a.m. "The house is too quiet."

"About that." Trey frowned when she stiffened. "I'm moving into the main house with you since you're basically there most of the time anyhow. There's enough gossip floating around." He should have relocated his belongings sooner.

"I'm not ready to give up my cabin, and I'm certainly not ready to live in the same house as . . ." Sydney rubbed the back of her neck.

"As what? Your husband?"

"Sorry. I'm just not ready. But I am willing to talk about it after the dispersal sale."

Would she ever be ready? He slumped, wanting the go-ahead to move in ASAP.

Sydney tapped her pencil on the table. "Do you mind overseeing the cattle then? That will free Chad and Rich up to concentrate on the horses and trail rides."

"Works for me." How many times would he have to repeat himself? And he wanted to be more than a ranch hand to her. Someday, she'd have to let him help with the books. They could split things up. She could handle the horses, and he could oversee the cattle.

"Can I look over your business plan? I might be able to offer a scrap of advice."

"I'll handle it. It's almost wrapped up anyway." She smiled.

Disappointed, he asked, "When do you meet with the financial planner to look things over?"

"Friday."

"Mind if I tag along?" He looked forward to the day they could have a discussion without her getting defensive. He'd need to be patient, trusting in God's timing and not his own.

She lifted a shoulder. "Sure."

Progress.

He stood, wanting to hold her and assure her life would eventually ease, and she would be able to move forward. Instead, he muttered, "See ya in the morning," and went back to bed with a heavy heart.

CHAPTER 37

Wednesday, July 19

She finished her business plan. Although her shoulders felt lighter, an awkward feeling rushed over her from the attached note announcing her marriage.

She'd decided to keep her wedding ring in a drawer. The last thing she'd wanted was to draw attention to the nuptials. Why couldn't Trey have done the same? That or remain in the truck while she went inside the post office.

But he'd insisted on going with her so they could check out the west pastureland along the Columbia afterward. He needed to take more photos and wanted a few with his new bride.

Since the tractor had broken down, the boys didn't need his help for a few hours. She wished they would have suggested he do something else. Check on cows. Deliver salt blocks. Clean stalls. Half a dozen chores needing to be done floated through her mind. Anything but escort "Mrs. Hardy" to the post office.

July heated the cramped lobby like a dry sauna, and an elderly woman ahead of them seemed like she had all the time in the world to get her money orders and visit with the postal clerk.

Once finished, the elder turned and smiled. "Sydney Moomaw. I haven't seen you in ages. How's the guest ranch?

Boy, I sure do miss your folks." She took Sydney's hand in hers. "How you holding up, dear?"

Trey cleared his throat. "Hardy, ma'am. Her name's now Sydney Hardy."

The woman's eyes widened, and a grin blossomed on her face. "You went and got yourself hitched? Good for you, honey. Marriage is a happy spot in life. At least it was for me. I wish you both the best of luck."

She hugged Sydney and shook Trey's hand.

He opened the glass door for her and smiled. "Thank you, ma'am. We're happy."

"That's good to hear." She patted his shoulder and made her way outside.

Sydney rolled her eyes and slapped the envelope on the counter. "Priority, please." Enough of the marriage hoopla. She felt everyone's eyes on her back, their snickers making her grow impatient.

The mail clerk chuckled. "Right away, Mrs. Hardy."

Trey grinned, pride shining in his eyes.

"Very funny." Sydney's neck and face heated. "You'll pay for that."

He grabbed her left hand and kissed her ringless finger. "I look forward to it."

Laughter droned throughout the small building. Sydney handed the clerk a five-dollar bill, told her to keep the change, and rushed out.

They drove nine miles to the pasture and parked. Trey shifted toward her. "Now that the financials are taken care of, I hope you can relax."

"Relax? As soon as I can, I need to schedule the dispersal sale. Then there's the farm auction. There's no time to rest."

She hopped out of the truck and strode to the edge of the property overlooking the river. Everything she had was invested in the guest ranch. Her sweat, heart, and soul were devoted to the land, animals, and guests. She felt light-headed and crouched on her heels. The swish of boots on grass revealed Trey had followed her.

He reached out to touch her but retracted. "Hey, I'm sorry. What I meant to say was you can rest easier with that one, overwhelming task checked off the list."

She nodded and rose. "I'm sorry too. Once these sales are over and I have a better idea where I sit financially, then I can unwind."

"Where *we* sit financially." Trey snapped a few shots of the river, bales of hay, and the tractor. He took one of Sydney with the river in the background. "Hang on." He jogged to the truck and back, tripod in hand. "Let's get a picture. Who knows, it might make a good Christmas card someday."

"Someday, huh?" She wiped a strand of hair from her eyes and squinted. "Do we need to face the sun?"

Trey tightened the screw holding the camera to the tripod. Sydney wanted to let him in, but there were too many red flags—his work and family and her fear of getting hurt again.

"Close your eyes until we're ready." He set the timer and ran to her side, draping an arm around her.

After the camera clicked, he went over and viewed the monitor. "Let's try again but at a different angle. You're right, we're both squinting." He repositioned the tripod to the south, and they took a few more photos.

When satisfied with one of the images, Sydney said, "That'll do," and started for the truck.

"That will not do. Let's get it right."

She went back and made sure she appeared happy for a few more pictures so they could get on with the day. She needed to make sure Twister was fully recovered before opening the stall turnout lane. There were more important things to do than take pictures.

Pastor Jake had parked his truck by the lodge when they got back. "I didn't call him," Sydney said. "Did you?" She pulled in and cut the engine.

"Maybe he came to eat. You do offer meals to the community, right?" Trey grabbed his camera equipment and got out.

The balding pastor sat inside the lodge with a piece of apple pie and a glass of iced tea, enjoying the comfortable leather chair and the view from the bay window.

Mandie sat across from him, her infant sound asleep in a cradleboard on her lap. Tan buckskin covered the board with beaded pink, purple, and fuchsia hummingbirds outlined in green on the flaps. A red willow branch arched overhead, a rattle hanging from it. Nona slept soundly, her tiny berry-colored lips reminding Sydney of a porcelain doll.

"Mandie, you're here." She gently kissed Nona on her head, taking in the soft hair. "How are you feeling?"

"Good. But bored out of my mind. I want to come back to work."

"Yep, when the doctor releases you." She gave Mandie a be-patient look and turned to Jake. "Surprised to see you, Pastor."

He swallowed, nodding. "No more surprised than I am."

Heat warmed Sydney's neck. More than likely he knew they'd gotten married. Glenda had probably squealed.

The pastor smiled at Trey. "Is there somewhere we can talk? The three of us," he said in a hushed tone, his glance landing on the stirring baby.

"The office is open." Sydney bent down and gently kissed Nona on the forehead again. The infant stretched and fell back asleep. Trey led the way through the grand room.

Sydney shut the office door, and she and Trey settled on the sofa. Pastor Jake turned a chair around to face them and eased down.

"How's Hazel?" Sydney asked, her leg jiggling with nerves.

"She's well," Pastor Jake said. "Busy with her goats and cats. Managed a nice garden this year. She enjoys puttering around the place."

"You ranch then?" Trey asked.

"We have a small hobby farm with a half-dozen cows, three goats, a handful of chickens, and a couple mouse chasers. Keeps us young." His jovial expression grew serious. "The reason I'm here is—well, I heard you two ran off and got hitched."

Sydney's eye twitched. *I knew it.*

"I'm not going to pretend to know why or tell you it's any of my business," Pastor said. "I simply wanted to make an offer for postmarital counseling if you want it. I've been your family's pastor for years, Syd, and wanted you to know you have marital support."

Trey grasped her hand and gave her an awkward grin. "We appreciate that, Pastor. I've never been married, and it wasn't planned."

"But we thank you for stopping by." Sydney tried to stand, but Trey held her in place.

"I have a few questions." Trey's tone carried gentle but firm.

She shook her head. "No you don't."

Pastor Jake crossed his legs. "It's fine, Syd. I know more than you think."

"Glenda call you?"

He hesitated. "I did receive a phone call."

She tugged her hand away from Trey. "I'd like advice on how to keep my sister out of my personal life."

The pastor nodded. "That can be hard. Have you talked with her about it?"

"Many times."

"Sometimes all we can do is pray for those who drive us crazy. Especially when they become defensive and won't listen. Let God handle her for a while and then try again. If need be, I'd be happy to moderate any squabbles you two may have."

"Or have had for years," Trey said. Sydney jabbed him hard in his ribs, and he groaned. Massaging the injury, he said, "If you can't or won't talk to me, then how about I leave so you can talk with Pastor Jake."

Sydney widened her eyes and turned to the preacher. "I'm sorry, Pastor. Thank you for coming. I'll keep the offer in mind. Who knows when I'll need a little guidance?" In her rush to the door, she stumbled over Trey's legs. He caught her arm as she righted, then let her go.

CHAPTER 38

Trey shook his head. "She's got that maneuver down."
With his wife out of the room, he could have a serious chat with the pastor. Tired of her impenetrable wall, he hoped Jake could help him begin to knock it down. He leaned forward. "How can I get through to her?"

"She's been through a lot," Pastor Jake responded. "I'm afraid she's not allowing herself to grieve. Even as a little girl, she stuffed her emotions. It's going to take time to crack her shell. And because you took the vows for what I'm assuming are the wrong reasons, the marriage may fold no matter how patient you are and how hard you try. In fact, you might be pushing her too hard and too fast."

"We did get hitched in a hurry. Did Glenda tell you about the deal?"

Pastor cocked his head. "No, she didn't."

Trey filled him in on the entire ordeal. His feelings for Sydney and her resistance. His commitment to her and his deepening love. How she drove him crazy. How he couldn't live without her. His desire for roots and to help her save the ranch.

"There's a lot to work out, Trey. If you ever need to talk, here's my number." He handed Trey a white card.

"I appreciate it." Trey put it in his wallet. "Guess it's time for a road trip."

"Why's that?"

"Most of my stuff's in Tucson." He had time to fly down, pack his belongings, and drive back before the dispersal sale.

He knew a woman who could sell his furniture since he no longer needed it. He'd give Sydney the money from the sales to help pay the crew's wages. At least Mandie's. With a newborn, she'd need the extra cash.

He prayed with Jake before the pastor left, then made a call to tell the storage unit manager that he planned on moving. Called his dad to pick him up at the airport. Made a plane reservation for that night and called Jim to come pick him up.

He searched for Sydney. Her cabin stood empty, as did the barn. He wrote a note telling her his plans and left it with Chad, who was taking him to meet Jim. He'd talk to her about moving into the main house when he got back. He might have to do it without her blessing and beg for forgiveness later.

It would be worth it.

CHAPTER 39

Thursday, July 20

On her knees by the creek, Sydney cried. The sound of shallow water tumbling over rocks and the brilliant purples of the sunset offered none of the usual tranquility. Nor did the chirping crickets.

He was gone. No note. No explanation. No one seemed to know anything about his whereabouts, and he wasn't answering her calls or texts. She should have told him she loved him. Now she'd lost her chance. Salty drops streamed down her cheeks.

The heaviness of managing a guest ranch without him clenched her chest. Later, when she could speak without breaking into tears, she would find a reputable Realtor and list the place. After the cattle sale, she would break the news to the staff. God help her.

The sound of horse hooves clomping on grass-covered ground came to a halt behind her. She wanted to be alone to think. Broken pipes or equipment were too much for her to handle at the moment.

"Broken hearts *can* be mended." Martin stood at her side. "Can I join you?"

Sydney nodded, glad it wasn't one of the ranch hands bearing bad news. "Sure." She wiped a tear with the back of her hand, rubbing the sorrow on her jeans, and pulled her knees to her chest.

He chewed on a blade of grass for a long moment. "Ruby and I divorced after only six years."

Sydney rested her cheek on her knees. "You did? Weren't you married for forty-nine years?"

"We were." He watched the creek for a while like most elders did when instructing younger generations. "She could slice me with the sharp edge of her tongue. Ornery at first. But once she quit the booze, she settled in to the kindest woman I knew." He chuckled. "'Course I wasn't always the easiest to live with. Living on the back of a horse, long days and lonely nights. She'd stay here with the babies while I chased cows on whatever ranch would hire me. After the divorce, I sold my saddle and fled to Alaska to fish. I lasted three months before realizing I couldn't live without my Rubygem."

"And when you got back?"

"I bought the biggest ruby-and-diamond ring I could afford, swallowed my pride, and begged for forgiveness."

"She took you back that easily?"

"Heck no." His eyes twinkled. "I bought my old saddle back from the secondhand store in Tonasket and wrangled up a handful of cows and an old tractor. Earned my keep until the day she took her last breath."

"I miss her." Overhead, two clouds in the shape of violet hands reached their fingers across the heavens, a small space between the tips. Images of her mother slid through her mind, as did images of Trey. She shuddered. "He's gone."

"Seek wisdom, not knowledge. Knowledge is of the past. Wisdom is of the future. Creator will guide you. But you have to let Him. Be still and listen." Martin rose. "Sometimes you have to stick to the power of the vows and swallow your pride."

Was he implying she rush after him like a desperate failure? Never. She scoffed. "What do you mean stick to the vows? I'm not the one who bailed." She twisted around.

"Martin?" She hated when he snuck around undetected, not even telling her goodbye. Her heart sank.

She mounted Cyan and rode back to the ranch. After tying her mare to a hitching post outside the barn, she checked on Twister. He played with another colt across the run. She haltered his mama and led her to the pasture. Twister bolted through the gate and ran in circles, bucking and kicking. He sniffed a filly and tore off, shaking his head.

A pinch of joy shimmied up her spine before sorrow squashed it. Letting him go would be hard. It would be tough to let it all go. She'd have to start fresh. Because she didn't see any other way.

CHAPTER 40

Friday, July 21

Since sleep had eluded her for the past several hours, Sydney rested on the porch lounge chair wrapped in a blanket. Had God heard any of her meager prayers? Did He want her to let go of the ranch? Was it too big a responsibility for one person?

Overhead, stars twinkled and danced in their ink-colored playground. She yawned and closed her eyes. Shifted until finding a comfortable spot. Her body pleaded for sleep, but her mind darted from Trey to Cooper. Her memory of him beating her bloody had jolted her from a restless sleep.

She rubbed her stiff neck muscles. Would she ever shed the images of her purple arms and legs? Cut and swollen lips? Black eyes? His snarled face? Was she better off alone? At least no one could hurt her that way. Not even Trey. She could finish her degree and get a job in another state. That way there would be no reminders of a failed past.

Around four in the morning, she showered and sat on her bed, wet hair dripping on her tank top. Her phone chirped, a reminder of her meeting with the financial advisor. A meeting she could cancel as long as she had the guts to let the ranch go. Unless the meeting would leave her a spark of hope. If she did have to sell, there might be enough money left over after covering bills and Glenda's and Robert's third to pay for her degree. She blew out a breath. In the kitchen, she brewed a cup of coffee and toasted bread. The thought of eating anything else made her gag. She took her breakfast to the living room. Her mom's Bible stared at her from the coffee table, so she picked it up and pondered notes her mother had made in the margins.

She read and prayed until confident her decisions were the right ones. Good thing Trey wasn't around to try to sway her to his way of thinking. Her cell displayed 5:30 a.m. Time to get cracking.

Inside the lodge, an elderly woman entertained Nona while Mandie scurried from table to table, pouring fresh coffee for the early risers. Though Sydney had encouraged her to take more time off, her cook had refused. "Sitting around is driving me crazy," she'd said. Sydney had to admit, having her back lifted her spirits. She took a moment to snuggle the bundle of cuteness before heading to her office.

She checked her phone. No messages from Trey, confirming he had no plans to return. What a coward.

"Here's coffee." Mandie set the cup on her desk. "I went to clean Trey's room, but his clothes were there. Any idea when he's coming back?"

"They are?"

Mandie looked confused.

"I—uh—I'll take them to my cabin and clean the room when I'm finished." Sydney printed out the incoming guest list and handed it to Mandie. "I think I'll take care of his things now. I have a meeting this morning in Omak. Get me a list, and I'll go shopping."

"Sounds good." At Nona's cry, Mandie rushed out.

Sydney slid the folder encasing her copy of the business plan into a purple-and-blue Pendleton briefcase and laid it on the desk. She rushed up the stairs two at a time. Sure enough, Trey's room held a packed bag. His razor lay on the bathroom counter, and there was shampoo in the shower.

Was he in such a hurry to escape, he'd forgotten his things? She gathered his items, changed the sheets, cleaned the area, and toted the bag to her office, shoving it in the closet. She didn't know what to think.

She grabbed Mandie's list, kissed the sleeping baby, and headed out. Would this meeting with the financial advisor seal the deal? Would she lose the ranch for good? She had a feeling she would. Tears distorted her vision. She wiped her eyes and turned up the music.

Luke Combs crooned on about leaving. She groaned and changed the channel. Lauren Daigle came on singing "Rescue." She clung to Creator's promise of giving her a future and a hope. Convinced herself it could be the beginning of something new and exciting. Trey wasn't the only adventurous one.

Her father would have expected her to be excited. Like the day she'd left for college. Pride had shone on his face. His daughter, off to Eastern Washington University—an eagle, the Native symbol of fortitude and honor. She could use his firm hug today.

But you have My strength.

If only she could feel God's presence.

Sydney turned left off Central Avenue and pulled up to the weathered office of Evan Moore. She took a deep breath and unbuckled the seatbelt. Her trembling hand tipped her purse off the seat, and its contents scattered on the floor mat. She picked up her wallet, hoping Evan would be able to help her. After placing the items back in her purse, she grabbed her briefcase and went to slide out when a business card on the mat caught her eye. She picked it up and turned it over. Ah, the card Krystal Hopkins had given her for James S. Kruger, Civil Attorney. She placed the card in her wallet and locked the truck.

Inside the building, the waiting area hosted a couple of chairs, outdoor magazines, and a small, shabby table. A woman who appeared to be in her mid-fifties, wearing red glasses and a short bob, glanced up from behind a podium-style desk. "Just a minute." After clicking computer keys for several seconds, she smiled. "How can I help you?"

"I'm Sydney Moomaw—Hardy." She sighed and smiled. "I have a nine-thirty appointment."

The woman tapped her computer keys. "Here it is. He'll be right with you." Her sparkly mauve nails gestured for her to take a seat.

Once settled, Sydney hid her hands in her lap. Her nails were short, dirty, and jagged, and her dry skin itched. She reached in her purse, pulled out a small tube of vitamin E cream, and squeezed a small dot on the back of her hand. It soothed her hide as she rubbed it in.

"Miss Moomaw, come in." Evan wore black slacks, loafers, and a blue dress shirt.

Sydney followed him to an office complete with a desk, laptop, two chairs for clients, and a bugling-elk picture hanging on the dingy wall.

"Forgive our office. We're preparing to remodel." He pointed to a tattered chair. "How can I help you?"

She handed him the folder. "Jade Reese gave me your name."

"I've known her for years. Smart as a whip," he said as he skimmed the numbers. "She called me about you. Said your folks passed?"

"They did." Sydney pushed her emotions aside. Time so far had not healed anything. Neither had hard work.

Evan nodded. "My condolences."

"As you can see, several months of payments have not been made. My mom had been ill. It's all there." Her mouth desert dry, she opened her bag. Shoot. She'd left her water bottle in her rig.

He closed the folder. "I have to be honest. This doesn't look good."

"I have a dispersal sale in three weeks. An estate auction two weeks after that. I've listed mares, foals, and a couple of studs. That has to be worth something."

He opened the folder again. "And then what? How will you sustain the ranch with most of your stock gone?"

The gift shop seemed dismal compared to what she needed to keep afloat. But she told him her ideas anyway.

He set the folder on his desk. "I see the documents list your last name as Hardy. Did you recently get married?"

Sweat formed on her palms, and she swayed in the chair. She looked at the worn green carpet. "Yes, but . . ." Should she tell him her doubts about it lasting? Out of options, defeat danced around her. Happy endings were nothing more than a fairy tale.

"Why don't you come back after the sales. We can see where your financials stand at that time."

Sydney stood and shook his hand. "I appreciate your time."

With shoulders slumped, she strode out the door. The heat hit her like a blazing forest fire. She wobbled to her truck and struggled to get the key in the lock. Once inside, the reality of losing the ranch struck hard. Grabbing the water bottle and uncapping it, she took a long drink, then winced from the hot liquid. She slammed it against the passenger's window. Water splattered the cab, and she burst into tears. "God, where are you?"

CHAPTER 41

How would she break the news to her employees? Sydney feared their reactions. After all, they'd been committed to the ranch for several years.

She couldn't hold Glenda off much longer. She'd been rejecting her calls the last few days. And now with Trey gone, how would she explain everything?

She missed her nieces and nephew, wanting to spend more time with them. They didn't deserve to be caught in the middle of a sisters' battle.

Her phone read seven o'clock. Time to get this over with. The guests had all left to take in an evening light show at Grand Coulee Dam. It had been a stretch to pull the excursion off—surely divine intervention.

The crew gathered in the dining room like sheep to slaughter. A thickness hovered over them. Mandie held a sleeping Nona in her arms.

"Thanks for coming," Sydney said, her throat thick. "I've . . . uh . . . discovered financial troubles. I didn't know about them until recently." Chad's exasperated sigh distracted her. "There will be a dispersal sale the tenth. And—"

"Of next month?" Robert asked, wide-eyed.

Sydney had wanted to make the announcement only once, but now she regretted not telling her brother in private first. "Yes. August tenth we will have an auction for items we don't use. I need you guys to fix whatever can be repaired. The rest we can sell for parts. I'll help make a list. Anything we don't need to run this place barebones has to go."

"Can you save the ranch?" Mandie's voice cracked. Nona snuggled next to her chest and Mandie patted her back.

"It doesn't look good," Sydney answered. "If you guys stick with me, I'll make sure . . ." For a moment she pressed a hand to her mouth and squeezed her eyes shut. "You'll get paid and one heck of a recommendation."

Mandie would be taken care of. She lived in Indian housing and the rent would drop to next to nothing without an income. Plus, she could use unemployment, WIC, and the tribe's low-income programs for food and energy.

As for the ranch hands, they could easily find work on the rez with tribal Fish and Game, Forestry, or Range with their good reputation and strong work ethic.

Mandie nodded. "I'll do what I can to help."

"I'll make sure the rooms are clean and help cook when I can." Sydney turned to Chad and Rich. "You two will have to do most of the work. Guests will thin out soon for a couple weeks, and the hay's about ready for the barn, right?"

"Yeah." Chad's voice cracked.

Sydney sighed. "Do any of you know a high schooler to help if we need it?"

"I have a handful of cousins who can load and stack hay," Rich said.

She frowned. "I can't pay them."

"They owe me. I've run their scrawny hides all over the rez on my dime most every weekend for months." He grinned. "It's payback time. They can pitch in and learn about volunteering."

"In the meantime," she said, "let's concentrate on getting panels in and move the cows to the northern pasture. We'll haul that hay out first and leave the river pasture till last. My uncle will help, and I'm sure a couple of his friends. We'll know more after the sales."

"What about the horses?" Robert asked.

"I've got several listed, including the broncs."

He shook his head and looked away.

"What about Camo?" Rich's voice wobbled.

"Him too." She hated having to release the colt Rich had been working with the last couple of years. The gelding finally had a solid stop and spin, taking right to cattle with little pressure on the reins. "I'm sorry. I have no choice. These sales are the only chance I have at saving this place."

He bumped a fist on the table. "I understand. Don't like it, but understand. You should get a nice price for 'im."

"I will. You've done a top-notch job with him. I'll make sure you get the credit. You've earned it."

"I'll try to round up a couple volunteers to clean rooms here and there so you can concentrate on the sales. I'll text them now." Mandie pulled out her phone from the diaper bag and tapped the keypad. "You and your folks have done a lot for this community. All the barn dances and kids' events. They'll be happy to pay it back."

Sydney pressed her lips together. What would she do without her good friend, big mouth and all?

"Where's your husband?" Chad's tone sounded more condescending than concerned.

How would she tell them he'd run off? "Remember, he's a photographer. He has a job to do." That should hold them at bay. For a while, anyway.

CHAPTER 42

Thursday, August 10

When Sydney entered the guest ranch the morning of the cattle dispersal auction, Mandie and two friends were busy cleaning rooms and checking guests in and out. Thank the Lord. Her cook had come through, and Robert could now complete most of his simple chores with the walking boot and crutches. Marcie and her mom's longtime friend, Georgie, helped prepare food for potential buyers coming to the sale.

"Three more ladies are on the way," Mandie said as she whipped past.

Sydney hoped they'd get more cooking done than storytelling.

Jim and Pam pulled up in time to carry trays of sandwiches to the tables set up under a tent. Behind them friends and neighbors donated cookies, water, and iced tea. Some stayed to help organize the smaller items for sale, keeping back a few that interested them.

Stock trucks swirled dust behind them as they rattled up the drive. The guys had erected panels by six and the last of the cows were fed and ready. Sydney's head spun. Never having hosted an auction before, she had no idea what to expect. She'd taken time during the early morning hours reading her mom's Bible and praying, asking for God's wisdom and favor.

She found Marcie and Georgie cleaning the lodge's kitchen, the aroma of ginger snaps and chocolate chip cookies lingering in the air.

"Remember to ask the guests to stay clear of the auction for a couple hours. I don't think we'll be able to keep them away." Sydney noted her clipboard, her hands trembling.

Marcie rubbed Sydney's back. "Creator will take care of it all. Trust Him." Her floral apron tied snug, she clasped her hands together in front of her midsection. "Your folks would be proud."

"Would they? Feels like I'm about to lose it all." She'd be lucky to salvage one bull and a few mom-calf pairs. She stepped toward the door but stopped at the sound of her aunt's voice.

"Don't be so hard on yourself. You're doing your best. That's all anyone can ask for. Besides, so what if you lose it? You and your sister's happiness were what they cared about most. This place brought *them* joy. It was their life. It doesn't have to be yours. You can have your own dreams, ya know."

"But it is my life."

Marcie stood nose to nose with Sydney, her worn hands on her niece's shoulders. "Well, then . . ." She admired her for a long moment. "Go work your magic."

"Don't forget your water bottle." Georgie waved it in the air.

"I don't know how I'd get along without you two." Sydney kissed them both on the cheek and left. She swung open the heavy wooden lodge door. Normally, she wouldn't have trouble opening it, but today it felt extra weighted. The only thing that would make her happy would be for life to rewind back to the morning her folks left. She would have stopped them from going.

Glenda and Chuck drove up and hopped out of their Toyota.

Sydney groaned, not bothering to smile and act happy to see her sister. "I got a lot going on today. What's up?" She strode past them.

"Wait!" Glenda waved a hand in the air.

Sydney turned around and arched a brow.

"We're here to help," Chuck said.

Glenda seemed sincere, her expression soft and caring. Sydney gestured to the guest house. "Auntie's in the kitchen. If you want, you can see if she and Georgie need help." She faced her brother-in-law. "Will you come with me?"

"But—"

"Not today, Glenda." Sydney strode off.

Chuck fell in step alongside her. "She wants to help."

"Yeah, help sell the place and get a chunk of cash."

"Try to give your sister a break," he said. "She's concerned all of this is too much for one person. She cares about you, Syd. Whether you believe it or not. This place was hard for all three of you to run. Now it's only you."

"Creator and me. I'm not alone." Her renewed conviction made her smile inside. She wanted her relationship back with God. She'd wandered away for too long. It felt good having Him back in her life.

After putting Chuck to work with Rich, Sydney went to find the auctioneer, Caliber trailing behind. She needed to know where he wanted to stage himself, hoping he'd brought his own sound system. If he even needed one. She rounded the corner of the barn and came to a standstill, face to face with her husband.

His smile faded into a blank look.

Sydney narrowed her eyes. "You're back?"

"Of course I'm back. I said I'd be back in time for the auction."

"What are you talking about? You didn't tell me anything. You just left. You didn't answer my calls or my texts. Why not?"

"Pastor Jake suggested I give you some space. So I did. Besides, I left you a note. Didn't you get it?"

"No note. No text. No call." She went to shove past him when Caliber growled and bit at his heels.

"Hey! Knock it off," Trey said to the dog, then took hold of Sydney's wrist and towed her into one of the empty barn stalls. "I couldn't find you, so I left a note for you with Chad. He said he'd get it to you right away."

"With *Chad*? Where did you go?" She clenched her teeth. "You know how busy we are. You left—without talking to *me*. I thought you'd run off. What were you thinking?"

"I'm sorry, hon. I couldn't find you. By now you should realize I'd never abandon you. I wanted my belongings here. With you." He combed his fingers through his hair. "This is my home now, and *you're* my world."

"Your things?" She leaned against the wall, inhaling the scent of fresh pine shavings.

"I told you I'm in this for the long haul." He stepped close to her. "And I meant it."

She placed a hand on his chest as a barrier. His musky scent and faithfulness made it hard for her to hold a grudge. "There's a lot to do. We'll talk later, OK?"

He wrapped his broad hand over her dainty one. "I have to tell you something." His finger outlined her cheekbone.

The longing in his eyes made her knees wobble. His fierce sense of commitment scared her, and she hated herself for allowing fear to control her. "I've got my hands full. I promise we'll have time to talk tonight." She fled from the stall and hollered for Chad.

CHAPTER 43

Trey strode out of the barn behind Sydney, his fingers curling into a fist. His news could wait, but his talk with Chad couldn't. A tall, thin man wearing a straw cowboy hat waved at Sydney. Ah, must be the auctioneer. *Please keep her busy.* But Sydney kept walking toward Chad. Darn.

Trey caught up to Sydney. "Let me talk to him first."

She grunted. "This should be good."

When they reached the ranch's stock truck, he said, "Hey, Chad, can I talk to you?"

Chad scowled. "Where have *you* been?"

"You give that note to Syd?"

"Yeah. Of course." Chad patted his pants pocket. "Oh, man. Sorry. It must have went through the wash."

"You stupid—"

Chad threw up his hands. "It wasn't on purpose, I swear." He jabbed a finger in Trey's chest. "You're the one who should have talked with her. Not left it up to me or anyone else."

"Guys, enough!" Sydney pointed at them. "Though you're right, Chad." She jabbed a finger at Trey. "You should have called and left a message." Glancing between the men, she added, "We have a lot to do today. Let's get at it." She swung around and marched toward the auctioneer.

Trey shifted his weight, his jaw clenched. "She's right. I should have called her." He set his hands on his hips, shaking his head. "No hard feelings?" he asked Chad.

Chad clapped Trey's shoulder. "You're in the doghouse, dude."

"Tell me about it." So much for Sydney receiving a love note. Why had he left it with someone else? What had he been thinking? That she'd be too busy to find it. Still. Stupid move.

"Where'd you go? You had her twisted in knots."

"Tucson. I need my truck now that I'm staying. And the rest of my stuff." He gestured toward the barn. "Any empty spaces in there?"

"Not right now."

Trey nodded. "I'll park the U-Haul trailer behind Syd's cabin and come back.

Chad waved him on. "Follow me."

For the rest of the day, Sydney directed her ranch hands and buyers as each cow and horse got sorted and loaded. Trey helped show and load, trying to keep his wife fed and hydrated. He planned to make good on the promise to take care of her, so he asked Marcie to surprise her with a nice dinner.

The auctioneer's voice had gone hoarse at the end of the day. The holding pens were empty and the last of the trucks rumbled down the drive. When all was said and done, Sydney looked more worn than usual.

Trey slipped out early and headed for the cabin.

An hour later, Sydney and Caliber came through the screen door. "Auntie said you needed to see me?"

"Dinner's almost ready."

"Looks nice in here." She glanced around. "Is there food?"

"It was supposed to be here by now." He liked the way she explored him with her chocolate-colored eyes. "You thirsty?"

Sydney nodded, took a glass of ice water from him, and placed it against her forehead. "Wild day, huh?"

"Yeah, but you handled yourself like a pro."

She scrunched her nose and fingered the purple phlox adorning a glass vase. "I had no idea what I was doing. Glad the auctioneer took over." She sipped the water. "This hits the spot."

He was glad she'd noticed the floral arrangement Marcie had helped him with. Her aunt had made sure he knew they were Sydney's favorite. "While you shower, I'll check on dinner." Out the window, Marcie and Georgie were headed toward the cabin, both packing covered trays. He draped an arm around his wife and led her to the hallway, trying to hide the busybodies. "By the way, all the photos are in. The editors are thrilled. That income should help."

"Congrats!" she said before disappearing behind closed doors.

He rushed to the screen door and took the tray from Marcie. "She's in the shower." He spoke in hushed tones, hoping they'd get the hint.

Marcie held the door open for Georgie, who pushed past Trey.

Georgie scanned the room. "Food's warm. And there's a little something special in there for you." She giggled, winking at Marcie.

Marcie held out a bottle of men's aftershave. "This worked for me, if you know what I mean. Harold wore it all the time." Her husband had died five years ago.

Mortified, Trey thanked the ladies as he ushered them out the door, then set the table. He fingered through Sydney's CDs and put one of R. Carlos Nakai's on, turning down the volume and allowing the Native flute tones to float through the room. He sat on the couch, trying to decide how to bring up him moving into the main house and his idea for a studio.

Sydney's floral scent reached him before she came into the kitchen wearing shorts and a tank top. He went to the table and pulled the chair out, leaning close to breathe in her fragrance. "Feel better?" He moved to his spot.

"I do." She scanned the table. "Mmm, this is Auntie's cooking." After Trey said grace, she forked in a bite of mashed potatoes and country gravy.

His wife's beauty captivated him. While enjoying the steak dinner, they spent nearly an hour rehashing the day's event. "I'm proud of how you handled yourself."

Her eyes lit up.

"You should be able to pay off a chunk of debt."

"I hope so. Now that I know what to expect, I'm ready to focus on the horse and estate sale." She gave him a shy smile. "Thanks for your help. I was beat when the last truck left."

"I wanted to draw you a bubble bath but wasn't sure when you'd be home." Would there ever be a day she'd want to grow old with him? He prayed God would soften her heart to the idea. And again give him the courage to bring up them moving into the main house.

CHAPTER 44

Home.

She wanted a family of her own so badly her heart ached. Daydreamed about children running around barefoot, leaving dirty footprints on the wood floor—laughing and playing. What had possessed her to give up her baby? How foolish of her to have thought her family would have been ashamed.

Would it be that bad to have a trustworthy husband to share dreams with? Take her riding and fishing. Be somebody she could count on. Was Trey him? There were days she felt as though her fear blinded her.

A pang of guilt swirled inside her for sneaking his belongings back to his room before meeting him for dinner. She should have trusted him. With most of the cattle gone, she felt empty. She crouched over and scratched Caliber's head, the only thing she had left of her daddy.

Her belly clenched as her thoughts went back to the auction. Auntie Marcie was wrong. Her father would have hated this day. More than she did. If they hadn't died in the car wreck, the sale would have put her mother in a grave. Had Creator allowed them to go away so they wouldn't have to watch the ranch fall apart? Was that a merciful act? Pastor Jake would know.

When dinner ended, she moved to the couch. Trey brought in two plates of huckleberry pie draped with whipped cream. Her mouth watered.

"Where are you going to store all your things?" How much did he have? There wasn't much in the back of the truck. "There are a couple different storage units at the Dam."

"Thanks. I'll look into them." He inspected the room. "Have you ever thought about turning this place into a bunkhouse for the hands? Or a studio?"

She didn't have the energy to put much thought into it. "Not really."

"I have an idea."

Her heart told her to fess up about Cooper. She couldn't let this drag on forever. Better he hears about her ex from her lips and not Glenda's. "I have something to tell you first."

"Sure."

She set her pie plate aside, not knowing where to start.

"We'll work this out, whatever it is." He placed a hand on her leg.

Sydney cleared her throat. "I, uh, I've been married before." She waited for a response and when he didn't offer one, she continued. "I met a guy, Cooper Payne, at Spokane Community College. We were both on the rodeo team. I roped, and he rode bulls. I'd talked to him off and on during the first year. Wasn't looking for romance or anything. Then the following fall, we hooked up. We were young. And he made all the right promises."

"So what happened?"

"We got married at the courthouse on a whim, and within weeks, he became short-tempered. The night we got married, he got drunk and never stopped. We were broke. Two days later I came home from class to find him snortin' coke with a couple greasy guys. Then the beatings started." Her voice hitched. Not wanting to relive the horror more than necessary, she kept her walk down memory lane brief and to the point.

Trey brushed hair from her face. "How'd he react to getting caught with the drugs?"

"I ended up in the hospital with a broken nose and two cracked ribs."

The vein on Trey's neck bulged, his lips forming a thin line.

"He promised he'd quit. But never did. Things escalated pretty quickly from there."

"Did Glenda know?"

"Yeah. That's why we don't get along. I swore her to secrecy, and she's never forgiven me for it."

"That explains a lot. How long did you guys stay married?"

With his invitation she cuddled up next to him, her head on his chest. "For about five months. I landed in the hospital two more times. Boy, he sure knew how to hide that side of him. But I didn't find out how wicked he was until the barrel racers came looking for me when I hadn't shown up for several practices and a rodeo."

"Why didn't they tell you before?"

"That's the thing about abuse—everyone's afraid to speak up. They were terrified of him coming after them for snitching."

"Did you turn him in?"

"Not at first. Not until after the third time he put me in the hospital. A domestic violence advocate tried to help me. But like my friends, I was petrified. So I went home. Then one night after a rant, he pulled a gun on me. I tricked him into thinking I would submit to him. Told him I needed to use the bathroom first, then crawled through the window. I called my friend Jaycee. She came and picked me up, and we went to her place. The next day she took me to the YWCA, and I got the help to get a no-contact order, then filled out divorce papers."

"How long was he in jail for?"

Trey's heart pounded in her ear. "The first time . . . less than a year because he had no priors. The second time, with proof of the coke, they kept him a year or so. Then he got out. Later, cops picked him up for theft. He got out again. Went back in for disorderly conduct. I should have never married the psychopath."

"You kept tabs on him?"

"I know it sounds sick, but I had to know where he was. So yeah, I'd scan the papers and check with the Department of Corrections and the US Bureau of Prisons inmate locator."

He kissed her head, tightening his hold on her. "I bet your dad was ready to castrate him."

"He never knew. I didn't tell my folks."

"You didn't tell them? Why not?"

"It would have broken their hearts to find out I married so quickly and ended up with a loser." Looking back, horses and their daughter were the only things she and Cooper had in common. She wanted to share the story of her baby girl with Trey, too, but wasn't brave enough. Simply thinking about it overwhelmed her.

"How did you keep this a secret for so long? It seems like you were close to your parents."

"That's how rebellious and independent I was in those days. Foolish, actually. But now that they're gone, I'm glad they never knew."

"I'm so sorry, honey. I'll never let him hurt you again. I promise."

But could he make that promise stick? Sydney closed her eyes, releasing years of pent-up fear and guilt and shame. He deserved better than the train wreck she'd become. But she desperately wanted his love and affection. Loved how he made her feel stable. Could the wall she'd put up to protect herself ever be shattered?

CHAPTER 45

Saturday, August 12

Sydney had found the perfect match for Camo. While Trey held the horse trailer door open, she led the colt inside. The blue roan stepped up like a veteran and stood without fidgeting while she secured him.

Today, she'd kill two birds with one stone. One, meet a savvy estate auctioneer in Moses Lake. Two, deliver the horse to a rancher in the area. The new owner planned to rope off him in the coming year and get him ready for the pro rodeo circuit.

Jim and Pam pulled up. Pam jabbered the minute she stepped from the Jeep. She joined Sydney in the old pickup, settling in the passenger seat.

"Here's a thermos of coffee and snacks." Trey set a cooler on the back seat of the truck, let Caliber in, and handed Sydney the thermos. The trip should be good for her. "You two be safe." He gave her a quick kiss and swung the door closed. He pushed on it until the latch clicked tight and clapped the rim of the bed twice.

Sydney pulled out, window rolled down. The ladies sang along with Garth Brooks's song "Shameless" as the truck and trailer rolled down the drive. Trey swallowed hard, shaking his head. He prayed she would eventually accept what he was about to do.

"Let's get this done," he said to Jim as he moved toward the cabin.

"Syd has no idea?"

"Nope." Trey opened his tailgate and tossed Jim a couple of empty boxes. "The rest is in the U-Haul behind the cabin."

Jim chuckled. "You're brash, my friend."

"I've never known a more stubborn woman than my wife. Nor a more tenderhearted one. I think once she gets used to the change, she'll be happy I took the initiative to make it happen."

"Easier to ask for forgiveness, huh? As long as you don't make it a habit." Jim clapped him on the back. "Let's do this."

Trey hesitated. "Think she'll ever learn to love me?"

"Depends how she reacts to this." Jim hopped up the porch steps. "If she smiles, you're home free. Pam, on the other hand, would kill me."

That's what scared Trey the most. But he'd never know until he tested her.

The colt rode as quiet as a mouse down I-90 as they headed west. Sydney flipped the visor to shade the sun, tuned in to 104.9 Shine, and turned down the volume.

"Trey seemed in a hurry to get me off the ranch this morning."

"Jim mentioned helping Chad and Rich fix equipment for the estate sale." Pam refilled both travel mugs with steaming coffee and pushed the lids on. "How's the marriage going?"

"Trey's pressuring for the both of us to move into the main house. He claims since the staff knows and the guests are figuring it out, there would be less gossip. I hate when the guests congratulate me."

"Because of how you got married? Or the reasons why you did it?"

The truth stung. "I suppose both."

"Not quite what you had in mind, is it?"

Sydney grunted. "It's the price I pay for keeping the ranch."

"Is it worth it? Will you be able to hang on to the place? You haven't told me everything, have you?"

Sydney cringed. "You know most of it. And I'm not sure if I can make this work or not."

Pam turned off the music. "You talking about the ranch or Trey?"

"Both. I feel like I'm in over my head."

"I can imagine you do. Someday you'll figure out you don't have to do everything by yourself. You have so many people who love you and want to help. Even God, Syd. When are you going to quit running?"

"I know." She sighed. "I'm sorry, Pam. For everything. For not keeping you in the loop. Not sharing my struggles. You were the one I wanted by my side when we got married, but we had to keep things quiet. I've been so overwhelmed. I guess I've been hiding out."

"But why? Why is everything on the down-low?"

"I'm ashamed . . ." Sydney fought to keep her composure. She hated hurting her best friend's feelings. They'd never kept secrets in all the years they'd known each other. Well, almost none. She felt most horrible about never telling her about Cooper or the baby.

She filled her in on the will's stipulations and her and Glenda's agreement. Her mother's cancer, treatments, mound of medical receipts. Whew, a relief to unload her conscience. "I don't trust my sister right now. I know if she can find one crack in our deal, she'll take me to court to sell to get her third. Especially, if I can't come up with it between the two auctions."

"Glenda has always had a vindictive streak." Pam sipped her coffee and pulled out a baggie of fruit from the cooler. She popped a grape in her mouth.

"She can definitely be self-absorbed." Sydney held out her hand, wanting something other than the bitter taste of regret to baste her tongue.

Two hours later, she pulled into the Coyote Ridge Ranch and unloaded Camo. After a quick tour of the ranch, the girls headed back to the rez. Sydney swallowed the knot in her throat, her finger's clutching the cool steering wheel. Camo had promise. The loss tore at her chest.

Pam gave her a compassionate grin. "Want me to drive? You look tired."

Sydney slid on her sunglasses. "No. The road's a good distraction."

"I know he's a big loss. But he's in good hands."

Sydney nodded. "Not sure I can take any more major changes right now. The farm auction is hard enough."

"If you get through all of this, nothing can sink you." Pam switched back to the CD. "For now, more Garth!"

"I'll second staying afloat. Now, let's go meet the bid caller." The estate auctioneer seemed to be a good choice. Thanks to a cancelation, she booked him for the following Saturday. She couldn't get Glenda off her back soon enough. Even if they now had to rush to get ready.

CHAPTER 46

Sydney pulled into the Seven Tine a little after five that evening, tired and hungry. Glad to be home, she looked forward to a cool shower and her own bed. Jim and Trey were on the lodge's porch. They rose as the truck and trailer rolled to a stop in front of the barn.

"You wanna stay for dinner?" she asked Pam.

"Would love to. I'll see what Jim has planned." Pam opened the door and hugged her husband.

"I see you two went shopping." Jim eyed the garden supplies and flowers in the truck bed.

"We found a few good sales." Pam winked.

"How was the trip?" Trey held open the driver's door.

"Uneventful." Sydney slid out.

"Hey Syd, we're heading out. A guy's coming over to look at a chainsaw Jim's selling." Pam went around and hugged her. "Thanks for letting me ride shotgun."

"Thanks for keeping me company." Jim practically dragged Pam to the Jeep. What was that all about? She shrugged and started toward her cabin, telling Trey, "I'll shower before dinner." He caught hold of her hand and laced their fingers together. "I have a surprise for you."

"Can't it wait?"

"Not this time. It's important." He led his groaning wife to the main house, stopping at the front door. "Hope you like it."

She bit her bottom lip, a pit forming in her belly. She prayed he had not disturbed her parents' home. She wasn't ready to let them go. Didn't want anyone else in the house with her. He opened the door, and she gasped as she stepped over the threshold. Her hand flew to her throat. "No . . ."

Sydney tore loose from Trey and sprinted to her cabin, remembering his remark about making it into a studio. She thrust open the door and stepped into her sparse home. A blue sofa and white end table replaced her living room furniture. Where was her kitchen table? In her bedroom were boxes of camera equipment and photos. The cupboards stood bare. What had he done?

Hands fisted, she marched back to the main house. Trey rose from the porch stairs as she closed in. His charm wouldn't soften her this time.

"What have you done?"

"Now, honey—"

Sydney flicked the palm of her hand up inches from his nose. "Do not *honey* me!" She brushed past him and stepped inside. Her horse photo replaced her mom's painting— daisies waving in a summer breeze. It had been her mother's favorite.

"I'm sorry you're upset. But it's time we act like a married couple. With separate bedrooms, of course. I didn't toss out anything. Only blended yours with theirs. Some of it's in the basement." Trey swept a hand over the house. "Look around. You'll see I'm telling the truth."

"You had no right." After taking a quick spin around the house, she perched on their green sofa and hugged a hummingbird pillow.

"Maybe not." Trey dropped to the coffee table. "But we can't be married with you keeping me at a distance. I'll turn your cabin into my studio. You're now the owner, not a partner or hired hand. The main house is where you belong."

Sydney took in a few deep breaths. When calmer, she said, "What do you need with a studio?"

"At the airport I ran into the guy who takes the rodeo photos during the Omak Stampede. He recognized me from the funeral. He's retiring and thinks I'd be perfect to take his place. He's willing to set me up for a meeting with the board. Said there are a ton of events he shoots and will hand them over to me."

Sydney's eyes widened. "When?"

"There's no hurry. I told him I needed to unpack and organize my portfolio first. He wanted me to shoot with him this weekend at the rodeo. But I told him I'd check with you first. We've got a lot to do around here, and I want to be available to help."

Too much. Way too fast. She rubbed a shaky hand over her forehead.

"I know this is moving quickly for you. But remember, it's the only way Glenda agreed to not contest the will."

"I need to come up with her share."

"And we will. If the next auction doesn't produce it, we can raise it. As I've said before, I have a little money in savings."

"But you may need it for travel expenses. If keeping the ranch is meant to be, God will allow me to have it."

"There will be plenty for traveling." Trey scrubbed the stubble on his face. "Did you ever think God placed me in your path for a reason? That I might be part of His plan? I'd like to think I'm an answer to your prayers. I know you're an answer to mine."

Sydney toed the cream carpet.

"I am?" Her voice slanting a hair above a whisper.

"Yes. You are."

CHAPTER 47

Sunday, August 13

Sydney bathed five horses and lined them up in the barn. She felt better after a good night's sleep. And had to admit, Trey did well blending her and her folks' belongings. But she still struggled with him being two doors down the hall.

She snatched a tube of coconut-scented detangler from the grooming caddy and worked it through the tail of a blue roan mare with a white star on her forehead and quiet eyes. The clean scent helped calm Sydney's nerves while singing along with the '90s country CD mix as she brushed. Keith Whitley came on and sang "Somebody's Doin' Me Right." Sydney swayed to the beat, twirling from one horsetail to the next.

She squeezed out more detangler and rubbed her hands together before running them down the ebony tail. The CD had been one of her mother's favorites. She sang and brushed and waggled, wishing her mom was with her. They used to bathe horses together while singing and dancing on many summer afternoons. Jennie's voice had rung clear and crisp.

Halfway through a particular twirl, she noticed Trey. He leaned against one of the stall doors, a wide grin across his face.

Sydney tossed him a mane-and-tail brush and waved him over. "I'm hoping if we make these guys shine, we'll get a higher asking price." She gestured to a plastic caddy on a hay bale in front of an empty stall. "There's another tube of detangler in there."

"Good to hear you say *we*." He got the grooming product and swaggered over to a fit blue roan sporting a brown muzzle. After rubbing in a liberal amount of the goop, he worked the bristles through the gelding's mane. "He's a dandy."

"Sure is." Sydney continued to move with the music as she spoke. "Chad's done an amazing job with him. I can't wait to show them off today."

"What time are they coming?"

"In an hour or so."

"Well, big boy, let's get you ready." After Trey finished brushing his mane and tail, he took hold of her hand and twirled her around. He caught her around the waist and slowed the rhythm down to a leisurely sway as "When You Say Nothing at All" crooned throughout the barn.

Liking his closeness, Sydney laid her head on his firm chest and drank in his horsey fragrance.

As Whitley sang about a woman speaking to his heart, they danced. Was God using Trey to touch her heart? Would God and Trey catch her if she fell? She pressed her hand against his chest, felt his heart beating slow and steady. Strong and reassuring. Yeah, they'd catch her.

Did the truth in Trey's eyes say he'd stick around? Yeah, he would.

In that moment, between his tender touch and his unwavering faith, he gave her the courage to believe in herself, in what they were trying to accomplish, and in their marriage.

The sound of tires crunching rocks ricocheted through the barn. Whomever needed to go to the lodge and leave them alone.

"You expecting anyone?"

"Not this soon." She tightened her grip on him and felt him return the pressure. He ran a hand down her back, causing her to shiver.

"How 'bout you get your hands off my wife." A leggy, backlit figure wearing a cowboy hat swaggered to the couple and halted.

Sydney spun out of Trey's embrace. "Cooper. What are you doing here?"

Shooting a sneer at Trey, he said, "Collecting what's mine." He tipped his hat back, the one he'd worn bull riding on the college rodeo team. "Time to come home, babe." He gripped her arm and yanked.

She ripped her arm out of his grasp and rubbed where he'd clutched her. "We're divorced, moron. I signed the papers after you were arrested."

Trey put his arm around her waist and drew her close. The men were about the same height and both lengthened their spines as they eyed each other. How'd he bust out of jail? He had two more years, or so she'd thought.

Two trucks and trailers pulled up outside the barn. Good thing the potential buyers had shown up early. Doors creaked open then slammed shut.

"Get off my property, or I'll have you arrested," Sydney said to Cooper, her voice thick.

"Not without you signing the papers." He jerked a thumb toward his truck.

"What papers?"

"What do you mean what papers? These are for our divorce."

"Those are phony. I signed them while you were locked up and so did the judge, you idiot. Get lost."

Trey stepped between Sydney and Cooper. "You heard the lady. Get out of here."

Cooper sneered. "I'll be back." He strutted away like a cock in a hen house, tipped his hat to the folks entering the barn, and disappeared. Seconds later, his truck sped off.

Trey turned to Sydney. "I'll go let Chuck know he's out." Trey held Sydney for an instant before walking away.

She plastered on a fake smile and greeted her guests. "How you all doing? I'm Sydney Moomaw—Hardy." She held out a shaky hand but retracted it, wiping them on her jeans so the visitors wouldn't notice her distress. "Sorry, I'm pretty dirty. But I've got them ready for you."

One by one, she saddled and brought the horses out to the arena and let them stretch their legs. When they seemed settled, she rode each one so the lookers could see how they were progressing in their training as three- and four-year-olds. Working with them calmed her nerves.

Within a couple of hours, all five horses sold with minor finagling. Sydney helped load three horses in one trailer and two in another. She signed over the papers and placed the payments in the safe. Weary, she crumbled on the office couch.

Two messages flashed across the top of her cell screen, both from Glenda about the kids coming for a visit. Though Sydney missed them, her reply would have to wait.

With Nona nestled in a front pack, Mandie poked her head into the office and handed Sydney a glass of lemonade. "Did you make a sale?"

"Sure did." She sipped her sour drink. "This hits the spot."

"Get a good price?"

"A few dollars under what I listed them for. But all five sold."

Mandie pressed a hand to her hip. "They should be happy having the best horses around." Nona fussed. "Better take the boss on a little walk. The fresh air will be good for both of us."

Oh, how Sydney wished she'd kept her baby. With a heavy sigh, she rose, took a manila envelope out of the minisafe, and went to the main house in search of Trey.

CHAPTER 48

Sydney found Trey on the couch in the main house listening to soft, Spanish guitar music. "Get a hold of Chuck?"

"Nope. But did leave him a message for him to call me back."

"OK, thanks. I-I have something to show you." She prayed he wouldn't be too upset for withholding pertinent information. She handed over the envelope and settled next to him. "I've wanted to show these to you so many times, but . . ."

He pulled out the contents and studied the picture, then read the notes. "We could have handed these over to Chuck."

"I thought maybe someone was sending them for him." She sighed and set them on the coffee table. "In the back of my mind, I'm terrified he'll attack me if he finds out I gave them to a cop. Having him show up today . . ." Fear blocked her words.

"I don't know what you're going through," Trey spoke in a compassionate tone as he laid the documents down, "but, babe, handing them over might have prevented him from showing up today. Chuck could have found out if he had been released and these notes and the photo would've put him back in jail."

"I'm sorry." She hugged herself.

He motioned to the speckled bruises on her arm. "He leave many of those back then?" His gentle touch caressed the purple marks Cooper's fingertips had left.

"Too many."

220

He rubbed her leg, his woody sent reaching her nose. "I don't know how else to convince you, Syd. For *us* to work and for me to be able to protect you, you have to find a way to trust me enough to be open and honest."

She didn't know how to trust him. Cooper's beatings had stripped that away from her.

"We'll work this out."

She melted when he pulled her into his arms. "He must have been recently released. I doubt he would have waited this long to show up. And I'm sure he had one if not two people spying on me."

"Who would have helped him?"

"His brother, Kris, probably found our address off our website and mailed the letters."

"And the photo?"

"I'm not sure. I didn't see Kris at the powwow." She couldn't think of anyone else who'd want to help him. Or destroy her. "Part of me hoped if I didn't respond they would stop."

Trey held her until she quit trembling. Then he found a cool rag in the bathroom and brought it to her. "What about the divorce papers? Are they valid?"

"Cooper's aren't, but the one's I turned in are valid. A domestic abuse advocate from the YWCA helped me fill out the forms and get the judge's signature." She laid across the couch, her head in his lap, and closed her eyes. She concentrated on the guitar tones for a long moment, then said, "The thing is, I burned my copy of the official divorce papers so my family wouldn't find out."

She burned them? Not real smart.

Sydney had fallen asleep on his lap. Trey wanted nothing more than to stay there with her all night, but sleep eluded him. So at eleven, he slipped from the couch and her sweet, soft scent, covered her up, and retreated to the kitchen table.

He swiped his cell screen and scrolled through his contacts, landing on Brad Talbot, a high school buddy from Tucson, now an FBI agent. He texted him what he knew about Cooper, then slipped on his boots and went to the cabin to find his laptop. He wanted answers. And to find out more about his wife and her past. What else had she kept from him?

After digging out a computer in the box-littered office, he settled on the blue couch in his living room and researched Cooper. Would he find what Sydney said to be true? Fifteen minutes later, he quit investigating. Her ex's old social media posts confirmed his scumbag status.

He typed in Sydney Hardy, then hit the delete key five times and punched in Moomaw. His hand hovered over the *enter* key. He wanted desperately to trust her.

What was he thinking?

With a deep groan, he closed the laptop with a *click* and took it back to his bedroom in the main house. If he planned to make this marriage work, he'd have to follow his own advice and trust her.

CHAPTER 49

Monday, August 14

Sydney tossed and turned on the stiff sofa. The wall clock above the fireplace in the main house's living room read 2:15 a.m. She groaned and covered her face with her arm. Where had Trey gone?

Last night, his strong arms had given her much-needed comfort and a sense of peace and protection. But it wasn't enough for her to sleep soundly. Cooper had desecrated her dreams all night long as she relived each beating. And their pathetic courthouse wedding. Not to mention the fire in his eyes when he'd threatened her if she ever left him. The images left her a frazzled mess.

3:47 a.m.

Getting up and dressed weighed heavy on her mind, but her body insisted she remain under the comfort of the blanket. Trey must have covered her up when he'd left. Such a good man.

4:17 a.m.

Why had her mom spent so much money on natural treatments? Why hadn't she remained with the oncologist? Why tax the ranch like that? For goodness' sake, Indian Health would have paid for chemo.

5:24 a.m.

Light streamed through the window, directly into her eyes. She rolled over, mad she hadn't pulled the curtains last night. Ideally, she should have slept in her bed. Her cold, lonely bed. What would it be like to have her husband's warm body beside her each morning? To embrace his love and strength.

Then get up, drink morning coffee together. Plan the day. Run the ranch side by side.

She tossed her blanket aside and padded upstairs to Trey's closed bedroom door. She sighed and went to take a shower. Once dry, she dressed in jeans and a yellow tank top, with the auction and Trey occupying her mind.

Maybe having him in the same house would be beneficial. Especially with Cooper on the loose. Sitting on the edge of the bed, she rubbed her temples, a migraine worming its way up the back of her neck and threatening to ruin her day.

She dragged herself to the kitchen. Every groan of the wooden stairs made her heart feel emptier. Oh, how she wished she would have awakened to him cradling her. She needed his sense of protection now more than ever.

After making a strong pot of coffee, she found pen and paper and settled with a steaming cup of brew at the kitchen table. She listed preparations for the combined estate and horse sale. Not having held or been to one before, she found herself with a small list.

Trey. He'd know what needed to be done.

She shot out of the chair to go find him and slammed into him as he rounded the corner. He caught her in his arms, his earthy scent tantalizing her.

"Where's the fire?" Trey swayed with her for a moment.

"I'm trying to figure out what all needs to be done for the horse and estate sale. And . . . well . . . I'm stuck." She rested her head against his chest, fitting perfectly in his space.

"Maybe I can help. Where's your list?"

She led him to the table and handed the pad to him, embarrassed by its sparseness.

A grin on his face, he perused the list, plopped the notebook on the table, and grabbed a cup from the cupboard. The aroma of coffee swirled in the kitchen as he poured it from the carafe. A bottle of salted-caramel-flavored creamer in hand, he settled next to her. "I'm glad you want to work as a team. Do you know how happy this makes me?"

Heat wiggled up her neck. "I suppose this is a baby step."

"That it is. But I'll take it." He took a sip and added a drop of creamer.

Sydney fingered her cup. "What about the old equipment?"

"What about them?"

"Are you much of a mechanic?"

Trey tapped the notebook a few times with his finger. "How about I make the list for you? Or is that a big-girl step?" He winked at her, suppressing a grin.

"Funny." She had a hard time concentrating on much of anything with his deep green eyes boring into her. That and her growing headache.

"On another note, I have a meeting with the stampede board after the auction. I believe on the twenty-first. You wanna come with? We'll do lunch, make a date of it."

A date? They'd been married for how long now, and the idea of dating had never surfaced. She nodded. "I'd like that."

"A date it is." He leaned back in his chair and took a drink.

Where would they go? What would they do? Places she could take him swarmed her mind.

"How'd you sleep?"

She yawned. "Not well." She rose and fetched a migraine pill out of a cupboard. After popping it in her mouth, she dropped a slice of bread in the toaster and went back to the table.

When the toast popped up, he slathered one side with butter and brought it to her. She took a bite, and he rubbed the back of her neck. "How about you rest, and I'll go make a list?"

"It'll pass."

"I wasn't asking." When she didn't respond, he continued on. "I'll make sure the animals are fed, including Daisy and her calf, and check on Twister." He studied her for a moment. "You need a second opinion. Maybe a different doctor."

He knew her all too well. What a sweet offer to take care of her animals. The headaches were another story. "I'm sure there's nothing that can be done."

"Have you tried a naturopathic doctor or chiropractor?"

"Don't know any." Other than Dr. Gordon. And after seeing what her mom had to fork out, no way could she afford it.

He escorted her to bed and tucked her in, pressing a warm kiss on her head.

Yep, she could definitely get used to having him around.

Three hours later and feeling better, she slid on her cowboy boots. A note by the coffee pot let her know Trey was with Chad and Rich. He also stated two tractors were almost fixed and ready for the auction.

She found a legal pad in her dad's office and started a list: tack, panels, balers, irrigation pipes, unused furniture, the old Ford with a bad radiator, and her first car—a 1964 blue Mustang that needed a new starter. She hated to let go of it. Too many memories had been made in that car. Like cruising the reservation with friends, their time filled with adolescent joy and peace and enthusiasm. If only she could find those traits in her life again.

She added the rest of the horses to sell, along with old lawn and garden tools her mother had collected over the years. Two of the hay trailers would have to go. One of which her grandfather had spent countless hours pulling her and Glenda and their friends around in the winter by horseback. After the ride, her grandmother would serve them warm cookies and hot cocoa in the main house by a crackling fire. All good memories about to be ripped away with a drop of the auctioneer's hand.

Why had they left her with such a mess?

Sydney found her sunglasses, put on one of her father's loose-fitting cowboy hats, and made her way outside. The ranch yawned to life under the heat of a cobalt sky. Stock nibbled on their hay, and birds sped from branch to branch, singing staccato tunes. Caliber found her in the barn. She took a moment to love on him before checking on the horses.

In their stall, Twister mouthed hay beside his mother. Before long it would be time to wean him, unless the pair sold at auction. The thought left an ache in her chest.

She opened the gate and strolled in between pairs of mares and their babies, stopping beside a gray colt. She massaged his neck and back, praying for strength to let him go if the interest arose. He relaxed and took another bite, swatting flies with his fluffy tail. She scratched his back one more time before going in search of the guys.

Trey and Chad tinkered with the aged International truck outside the shop. Rich lay under her car, singing to a country song on the radio.

Sydney ran a finger over the Mustang's fender. "Polly's been good to me."

Rich rolled from under the car, grease staining his face. "Starter's in and oil's changed. She's 'bout ready."

"The Mustang's yours?" Trey gave a low whistle and wiped his hands on a rag. "I'd always wondered what was hidden under that tarp."

"She's mine for another week, anyhow. I'm sure she'll bring me a nice price." Sydney polished a spot with the inside hem of her tank top. "All she needs is tires." She kicked the bald rubber.

"You sure you don't want to keep her?" Trey tossed the rag on the tractor seat.

"Yeah." She had to pay off Glenda.

CHAPTER 50

More than watching his wife have to give up her Mustang, Trey hated to see her in pain. Stinking migraines. There had to be a way to relieve her agony.

He went to the lodge for cool drinks for him and the crew and searched for a local naturopathic doctor on this cell. Finding one in Omak, he went to the ranch office and scribbled the number on a sticky note. He slipped the paper in his pocket, noticing a large envelope on the desk from the appraiser. Why hadn't she opened it? Should he? No. He'd give her the chance to do it and share her findings. Hopefully today.

He strode to the kitchen and grabbed five chilled Cokes out of the fridge.

Nona fussed in her gray-and-white Pack 'n Play as Mandie rolled pie dough, so Trey set the drinks on the counter and lifted the little one out. He patted her back, catching a whiff of her clean baby scent. She settled down and rested her head on his shoulder.

"You'll make a great daddy," Mandie said.

"Never considered having kids until recently." His heart melted every time he caught a glimpse of the sweet, chubby child.

"Until recently, huh?" Flashing him a grin, she rolled out a lump of dough. "You getting an itch to settle down?"

"Maybe a little."

"Sydney has that effect on people. Trust me."

She sure did. "What do you want me to do with Nona?"

"She's getting hungry. Put her in the high chair, and I'll feed her."

Trey pulled the chair closer to the counter, unhooked the tray, and bent over to set Nona in. She clung to him and wailed, drawing up her legs. He hugged and soothed her, not liking to see her upset.

"She's got your number."

"Is that a bad thing?" he asked as Nona again nestled against his chest, wiping her snotty face on his shirt.

"Uh-oh." Mandie laid the dough in a deep-dish pie tin, tossed him a flour-dusted hand towel, and washed her hands. "I'll take her."

He passed Nona to her mother.

"Hey, Trey?"

"Yeah?"

"Is she gonna lose the ranch?"

He scrubbed his shirt. "Not if she lets me help her."

Mandie gave him a lopsided grin.

"Don't worry. I'm wearing her down." He gathered the icy Coke cans, and on his way out, tossed the towel in the laundry room. The guys were working hard when he entered the shop. He passed out the beverages. "Where's my wife?" he said in a confident tone. Instead of teasing him, they all pointed toward his studio.

He rushed back to the office, grabbed the assessment, and found her in the cabin hanging one of his desert cactus photos on a wall in the main room. Two more lay on the floor beside her. One illuminated a stunning orange and black summer sunset he'd taken in the desert last year. The other highlighted a Navajo elder with brilliant white hair and deep facial creases. She wore and sold turquoise squash blossom necklaces and cuffs. They'd met five years ago at the Santa Fe Indian Market. Her kind eyes had burrowed into his heart and stayed there.

"Where'd you take this?" Sydney stepped back and admired the photo she'd hung.

"Sonoran Desert. The sunset is from there too." He handed her a soda. "How's your head?"

"Fine."

Fine? Her baggy eyes and faraway look said otherwise. Evidently, her morning nap wasn't enough. He handed her the note with the clinic's phone number on it. "I found a naturopath in Omak who may be able to help with your migraines."

She took it. "This is the same guy my mom went to." She filled him in on what she and Glenda had uncovered. "There's no way I can afford him, and Indian Health doesn't pay for it."

"That's the only medical coverage you have?" When she nodded, he asked, "How long have you been having these headaches?" They had to be related to her ex.

"Since college."

"Exactly." Trey worked his jaw. If it weren't for his ability to forgive and let God deal with Cooper, he'd find a way to make him disappear for good. "Listen, you need to do something about your headaches. I'll go with you. Please, make an appointment. I'll pay."

"I'll think about it. According to my mom's journal, the cancer was about gone, so yeah, maybe it will work."

"Almost gone, huh?"

"Yeah. She'd written in her journal that she no longer could feel the lump. Plus, a second mammogram confirmed it. Oh, she also traded coffee for green tea about a year ago. I'll have to find out why."

"Why don't you make an appointment right now?"

"I'll do it later."

Oh, she drove him crazy. He handed her his cell. "Why wait?" After a long moment, she took the phone and tapped in the number. After making an appointment, she said, "Maybe

I can persuade him to tell me about my mom. It won't hurt to ask." She motioned to his hand. "What's in the envelope?"

"The assessment." He gave it to her.

"It came in? Robert must have picked up the mail." Sydney ripped it open and scanned the page. "This can't be." She handed it to him. "We'll never come up with the money to pay off Glenda."

Trey considered what they'd already sold and what would be auctioned off. "Is she willing to make a deal?"

"She said so, but I'm not sure."

He leaned against his four-drawer cedar desk and crossed his arms. "We'll figure this out."

"You sure about that?" Red faced, Sydney rose and hung the sunset photo on the wall, then picked through several desert canvases. Her hands shaking, she pulled out a few and arranged them on the carpet: a single saguaro cactus with three stubby arms in bloom, a roadrunner perched on a rock, a full moon hovering over rock canyons dotted with saguaros and prickly pear cactus.

Trey sighed. How would they come up with seven hundred thousand bucks? There had to be a way.

CHAPTER 51

Saturday, August 19

Sydney rose bright and early, feeling refreshed, glad Trey had talked her into resting more the past couple of weeks. Because she'd need her strength and wits for the day. The auctioneer was scheduled to arrive at seven thirty. After a quick shower, she plodded into the lodge to find Mandie organizing food in the refrigerator.

"Where did all this come from?"

Mandie pointed at Trey, who sat on a bar stool jiggling Nona on his knee. "Ask him."

Shifting Nona to one arm, Trey stood as his wife approached. "Good morning, babe." His face shone with excitement.

"Hey there." She hugged Trey, then took Nona from him and pressed several kisses on her face and neck. Nona giggled and squirmed. "Where did all this food come from?"

"I went shopping. Figured the crew would need lunch and snacks. It's supposed to be pretty hot today. There are a couple of coolers of ice and water in the barn."

"That's sweet. Thanks."

He inhaled a sharp breath. "Could it be? Is she learning my money is her money?"

"Very funny."

His smile turned serious. "You got your pills in case you get a migraine today?"

She patted her pockets. "Nope."

"Want me to get your meds?"

"I'll get them. You go meet the auctioneer. I'll catch up with you guys."

Trey kissed the top of her head and let out a soft groan. "Love you," he whispered and walked away.

His touch sent a charge of electricity through her. *Love you too.* Someday those words would roll off her tongue. Her mind shifted to the auction, and her belly knotted. Only Creator knew how much money they'd make. Would it be enough?

Sydney settled Nona in the high chair and went in search of her meds. Marcie and Georgie would be here soon to help. What else would she need? Her mind reeled too fast to think.

With her medication secure in her front pocket, she found Trey and Tim, the auctioneer from Moses Lake, in the north pasture discussing the list of sale items. She pushed her sunglasses up on her nose and tugged the brim of her hat lower to dim the sun.

Trey draped an arm around her. "You remember my wife?"

"Nice to see you again, Tim. How was your drive?"

"Beautiful. I think we're ready to go. What time did you advertise the sale to begin?"

"Eight sharp," Trey answered.

Tim rubbed his hands together. "I'm ready."

Tractors and other equipment arced the top of the sale area. Furniture and any other item Sydney deemed useless sprawled across the south side of the pasture. Ranch guests milled about, picking up items here and there. A round pen stood in the middle.

Sydney couldn't have asked for better help. Auntie Marcie and Robert manned a table under a blue canopy tent, ready to collect money. Martin and Trey were to assist the auctioneers. Chad and Rich were in charge of handling the sale horses, leaving all list check-offs to Sydney. Kidless, Chuck and Glenda had insisted on being gofers.

A large crowd gathered, and when the auctioneer called out his first bid, a sharp pain weaseled its way up the back of Sydney's neck. *No! Not today.* She grabbed her clipboard and went to make sure the horses were ready.

Two hours later, Martin called her over to the barn. She dipped her cooling pad in a bucket of ice water and wiped her overheated face with the chilly ends before joining him.

"How are you holding up?"

She swallowed the boulder in her throat. "Daddy would hate this."

"Your father would be proud. You're fighting to breathe life back into this place, Syd. Believe me, it's going to happen." He shuffled toward the equipment.

Believe. "Easier said than done," she mumbled as she walked inside the barn.

Chad had three geldings haltered and bathed, their coats shining. Rich hosed off two tied to the hitching post.

"How's it going out there?" Rich asked.

"They're almost ready for a round of horses." Sydney haltered a blue roan tobiano mare with a quarter moon on her shoulder, her mane a mix of white and blue-gray. The filly at her side had a white patch the size of Texas that started at her withers and tipped at her belly.

She led them to a padded-floor stall in the barn where she bathed the mare and fixed white ribbons in the foal's fluffy mane, then sprayed orange-and-coconut-scented homemade coat shine on the mare's damp hair. "Bring in the cash for us, girl." She laid her head against the mare's silky neck and sighed.

Thirty minutes later, the auctioneer's voice carried into the barn. He called for the first horse. Sydney wanted to start and end the auction with a mare and foal. Who could resist the temptation of motherhood?

She led a pair to a small section of panels and untied the filly, hoping the spunky youngster would do the selling. Sure enough, as she led the mare in circles, the foal hopped around, stopping to sniff buyers' outstretched arms. After one young girl thrust her hand through the panel, the filly sprang and trotted toward its mother. Laughter wove through the crowd. A couple of times she had to signal for Caliber to lie down and not chase the foal.

The rest of the sale went without a hitch. Equipment sold for fair prices, as did the sale horses. Her beloved Mustang brought in an exuberant chunk of change. Sad but worth it. She was now down to five saddle horses and one mother-foal pair—Twister and his mother.

Sydney leaned against the counter in the tack room, surveying what little horse equipment she had left. Most of the buyers were gone, and the last of the sold horses were being loaded. She wasn't sure what hurt more, her fingers from signing titles and registration papers or her heart.

Trey entered and announced, "A woman's interested in Twister."

"I told you he's not for sale. I thought you understood that." She wasn't about to sell the only horse that could rebuild her stock.

"At least hear her out."

"How does she know about him?"

"Rich saw her lurking in the barn."

Torn between needing the money and keeping her tie to her father, she gave in. "Let's get this over with." Her gut told her she'd never have a second chance at a Blue Valentine grandson. Not one with Twister's caliber.

They stepped outside, and Trey pointed to a middle-aged woman by the empty auction pen. "That's her."

Sydney got Twister and led him to the gate. His mama let out distressed whinnies, so Trey haltered her and met them at the pen. A pit formed in her belly from the potential sale. Her mouth parched, and she greeted the prospective buyer with a forced smile.

"What are you asking for him?" The woman's confidence towered her height. She didn't even need to bend her knees when leaning over his back. "This is a first ride, ya know." Her tank top revealed tan arms that knew hard work. She tucked a wisp of blonde hair under her turquoise cap with a horse turning a barrel stitched on the front. Her short ponytail resembled Twister's.

Sydney wet her lips. "What are you looking for?"

"My daughter turns cans." The woman ran a hand over Twister's back. "Her horse will be ready to retire when this one comes of age." She stood back, scrutinizing the colt's legs as though a vet with an injured patient. "Blue Valentine, huh? Still on the mare?"

"He is. To both questions. We're late weaning this year. I plan to use him as an upcoming stud."

The woman eyed Sydney. "He's not for sale?"

"I hadn't planned on selling him." She turned to the mare. "His mother on the other hand—"

"You spoke as if he was." The woman scowled at Trey.

"He is." Trey nodded to his wife.

"I . . . uh . . ." Sydney rubbed her temple, wishing her pesky headache would go away.

"What she's trying to say is, we hadn't planned on selling him, but if the price is right, we'd consider it."

Sydney glared at him. But an inkling told her to wait and see how this played out. Maybe if she insisted Twister and his mother had to go together, the buyer would back out. "They come as a pair."

The woman examined Sydney and Trey as though they were out of their minds. She circled the colt, and then the mare, picking up her hooves and making affirming noises, and then did the same with the colt. She pounded a rock against each of his soles. Twister stood quietly, making Sydney squirm. Darn if he wasn't impressing the potential buyer. The woman looked in both horses' mouths and stood back. After a long moment, she made an offer.

Sydney's jaw dropped.

"Done." Trey shook the woman's hand and led the colt to her trailer.

The woman followed him, leading the mare, as though afraid Sydney would back out.

This would be the last time her husband showed her up. Especially the way he promoted "teamwork." Too weary to object, she marched to the lodge office and found the horse papers, signed them both, and brought them out to the new owner.

Once the horses were loaded, Sydney hightailed it into her house and fumbled in her purse for her medication. Trey caught up to her, took the blister out of her hands, and popped out a pill. She opened her mouth, and he dropped it in. She sank onto the rigid sofa and hugged a pillow.

Trey handed her a glass of ice water.

She took a sip and held the glass against her forehead. "I feel stunned." She winced and tried to keep calm, knowing anger would only increase her pain.

He laid an ice pack on the back of her neck.

She squeezed her eyes shut. "Why did you underhand me out there?"

"Good colts come and go. We can replace him down the road."

"I don't want to replace Twister. I want *him*."

He handed her the check. "This will pad your account."

Sydney tossed it on the couch between them. "Nothing will pad the account. It's too far gone."

She tried to stand, swayed, and tumbled forward, catching the edge of the coffee table on her arm. She cried out and rolled to the floor, landing on her side.

"Syd . . . !" Trey crouched beside her. "You need to take it easy." He helped her back to the sofa and sat beside her, cradling her in his arms.

She clung to him, her head and arm burning, and cried.

"What can I get you?"

"Just hold me." She squeezed her eyes shut, her head spinning. She clutched one hand on his T-shirt and the other over her stomach. "I think I'm gonna be sick."

He left and came back with a bowl. She took it and clutched it like a football, ready to retch. He closed the curtains and rubbed her back. When done vomiting, she curled into a fetal position, her head on Trey's lap.

Why had she let him convince her into selling Twister?

CHAPTER 52

Sunday, August 20

Sydney jerked awake at the thick smell of smoke. Through a murky blur, the clock glowed 2:17 a.m. Heart pounding, she thrust the blanket aside and raced downstairs. Her hands trembled as she pulled back the curtains. No. This could not be happening. She darted to her dad's office and swept open the curtains. Her breath caught at the sight of the orange glow over the hay barn.

She yelled for Trey as she dashed outside to an eye-burning haze. Covering her nose with her arm, she sprinted to the lodge and shouted through the great room, "Robert—fire! Get up!" She bolted outside again and bounded down the stairs. Fingers of flames stretched, crackled, and clawed at the starlit sky.

She flipped up the lever to a spigot closest to the wooden hay shed and sprayed, the pitiful stream doing nothing against the blaze before her. Stepping back from the heat, she tapped 911 into her phone then shouted for dispatch to send fire trucks to her physical address. "Hurry!"

Trey scrambled for the hose between the horse pens. "Stay back," he yelled to her.

Using only one crutch, Robert tried to drag another hose over from the spigot between the barn and the lodge. Dumping the crutch, he finished the job. They might as well have been shooting water guns at a wildfire. "We can't save it."

"We have to try!" Sydney shouted.

"It's too far gone!" Trey jabbed a finger toward the inferno.

Robert hollered, "He's right!"

"Don't you guys quit on me!" Hot ash burned Sydney's eyes. She wiped them away and swept the meager spray over the flames.

The mares and foals huddled in the south end of their pen. The geldings stomped around in their corrals, their fearful cries reverberating through shadows and shards of light. Ash floated over them, covering their backs.

Sirens blazing, lights flashing, two firetrucks pulled in. Sydney waved them over to the blaze. Firemen jumped down and took over. Sydney hosed down the horses to cool them off, then, hot and tired, she turned off the spigots. The flames taunted her. Everything felt numb, her mind, body, and heart.

From behind, Trey wrapped his arms around her and held her tightly.

"We could have sold the extra hay." She leaned the back of her head against his chest, glad he hadn't tried to convince her everything would be all right. Because it wasn't.

All hope burned with the barn; she'd call the Realtor in the morning. She could have made it with life insurance.

Come to think of it, she wasn't sure her parents had kept up with the farm and auto policy either. Her heart sank to her ash-covered boots.

She turned to see the guests gawking, their eyes wide. She strode over and assured them all the animals were safe and encouraged them to go back to bed. But they stayed and watched. She rubbed her forehead, feeling a pulse of pain in her temples, and went back to Trey.

Embers rained down on them as a crackle of fire escalated. She stomped back to the spigot and sprayed the horses again as firemen doused the eruption.

Once the fire crew could get to the bales, they broke them apart with their axes. Little by little, they raked and saturated the hay, taking three hours to cool down every last hot spot.

Sydney stayed until the last coal had been submerged. Only then did she stop intermittently showering the horses with water. The smell of smoke hovered over the charred debris. She wiped her eyes, soot stinging them.

"Sorry, Syd. Let me know what I can do to help," Gary, one of the smoke-stained firemen, said. He'd been a longtime friend of the family.

"Thanks. I appreciate it."

One by one, the guests returned to the lodge.

After the firemen left and Trey and Robert went to clean up, Sydney stayed and surveyed the sloppy remains. Honey-colored light crept over the knoll behind the ranch and spread overhead. Smoke clung to the canopy of pine and aspen trees, giving her an eerie feeling.

She toed the mud, looking for signs of what could have started the fire. Coming up empty, she figured the hay must have been put up too wet and combusted. Good grief. What more could go wrong?

After showering and slipping into clean clothes, Sydney strode to the lodge. A few milling guests approached her with condolences. They visited for a few minutes, then Sydney headed for the dining hall. Robert sat at a table with a cup of coffee.

Trey pulled out a chair. "I'll get you a cup, then I'm headed outside to start cleaning up the debris."

She settled at the table and with her steaming brew asked, "How're the horses this morning?"

"They've settled down." Robert laid a scorched pocket knife on the table. "Found this in the ashes. You see it before?"

She picked it up. "It was Dad's. He'd been looking for it for a few months. You can have it. He got it from Grandpa Moomaw for his thirteenth birthday."

Robert's eyes lit up as she handed it to him. "Thanks."

She'd make sure he got more of their father's belongings. Wound up, she took a sip of coffee and moseyed out to check on Twister. Her shoulders slumped at his empty stall. She sighed and turned to where the hay barn had stood the day before.

The smell of burned hay and barnwood filled her eyes with moisture. She sniffed, wiped her eyes, and found a shovel.

Tuesday, August 22

The next morning, Trey and Sydney headed to Tonasket for hay, stopping at the Omak Naturopathic Clinic on the way. Thank goodness she had snagged enough bales of orchard grass from a local farmer for the morning feeding.

"Sorry you missed your meeting with the stampede board." Sydney snuggled close to him.

"No worries," Trey said. "I got ahold of one of them, and they understand. I'll catch up with them when things settle down."

"Good deal."

His wife looked worn-out. But her natural beauty shone, her face free of makeup.

"I don't know where we're going to store hay for the winter. There's no way I can afford to build a new barn."

"Did you find an insurance policy?"

"Glenda's looking into that for me. But when I was searching for the will, I never came across one."

"We can build a roof over the hay for now. Tarp the edges."

"With what money?"

"Our money." He kept his focus on the windy pass.

She gnawed on her bottom lip. "Thanks for coming back from Arizona. I assumed you'd abandoned me. Having you by my side has made a big difference."

"Leave you? Never. I'd be bored." Trey smiled, trying to lighten the mood. He was proud of her for opening up to him—a big step. "That was hard for you to admit, wasn't it?"

"Admit what?"

"That getting help from your husband is a good thing."

She blushed and turned her face to the window. "What hurts the most is to have watched what had been in our family for three generations burn to the ground."

"I know, honey. It's not easy." He wished he had the money to build her a new, fancy barn.

"I'm not sure I can take much more."

"You don't have to go through this alone. I'm here for you. As are Glenda and Robert and Pam."

"I know. And I'm grateful. It's . . . hard."

Until Cooper was out of the picture, he figured it would be tough for her to trust him enough to lean on him. Now that their line of communication was unclogging, he should see improvements in their relationship. Though it wouldn't be easy, she was worth the wait.

When her cell lit up and buzzed, she answered. "Hello, thanks for calling back. I'm inquiring about hay for sale."

How could he make her feel comfortable enough to share ranch finances with him? Finding out what they could pay off first would be nice.

Sydney ended the call. "No luck there."

"I have a few leads. I'll call tonight. The good news is, we don't need nearly as much hay. We're down to the bare bones. We can take the winter to regroup. Between guests, the gift shop, and my photography, I think we'll stay afloat."

"Yeah, but I'd rather have too much than not enough. That was only the first on my list of ten." She punched in another number and left a message.

There had to be a way to get rid of Cooper, so she could relax and settle into their marriage.

Inside the naturopathic clinic, Sydney shared her medical history with a thin, middle-aged Native man who had introduced himself as Dr. Gordon. She told him about the migraines, including when they started. He took her into an examination room and adjusted her spine and neck. While he worked on her, she got her nerve up enough to make a few inquiries. "You treated my mom."

"Oh?"

"Jennie Moomaw."

He made another adjustment on her neck, then helped her sit up and took a seat beside her on the padded exam table. "Yes. I saw your folks' obituary in the paper. My condolences."

"Thanks. I'm wondering if you can tell me about her cancer. Was she ... how was ..." She didn't know how to ask what condition she'd been in during her last appointment.

"Because of HIPAA, all I can say is that the methods I use to treat my patients are known to heal people."

Thinking of her mom tugged at her heart. Had she beat cancer to die in a car wreck?

"Why don't you come back in a week or two, and we can do allergy testing. I think you'll see a big improvement. Diane will give you more information about the Nambudripad's Allergy Elimination Techniques I use. Sound good?"

The what techniques? Oh, my. What was she getting herself into? "Um—yeah, I'll check it out." If her mom trusted him, why couldn't she? After all, her journal entries had indicated the tumor had significantly decreased.

CHAPTER 53

Friday, August 25

Not yet having enough hay for winter, Sydney found it hard to celebrate the gift shop's opening day.

Her belly tangled as she fixed a purple-and-green beaded necklace around Kimberly's neck. June, Glenda's five-year-old daughter, stood on a pink folding step stool, smelling soaps and lotions, Glenda rubbing testers on both of their hands.

"I like this one." Glenda stretched her arm out to Sydney. "It's sweetgrass."

"Mmm. That is nice. I've been so busy setting up, I haven't taken the time to check anything out." Sydney squirted rosemary lotion on the back of her other hand.

June tugged on the leg of her jeans. "Lemme smell, Auntie."

Sydney knelt, allowing her niece to sniff her skin. "What do you think, Junie Bug?" The girl nodded, a bright smile on her face. She rubbed a dab of lotion on the girl's arm.

"Don't you look pretty," Trey said to Kimberly. "Where's Chuck and Franky?"

Glenda snorted. "In the kitchen. Where else?"

"Uncle Trey, smell me." June ran to him. He lifted her up and sniffed the arm she held to his nose.

"You smell as sweet as sunshine on a spring day. Good enough to eat." Trey tickled her, making her squirm and giggle. He set her down before she toppled headfirst to the floor. "How's it going in here?" He strolled over to Sydney and whispered, "That necklace looks stunning on you."

She fingered the beads, heat rising not only from the compliment but also from his electrifying touch. "It's a nice day. Maybe too nice. I'm not sure I'll have many customers today."

"Of course you will. There are a lot of folks out there who want to support you." He kissed the side of her head, squeezing his warm body close to hers.

Goosebumps danced across her arms, and she rubbed them. And he'd been right. Fifteen minutes later, ranch guests and customers filed into the shop. Trey gave her a reassuring nod that about made her heart stop. She relaxed and passed out jerky samples, thanking the patrons for coming.

By two that afternoon, family, friends, and those passing by continued to browse and purchase, leaving her stock depleted. While Trey, Chuck, and Glenda assisted customers, Sydney went to the dining area, called a friend at the tribal government building, and asked her to broadcast the need for more merchandise. Bare shelves would leave the place with an empty feeling. She'd learned from crafty friends that sparse tables produced little interest.

She was confirming the ad information when a leggy teen approached her. "You Sydney Moomaw?" Sydney lifted a finger for the girl to wait a moment. The black-haired, heart-shape faced teen, who stood about the same height as Sydney and visibly a nervous wreck, held out a folded piece of paper, her hands trembling. Sydney nodded and took the document. After a short moment, the girl blurted out, "I think I'm your daughter."

Sydney stiffened, still on her call. "What?" She unfolded the document. "No, not you, Steph."

The girl's gaze dropped to the floor. "I think you're my mom."

"Steph, yeah, send the message like I said. Gotta go." *I think you're my mom?* "This has to be a mistake. Who are you?"

Glenda approached Sydney. "What's going on?"

Turning to the girl, Sydney asked, "Where did you get this?"

The girl lifted her eyes to Sydney. "I petitioned the court to open my files."

Glenda's brows shot up. "What files?"

"Not now, Glenda." After all these years, could it be her? Oh, how she'd prayed for this day. This moment. "When were you born?" Sydney studied the girl's petite frame, similar to her own.

"May fifteenth."

"Where?" Her hands shaking, she scanned the birth certificate—three times because her mind fought to wrap itself around the words. Until her eyes landed on the year. And the location.

"Spokane Valley Hospital."

The document listed her as the birth mother. Moisture collected around her eyes, blurring her vision. "Leena *Morgan?*"

"Morgan's my foster parents' last name."

She'd been fostered all this time? How many homes had she been in? She'd hoped a nice couple would have adopted her. Her pulse pounded in her ears.

"I'm so sorry . . ." Leena broke out into a cluster of sobs.

Trey stood with his hands in his pockets, his shoulders drooping.

What on earth could Leena possibly be sorry for? She placed a hand on the girl's trembling shoulder. "For what?"

Leena shook her head and squeezed her eyes closed, her chin trembling.

"Hey, you can tell me."

"I killed your parents." Leena burst into tears.

Sydney sucked in a sharp breath. Her head spun, her body unable to move. There must be a mistake. They'd arrested a boy.

Glenda blinked several times. "*What?*"

"How's it going in here?" Chuck pushed his way through those who'd gathered around Sydney and the girl, twelve-year-old Franky at his side.

Leena covered her face with her hands as Chuck pulled her into a hug. Sydney's chest constricted. Was it true? The baby she'd given up now stood before her, claiming she'd killed her parents?

She pressed a hand to her throat. "I, uh, I . . . can't . . ." She dashed to the bathroom and locked the door. This couldn't be happening. She fell to her knees, her hands on either side of the toilet, and gagged. Her vision blurred, and she vomited. A knock sounded on the door.

"Syd, honey . . ." Trey's husky voice floated through the wood. The brass knob jiggled. "Can I come in?"

She couldn't face him. Not anyone for that matter. What would they think of her tossing her daughter out like dirty water? This was the worst day ever. Half the town had shown up. Watching. Whispering. She'd be the talk of the reservation.

"Syd, honey, it's Pam. Talk to me."

Voices mumbled on the other side of the door. "Sweetheart," Trey said, "we're clearing the lodge. Come out when you're ready."

Thank God Pam had finally arrived. A commotion came from the heart of the lodge, but she had no desire to check it out. She wasn't ready to face anyone. Minutes later, everything went quiet. After splashing cold water on her face, she opened the door. Pam and Trey were huddled around Leena.

She steadied herself by leaning against the wall, not able to wrap her head around what she'd been told. When steady on her feet, she opened the door as Leena collapsed to the floor.

"I didn't mean to kill them . . ." Leena paled.

Trey lifted her into his arms and carried her toward the main house.

"We're gonna get through this," Trey whispered as he strode past his wife, his face twisted.

Pam and Glenda ushered the last of the customers out, promising the doors would be open the next morning. A couple staying at the ranch made their way up the staircase. Pam promised to help clean up while Chuck led his family to their truck.

Sydney sighed, thankful her sister didn't hang around to get the scoop.

CHAPTER 54

In the main house, Sydney found Leena on the couch with a cool washcloth pressed against her face. Trey sat in an overstuffed chair to her right. Sydney took a seat beside the girl, feeling light-headed.

"I didn't mean to ruin your open house," Leena said.

"There has to be a mistake." The flesh between Sydney's eyes pinched. "Why do you think you're responsible for my parents' death? And when did you find out I'm your biological mother?"

"Because I was the one driving. I . . . uh . . . found out soon after . . ." Leena chewed on her bottom lip.

Sydney took her hand. "I don't blame you," she whispered, emotions clogging her throat. "From what I understand, it was an accident."

"It was . . . He took the wheel . . ." A fresh round of sobs kept Leena from continuing.

Trey handed Sydney a box of tissue. She tugged one out and passed the box to Leena. After dabbing her own eyes, Sydney asked, "Why don't you tell me a little about yourself?"

After a long moment, Leena sniffed and wiped her nose. "Well . . . I've lived with the Morgans all my life."

"Do they know you're here?"

"I left them a note."

Trey's eyes widened, but he kept silent.

"Oh?"

"They won't care." Leena's glance fell to the floor.

"Why don't you think so?"

"They're . . . they're not interested." She hugged herself.

"In you?"

"In anything I do. They've never adopted me, although they gave me their last name. Which is weird. They won't let me join sports. Rarely let me hang out with my friends. They fight a lot over money and make me do most of the chores."

"They probably got to name you because . . . because I didn't." Which would be the reason she'd been able to remain under everyone's radar. The look of disappointment on Leena's face stabbed at her heart. "What are you interested in?"

"Basketball."

Huh. Like me. "Anything else?"

"I'd like to learn to play the guitar." Her eyes brightened.

They talked about music for a while. When Leena appeared to be more comfortable, Sydney asked, "You mentioned opening your files. Can you tell me more about that?"

Leena peered at her palms. "After the accident, the cops took me to the police station, and the Morgans picked me up. That night, I overheard them talking on the phone to Angela, my social worker. They told her to place me with another family. Claimed I'm negligent and don't listen. But that's a lie." She looked Sydney in the eyes. "I do everything they ask in that suffocating place. I don't think they want to put the time into helping me out. By their reaction, I know Angela suggested I get counseling. But they didn't seem thrilled about it. Knowing them, it'd be too much effort."

She cried more, blotting her nose with a tissue. When composed, she went on. "They told her I've become 'too hard to handle.' Talked about me being old enough to strike out on my own and about me killing my own grandparents. That got my attention."

All the years Sydney had prayed and believed her daughter would be adopted and raised in a loving home.

Better than she could offer. Those faith-filled assumptions were now shattered. What had she done? She should have kept the baby. Went home and gotten help from her family. Oh, how wrong she'd been.

Leena took a deep breath and peeked between Sydney and Trey, then scowled at the ground. "They kept Angela's business card in the front page of the phone book, so I called her and asked what my rights were. She told me at my age, I could petition the court to open my files. Said with a job and a place to live, I could even strike out on my own. But I was too scared to live alone. So she went to court with me." She stole a shy glance at Sydney. "When I got the files, you were listed on the birth certificate as my mom."

Sydney's eyes burned. "I was young and in a horrible marriage. I didn't want you raised in an abusive environment. I thought I was protecting you by giving you away."

Trey's red-rimmed eyes watched her, his face flush with compassion and respect and love. At least that's how she translated it. But when he rose and eased to the coffee table between mother and daughter, took Sydney's left hand and Leena's right, and said, "We'll do whatever it takes to help you," she understood his commitment to their vows.

At that moment, every barrier for her husband exploded and profound love for him spilled over her. But she needed to focus on Leena. "Can you tell me about the accident?"

"I was with a friend. We went swimming at Spring Canyon. A guy from school was drunk and asked for a ride home. I wanted him to be safe, so I said yes. When I pulled out of the park, he joked around and grabbed the wheel of the Morgans' car. I overcorrected and slammed into—"

A loud knock on the door turned heads.

"Sydney? Can we come in?" Pam asked.

We? Who could be with her? She wanted to tell them to come back tomorrow. She had more questions. Needed more information. Then again, knowing Pam, she wouldn't have asked if it wasn't important. Trey nodded his approval. "Yeah." The door opened.

Leena's expression turned cold as a middle-aged couple entered the house behind Pam.

CHAPTER 55

It took guts for Leena to reach out to Sydney and reveal her lousy upbringing. But Trey was furious at his wife for not trusting him enough to reveal she had a daughter. They'd have to discuss the matter later—in private.

He stood as the couple entered the house. "I'm Trey Hardy and this is my wife, Sydney." He motioned for them to sit in two chairs bookending the fireplace.

Pam patted Sydney's shoulder before excusing herself.

Leena introduced her foster parents as Beth and Tim Morgan. Dressed casually, Beth was a tall brunette with cropped hair. She nervously wrung her hands, her face pinched. Tim, with a receding hairline, watched his daughter through thick glasses.

Beth held up a crinkled paper. "We found your note." Her light blue eyes shifted from Leena to Sydney. "I'm sorry to have caused any problems. We never . . ." She pressed a hand to her mouth and glanced away, her eyes moist.

"We didn't know she'd overheard us talking," Tim said in an ominous tone, his face turning red. He turned to Leena. "You have a lot of explaining to do." His hands in his lap, he curled his fingers into fists.

Leena nodded, staring at the carpet.

Tim Morgan obviously ruled his home with a strong upper hand. Had he abused Beth and Leena more than emotionally and psychologically? Although Trey could see no physical signs, that didn't mean there weren't any. Sydney had mentioned how Cooper used to leave marks in places her clothes would conceal.

"She hasn't caused any problems." Sydney briefly shared why she'd given Leena up. *Smart thinking on her part.* Hopefully, it would open dialog and trust.

"I'd like to be a part of her life," Sydney added, "if that's all right with you. And on your terms, of course."

On their terms? No way. He had an urge to protest but kept his mouth shut, not wanting to cause added tension.

Beth and Tim exchanged glances. Trey hoped they would agree. However, watching their defensive body language—particularly Tim's—caused doubt to flood his mind.

"I don't know." Beth shook her head. "It's hard."

"Let's take things slowly," Trey said. "How about we exchange contact information and give it a few weeks?"

The Morgans agreed, and they swapped numbers.

Tim stood and held out his hand to Leena, who ignored it. Instead, she leaned close to Sydney. "I'll contact you even if they don't," she whispered before rushing out the door. Her parents trailed behind.

Sydney sniffed and blew her nose.

"Give them time," Trey said. "If Leena is anything like you, she might be able to convince them that having a relationship with her birth mother is best. Especially, since she claims they want to get rid of her."

"I don't trust them. I think she'd be better off with me."

"But you gave up your parental rights."

Her body language suggested she wanted to run after her daughter. One thing he'd learned from watching the local Natives was their family bonds were stronger than a three-strand cord.

"I can't believe you said that."

"But it's true," he responded. "You can't go marching over there and demand they give her back."

"I don't intend on demanding anything. But you heard Leena. They don't support her. In fact, I think she's afraid of Tim. Did you see the look on his face? And Beth . . . She looked afraid of him. Do you think they're safe?"

"I think you're overreacting."

"You heard Leena. It's all about the money. They use her for child labor. There's no love. No affection whatsoever. They acted mad, not concerned. If my child ran away, I'd be scared out of my mind."

"I would be too. But let's be reasonable and not let our thoughts run wild."

Sydney paced the living room. "She needs to know her family. Learn her culture. Does she even know she's Indian? That's another thing—is she enrolled? That might help us get her faster."

"Whoa, slow down. Yeah, they don't seem to support her, and yeah, Tim seems a little intense, but the question is, does *she want* to be with you? Or did she come to ease her conscience?"

"Ease her conscience? Is that what you think?"

"I didn't mean it like that."

"Then what did you mean?"

Trey sank onto an overstuffed chair. "I think it would be wise to dig into this a little more and not take Leena at her word."

"You think she's lying?"

"That's not what I'm saying, Syd. We need time to process this. I don't know, maybe we can talk to Chuck. Corroborate her story with the social worker."

"We don't need to corroborate anything. It's plain to me we need to get her out of that home as soon as we can. She's a Moomaw. My daughter—"

"But that's it. She's not yours. She's a Morgan. That's how she was raised. They've had her since birth." He cringed when her chin quivered.

Sydney closed her eyes and rubbed her temples. "At least we both agree they take in fosters for the money and not the love of children." She plopped down on the couch. "They can't love her like I can."

"Your right. They can't." Trey moved to her side and held her.

Maybe he was wrong. Maybe they needed each other to help heal the loss of Lester and Jennie. *God, tell us what to do.*

CHAPTER 56

Sydney did her best thinking from the back of a horse. And boy, did she need to get away to reflect. Decide what she wanted in life. She checked the weather on her cell. Darn if a storm didn't flick in the forecast, but according to the radar, she had enough time before the downpour attacked.

"I'm going for a short ride. I need to figure this out." She broke away from Trey and started for her room to select a suitable jacket.

"Please don't be gone too long."

When she came back, Trey walked her to the barn and helped saddle Cyan. Outside the barn's west entrance, a truck raced up and skidded to a stop. With a sloppy grin on his face, Cooper jumped out holding a manila envelope and strutted toward them.

Trey glared at him as he approached the barn. "What on earth?"

"Sheesh, he needs to understand we're divorced."

"You stay here." Trey met him halfway.

Whatever. Sydney wasn't about to stay behind. She followed him, curling her fingers into a fist.

"What are you doing here?" Trey set his hands on his hips and lengthened his spine.

"I've come to see my wife. You stay out of it, punk."

"She's not your wife. You need to get that straight."

Cooper motioned to Sydney. "I'm in no hurry for her to sign the divorce papers, if you know what I mean."

"Scum like you don't deserve her. She's mine now." He held up his wedding-ring-covered finger like a kid wet behind the ears.

Mine? Had she been reduced to a piece of property? "You need to leave, Cooper."

"You deaf, man?" Trey said. "She doesn't want you around. And neither do I."

Before Sydney could step between them, Trey moved her out of the way. She scooted closer to her mare, wishing Cooper would go. Instead, he flung the papers aside and lunged at Trey, taking him by the waist and slamming him to the ground. Cyan shied to the side and pulled back on the lead rope.

Sydney reached for her. "Whoa, girl!" She moved her into a stall. Her pulse hammering her ears, she stepped from the stall to find Trey rolling Cooper off him. He then pushed to his feet, grabbed Cooper by the collar, and pinned his neck to the stall with his forearm.

"I told you to leave her alone," Trey said.

Cooper kneed Trey and tossed him onto the barn floor. Red-faced, Trey jumped to his feet and started pounding on Cooper. After getting in a few licks himself, Cooper stumbled backward, tumbling to the ground. Trey hunched over him, hitting his face, red staining Cooper's skin.

Sydney pulled on Trey, but he wouldn't budge. "Help!" She tugged as hard as she could.

An instant later, strong hands pulled her aside. "What's going on?" Chad asked, his chest heaving.

Robert yanked Trey off Cooper, his face covered in blood and cuts, his eyes starting to swell. Trey had a cut over his eye and a bloody nose.

Cooper sat up and spit red saliva in the dirt, then wiped his mouth. "Just trying to keep what's mine."

"Yours?" Chad's eyes swept to Sydney.

"She's not yours." Trey lunged for Cooper, but Robert blocked him. Chad hauled Cooper to his feet.

"I'm not anybody's!" Why couldn't they get that through their thick skulls?

"Syd," Chad said, "Call Chuck."

Feeling nauseated, she patted her back pocket. Shoot, she'd left her cell in the main house.

"Go ahead," Cooper said, "I can get to you no matter where I land."

Yep. He'd used someone else to get to her. And he could do it again. Fear swirled inside, lodging in her throat.

"Shut your mouth, Tough Guy." Trey wiped his nose with his shirtsleeve, smearing blood on his cheek and staining the fabric.

"Give me a hundred grand, sign the papers, and I'll go away."

"You can get out now, or I'll call the cops." Robert held up his cell and moved beside Sydney.

She clung to his arm, still unable to speak, and Chad inserted himself between Trey and Cooper.

Cooper sneered. "Reservation cops won't do anything. I'm white."

"Get your rotten hide out of here and don't come back," Trey said, "The divorce is legal. Get over yourself."

Cooper sprang at Trey, knocking Chad to the ground, and whacked him in the side of the head. Trey recoiled, then jabbed Cooper in the ribs three times, slamming him against a stall. Cooper pounded Trey in the gut. Sydney found her voice and screamed. Robert dropped his cell, and again he and Chad broke them apart.

"I'm not through with you, honey." Cooper stumbled to his truck, the bogus divorce papers crumpled in his fist.

Robert went after him, but halted when Cooper leveled a shotgun at his head.

"Stay there, or I'll shoot." He got into his truck and sped off.

"Got his plate numbers. I'm calling Chuck." Robert tapped his phone.

Chad turned to Syd. "Who the heck was that?"

Feeling like her knees would buckle, she said, "My ex-husband."

"When were you married?"

"Never mind." About to come undone, Sydney turned to Trey. "He can never learn about Leena. He'll use her against me." She gritted her teeth. "If he ever lays a hand on her, I'll kill him."

"Who the heck is Leena?" Chad shifted his weight.

Robert held up his phone. "Chuck put out an APB on him."

"Why don't you guys finish your chores." Sydney didn't have the energy to explain Leena. Not that she was anyone's business. "Trey and I need to talk."

Nodding, Robert tapped Chad's arm, and they left.

Red-faced and breathing hard, Trey drew her into his embrace and whispered, "I won't let him hurt either you or Leena."

Sydney felt his heart pounding. Hers kept pace. "I need to get out of here. Go for a ride. Clear my head."

He released her. "I'm coming with you. There's no way you're going alone."

When he turned toward the tack room, she grabbed his sweaty arm. "Please, no. I need time to think."

Drops of rain pinged the barn roof. "Bad idea."

"I'll stay close and won't be gone long." She led Cyan out of the barn and mounted. Trey and the hands had gathered into a tight circle, probably talking about her, Leena, and Cooper. Fine. That way, she wouldn't have to.

She kicked the mare into a lope and didn't stop until she'd reached Nespelem Creek. Dismounting, she dropped the reins and glanced around. God help her if Cooper had followed behind. Bursts of orange and yellow lined the mountains and streams. Squirrels scampered up and down pine trees, nuts in their mouths, and dark clouds loomed overhead.

Feeling uneasy, she perched under the cover of a grove of aspen trees, their green leaves once attached now floated down the creek. Sparse raindrops rippled rings on the surface. She closed her eyes, trying to shut the barn fight out of her mind. Darn if Cooper's bloody face didn't show back up. And it made her want to puke.

What would it take for him to disappear? Would Chuck find him? Toss him back in jail? She could only hope so.

But what if he finds out about Leena? Would he actually use their daughter as a pawn against her?

What am I supposed to do? Besides fuel Cooper's rage.

She opened her eyes to curious calves sneaking up on her. A mist of rain pricked her face. Too upset to go back, she hopped into the saddle and continued north.

CHAPTER 57

The farther Sydney rode, the harder the rain pelted her face. But she couldn't go back. Not without a plan. Ten more minutes and she'd be at an old cabin that would at least get her out of the storm.

She kicked her mare into a nice long trot and pulled the zipper of her jacket up to her chin. Her red fingers stung as she wiped soggy hair from her face.

Her cold bones made the ride seem to drag on. Her teeth chattered as she tried to figure out what would make Cooper vanish. For good. Couldn't be money. He'd only demand more. Bile burned her throat as her mind spun.

By the time she made it to the cabin, the rain and wind had intensified. As quickly as her frigid fingers would work, she unsaddled her horse and hauled the tack into the rickety structure. Finding a flashlight in a saddlebag, she turned it on. Rain dripped down the walls and through cracks between weathered wooden planks. If she could only stop shivering. She paced the room and rubbed her arms, her mind growing lethargic. Matches. She riffled through her tooled leather saddlebag and pulled out a plastic baggy with a tin of waterproof matches and tinder tucked inside. Now for dry wood.

Rat droppings, beer cans, and nesting materials filled the damp, musty space. She toed around and found an old tin plate. Outside, she found a stick and flicked varmint bedding onto the plate. She shuddered, scooped up added tinder, and lit a match. Smoke and small flames spiraled and flickered. She fed the fire until enough warmth and light scared potential rattlers from sharing the room.

When her tummy growled, she dug a protein bar from her saddlebag, took a large bite, and stuffed the remainder in her coat pocket for later. No telling how long the storm would last.

Flashlight in hand, she scanned the place for anything burnable. Twigs and pinecones were what she needed. Rain pounded the roof. One drop landed on Sydney's head, making her flinch. She went outside again, scavenged for what fuel she could find, and laid it on the floor. A small puddle formed under the debris. The twig she laid on the now-dying flames remained too wet and doused the fire. After tossing a small heap of rat bedding in the tin, she lit another match, gently blew on the growing fire, and again killed the flames with wet pine needles.

With her soggy boots, she cleared a place to sit and leaned against the inside of her saddle. The saddle blanket wasn't enough to keep her warm. Tired and cold, she closed her eyes for a moment. *Oh, Lord, what now?*

A faint whinny caught her attention.

She reached for her pistol, then gave a stiff grunt. Shoot. She'd left it in her purse. The porch steps groaned against heavy clicks. Cooper? Her heart pounded as her breaths came in short spurts. She searched for something, anything, to defend herself with. The door creaked open.

No, no, no! She pulled out a deer-skinning knife from the saddlebag, her hands shaking.

A tall figure came through the door. "Sydney?"

A light shined in her face, causing her to squint. "Trey?"

He dropped his saddle and pad on the floor and slammed the door shut. "You crazy—stubborn—determined—irrational woman! You said you were going on a short ride."

She wanted to hurt him or hold him. Anything to calm the terror clawing at her insides. "Stubborn? Irrational? With everything I've been through, the length of my ride is all you're concerned about? You arrogant—cocky—egotistical—"

He reached her in two strides, tossed the knife aside, and pulled her into his grasp. "You scared me half to death." His voice soft, it felt more like a breath whispered deep in her soul.

Her chest burned. "I didn't mean to." She captured his mouth, a low groan escaping her throat, and he deepened the kiss, his firm hand cradling her head.

She wrapped her arms around his soaked waist, the kiss tasting of regret. Of desperation and remorse. Needing his strength and comfort, she pulled his taut body snug against hers. Then gathered her wits and pushed him away, breathing hard. "Sorry. I can't."

"Can't what? Love? Trust? For how long, Syd? Until you grow old and alone? What will it take for you to let me in?" He shed his hat and raked his fingers through his hair. "I'm tired of being on the road all the time. I want roots, and I want to plant them with you."

Oh, Lord, how she wanted a life with him too. But could she ever heal the scars Cooper had carved in the depth of her being? With a shaky hand, she went to trace the cut over Trey's eye with her finger, but he took her hand in his.

"When I'm with you . . . It's—it's my best day rolled out for the rest of my life. I see your smile, smell your sweet scent . . . Feel your touch. Not sure I can live without you, honey."

The loving look in his eyes started to chip away the hard shell around her heart. "I want roots, too, and I want to make them with you." She pulled away and folded her arms over her chest. "But I'm not sure I can focus on us and the ranch while living in constant fear. Cooper . . . he's dangerous and vindictive. And now with Leena in the mix—"

"Chuck will find him." He strode to her and again drew her close. "And I can take care of you. And Leena. Let me prove it."

"You can't—"

He pressed his finger against her lips. "When we're apart, I feel like I can't breathe. It's as though I'm drowning, and no one's around to rescue me. I love you, Syd. Like I've never loved before. And I'm scared too. Scared of losing you. I want this marriage to work. Don't you?"

Of course she did. Once Cooper gets out of the picture.

When she didn't answer, he continued. "When we stood at the Hitching Post, I knew I wanted to grow old with you. Riding and running the ranch together. Your fight to try to save the ranch made me believe if I could somehow chip through the cracks, you could learn to love me. You see, you don't have a small piece of my heart—you have it all."

Sydney melted into his embrace. Let his tender lips find her. Let him deepen the kiss. And when she got too heated, she broke away. "I'm scared to give my heart to anyone."

"I know. We can take things slow. Figure it out as we go."

She pressed her head against his chest, shivered. He rubbed her arms. "We need to get you warm."

He released her and went to the tin. "You tried to build a fire?"

"Yeah. But I couldn't find any dry fuel." She stepped from side to side, swinging her arms, trying to get her blood flowing.

"And I doubt we'll find any in this storm. Come on, we can use our body heat to keep warm." He led her to the saddles, spread the pads out as cushions, and used their coats as blankets, then settled her back against his chest and wrapped his arms around her. "So tell me what you're most afraid of."

"Besides being in this rat-infested cabin?" Sydney sighed. The craving to be open and honest pulled at her. But talking about feelings was like letting a rabid dog use her leg as a bone.

In reality, she missed long walks and talks with her mother. She hadn't had anyone to share her plans and deepest desires with for a long time.

Something scuttled across the floor, and she screamed. Trey grabbed the flashlight and pointed the beam in a corner. A mouse cowered behind a crumpled beer can. Trey tossed a pinecone at the rodent, and it fled through a crack in the wall. "It's gone." He went back to his saddle and set the light on the floor, beam up.

"I hate mice!" Sydney shuddered and rubbed her stiff fingers. "OK, what concerns me the most?" She crossed her legs. "Cooper finding Leena."

CHAPTER 58

What a stupid question. Trey should have known keeping Leena safe would be his wife's biggest fear. With or without the cops, he would make sure Cooper would disappear for good.

Sydney looked peaceful as she slept under her coat, her head on the saddle. How could he convince her he could handle her ex? His type was common—a cowardly bully who preyed on innocent women.

How could one man cause so much damage?

Trey's time at the Seven Tine made him realize how much he longed for a family of his own. He wasn't about to let anything happen to Sydney and Leena. She needed to get back to the ranch. Get warm. He eased to his feet, not wanting to disturb her, and checked the weather outside. Darn. The storm had gathered speed.

He went back to his saddle, pulling his jacket over his shoulders, and rested next to his wife. Curled up on her side with her back to him, she stirred.

"Looks like we'll be here all night. No sense in going out in a downpour. At least in here, we're dry," he said. When she sniffled, he asked, "You cold?"

"A little. But I'll be all right."

"Everything will be fine." He pulled her back against him, arranged the coats so they covered the length of their bodies, and held her close. Her hands were ice cold.

"What if he goes after Leena?"

"We'll get her into protective custody."

"What if he beats us to her? What if he's already got her?"

"You can't keep letting your mind wander like that. It'll drive you crazy. Let's trust God to keep her safe."

"I can't get him out of my mind."

"Sshhh." He stroked her arm. "I'll keep him away." And he planned to. Whatever it took.

"How?"

"I have a few ideas."

"What are they?"

"Syd, stop. Get some sleep so we can be fresh in the morning."

"I need to know."

What he felt like doing to her ex would land him in prison. "Get the notes and photo to Chuck. Make sure everyone has a gun in case Cooper shows back up. Even Mandie. Nona can stay with extended family until he's apprehended."

"Sounds like a good plan." She snuggled closer to him, her body tense. He rubbed her arm and leg until her muscles relaxed, disregarding his desires for her. It would be a long night.

Minutes later, her breathing became shallow. Later, she jerked and mumbled in her sleep. He couldn't make out the words but knew her restlessness came from a deep place of terror. He rubbed her back until she stilled, praying God would ease her mind.

He remained wide awake. Thinking. Planning. Preparing.

CHAPTER 59

Saturday, August 26

They had ridden halfway home when Sydney pointed. "Look."

Martin rode through a curtain of mist. Steam blew like a cloud of smoke from his horse's nostrils at rapid intervals. Rain dripped from his oilskin cowboy hat, his eyebrows drawn together. He waved them forward. "Hurry. It's your daughter."

"What's wrong?" Sydney shivered so hard her teeth clinked. She wiped water from her eyes. "What happened?"

Martin hesitated. "She tried to kill herself. She's in the hospital."

"Tried to kill herself?" Was she that distraught? *Oh, Lord.* . . If only the Morgans had gotten her help after the accident.

"Yeah. I have a friend who works there. She called after overhearing Leena shouting for her parents to call you. But they refused. She figured you would want to know."

Sydney's chest clenched as she kicked Cyan into a lope.

As she rode, her mind dragged her back to the day she had attempted to take her life.

Back to the third time Cooper had put her in the hospital. Deep red liquid had filled the pan beside her sterile bed. Her nose and eyes were purple and swollen. Stitches closed skin in her bottom lip and head. The doctor warned her about men like him. He gave her a number to call for help. She'd tucked it in her pocket and forgotten about it.

She'd hidden the lunch knife under her pillow, planning to slit her wrists that night. Since she wasn't hooked up to anything to alert nurses, they'd leave her alone long enough to get the job done. She'd read how to do it so she would die in a couple of minutes.

That night she lay in bed, scared to death. Afraid he'd find her. Come after her again. A night nurse took her vitals about midnight. When she left, Sydney slid the knife from under the pillow and rubbed it against her wrist, fingers quaking. It would only hurt for a short while. Seconds at best.

A slight crack at the door revealed faint light in the hallway. When the knife pressed against her wrist, ready to slice, she felt a flutter. A light sensation like butterfly wings brushing against the inside of her womb.

Her focus shifted to the knife. Then her midsection. She hadn't had a cycle for three months, convinced stress was the culprit. The impression surfaced again. She pressed a hand to her belly. A voice in her head told her to drop the weapon. Another life needed her to live.

The knife slipped from her hand and clinked to the floor as tears cascaded down her face. How would she take care of a baby? And if Cooper ever found out? What would he do? Fight for custody to only beat the baby when it cried? She couldn't take the chance.

Yet for her, abortion was not an option. That night in the dark room, she vowed to give the baby a fighting chance the only way that made sense. By giving the child up for adoption.

And now her girl tried to take her own life.

"What do you think, honey?"

The sound of Trey's voice pulled her back into the conversation. "About what?" She wiped her eyes with the back of her hand.

"Martin will take care of the horses so we can get to the hospital."

"Yeah, sounds good." The corrals appeared through a frosted haze. She halted her horse beside a hitching post and handed the reins to Martin. "Please call Pam and have her start a prayer chain." She rushed to Trey's truck.

Inside the pickup, Trey started the engine and turned up the heat.

On the way to Coulee Community Hospital in Grand Coulee, she prayed she could have a relationship with her daughter. She asked God to forgive her for abandoning her as a newborn. Feeling as though she was losing Leena all over again, she scooted next to Trey and leaned her head on his shoulder, her fingers clinging to his soaked shirtsleeve. *Help her, God. Please.*

Sydney marched to the emergency room nurse's station and asked to see Leena Morgan.

"Are you family?" The overwhelmed nurse wearing her blonde hair in a ponytail snapped at her.

"I'm her . . . her biological mother." *For crying out loud.*

The nurse studied her. "Hang on a moment, I'll find her parents." The packed waiting room hummed with distraught murmurs. A few cried while others paced. Sydney wanted to do both but steeled herself.

"How do you think Leena's doing?"

Trey shrugged. "I think she needs to get counseling."

"Yeah, me too." Sydney could have used sound advice during her college days.

Fifteen minutes later, the nurse came back and said to her. "We can't find Leena or her parents. It appears they've left."

"They left? Why? Where'd they go?" What now?

"We've been swamped." The nurse blushed. "Sorry, I can't tell you anything more." She disappeared around a corner.

Sydney stormed back to the truck with Trey on her heels and slammed the door after she plopped into the passenger seat. "Something's up."

Her cell buzzed. She tapped the screen. "Hey, Pam."

"How is she?"

"Not sure. They weren't there."

"What? Do you think they took her to Spokane for a psych eval?"

"I don't think so. The nurse seems to think they up and left. Leena wasn't discharged, that's for sure."

"Keep me posted, sweetie. She's on three prayer chains. Call me if you need anything."

Sydney ended the call then turned to Trey. "Pam thinks they may have taken her to Spokane for a psych eval."

"I'll call." Trey tapped his screen and put the cell to his ear. "I'm looking for Leena Morgan. Has she been admitted?" After a short moment, he hung up. "She's not there." He opened his wallet and pulled out a slip of paper. "I'll try the number Tim gave me." He punched in the digits and gave Sydney an encouraging grin, then scowled. "The number's no longer in service."

"We need to find out where they live. Chuck can look into it."

Trey started the truck. "He can get ahold of the social worker. What's her name?"

"Angela."

"I gave Leena both of our cell numbers before you walked into the house that day. Maybe she'll call." He pulled out of the parking lot and headed toward Nespelem.

"What if she lost the slip of paper?" Sydney tapped in her four-digit lock passcode. There were no missed calls.

"We'll find her, babe."

"I hope you're right." God felt miles away. She turned her head to the window, trying not to cry. As soon as she dropped her cell on her lap, a notification for a text flashed. Not recognizing the number, she swiped the screen and read it. "I'm Leena's friend from school. She told me to get ahold of you. She tried to slit her wrists this morning." Sydney's voice wavered. She took a breath and kept reading.

"The Morgans took her to the hospital, but when the doctor said he was sending her to a shrink in Spokane, they snuck her out and are heading to Beth's sister's place in Oregon. When they get there, she'll text me the address, then I'll get it to you. She doesn't want Beth to know she's contacting you. Says it will make things worse."

Sydney shuddered.

Trey pulled over in a parking lot overlooking the top of Grand Coulee Dam. "Make what worse?"

"I don't know. Leena said the Morgans fought a lot. You saw how timid Beth was at the house. Do you think he's escalated to physical abuse?"

"Probably not. I didn't see any bruises on either Leena or Beth. I have a feeling he uses coercion and isolation to keep them in line. But why they left the state is what worries me."

She hated to assume his anger or fear might have heightened to beatings. But it had with Cooper. And taking Leena to Oregon. Was that even legal? She tapped in Chuck's cell number and left a voice message for him to call her back.

By the time they reached the ranch, exhaustion overtook Sydney. Trey stopped in front of the lodge and killed the engine. Guest parking stood empty. "Where is everyone?"

"Good question."

Inside, Mandie, Martin, and Robert sat around one of the dining room tables, and Nona slept in a portable Pack 'n Play near the fireplace.

Martin caught Sydney's eye and stood. "How is she?"

"By the time we got there, she was gone." Sydney and Trey joined them at the table.

"Gone?"

"Seems they fled at the mention of a psych eval."

"You have a kid?" Robert arched his brows. "When were you gonna tell us?"

"I hadn't figured that out."

"How old is she?"

"Sixteen."

"And she tried to kill herself?"

What was with the third degree? "Apparently so, Bobby. Anything else you need to know about her, or maybe I need to explain why I gave her up in the first place, huh?"

He held up his hands, his face reddening.

Trey touched his wife's shoulder, and she breathed in deeply to calm down. "Sorry. I'm a little stressed right now."

"A friend texted Syd," Trey said, "with news of the Morgans taking Leena to Oregon. Apparently, her foster mom has a sister there."

"Where in Oregon?" Martin leaned forward. "I know a lot of people on the Umatilla rez."

"Leena's friend is supposed to let us know."

"Why the friend?"

"All she said is that Leena contacting me would make things worse." Sydney answered. "Leena must be afraid of what will happen if they catch her contacting me."

"Yikes." Mandie's eyes widened. "*Make things worse?* That doesn't sound good. What kind of people are these guys?"

One of Sydney's shoulders inched up. "That's what we're trying to figure out."

"Do you know they aren't supposed to take foster kids across state lines without permission from their social worker?" Mandie asked.

Martin turned toward her. "How do you know that?"

"I have a cousin who's a social worker. If you want, I can give her a call. Maybe she can contact Leena's and find out what's going on."

"Chuck's on it." Sydney consulted the time on her cell, sure Chuck had gotten her message and was indeed looking into things. She set her phone on the table. "Where are all the guests?"

"Gone." Mandie frowned. "Everyone checked out today and all the reservations have been canceled."

"Canceled? Why?" Was this a sign that selling was the right choice? Or was it from the chaos on opening day?

"I don't know. They all had different reasons, and none of them wanted to reschedule."

Trey leaned forward. "So there are no reservations at all?"

"Not one."

He slid his cell out of his back pocket and swiped the screen. "I wonder if the barn fire made the papers."

Had it? She too picked up her phone and searched "Seven Tine Ranch fire." Scrolling down, she clicked on a thread. "Yep, it's in *The Star.* Oh, great, they claim the lodge burned to the ground, not the hay barn. And there's a photo that makes it look like the lodge is on fire. Who the heck took it?"

"Looks like the same mistake hit several papers." Trey flashed his screen toward her.

"Everything's falling apart." Including her. "What are we going to do?" This was too much. Her body numb, she couldn't think.

"Nothing we can do about it now," Robert said.

How could the ranch survive without any guests? She dropped her head in her hands and rubbed her temples with her thumbs. "I hate to have to say this, but I'm going to have to lay everyone off." She dreaded having to call Chad and Rich.

Mandie peered at Nona. "For how long?"

Trey sighed. "Until we figure this mess out and get guests coming back again."

Sydney was at a loss for words.

"Let's rest." Trey patted her leg. "We can start fresh in the morning."

Nona fussed in the Pack 'n Play. "I'll take her home and call my cousin," Mandie said. "See what I can dig up." She collected her baby and the diaper bag and followed Martin out the door.

"I'll go check on the horses." Robert limped outside, his shoulders slumped.

Sydney's heart ached for them all. "What are we going to do?"

"Figure this out, that's what."

"I'm going for a ride."

"I don't think that's a good idea—"

"Sitting around will drive me crazy. I'll stay close this time." Through the bay windows, it looked as though the worst of the storm had passed. She leaned over and kissed him. "You're the best." Her chest fluttered when his face lit up. "I'll be back by dinner."

CHAPTER 60

How could the papers have gotten their facts wrong? Could Cooper have dropped the misinformed leak? It would have been easy to take a photo from the knoll and doctor it. Which made Trey wonder if the psychopath had started it.

With Sydney out riding, Trey went into his studio and wrote a short press release, clarifying the Seven Tine was indeed open for business. He googled *The Star*, Grand Coulee's newspaper, and other area periodicals. Then stretched the reach to central and western Washington, northern Idaho, Montana, and eastern Oregon, sending numerous announcements with attached photos of the ranch and Sydney working cattle. He also sent the statement to local news and radio stations.

When done, he leaned back. *What else could we do?*

He opened a Word document and typed the header, *Ways to Save the Seven Tine.* He listed ideas: put merchandise from the gift shop online, make more jerky, call photography contacts, take and sell more photos, run ads, host barn weddings and other events, offer family photo sessions of guests, look for a Valentine colt to replace Twister. OK, that one would make his life and wife happy.

He regretted pushing her to sell the colt. Especially because of the time, money, and energy she'd put into keeping him alive. He'd never make that mistake again.

279

What else could they do? Spruce up the place, more flowers, fresh coat of stain on the barn and lodge, finish setting up his studio. He checked his bank account. Yep, he had enough to cover most of the list.

He scrolled through his email. The inbox revealed multiple photography callouts from several magazines. Most he could cover locally. For others, he'd have to travel. For now, he'd concentrate on regional ones. Then shift to fall senior pictures in late September and early October. At some point, he'd have to travel again. Even if only in the states. And Canada. Maybe Mexico too.

A message from Brad Talbot made him pause. He opened it. Shoot. Nothing new on Cooper. He had assumed they could stick him for more than breaking parole and harassing his wife. He wrote a quick reply of appreciation, not wanting to lose hope.

With God all things are possible. But was it God's will to save the ranch? Or his and Sydney's? She was losing her will to fight. He'd have to battle for her. At least until she regained her drive. Then they could work together.

His cell chimed, and Chuck's name glowed on the screen. He tapped the On and Speaker icons. "Hey, what's up?"

"Where's Syd? She's not answering her phone."

"On a ride. Why?"

"I found Leena's social worker. Her name's Angela Ward. She's working on securing a warrant so we can go and pick her up."

Trey darted outside to see if he could spot his wife. This might be the one thing to spark her motivation. "How long will it take?"

"We should have it sometime tomorrow."

"That fast, huh? How'd you find her?"

"One of the Coulee Dam officers is a good friend. I called in a favor."

"Good deal." Sydney should have been back by now. She hadn't planned on being gone long.

"Have her call me."

Trey hung up and texted her to call Chuck, then went to the main house to make a pot of coffee. Like Sydney, he wasn't good at waiting and decided working in his studio would be a good way to pass the time. When the brew finished, he poured a cup and took a sip, his mind on the warrant and how excited Sydney would be. Burning his mouth made him jerk and spill the steaming liquid on his shirt, burning his skin.

He jogged upstairs and ripped off his shirt, then parked on the edge of the bed and looked around. "This has to change."

CHAPTER 61

Sydney trotted up the stairs to take a shower and change into something more comfortable. The ride had been invigorating, and she came back ready to fight for the ranch and rescue her daughter.

At the top of the stairs, she caught a shirtless Trey in the hall carrying an armful of his Western shirts toward her room. His fresh scent lingered. Her eyes locked in on his brawny, tan biceps. She wet her lips, wanting to kiss him senseless.

"Hey." He strode past her.

"What are you doing?" She ran ahead of him and blocked the entrance.

"What I should have done when I said 'I do'." Trey moved her aside and plopped his shirts onto the bed.

Sydney gathered his attire in her arms and thrust the wad at him.

"You didn't hear me." He dropped his garments back on the bed. "I'm movin' in."

"No, you're *not*!" She struggled to rip her focus from his bare chest. She reached for him but quickly snapped her hands back, hugging herself.

He wrapped his arms around her shoulders and gave her a tender kiss. "We are legally married. It's time we act like it."

"But—"

Trey kissed her until she quit resisting. Her fingers found his damp hair. She inhaled his minty scent, melting into his solid chest. He released her and went for another load of clothes. "You might want to find a spot for those," he hollered from down the hall.

She stomped into his room, empty-handed. "I'm not ready. Besides, I have enough stress. I want to be alone to try to figure it all out. I need more time."

"I don't care." He dug in a drawer, pulled out a handful of socks, and faced her. "By the way, how's lone wolfing working for you anyway?" He strode down the hall and dumped the footwear on the bed.

Sydney trailed behind. "I've done fine so far."

He whirled around. "Oh? Let's recap, shall we? In the beginning, your parents brought you into this world, gave you a good home, provided for your needs, and loved you unconditionally. A social worker helped you in your time of need. Pam and Jim were here for you when your folks passed. Martin has been looking after you since the accident and probably way before then. The vet helped save Twister. Chuck has located Leena. Your brother and employees have battled right alongside of you to keep Glenda from ripping this place away from you. And I . . . I'm trying my best to help you find love again." He reached her in one long stride, pulled her close, and gave her a thorough kiss.

"But . . ." She couldn't think clearly enough to spit out the words, her mind stuck on his warm lips.

"I was going to move in and tell you, well, after."

"Tell me what?"

"Did you get my text?"

"No." She patted her back pockets. "I must have left my phone in the tack room."

"Chuck talked to Leena's social worker. She's in the process of obtaining a warrant to get her back."

"When can we go?"

"Sometime tomorrow."

He kissed her neck.

"Can we bring her here?" Her fingers slid up his chest and wound around his neck.

"I don't know." His mouth took hers.

She shoved him back. "What all did Chuck say?"

He groaned and walked out of the room.

She followed. "Well, aren't you going to tell me?"

Trey gathered another armload of clothing, carried the wad to her room, and moved the clothing to the floor. He sat on the bed and patted the spot next to him. "Sit down, and we'll call him."

She gnawed on her bottom lip.

He held out his hands. "I won't touch you. I promise."

She eased beside him, eyes narrow.

Trey punched in Chuck's cell number and handed her the phone.

She tapped the Speaker icon. When he answered, she asked, "Is it true? You found her?"

"Sure is. We should have a warrant tomorrow. I've already contacted Oregon PD. They'll meet me at Beth's sister's place."

"I'm coming with you."

"I think you should stay here. It could get ugly."

"You know I can't do that. She's been through enough. I want to be there for her, Chuck."

"I know, but—"

"But nothing."

"She can't go home with you, Syd. She'll have to go to a halfway house in Omak."

"For how long?"

"Until the court approves her living with you. If that's what you want."

With me. "Yes, of course!" She blinked back tears and hung up.

Trey took her hand and kissed her palm with his soft lips. Goosebumps danced up her arms. "We can't sell the ranch now. She'll need a safe place to call home."

"Here?"

"Yes. This is our home. Let's build a family, starting with Leena." He rubbed her arm. "I love you. More than you realize. And I know you love me."

He smiled at her with his alluring hazel-green eyes. She drank in his intimacy, longing to purge all remnants of fear. Yep, his love proved real. He was nothing like Cooper.

He traced a finger down the inside of her forearm. "How can I show you?"

"How?" She smoothed the floral quilt, feeling like a teenager on a first date.

"You do love me, don't you?" he whispered, his voice husky. "Is there the slightest hope we can make this marriage last?"

This time she drew his hand to her lips and held it for a long moment. "I do love you, Trey. So much it hurts."

The light in his eyes brightened. She allowed him to lay her on the bed. Kiss her with tender lips. Validate their marriage.

CHAPTER 62

Sunday, August 27

The strong aroma of coffee woke her up. She rolled over and reached for her husband, but his side of the bed had turned cold. *The warrant.* She jumped out of bed, showered, and padded downstairs.

"Trey?" The kitchen stood empty.

A note by the coffee pot stated he'd gone to help feed the animals. She poured herself a cup and went to the lodge office. She hadn't had a migraine since she'd seen Dr. Gordon. Maybe his treatment had worked after all.

Even though last night's intimacy with Trey thrilled her, the reality of the ranch deficit threatened to fizzle the bliss. After paying off a big chunk of debt with auction funds, she didn't have enough to hire back the employees. Not unless guests started booking again.

She ended up having to pay for hay from the gift shop income.

How could little to no revenue provide for her, Trey, Robert, and Leena? She didn't know how much Trey had in his account or had coming from his freelance profits. He hadn't sold any additional photos, not that he'd mentioned anyhow. Either way, she felt certain it wasn't enough to keep a bleeding guest ranch alive.

A deep sigh escaped her lips as she typed the last invoice into the accounting software. Then she called Lynda Picard, a local, reputable Realtor, about listing the ranch. She picked the framed photo off the desk and studied her folks' young faces. "I hope you can forgive me," she whispered, hoping Trey would too.

When Lynda answered, they agreed on a date and time for her to take a look at the ranch and sign a contract. In three days, the Seven Tine would be officially on the market. Sydney hung up and let out a deep breath. Was she doing the right thing? A knot formed in her belly.

With shaky hands, she opened the ranch's website dashboard, typed in a few words on the Home and About pages, and scheduled a new blog post. At six the following morning, an announcement would release, notifying the public the Seven Tine Guest Ranch would no longer be taking reservations.

Effective immediately.

Pursed lips couldn't stop the flow of tears. Sydney never promised Trey she'd stay, only that she'd think about it. And she had. Time to move on. She wiped her face and strolled to the deserted gift shop. She couldn't even hire anyone to help run it. But what she could do is open one of those Etsy shops and sell the merchandise online.

She picked up the yellow-and-purple beaded necklace her grandmother, Abigail Moomaw, had made as a young woman. She'd been an exceptional jewelry maker. Sydney placed it around her neck and closed her eyes. "Tell me what to do." She walked around the merchandise-deficient tables and stopped by a floral photo album. "Where did you come from?" Had Glenda brought it over during opening day then forgotten about it?

Inside were faded photos of her parents and grandparents and the original two-room cabin. A picture slipped to the floor. She picked it up. A dark-haired woman with an easygoing expression in an above-the-ankle dress sat in a chair. The back of the photo displayed the name Esperanza. Where had she seen that name before?

Taking the album back to the office, she unlocked the safe. In a plastic sack lay a beaded purse with six running horses adorned on the front in multiple colors. Black letters spelled Esperanza across the top. Who was she? Could she sell the bag for a good price?

Sydney put the album on the desk and sat down.

Robert knocked on the door, Caliber at his feet. "Sorry to interrupt, Syd, but what do you want me to do with Cyan? She's pretty restless in her stall."

"Put her in the mare-and-foal pen. It's empty." She tapped her palm with the photo. "Have you seen this woman before?"

"Let me take a look." He took a glance, then snatched it out of her hand. "Where did you get this?"

"Do you know her?"

He pulled a photo out of his wallet and handed it to her. "That's where I've seen her."

"You've been in my wallet?"

"Yeah, once. Remember last year at the fourth-of-July rodeo when you got dumped and I had to take you to the hospital for X-rays? You had me get it out of the jockey box and find your insurance card. The photo fell in my lap." Her brows furrowed. "Who is she?"

"My mother."

She reached for the beaded pouch. "Have you seen this bag before?"

"No." He looked it over and ran a finger over the name. "My mom told me when they were first together, Dad used to call her his Esperanza. His flower of hope."

"Aw, that's sweet. But why a Spanish name if she's Indian?"

"Because she's part Mexican."

The name and bag now made sense. "Dad must have kept it for you." She pointed to a picture in the album, an image of a young man and woman in their early twenties with their arms around each other. "Here she is again. This is our dad with your mom. I've never seen a photo of them together before."

"Me either. They were a handsome couple."

Was their connection a sign to keep the ranch? But she'd already called the Realtor. She felt pulled in opposing directions.

Would it be wrong to want to sell the beaded bag? Would Robert want it? She exhaled. "I guess this belongs to you then."

"You sure?"

She nodded. Though she could have gotten a pretty penny, it was the right thing to do. She needed to let the valuable handbag go. Like she needed to let the ranch go. When about to tell him she'd listed it, Trey bounded in.

"There you are." He held up his cell. "Chuck called. He's got the warrant."

Sydney squealed, and Robert stepped aside as she hurried to Trey. They clung to one another for several seconds. Was this for real? Her chest fluttered. "So . . . ?"

"We go get her."

"How do you think the Morgans will respond?"

"Not real well. But they've broken several laws, so they don't have a choice but to give her up."

Sydney turned to her brother. "Bronco Bobby, you're in charge."

"Copy that." Robert smiled. "You guys better get on the road."

Headed south toward eastern Oregon, Sydney and Trey sat in the front seat.

Chuck rested in the back. "Settle in. We've got a long trip ahead of us."

"Where is she?"

"Danner. A couple of hours south of Ontario."

Sydney called up Google Maps on her cell and typed in Danner, Oregon. "It's over five hundred miles away. Eight hours and thirty-eight minutes." Way too long. Her daughter needed to be safe. Tim and Beth's impending reactions upon their arrival left a bitter taste in her mouth.

Trey turned up the radio. "May as well enjoy the ride."

"We're going to get her." Delight clashed with anxiety in Sydney's chest.

Trey took one of her hands and pressed his lips to her skin. "We are."

"I hate to spoil the mood," Chuck said, "but do you two realize you'll have to remain in the rig while I go get her?"

"Why can't I tag along?" Sydney asked. "I'll stay out of the way. Simply be there for Leena. She'll need the comfort and—"

"Syd, no. This is official police business, and you're a civilian. You wait in the rig until I bring her to you, then you can take over. Got it?"

Of course she didn't get it. But she'd do as told. Or at least try.

"I'm predicting it will get ugly."

"More reason for me to go with you."

"Syd . . ." Chuck leaned his head back and closed his eyes.

She never could win an argument with him. She consulted the dash clock. Eight hours and thirty-eight minutes to go. Plus bathroom breaks. She groaned. They couldn't get there fast enough.

CHAPTER 63

Along the side of the road taking them to the Ontario State Recreation Site, plumes of orange, green, and yellow reflected off the Snake River. Trey pulled over and cut the engine. Sydney hurried to the restroom. He rolled down the window—a rush of heat blasting the cab—and stepped from the pickup.

Chuck got out and stretched then went around to the other side of the truck. "You'll need to keep Sydney outside."

"Easier said than done." Trey headed for the river. Cottonwood trees swelled in standing water, their golden leaves glimmering in the sunshine.

Chuck joined him. "Not sure what we'll walk into when we get there."

"I'm thinking we should have stayed at the ranch. My wife's gonna be a handful."

"Pfft. She would have followed and messed things up. She's a determined woman."

"That she is. And that's what I love about her most."

Sydney waved them over to the truck. "Let's go!" When the guys didn't move, she trotted over to them.

"What's going to happen when Leena gets back?" Trey asked Chuck.

"Her social worker's setting up a psych eval now, then she can petition the court for her to be placed in Sydney's care. That or Leena can petition the court and become emancipated. All she needs to do is prove she can hold down a job.

"Seems simple enough."

"Like I said"—Chuck closed his eyes for an instant—"it's not that easy. They're the only parents she's ever known. It might be traumatic for her, even as a teen, and even if it's her idea. More than likely she'll have to deal with PTSD from the accident. She may even have a harder time living with Sydney because of who she killed, accident or not."

"Or they can help each other heal." Which had been Trey's prayer.

"All she needs is a little time," Sydney said. "I understand she's going to need counseling, and I'm prepared to get her the help she needs. Now, come on, let's roll!"

Chuck leveled his eyes on her. "This isn't going to be easy, Syd."

"I never assumed it would be. You know how much family means to us. It's our culture. Our Indian kids need to be with us, not with . . ." She gave Trey a sideways glance and blushed, but recovered quickly. "Listen, I have a second chance with my daughter and am not about to let anyone steal it from me. I realize we won't be together right away. But surely I'll be allowed visitations to start forming a relationship with her."

"Yes, you will," Chuck said. "But do you realize how long it may take? You know tribal court—any court for that matter—is no simple process. You two will have to get blood tests for her tribal status, and I don't know how the outcome of her psych eval will affect things."

"That doesn't matter." Sydney waved away his concern and stalked back toward the truck with the guys in tow. "As long as she eventually gets to live with me. I want her to have the loving family she's never had. She told us the Morgans were only foster parents for the money, which they fight over all the time. They never felt like family to her, and it's obvious

she's no longer safe. She deserves a *family* who will love her."
Sydney sighed. "Can we please go now?"

Chuck climbed to the driver's seat as Trey caught
Sydney's arm. "You sure you want to do this?"

"Of course. Why would you even ask?"

"Because this is going to change your life. There's no
going back. She's a teenager, not a baby."

"Don't you think I know that?" Sydney narrowed her
eyes. "Or is this about you not being ready to be a dad?"

"Stepdad."

"Whatever." Their gazes locked.

"I'll admit, I'm scared as heck."

"Please tell me you're not going to quit on me now. Quit
on us."

"Good Lord, Sydney. Have I ever quit on you?" He shook
his head. "I'm here, aren't I? All I said is that I'm scared. I don't
know how to raise a kid, and my dad wasn't the best example.
When are you going to stop blowing things out of proportion?"

She stepped into his arms. "I'm scared too. This is real,
isn't it?"

"It is." Just because his dad acted militant didn't mean he
would too. Leena seemed like a great kid. But did Sydney
realize how much work would go into raising a traumatized
kid? "I know you'll be a great mom."

"And you'll be a wonderful dad."

But would he?

"Now, can we go get her?"

Trey gave her a quick kiss of reassurance before she
climbed into the truck and scooted to the center. His—
their—lives were about to veer into uncharted territory.

CHAPTER 64

Only a smidgen of light remained when they pulled into the small community of Danner, Oregon. Sydney's nerves fired. "There's nothing here."

"That's because it's an unincorporated town," Chuck said as the fields rolled by while they cruised south on Danner Road. "It's nothing but a small, historic site."

He jutted his chin at two state troopers on the side of the road and pulled into the driveway of a little, yellow farmhouse with a small covered porch and a weedy yard. The police cruiser stopped beside them.

"Remember what I told you, Syd," Chuck said in a stern voice. "Stay put."

She nodded.

He got out and talked with the officers for a moment before they all headed to the house. He'd checked in with them before they'd arrived, and one of the officers told him they'd been there all day and no one had come or gone.

Sydney slid over to the driver's side. "You think they're still in there?"

"I don't see why not."

Chuck knocked on the Morgans' door. A moment later, it opened, but not far enough to see who had answered. Sydney chewed on her nails. When she couldn't stand it any longer, she jumped out.

Trey met her by the hood. "Syd, what are you doing?"

"I can't breathe in there. It feels claustrophobic. I need air."

The house door slammed in Chuck's face. "Open up, Mr. Morgan. I have a warrant. Leena's coming with me." When no one responded, he wiggled the knob. "It's locked." He backed up, and one of the state troopers kicked in the door, then all three officers darted inside.

Sydney crept closer to the house, her hand pressed against the base of her neck.

Trey caught her arm and pulled her back. "Don't do it."

Shouts, foul language, and accusations vibrated out the open door. Were they resisting arrest? Where was Leena? Sydney's pulse raced. More shrieks sounded along with the crash of heavy objects like glass vases or lamps smashed against a wall. She jerked away from Trey and raced for the door.

"Sydney!" The call came two more times.

The voice made her halt and face the sound. Leena rounded the corner, running for Sydney. Both wrists were bandaged, one eye red and swollen, and a navy blue pack bounced against her back.

Sydney rushed to her, arms open, and caught her. "I've got you." She held tight, feeling Leena's trembling body against hers.

Moments later, the state troopers appeared and escorted the Morgans to the cruiser, their hands behind their backs.

"You threw her away!" Beth Morgan shouted. "We're the ones who raised her! We're her parents, not you!"

Her words stung Sydney's heart.

"Shut her up and put her in the car!" Chuck shouted.

Beth was right, she had given her daughter up, and she'd regret it the rest of her life. But she wasn't about to believe she didn't deserve a second chance.

Leena broke loose and went after Beth. Trey blocked her, but she shouted toward the patrol car, "You only wanted me for the money! This"—she pointed to her swollen eye—"is not love! You didn't even care when I tried to kill myself!"

Sydney rushed over to help Trey.

"That's not true—" Beth called from the backseat.

"Yes, it is!" Leena yelled.

Sydney touched her arm, but she brushed it away.

Leena pushed into Trey. He stood his ground and held her in place. "You didn't even ask me if I was OK after the accident. You never called Angela. She's my social worker, she's supposed to help me. You're supposed to help me."

"Let's go home." Sydney wrapped her arm around Leena and led her to the truck. Once in, she held her daughter's hand as she cried. And cried right along with her.

Chuck and Trey talked with the state troopers for several minutes before joining the girls, Chuck in the driver's seat. Trey leaned over and handed Leena a few napkins.

"What's going to happen to them?" Leena said as she wiped her face.

"They'll be booked, then go to court," Chuck said as he turned around. "As foster parents, they are legally responsible for getting you an evaluation after the suicide attempt. And they weren't supposed to take you across state lines without permission."

"So, they basically kidnapped me?"

"Something like that. You want to tell me how you got that black eye?"

Leena looked at Sydney, and she nodded back at her. "When we got home from the hospital, I told them I knew I could emancipate from them. Tim hit me and told me that wasn't an option."

Emancipate. Sydney couldn't imagine. Providing for oneself at sixteen would be a lot to handle. Would she want to be on her own? Or would she be open to living at the ranch? For now, she'd leave it alone. Give her time to heal.

"Where are you taking me?" Leena asked.

"To a halfway house in Omak until Angela finds you a place to stay," Chuck responded.

"I'm not staying with a bunch of juvies. I want to live with Sydney."

"You do?" She squeezed Leena's hand, and she returned the pressure. Surely that would speed up the process.

"Right now, I have to take you to Omak. But I'll let Angela know." In the rearview mirror, he winked at her. "You're in good hands, kid."

CHAPTER 65

Thursday, August 31

The all-female halfway house looked cleaner than Sydney had assumed. And less chaotic. Its furnishings were modest but in good condition. Soft music played in the background as teens roamed in and out of the waiting room. She waited for Leena in a green overstuffed chair and set a toiletry bag adorned with musical notes on the floor.

After ten minutes, Leena appeared wearing cargo shorts and a long-sleeved tee covering her wrists. She settled into a chair across from Sydney and hugged herself.

"How are you?"

"OK." Leena glanced down as if not knowing what more to say.

"How do they treat you here?"

"Good. The counselor's nice."

"How'd your evaluation go?" Because Sacred Heart Medical Center's psychiatric center was full, Angela had pulled strings and gotten her in with someone she knew. Good. Because Angela had mentioned the quicker Leena got to the ranch the better.

Leena shrugged. "Good, I guess."

Which could only mean she was on the road to recovery, right? "Got my blood work done." Sydney had to get a maternity test in order for Leena to get enrolled in the Colville Tribe.

"Me too. How long will it take?"

"A week or two."

"No, I mean how long until I can come live with you?"

"Oh." Sydney had never heard such wonderful words. "I'm not sure. I did talk to Angela, though, and she's pretty optimistic. She came to the ranch last night, and we had a good visit. She's in favor of you living with us. In the meantime, we can keep meeting. Go to lunch if you want."

"I'd like that." The light in her eyes brightened.

"Maybe Trey can come too?"

"Yeah, sure." Her shoulders inched up and down.

Sydney handed her the bag. "I brought you these. Wasn't sure what you like." How would she provide for a teenager? Jerky sales certainly wouldn't cover anything. Now that Leena was safe, her focus would be on selling the ranch, paying Glenda her share, and finding an affordable place to live. And looking for a job.

Leena peeked inside, then held it on her lap. "Thanks."

"Do you have any questions?"

"About?"

"Me, the ranch, Trey?"

"No. But I do wanna get outta here."

That didn't sound good. "How come?"

Leena took a quick look around the room, then leaned forward and whispered, "I'm sick of the drama around here."

"You can call me anytime. Any hour."

"I don't have a cell."

"Oh. Guess I better check into getting you one. That way we can stay in touch."

"You might want to check to see if it's allowed." Leena lowered her voice again. "They're pretty strict here."

Sydney bet it seemed strict compared to the Morgans' dysfunction. She'd have to learn to strike a balance. After another thirty minutes of visiting, she left with an empty space in her heart. She spun back to the hospital sixteen years ago, leaving her child behind.

Sydney found Trey at the riverside pasture, shooting photos of the sunset against the Coulee's jagged rock formations lining the river. "How's it going?"

"Great. Take a look." He lifted the strap over his head and handed her the camera.

"These are nice. You selling them?"

"Yep. *Country Lifestyle* wants 'em. How'd your visit go?"

Maybe his sales were picking up speed. "Good. Maybe next time *we* can take Leena to lunch."

"Sounds good. I'd like to get to know her better."

Yeah, they both needed to. "She's pretty eager to live with us."

An eagle glided overhead on a light current. "They must have been pretty neglectful for her to want to come live with us so badly."

"Because we're . . ."

"Because *she's* insecure."

"She'll need a lot of support. It's going to be an adjustment for everyone." She gave him back the camera. "You sure you're good with this? New wife. New kid. New life?"

He drew her close. "We'll adjust. It'll take time and patience, but she's better off here with us, that's for sure."

She tipped her face to him. "That's why I love you. You're so understanding."

"You love me, huh?"

"Yeah, I do."

He leaned down and kissed her. Long and sweet. Now she needed to confess the ranch was again up for sale. Would he be as understanding?

Trey broke the kiss. "Oh, hey, a handful of reservations came in today. Isn't that great? They'll arrive Friday. My plan worked."

"Your plan?"

"You might say I set the media straight."

Oh goodness, reservations? How many? Would more follow? Would there be enough to salvage the Seven Tine? Mixed feelings warred inside her. Maybe she wouldn't have to tell him after all. A sprig of hope broke through.

CHAPTER 66

Friday, September 1

Flames crackled in the lodge's dining room fireplace, warming the great room. Sitting on furniture by the bay windows, Sydney and Trey, the Gibbses, and Chuck and Glenda visited after a nice lasagna dinner Pam had provided.

They had no idea Sydney had again listed the place. Guilt pricked at her. Had she made the right choice to keep the ranch listed, even though Trey had run the articles and ads? Bless his heart. She should have come clean that night. With Robert too.

Glenda snapped her fingers. "Syd, did you hear her?"

"Huh?"

"How's Leena?" Pam crossed her legs.

"She's hanging in there. I think she's doing better than expected but is awful quiet."

"These things take time," Glenda said. "Let us know how we can help."

Her mouth fell open. She couldn't recall the last time her sister had supported her. "We'll need it."

"It's good you have guests lined up," Jim said. "How many?"

Trey nodded. "A group of sales execs from Seattle is scheduled to arrive on Monday for a weeklong retreat."

Guests booked reservations even with the website announcement they were no longer taking them? Wow. Should she take down the notice and see what happens?

"Any more scheduled to come?" Chuck asked.

Sydney wished. "Not yet."

If she did keep the ranch, how would they sustain it? What would be the attraction for visitors to stay at the lodge and not a cheap hotel? Only a few at a time could go on trail rides. Unless she rounded up some of her friends' horses. She could kick herself for having sold most of her bombproof animals. They were hard to come by.

She had two days to clean the lodge and shop for groceries. Thank goodness Mandie and the hands had been available to come back and were hard at work getting the place ready. She'd missed them. And Nona too.

"So, I've got a few ideas," Glenda said, "if you're open to them."

Sure. Open but not hopeful. "What are you thinking?"

"Until you can rebuild your stock, why not turn this place into an event venue. There's nothing like it around here. I've been talking to my friends, and they think it's a great idea."

Sydney cocked her head. "Is it too late in the season?"

"Maybe for weddings," Pam answered, "but not other occasions and parties. You could have a new-and-improved open house."

"Improved how?" The first one humiliated her.

"A fresh start," Pam said. "Open Trey's art studio, advertise for that and the event venue. Imagine what we could do with this place for Christmas, New Years, and Valentines."

Valentines?

"Yeah," Glenda said, brightening with enthusiasm, "and focus your advertising on those business retreats throughout the winter and come spring, you'll have enough money for new stock and trail horses and money ahead to build another barn and put in a loft for weddings and dances. Remember Grandpa Moomaw hosting a few barn dances? They were a blast."

First Glenda was encouraging, and now she's a visionary too? What had come over her?

"And I could pass out brochures at ATNI and other tribal meetings." ATNI conferences were quarterly Affiliated Tribes of Northwest Indians conventions where members convened for the future of Indian Country in the Northwest.

Sydney pulled at the sleeves of her shirt. Should she tell them about the listing and get it over with in one fell swoop? Or pull Trey aside and let him know first? Then again, it was sometimes easier to ask for forgiveness afterward. "I-I-uh . . . listed the ranch."

"You what?" Glenda leaned forward. "Why on earth would you do that? You've fought like a dog to safeguard the family legacy, and now you're willing to cut ties and let go? Did you know about this, Trey? What's gotten into you?"

And she's back.

He shook his head, fury in his eyes.

Sydney swallowed the boulder in her throat. By the look on Trey's face, she'd have to work hard at begging for forgiveness.

"I can't believe you didn't tell me." Trey paced the bedroom.

Sydney sat on the edge of the bed. "I honestly didn't see any other way."

"Not sure you wanted to." Did she have no faith in him whatsoever?

"I'm a rancher, not an event planner."

"I agree with Glenda. You've fought too hard to throw up your hands and quit."

"Sounds like you two plan on double-teaming me."

"You've fought tooth and nail to rescue the ranch. Why are you giving up so easily?"

"Can you guarantee we can pull through?"

Trey scrubbed his hand over his face and sat beside her. "Nothing's guaranteed. But c'mon. Have a little faith."

"In what? I don't know how much money you have, and you've never seen the ranch books."

He snatched his cell from the side table, tapped the screen, and showed her his bank account. "This is what I—*we*—have."

"Oh, that could definitely help."

"I've got both feet in, sweetheart, and I'm committed. I don't plan on getting a divorce, so what do you say? You want to keep this place? If not for you, think about Leena."

"I don't have your kind of faith to go out on a limb. And by the way, Leena's why I want to sell. We can get rid of the ranch and start over with cash in the bank. I can get a job."

Trey tossed his head back and let out a hearty laugh. "What—in an office? That'd drive you crazy. Like you said, darlin', running this ranch is in your blood."

Her mouth twisted.

"At least consider the event stuff," Trey said. "In the morning, let's go over the books. Show me everything, then we'll see what we can do. Maybe all we have to do is tweak your business plan."

"Fine. But don't hold your breath."

CHAPTER 67

Saturday, September 2

The following morning, Sydney woke up feeling drained. She'd slept like a colicky horse. She wanted to fold, but her gut told her to keep a hand in the game. After a strong cup of coffee, she and Trey went to the office and combed over the books.

"So you never found insurance on the place, huh?"

"No. I forgot to tell you, when we were in Oregon, Glenda found out that, too, had been canceled."

"That's not good. Well, here's what you have."

Sydney sighed. "It's not much."

"No, but I can cover the first few payments. We have to have insurance on this place."

"I can do that now." She picked up the ranch phone and made an appointment for the following Tuesday. She had to admit, she felt better. "Now what?"

"Let's rework this business plan before we head out to pick up Leena."

He did have enough faith for both of them. Was that a good thing or not?

Trey and Sydney took Leena five miles south of Omak to Burke's Western Store in Okanogan to get her more jeans and a couple of shirts before going to the Breadbasket Café for a late lunch. He insisted they buy her a pair of riding boots. It was all he could do to keep his cool at her resistance. Was her faith that depleted?

They walked into the café and went up the stairs to the main floor. The scent of barbeque made his belly rumble. The place resembled a Western museum. One family and two couples were the only other patrons in the room. With their order placed, Sydney excused herself and went to the restroom. He sat back. "You like your boots?"

"Yeah. But I don't ride horses."

"By the time Syd's done with you, you'll be a pro."

Her face paled. Was she afraid of them? Was she nervous to be alone with him? The waitress brought them baskets of bread and ice water. Leena took a drink.

"I hear you're excited to come live with us."

"I'm excited to be in a place I can roam around and not feel closed in."

"Well, then, let's hope Syd doesn't sell the place."

"She's getting rid of it?"

Oh great. Her face wanned. Apparently Sydney hadn't told her. "There's a chance. But I'm trying my best to talk her out of it. How about we keep this between the two of us?"

"Keep what between you two?" Sydney settled in the chair between them.

"Why would you sell the ranch?" Leena asked.

Sydney's face turned red as she leveled a glare at Trey.

"Why would you buy me boots if you don't plan on staying?"

"Because you can ride until, well, you know . . ." She shrugged a shoulder.

They ate a quiet meal, only making small talk, then took Leena back to the halfway house.

When out of Omak, Sydney spoke up. "First you tell her I plan on selling the house, then you ask her to lie about it? What the heck were you thinking?"

"*Lie* is a pretty strong word. Honestly, I thought you would have told her by now so she could have time to prepare for the change. I asked her to keep quiet so we wouldn't ruin lunch. Why hadn't you told her?"

She lifted a shoulder. "Because deep down I'm hoping there's a way I can hold on to it."

"Sorry for opening my mouth."

"I'll call her later. In the meantime, please, let me do the talking when it comes to *my* ranch."

"If I'd known you hadn't told her yet, I wouldn't have opened my mouth. You need to communicate with me so we're on the same page. And darn it, Syd, I know the ranch is yours. I'm not trying to take it. But I do want to help you run it. I've got more experience than you realize. And seriously, why are you in such a hurry to sell?"

"Because I inherited a mess," she said with a hitch in her voice. "And yeah, I was on fire to keep it, but the idea of getting Leena changed my mind. We can make a home anywhere. She deserves a good, simple life, and I'm not sure I want to bring her into this chaos."

Darn her stubborn hide. "What if you can have it all? The husband, the daughter, the ranch, filled with guests, and a fresh start?"

"Things like that don't happen to me."

Her words cracked his heart. "Can't you see that they are? You have me. You're about to get your daughter back, and we have the start of a fruitful business plan."

She rubbed her temple. "I'm tired. Can we talk about this later?"

"You getting another headache?"

She nodded. "At some point, I suppose I need to go back to Mom's doctor."

He'd make sure she did. "I have one last thing to say. With Pam and Glenda rearing to help, and Robert too, we have a good chance of building the Seven Tine back up. It will take time and effort, but I truly believe it's doable. And remember, the ranch is all your brother has left of his dad. Please, think about it." Only God could reach her now.

CHAPTER 68

Sunday, September 3

Sydney stood in front of the lodge, shades of purple, red, and copper splashing the western horizon, and waved goodbye to Mandie. It had been a long day of organizing and cleaning the lodge, and baby Nona had been a trouper. Guests were scheduled to arrive early afternoon, a good thing.

But after what Cooper had done to her, she'd never been a risk-taker and was scared the revised business plan would flop. There were no quick fixes when it came to overcoming the mental and emotional scars of abuse.

Glenda held out a glass of iced tea. "Come sit with us."

Sydney inhaled the dusty air, then dragged herself up the steps and sat on the horsehead bench beside her. Pam enjoyed the rocking chair, her head back and eyes closed.

"You serious about selling this place?" Glenda asked. "We've had a lot of good times here."

"If we take the risks and fail, we all stand to lose a lot." She took a drink, the cool liquid trailing down her throat. "If we sell now, I'll get enough to start over with no debt, even if the money is split three ways."

"What if we pool our funds? Chuck and I have quite a bit in savings."

"I can't take your money," Sydney said. "Besides, it wouldn't be enough."

Pam stopped rocking. "You letting Trey help?"

"Yeah. He promised to help me get insurance."

"As your best friend, and I say this in love, stop behaving like a lone wolf. It's his job to help."

Ugh. Not again. "I—"

"And another thing, he's nothing like Cooper and you know it. So quit comparing them and start behaving like a married woman. Work as a team. It's the only way anything will survive."

Was she talking about the marriage or the ranch? "That's what he keeps telling me."

"He's right." Glenda took hold of her hand. "He loves you, sister. Let him in."

"You guys don't understand."

"You're right. We don't," Pam responded. "But, sweetie, you can't live in fear forever. Trey is a good, kind, faithful man. Do you not see that?"

"I know he is. That's the problem. I don't deserve him."

"Stop allowing guilt to control you," Glenda urged. "We all make mistakes. Don't let them define you. You're smart, courageous, and talented. I wish I could have an ounce of your bravery."

Had their parent's death changed her? Or maybe their mom's cancer scare? Or both? She leaned her head on Glenda's shoulder. "I'd always thought that about you. Fighting your way onto council. That takes determination."

"It's going to work out," Pam said. "You wait and see. God will work it out."

After the girls left, Sydney showered and pulled on a tank top and stretchy shorts. Her hair in a towel, she went downstairs and scrolled through her emails and text messages before turning in for the night. The last text caught her attention. She held her phone to her chest. "I've got to tell Trey."

She sprinted upstairs, securing the hair wrap with her hand, and bounded into the bedroom. Leaning against the headboard, Trey lay stretched out, his eyes closed. She jumped onto the bed, startling him awake, straddled him, and held up the cell. "She's coming!"

"Who's coming?"

No longer able to hold the towel on her head, she tossed it aside. "Leena. Angela left a message. The court decided she can live with us. Angela promised to call tomorrow with more details."

"Here goes nothing." Trey leaned up and kissed her, then settled back against the headboard.

"We need to get a room ready for her. Glenda's old room in the basement will do."

"You think she'll feel valued in a basement?"

"You're right. She can have my old room down the hall." Sydney clapped and planted a juicy kiss on Trey's lips, then rolled off him.

"Hey, where ya going?"

She giggled. "There's so much to do." With what little money they had, she wanted to get Leena a little something special for her room. "I have a friend who's an artist. I bet I can get her to help us with a musical theme."

"Good idea. We can go to the dam and see what they have."

"Yeah, there's a cute little shop on Main Street with fun décor. They're not overpriced either. I'll see if Pam can check it out for me."

"You ready for the guests?"

She curled up next to his warm, spicy body. "I suppose so. It feels weird not having all the stock and trail horses."

"Yeah, it does. But that's temporary. As long as we're together, everything'll work out."

"That's what Pam said."

"You know what I think?"

She braced herself. "What?"

"I want to give you one thing you haven't had yet."

She tilted her face to him. "What's that?"

"A real wedding."

"What do you mean? We had one."

"A ceremony with family and friends, here at the lodge. With a reception and the works. It could kick off the event stuff Glenda and Pam talked about."

She dropped her chin. "I don't know. It's kinda past the point, don't you think? Plus, I don't want to waste money."

"Consider it?" He lifted her face with his finger and peered at her. "I want you to have what every little girl dreams about." He kissed her head. Kissed her temple. Scooted down and kissed her neck.

Tingles ran up her arms as she let him take her as his wife, a soft moan escaping her lips.

CHAPTER 69

Thursday, September 7

Sydney paced the log planks of the lodge's front porch. She confirmed the time on her cell. "They should be here any minute." She never dreamed she'd see her daughter again, let alone—and by the grace of Creator—reconnect and have her move in too. Her heart would not stop pounding.

Trey observed her from the rocking chair, one hand scratching Caliber's neck. Having insurance seemed to make him feel more secure. Her too.

The week-long guests, who were inside brainstorming, had one more day. Thankfully, that morning, a few more bookings had come in for the following weekend. Good thing she'd updated the website, again welcoming reservations. Was this God's way of telling her to take a leap of faith? Keep the Seven Tine so Leena could have stability in a place she had her heart set on living?

Angela's car rumbled down the driveway, a wake of dust billowing behind her. Sydney clung to a log column, anticipating. Waiting. Wishing her driveway was shorter. When the silver Kia pulled up, she trotted down the stairs and went to the passenger's side.

Leena waved and hopped out of the car. Caliber raced down the stairs, sniffed her pants, and wagged his tail. She crouched down and petted him. "He's cute. What's his name?"

"Caliber." She gave Leena a hug, then grabbed two suitcases, a backpack, and the music-emblazoned bag she'd given her.

"I'll get the rest of Leena's belongings to her next week," Angela said. "I'll need a truck for the rest of it."

"The rest of it?"

"Yeah, the judge said she could have her bed and desk—"

"I don't want anything from there." Leena grimaced.

"You sure?"

"Yeah."

"We have a room set up for her," Sydney said to Angela, then turned to Leena. "I hope you like it. Come on. Let's go take a look."

Trey gripped her luggage and followed everyone to the main house, Caliber sticking close to Leena. Inside, Sydney led her to the upstairs room. Her eyes widened as she walked over the threshold. A purple pillow adorned with a whole and three-quarter notes stretched from corner to corner sat on the green bedspread. Sydney's artist friend had painted colorful chromatic scales and other note sequences on three of the walls.

"This is so cool!" Leena set her matching bag on the bed. "I can't wait to show my friends."

Friends. Something they hadn't talked about. Should they invite them over? What were they like? Were they good influences? Were some of them boys? Oh, Lord, she wasn't ready to deal with dating.

"Let's let Leena settle in," Angela said. "Is there somewhere we can talk?"

Sydney led the way to the kitchen table, and Trey served coffee, then settled next to her.

Angela gave them a bright grin. "The room's wonderful. I think she'll adjust well here. All she's been talking about is how happy she is to have found you, even under such horrifying circumstances. She feels a strong connection to you, Sydney. And likes you, too, Trey."

Sydney couldn't stop smiling. "I feel the same way about her."

"She seems like a great kid." Trey gave Angela a reassuring look, then turned somber. "I am a little nervous about having a teenager though."

"You'll be fine. You have a strong support system. Use it. And I suggest you both remember when you were her age. How did you feel? What sound advice did your folks give you? What advice made you want to rebel? Call me anytime. I'm here for you all."

"Thanks, I appreciate that." She'd have to ponder possible reasons for her teenage rebellion.

"Your apprehension is to be expected. Be patient with her and each other."

"I have a question," Trey said. "We had a private wedding."

Sydney closed her eyes, pursed her lips. *Oh, sheesh, not this again.*

"I want to give Sydney a proper ceremony. How would that affect Leena? Would she want to be part of it? Should she be?"

"I don't think this is the place," Sydney murmured.

"Actually," Angela said, "this is the perfect moment. As you know, her evaluation went well. She's a bright, healthy girl who needs stability and support. For now, she's on an antianxiety medication and is being treated for insomnia. Every person and family are different. I would wait to see how Leena adjusts. Talk to her about the ceremony when you think she's ready and go from there. Including her in the decision-making process might be what she needs. But I do caution you, don't rush into anything. She's been through a traumatic experience and will need plenty of time to adjust.

She's had a lot of nightmares, so be prepared for that. You have the counselor's number, right?" she asked Sydney.

"I do."

"Any more questions?"

Sydney shook her head. "But I do want to confirm that she'll go back to school when she's ready?"

"Yes," Angela said, "for now, online classes through the alternative school are fine. Anything else?"

"I don't think so."

Trey shook his head. "I'm good."

"Great. Call me if you need anything." Angela stood and shook their hands. "I'll see myself out."

Trey went to check on Leena while Sydney went to make her a counseling appointment. He found her sitting at the top of the stairs, a frown on her face, and took a seat beside her. "You settled in?"

Leena nodded.

"You like your room?"

"Yeah, thanks," she muttered.

When they'd left her, she'd been elated. Now she acted like she regretted staying. *Think, Trey. What could be bothering her?* "Did you overhear our conversation?"

She nodded again.

"What's on your mind?"

She lifted her shoulders toward her ears, then let them fall.

Yep, a huge adjustment. How did he feel at her age? Absolutely frustrated with a father who liked to work him to death. So, yeah, he should know how she feels. "I'm here if you need to talk."

She tugged her long sleeves over her hands.

"You want to go see the horses?"

Her face brightened. "Sure."

Ah, he got somewhere. After she slipped on her new boots, Trey took her to the barn. Caliber trailed behind them. "This is Sydney's horse, Cyan."

"She's pretty."

He found a bag of horse treats in the tack room and gave it to Leena. "Feed her a few of these. She loves them." When she hesitated, he fed the mare a couple and winked at Leena. "She's gentle as a butterfly."

Leena dug out a few, held her hand out flat, and giggled as Cyan gently took them with her lips.

"Come on, I'll show you something else."

After Trey put the bag of treats away, Leena followed him to the Jersey's pen, making sure Caliber trotted beside her. He bet the cow dog would reach her in a way neither he nor Sydney could. "This is Daisy, she's the milk cow."

Leena scrunched her face.

"C'mon now, don't knock it till you've tried it."

"No thanks." Boy, did she resemble her mother—both in beauty and bullheadedness.

"You don't know what you're missing. It's the sweetest, smoothest milk you'll drink."

"I'll stick to 2 percent."

Five words. Progress. "Do you have any questions about what we were talking about with Angela?"

"If you're already married, why have another ceremony? That doesn't make sense."

He chuckled, careful with how much to divulge. "We decided to have a small ceremony, just the two of us. She claims it was enough, but I think she regrets it. I want to give her a bigger, better one with family there to support her."

Leena rubbed Caliber's head. "I don't think I wanna get married."

"Why not?"

"All Beth and Tim did was fight. What's special about that?"

"I see your point. But not all marriages are filled with strife."

"What does that mean?"

"Chock-full of conflict." Was he making any sense? "Maybe you can help me plan the ceremony? When we're all ready, that is."

"Maybe."

Yep, too soon to talk about it. "Let's work on getting you settled in. If we do have a do-over, I hope you'll be part of it."

She glanced away.

Two against one. He wasn't about to give up so easily though. Once things settled down and they had more time to consider his offer, he was sure he could convince those noes to become yesses. And maybe, just maybe, planning a wedding at the Seven Tine would convince Sydney it would be a great event venue.

CHAPTER 70

Tuesday, September 12

Sydney zipped her jacket and headed down the lodge steps. She promised to be open. And she had been. All she needed was a small place that would ensure their seclusion.

A young, eager-looking couple stood next to Lynda Picard, clad in jeans, vintage cowboy boots, and a lilac-and-lace shirt. Sydney felt good about working with Lynda. It took a load off her shoulders to have a compassionate Realtor at her side. And it wouldn't hurt to hear an offer.

"Thanks for coming." She shook Lynda's hand, then greeted the couple, who by their Western clothing and weathered skin appeared to know a thing or two about ranching. "I'll show you around, and then we can go into the lodge and talk."

The first stop being the horse barn. She fessed up about the fire that had destroyed the hay barn, but it didn't seem to faze them. Especially when Sydney promised to have at least a cover up by the time they moved in. Next were the outdoor pens, corrals, cabin, main house, garden, and finally the lodge. Around a dining room table, the couple asked questions. She answered them the best she could, a twinge of guilt and uneasiness creating a pause now and again.

"Your price is firm?" The gentleman glanced at a document, at his wife, and nodded.

"Yes, sir. That's what the appraisal came in at for two-hundred-and-ten acres, equestrian facilities, cattle pens, arena, hay barn, lodge, main house, and cabin. Although we could reduce the price and let you take care of the hay barn." Sydney showed them various photos during the four seasons as she talked. Their eyes flashed at a fall photo—orange, reds, and yellows reflecting off the creek.

He smiled at his wife. "We'd like to make an offer."

Suddenly, Sydney felt like retching.

Trey came through the door, Leena and Caliber tight on his heels, and strode to the table. "Hey, what's going on in here?"

Sydney's face flushed. "These nice folks are taking a look at the ranch."

"Why?" Trey worked his jaw.

"They are prospective buyers."

"I thought we were going to work on this issue together."

She wanted—hoped—there'd be a way to clamp the ranch's bleeding artery. But she just couldn't see a trail out of the heap of debt. "We need to sell, Trey. It's the only way."

"No, it's not."

Lynda's eyes grew wide, and the couple's jaws dropped. The wife touched her husband's arm.

"I kinda like it here," Leena said. "Caliber and Cyan and Daisy, they might help me"—red bloomed on her face—"you know."

"You can't give up that easily," Trey said. "You haven't given it a fair shot, have you?" His expression pleaded with her.

"Please." Tears pooled in Leena's eyes as she dropped to one knee and hugged the cowdog.

Sydney hadn't realized Leena liked it here. Had Trey said something to trigger healing in her heart? Or perhaps she was connecting with the animals? She'd heard animal therapy had a way of mending shattered lives.

"Perhaps we should leave you alone for a moment." Lynda rose, motioning for the couple to do the same. "Better yet, let me know your final decision in the morning."

Leena watched the lodge door close behind them. "Mom?"

Mom? Sydney's heart melted. She walked around the room, imagining herself growing old with Trey. She'd have a few years with Leena before she was swept off to college. She stopped by the bay windows, her face heavenward. *If I trust you, will you save the ranch?*

She made a cup of instant coffee, giving her more time to think. Raked through the pros and cons of staying put. Could she afford all the insurances? Breakdowns? Vet and feed bills? Payroll?

More and more questions hounded her. She went to the fireplace where she could get a good look at the tree-covered land. After several minutes, she asked, "Why here? Why not somewhere simpler? We can take a few horses, Caliber, and Daisy."

Leena made her way to Sydney's side. Trey leaned against a log post and gave her a supportive nod. "The last sixteen years are gone," she said. "I mean, we can't get them back. But we can have a new beginning. As a family. A *stable* family. You're my real mom. Beth was superficial. I need parents I can depend on." She played with the cuff of her sweatshirt. "I like it here. I've dreamed about living on a ranch like this one since I was a little girl."

"You have?" This made selling so much harder. "I'm not sure we can afford it."

Leena sank to the sofa. "What do you mean?"

Sydney sat beside her and shared where the ranch stood financially.

"I can get a job," Leena said.

"Good idea." Trey nodded.

"What about helping out around here," Sydney offered. "Maybe in the gift shop after school and on the weekends?"

"That would be so much fun."

"And by the way," Trey said, "I ran into Landon Peters the other day in Omak. I also talked with the stampede board."

Sydney lifted her brows. "And?"

"You're looking at the new photographer." A broad grin broke out on his face.

"That's big," Sydney said.

"It's a good start and will lead me to additional rodeos. Landon's packing his bags. Said he'll be moved to New Mexico by Christmas. But I'll shoot with him this year."

"How cool is that!" Leena's face brightened.

Maybe Creator had been listening after all. "Then it's done. I'll call Lynda in the morning and tell her we're keeping the ranch."

Trey held out his cell phone. "Why wait? Call her now."

"Yeah," Leena said, "before you change your mind."

Sydney took the cell and called Lynda. Trust. She'd have to work on it being her new mindset.

CHAPTER 71

Wednesday, September 13

A bright vein of sunlight cut through thin clouds and spilled into the kitchen window. Trey sang along to a country song as he cooked scrambled eggs in one pan, bacon in another. He scooped up the last of the pancakes and flopped them onto a plate. After turning off the griddle, he slid the eggs into a small bowl and pinched bacon onto a plate with metal tongs. Their first day as a family.

"Breakfast's ready," he shouted up the stairs.

Leena came down first. "Smells good. What do you want me to do?"

"Pour some OJ?" Trey pointed to the fridge with a spatula and kept singing and dancing.

Leena grabbed glasses and poured the juice.

Sydney leaned against the wall, brows arched. "What's all this about?"

"We're celebrating." Trey danced his way to his wife and twirled her around. Her hair was pulled back in a clip, and her skin glowed. He was the luckiest guy around. Married to the most striking woman he'd ever laid eyes on.

Sydney kissed Trey and poured herself a cup of coffee, adding a splash of vanilla creamer.

Trey put the food on the table, blessed it, and took a bite of bacon. "Mmm."

Leena giggled and dug into her eggs, her eyes twinkling.

Trey said, "I think it's time for us to take a family vacation. We don't have to do anything fancy."

"There's no time," Sydney said. "We'll have to get ready for an open house, find more horses for trail rides, and get up a new hay cover before the snow flies. Not to mention getting the gift shop ready to reopen. Which means I have to make more jerky." She took a bite of syrupy pancake, closed her eyes, and let out a low moan. "This is good."

Leena leaned back in the chair, her mouth ajar.

"What?" Sydney swallowed and took a sip of coffee.

"We're a family now," Trey said. "We *will* take family trips. When was the last time you went anywhere? Spokane doesn't count."

"I've never had a vacation," Leena said quietly.

Trey twisted his face. "Never?"

She shook her head.

"What about you, Syd?"

"Define *vacation*. We've taken a few days here and there to fish and camp."

"A week," he said. "Either on the coast or in another state. No work or school involved."

Sydney pursed her lips. "Then I guess my answer is never."

Leena turned to Trey. "Did you give her one? I mean when you first got married?"

A twinge of regret tapped his chest. "Not yet."

"Why not?"

C'mon, Syd, jump in. But she leaned back in her chair, a devious smile on her face.

He let out a nervous chuckle. "I, uh . . . You guys think about where you want to go, and we can take a vote." He wasn't about to let the conversation swing to the marriage.

"Speaking of school," Sydney changed the subject. "We need to talk about when you want to go back to Lake Roosevelt."

Leena frowned. "I'm not ready. Can I do fall quarter online? Or try homeschooling? I really don't want to go back to LR."

Sydney nodded at Trey. "I don't see a problem with that, do you?"

"Not at all. Heck, I'd be in favor of homeschooling her if you want."

"That's something to think about," Sydney said. "What about your friends? And sports? Or music?" Students in the small towns of Nespelem, Coulee Dam, and Grand Coulee attended Lake Roosevelt High School in Coulee Dam.

Leena shifted her weight, her eyes cast sideways. "I can hang out with them on the weekends. Or they could come here, right?"

"They sure can," Sydney promised. "Is there something you're worried about?"

"They'll ask questions. Some of the girls . . ." Leena stuck her hands in her pockets. "They . . ."

Trey leaned closer to her. "They what?"

Tears pooled in her eyes.

"They what?" Trey's voice grew rigid.

"A few of them can be pretty cruel."

Trey's gut clenched. Maybe homeschooling would ease her stress. He could help her with the lessons. With all Leena had gone through, maybe staying home a year would help her gain her confidence back.

"Would family counseling help?" Sydney asked. "We could all learn how to navigate our new situation. Even though I'm your mom, I'll admit I don't know how to be one."

"I'm in," Trey said. "Don't worry, Leena. We'll get through this."

Leena seemed to relax. Having her around would give them more time to connect.

After breakfast, Sydney and her little family headed to the barn to feed. Overhead, cool air pushed gray clouds north. According to Trey's app, a 30 percent chance of rain threatened their ride. Hopefully, their light pullovers would keep them warm.

She showed Leena the ropes. She seemed interested in learning how much hay and what grain concoction each horse received. With a bright smile, she fed the two remaining chickens and screamed as one hen flapped at her when she reached for an egg. Timid around Cyan, she stood back as Sydney pitched hay into her wooden feeder, its scent pulsing. But Leena jumped in eagerly with the Jerseys.

"You wanna milk Daisy?"

Her eyes grew round. "Sure." She pulled up her sleeves, exposing the red, raised scars on her wrists.

Heart threatening to break at the sight, Sydney gathered a stool and a bucket and showed Leena what to do. When the bucket grew half full, she had Leena take it into the lodge fridge. The cowdog trotted beside her.

Trey leaned against a post. "She will get along fine around here."

"I think so too. But seeing those scars . . ."

"I know. But she's a strong girl. Like you. I think she'll heal just fine. Caliber will make sure she does."

"Good point."

Trey gathered her in his arms, backed her up against a stall, and pressed his lips to hers in a tender kiss. When footsteps crunched outside the barn, he let her loose.

He took Leena to feed the cows while Sydney watered horses. She watched as he taught her how to run the tractor, spear a bale of hay, and dump it in a big round feeder. He marveled at how quickly she picked up on the morning chores. She'd make a great summer hand.

Sydney led three horses toward them.

"Hope you ride."

Leena took a step backward. "I've always wanted to, but I don't know. They're pretty big."

Trey laughed. "If you're anything like your mother, you won't have a lick of trouble."

She gestured toward her new cowboy boots. "I only have my good ones, and I don't want to get them dirty."

"I can take care of that." Sydney went to the lodge and found her a pair of old boots. "These should fit."

Looking hesitant, Leena changed footwear.

Sydney handed the reins of a middle-aged sorrel to her daughter. "We'll be by your side until you feel confident enough."

Leena kept her arms to her sides.

"Are you scared?"

"Kinda." Leena's shoulders drooped.

"We don't have to ride today, ya know."

Trey took the gelding's reins. "You ladies have fun. I'll put this guy away. We can ride together another day. While you work with her, I'll run to Omak for a few supplies. Need anything, babe?"

"Not that I can think of."

He kissed Sydney and headed to town.

CHAPTER 72

It was a perfect day for a lesson—brisk weather and overcast sky. Leena held a gelding by the reins while Sydney showed her how to one-rein stop her horse. "When in a circle like this," she said from atop her mare, holding her rein hand near her knee, "she can't buck, bolt, kick, rear, or take off. This is your safety net. Remember to trust him and use soft, slow hands. Don't jerk his mouth. Hundreds of kids have ridden that gelding, and he's as safe as they come." She nodded her chin at the horse. "Your turn. Go ahead, get on."

Leena rubbed the gelding's neck. "What's his name?"

Not wanting to increase her daughter's angst with a name, Sydney hesitated. Then cleared her throat. "Tumbleweed."

"Oh?" Leena stepped back, eyeing her mother.

"Don't let the name fool you. He's bombproof." Sydney dismounted. "Come on, I'll give you a leg up."

"How'd he get the name?"

"The night before he was born, I'd watched an old Western with my dad. Your Grandpa Lester. The final scene rolled tumbleweeds across the screen. It seemed like a good name to an eight-year-old." Sydney patted the saddle. "He's never bucked, bolted, or reared. Nothing since day one. I'd never pair you with a bronc. Trust me. I want your first ride to be successful."

Leena set her foot on Sydney's bended knee and swung into the saddle. The circle of her lips flipped into a wide smile.

"Rub his neck. Let him know you want to be up there. Remember, relax and enjoy the ride. Look ahead, not down, or you might end up in the dirt." Sydney smiled. "Ready?"

Leena gave her a nervous nod.

"Let's ride in circles. He's not going anywhere in the arena."

With her hands on the saddle horn, Leena waved her legs, and Tumbleweed plodded around the dirt-covered area.

"Use one hand to steer him."

She dropped a hand to the saddle horn and pulled to the left. Tumbleweed followed the feel of the reins.

"That a girl. He's not going anywhere. Relax. And smile."

Dirt rolled behind a roaring truck rattling down the driveway. Sydney squinted, not recognizing the rig. "Keep going. You're doing great." She guided the horse to the side of the arena and stopped by the wood fence encasing the rectangle. The truck sped past the barn, which blocked the view. "Whoa! He needs to slow down! I'll be right back." She rushed out of the gate.

"Wait!"

Sydney stopped and turned around.

Leena scrambled off Tumbleweed and caught up. "I don't want to be in there by myself."

"You can come along." Sydney closed the gate. "But remember, he's a plodder. He'll keep you safe when you ride." She walked around the barn and stopped by a brown Ford pickup.

A guy stepped out, his black cowboy hat hiding his face. Caliber let out a low growl, causing goosebumps to dance over Sydney's arms. Leena crept close to her mother. She gave her daughter a reassuring smile and signaled for her dog to sit. The man strode around the hood of the truck and lifted his face.

Sydney sucked in a lungful of air. "What are you doing here?"

"I've come to meet my daughter." Cooper staggered over to them. "This her?"

The pungent scent of a day-old drunk wafted up Sydney's nostrils. Normally, his appearance mattered. Not today. His unshaven face, dirty jeans, and crumpled Western shirt made him look as though he'd come from a rodeo and a bull had gotten the best of him.

Hunching low, Caliber bared his teeth and snarled.

Sydney stepped in front of Leena. "Get outta here."

As she reached for her phone holstered in her back pocket, Caliber lunged for Cooper. He reached behind him, brandished a revolver, and squeezed the trigger. The blue-and-brown Aussie let out a yelp and dropped to the ground.

"No!" Sydney crouched beside him. She pressed a hand to his side. *Where's Bobby?*

"You try to call for help, I'll put a bullet in you." He wobbled a step toward her daughter. "Leena, is it?"

Stiff and big-eyed, the girl nodded. Sydney stood, putting a barrier between Leena and her sperm donor. Trembling, Leena clung to Sydney's arm.

"You're a pretty little thing," he slurred, "like your mama. But you're mine too." Cooper turned to Sydney. "You tol' her I'm her father, didn't you?"

"We told her what kind of scum you are and warned her to stay clear of you." She reached for Leena's hand and squeezed.

His face twisted, and he vacillated. "Now. That wasn't nice of you. Since she's mine, too, I figured I'd come back and get to know her. Weigh my options."

Sydney scoffed. "You don't have options."

"She's got the right to get acquainted with my family. My mom's dying to meet her granddaughter." He pulled out his cell phone. "How about a quick picture to commemorate this day? Us getting to meet an' all."

Yep, he saw their daughter as property to be owned. And his mom? Sydney had met her once. A bitter, crotchety woman who seemed thankful for nothing.

"Have you gone mad?"

"Don't make me do it," Leena muttered.

A fist-sized rock near her right boot snagged her attention. "Stay behind me."

"What are you two whispering about?" He waved Leena over. "Come on over here, girl. Let's get a picture."

"He's scaring me." She had a death grip on Sydney's arm.

For Leena's safety, she'd have to use her words wisely. Him drunk with a gun was like a baby on a bronc—nothing good would come of it.

"If you cooperate, there'll be no need to use this." He oscillated his pistol in the air.

"Do you think she wants to come over there with you waving that thing around? Think about it. She's a kid, Coop." Her father kept a loaded shotgun in the tack room. It'd help if she could get to it.

She hated this in-between stage of his drinking. Enough beer in him to ignite false courage but not drunk enough to pass out. This time she would stand up to him. Gone was the chance to toss her to the ground and kick her until she passed out.

After studying them for an instant, he tucked the gun into his waistband and held out his empty hands. "Is this better?"

When the squawk of a low flying hawk snatched his attention, Sydney lunged for the rock and heaved it at his head. "C'mon!" She grasped Leena's arm and raced to the tack room.

She found the shotgun, made sure it was loaded, then grabbed a handful of cartridges and stuffed them into her pants pockets. Leena screamed, and Sydney spun around. With blood running down the side of his face, Cooper had his arm around Leena, his pistol pressed to her head.

"Let her go." Sydney's body wavered, but she tried to keep her voice calm.

"You can't keep her from me, Syd."

"Mom!"

"Stay calm, Leena. Trey should be back any minute. Chuck's with him." She shifted her eyes to Cooper. "You remember me telling you about my brother-in-law, the cop, don't you? I can't wait until he arrests you." She leveled the shotgun at him. "You leave one mark on her, I'll pull the trigger."

Leena screamed and head butted him, slamming him backward, then broke free and ran to Sydney.

Sydney cocked the hammer and squeezed the trigger. But missed. Cyan reared up, kicked a wall, and darted through the door leading to the run. Cooper lunged at Sydney before she could insert another cartridge, and they wrestled for the shotgun. He ripped it out of her hands and hit her in the head with the stock. Leena screamed her name.

CHAPTER 73

Sydney?" Trey sprinted toward Caliber. The dog lay dead, a bullet hole in his ribs and blood on his fur. He stopped in front of tire tracks he didn't recognize. "Leena," he hollered.

He should have stayed. Getting the poles for the roof-only hay barn could have waited. And he shouldn't have given Robert the afternoon off before he'd gone.

Someone had left in a hurry. Trey studied the deep imprints, then hollered, "Sydney, Leena, where are you guys?" After checking the barn and finding three of the horses gone, too, he pulled out his cell and punched in Chuck's number. "Someone shot Caliber, and Syd and Leena are missing."

Sydney's truck stood in the parking lot. He ended the call and searched for them in the lodge, main house, and cabin. No one answered his calls. He phoned Jim and filled him in, urging him to hurry.

He raced back to the office, searched the desk, and found Martin's cell number in a floral, wire-bound address book. He punched in the digits and paced. "Hey, Sydney and Leena are missing. Caliber's dead. How fast can you get here?" The clock on the cabin wall read 2:00 p.m. He ran trembling fingers through his hair. "I'll have horses ready."

Trey went back to his truck and packed in sacks from Bar C Western Wear to the main house. He laid out Leena's new western clothing and boots on the kitchen table. He would make sure she'd live to get them. He slammed a fist on the table. It had to be Cooper. He stormed back to the gallery, pulled his revolver from a minisafe, and loaded it, stashing extra bullets in his pocket. By the time he got back to the lodge, Chuck and Glenda had pulled up. They got out and met him between the barn and the lodge.

"Oh no, Caliber!" Glenda rushed to the dog and dropped to her knees, stroked his head. After a moment and with red-rimmed eyes, she came back to the guys. "We have to find them."

"We will." Trey took them over to the tire tracks. "I don't recognize these. It has to be Cooper." He pointed to the north pasture. "They lead that way."

"North?" Glenda quirked a brow. "Why would he head toward Canada?"

"I don't know why. He didn't seem real bright when he showed up the other times. Anyway, Jim and Pam are on their way."

"I called in an Amber Alert on our way here," Chuck said. "Let's go to the lodge and set up base camp. The girls can stay here in case they show up." He went to his truck and pulled out a rifle and bullets for his wife.

Trey headed for the lodge but stopped and turned toward the hitching post. "One of the horse trailers is missing." Hoofprints led him to a spot outside the barn then disappeared as if loaded into a trailer. He and Chuck checked the stalls. Trey said, "Any hits from the notes and photos Cooper has been sending?"

"Not yet," Chuck answered. "I bet someone was sending them for him. Probably a relative or friend."

"That's what Syd suspected."

Chuck pulled out his pad and pen. "What's the license number?"

"Heck if I know." Edgy, Trey led Chuck and Glenda to the lodge. Glenda made sandwiches and coffee while Chuck and Trey spread out maps and packing supplies on the dining room tables.

"I'll saddle up and head north," Trey said. "Martin should be here soon."

Chuck nodded. "Good. He's the best tracker on the rez."

Jim and Pam burst through the doors. Two tribal officers and a thirty-ish Native guy in camo trailed behind. The bays of hounds bounded through the open doors.

Pam rushed to Trey and hugged him. "Any word yet? We heard the Amber Alert on the radio."

Trey shook his head as he reached for Jim's hand. "Thanks for coming, man." He turned to Pam. "Glenda's in the kitchen."

"I'm on it."

"What do you have so far?" Jim studied a map.

"Tire tracks lead north."

"You sure it's Cooper?"

"Who else could it be?" Trey pointed to the map. "There's a lot of rugged country out there. Nothing to head to. They can't cross the border. I'm not sure what he's thinking."

Glenda set a tray of sandwiches and chips on the table. "My sister's smart. She'll come up with something. He's on her turf. She knows this country better than most. Lived in those mountains many summers, watching cows instead of hanging out with her friends." Moisture gathered in her eyes. "She'll find her way home."

Pam set down two thermoses. "Glenda's right. If anyone can get out of this, it's Sydney. Cooper should have known that."

"The question is, will she be a wild card with Leena in tow?" Jim said. "Or will she play it safe?"

CHAPTER 74

A rancid stench of mold and vermin filled the damp room. "Leena?" Sydney's lids managed to lift, and she squinted against blurred light. Her maternal instincts ordered her to spring to her feet, but the sting in her head and her sluggish body held her to the hard floor. As did her bound wrists and ankles. She struggled against the zip ties. When they didn't budge, she rolled onto her side and groaned.

Chewed pinecones and rat droppings littered the floor. She wet her lips, her tongue brushing against a metallic taste. The last thing she remembered was Leena yelling for her. *Oh, God, had he taken her?* She struggled to sit up, but a dizzy spell made the room spin and her gut roil. "Leena?" Where was she?

"I'm over here." She slumped against a wall on the opposite side of the dilapidated two-room cabin. She, too, appeared restrained.

As far as Sydney was concerned, Cooper was a dead man walking.

Next time, she wouldn't miss. "Are you all right? Did he hurt you?" She fought to keep her cool. She wanted to scream and cry and pound a wall.

"I'm cold is all."

A draft drifted through the cramped space, and the rhythmic tap of a drizzle on wood sounded.

"What happened?"

"After he hit you over the head, he loaded the horses in a trailer and brought us to a camp with small corrals. When you started to wake up, he gave you some kind of shot he said would put you out for a while. He made me help him get you on Cyan, and he tied you to the saddle. We rode the rest of the way here."

Poor girl looked terrified. "Don't worry, honey. We'll get out of this." *He gave me a shot? Of what?* Sydney struggled to focus. Then it hit her—ketamine. Vets used the drug to put horses out for surgery; monsters used it for date rapes. Her body shook as she studied her daughter. "Have you been awake the entire time?"

"Yeah."

"Has he touched you?"

"No."

Sydney blew out a breath. "Did he say where he was going?"

"No. He tied us up and left."

"What direction did he take us?"

"North."

"Good." She could travel this country with her eyes closed. "How about we talk this through, huh? Up here, we have Moses Mountain. Colby Trail. Strawberry Mountain. Roaring Creek. Aeneas Valley. I know a way out. But first, we have to cut these zip ties."

Cooper had outdone himself this time. Sydney feared Leena's PTSD would get worse. Would she attempt suicide again? Sydney hoped not. She prayed Creator would protect her daughter's mind and emotions and get them out of there.

"He told me . . ."

The alarm in her daughter's voice scattered chills across the back of her neck. "What did he say?"

"He, um . . ."

"You can tell me, sweetheart." Sydney hated Cooper for putting Leena through this horror.

"He said he'd make sure Trey would never be in our lives again."

"Trey can take care of himself, trust me. He's smart. I'm sure by now he's got a search party out looking for us."

"Was Cooper like this to you? I mean before?"

Sydney cringed. Should she hide the truth to protect Leena? So far, lying hadn't done much for her in life or with Trey. "At first he was nice. Over a year's time, we became friends. I wasn't looking for a relationship. Then the following fall, we hooked up out of the blue. It was a whirlwind romance, and before I knew it, we were married. Then the heavy drinking began. And drugs and beatings."

Leena watched her as though she understood the pain.

"I was young and dumb, and he was charming. I'd always had an eye for cowboys, and he seemed to check off every item on my list. Once we got married, his true colors surfaced, and he turned vicious. Put me in the hospital a few times after he got into heavy drugs. When I found out I was pregnant, all I could think about was keeping you safe. That's why I gave you up." Her voice wavered, but she put on her best grin. "Let's not think about that right now. How about we work on finding a way out of here, huh?"

If they got out alive—which Sydney swore they would—she vowed to safeguard their relationship.

CHAPTER 75

By the time the search party returned to the ranch, daylight was fading fast. There'd been no sign of the girls. Muddy tire tracks had covered logging roads like tread marks on a racetrack.

Trey turned up the collar of his oilskin duster and pulled his Stetson low. "The horses are pretty tired. We need to let them rest then get back out there." Sprinkles of rain splattered his chaps and rolled to a puddle. Any hope of tracking a rig would soon be gone if the weather didn't clear.

Martin inched out of the saddle. "Let's get coffee and think this through."

Trey dismounted and led his wet horse to the barn. He answered his vibrating cell, talked for a moment with his brother-in-law, then turned to Martin and Jim. "That was Chuck. Someone called in an abandoned brown Ford and white three-horse trailer north of Moses Mountain. He's on his way there now. Forget the coffee, we need to load up. We can drive to the location in an hour and head out on horseback from there." He focused on Jim. "I don't know the last time my girls ate. Will you have Pam and Glenda fix them something to take with us?"

"You got it, buddy." Jim clapped him on the back and jogged to the lodge.

"I'll hook up the horse trailer." Martin headed for Trey's truck.

"Keys are in my rig," he said over his shoulder.

Trey burst into the tack room, his gut twisted and his hands in tight fists. Where were they? Where had that idiot taken them? If Cooper had hurt them in any way, by all that's holy, Trey would make him pay. He would pay.

Trey reared back and slammed his fist into the gray wall, splintering the old wood, absorbing the pain that shot to his wrist.

After a deep breath, he shook his hand out and lowered his head to stare at the plank flooring. "I should've stayed. I should never have left them alone here. I *knew* Cooper was snooping around here. What was I thinking?"

"You know it'll be dark by the time we get up there."

He spun around to Martin, leaning against the doorjamb. "I'm not waiting."

"I know." Martin joined him and motioned to the counter. "What's that?"

"Huh?" On Twister's medical chart lay a photo of Sydney and Leena riding horses in the arena. He picked it up and turned it over. *They're mine.* He handed it to Martin. "Look at this."

"Seems as though he wants his family back." Martin grunted. "He's a special kind of stupid."

"Looks like he took it from the east bluff." Trey took the photo and stuffed it into the inside pocket of his duster. "We need to find them. He's crazy enough to ..." The words stuck in his throat. "Who knows if and how much he's been drinking."

Martin faced the wall holding halters and bridles. "The shotgun's missing."

"What?" Trey's jaw muscles twitched. "Let's get a move on."

They loaded saddled horses and gathered at the rear of the horse trailer.

"Do you think he's up there?" Martin asked Trey.

341

"Don't know. I figured he'd head south. Not sure if he's playing us or what. But we have to follow the tracks."

Pam and Jim approached and handed thermoses to Trey and Martin, then Trey started the truck and turned up the heat.

Jim plopped a box on the back seat and tied a silk wild rag around his neck. "I've got food, gloves, and wild rags." They'd have to load their saddlebags at the base of the mountain.

Trey made sure his flashlight worked, as did the other men.

"Do you think they're OK?" Pam hugged herself.

"I wouldn't put it past him"—Trey's hands clenched and unclenched—"to rough Syd up a bit." He could hardly get the words out, wanting to scream and punch something. "But she can handle herself." Yeah, she can handle herself, but a man has the right to protect his woman so she doesn't have to. "For his sake, I pray he hasn't touched Leena." Trey kept the missing shotgun to himself, not wanting them to freak out even more.

By the time they were ready to head out, the temperature had dropped and a misty drizzle had turned into a downpour.

"Come back with her." Moisture pooled in Pam's eyes as she shivered.

"That's my plan." Trey and the other men jumped in the truck, and he headed for the north pasture, mud and rain pelting the windshield.

Trey pulled into a clearing with a small corral and parked by an unfamiliar truck and the Seven Tine horse trailer. He shot out of his pickup, and Chuck showed them fading tire and horse tracks.

"The rain sent the hounds home, so it's just us."

Martin knelt by partial muddy imprints. "Think he's headed up Strawberry?"

Chuck nodded. "There's a good chance that's where he's hiding 'em."

Trey pulled out the photo Cooper had left in the tack room and handed it to Chuck. "Here's more evidence."

"What is it?" Chuck studied the image.

"Cooper's death sentence." Trey moved to the back of the horse trailer and swung the door open. He unloaded the first horse and handed the reins to Martin. "You think we need to head up Strawberry?"

"There's an old, abandoned cabin up there. It's possible." Martin glanced at the gloomy sky. "We don't have much time."

Trey unloaded the other two horses. "What does your gut say?"

"He's got them up there."

Trey, Martin, and Chuck mounted, leaving Jim behind to deal with the truck and trailer, and headed north.

CHAPTER 76

Sydney battled the sting on her face, the agitation in her gut, and the thrashing in her head.

"We need to find something sharp to cut us loose with." Rat scat and mountain debris covered most of the rickety floor. "I don't see anything. Do you?"

"What about in there?" Leena tipped her chin to a second room behind Sydney.

"I'll check." Cringing at rat scat, she scooted into the other room, maneuvering around missing sections of the floorboards. It must have been used as a kitchen at one time. Dilapidated cupboards and a counter stood against one wall, a rickety table and two chairs beside the opposite one.

"Find anything?" Leena poked her head around the corner and inched forward. "This is gross."

"See that beer bottle under the table? We can break it and cut the ties."

Leena scrunched her nose.

"I'll cut you loose first. Don't worry, I'll go slow." Sydney scooted under the table, shifted until she could take hold of the bottle, and struck it against a table leg. It shattered on the third try. Moving to where she could inspect the pieces, she picked out a long, pointed shard, carefully made her way to Leena so she wouldn't slice her own fingers, and used the edge to saw through the wrist ties.

After she'd dropped the chip a few times, the tie broke loose.

"You're bleeding." Leena rubbed her wrists.

"It's nothing. Now, get the ties off me."

Leena wiped the blood off the glass and went to work. "Do you think he'll come back?"

"You bet he will. We don't have much daylight left, so hurry." She felt the ebb and flow of pressure as Leena worked.

Minutes passed as the cold rain dinned around them.

"Ouch!" Sydney jerked as a sharp pain sliced through her wrist.

"Sorry."

"Don't worry about it. Keep going." She felt the jigging pressure of Leena cutting.

"It keeps slipping."

"Hold it with your shirttail."

"I'll try."

The rain picked up speed. Thunder cracked, and they both startled. Sydney felt another sharp pain, but this time stifled the urge to shriek. "Keep going."

A long moment later, the ties broke. Sydney took the shard and cut the binds off their ankles. She stood and swayed, feeling woozy. When steady, she wiped her bloody fingers on her jeans and took in the room. Wood chips cluttered the top of an old countertop. Open cupboards above it stood empty. There were two mangled drawers next to a dilapidated worktable. A small window had glass in it.

"Think this will open?" Sydney climbed up a chair she'd dragged over, but the legs gave out, and she tumbled to the floor.

"Mom!"

Sydney eased to her feet. "I'm fine."

Outside, horses whinnied. Armed with a large glass shard, Sydney rushed to the door and pressed an ear to the wood. "I think he's back." Sweeping Leena behind her, she backed away from the sound of heavy steps on the other side of the wall. "Stay behind me, and no matter what happens, get on Tumbleweed and get out of here. You hear me?"

"I can't leave you."

"Do as I say, Leena."

At the click of the latch, the door creaked open. Cooper stepped in and dropped a soaked leather bag on the floor. Water pooled around it. "Time to go, girls."

Sydney lunged at him, swiping the jagged edge of the glass over his face.

"You wench!" Blocking the door, he yanked his pistol from the front of his pants, leveling it at Sydney's head. Blood ran from a gash above his eye. "You must think you're pretty smart."

Sydney lifted her chin, moving between him and Leena, and kept her eyes locked on his.

He put the gun to her temple. "I hadn't planned on killing you until now."

"No, don't," Leena shouted. "I'll do whatever you want. Please, don't hurt her."

"Stay back." Sydney swung her hand out to block her. "You so much as touch her, and so help me God, you're as good as dead."

"Dad, please . . ."

Dad? Smart girl. Way to make it personal.

A slow grin spread over his face. "You cooperate, and you'll stay alive," he said to Sydney. "We have enough time to get off this mountain and hit the Inchelium ferry. I'm sure your man thinks we're headed south. This should be enough time to confuse them."

She snorted. "Hit the ferry and escape the rez? Brilliant plan, genius."

He backhanded her. "You should know better than to sass me like that. Especially in front of our daughter."

"You're right. I'm sorry." She bit back the pain in her mouth. The smell of stale beer seeped through his pores and wafted up her nostrils. She turned her face to the side, breathing through her mouth. "We haven't relieved ourselves in a while."

"Not a chance." He grabbed her arm and took a step for the door.

She yanked free. He spun around, exposing a knife in his back pocket. Leena's gaze swept from his waist to Sydney. Hopefully, she saw it.

"Dad. I have to go bad." Leena pleaded with her eyes.

"Fine. But don't try anything." Cooper brushed her jawline with his bloody finger. "You hear me?"

"I promise I won't try anything, Dad. You can trust me."

Good girl. Keep him busy.

"I don't—"

"Please?" Leena bent over and held her fisted hands between her knees like a toddler who needed to pee.

"Fine. But I'm going with you guys."

When he turned to the door, Sydney shoved him, knocking him off balance, and grabbed the knife. Cooper spun around and kicked it out of her hands. Leena went for it and tripped. Able to clutch the wooden handle, she rolled over and propelled to her feet.

Cooper pressed his gun to Sydney's head. "Give me the knife." He stepped toward his daughter, shoving Sydney along.

Leena shook her head as she backed up.

"Don't give it to him. He won't hurt you. He loves you, don't you, Coop? You wouldn't hurt your own flesh and blood, would you? Your baby girl?"

"I'll do what I have to. You should know that by now, Syd." He took another step toward Leena. She kept her eyes glued on her mother.

Sydney gave her a small nod and ducked. Leena lunged at Cooper, slicing the other side of his face with the three-inch blade. He shrieked and pressed a hand to the wound. The pistol clanked to the floor. Sydney shoved him away, seized the knife, and plunged it into his side. When he dropped to the ground, she thrust Leena out the door.

"Get outta here!" she yelled as she yanked the knife out of Cooper. She caught up with Leena by the horses. They mounted, and Sydney twirled the mare around. "Kick him."

Cooper slumped against the entry with one bloody hand pressed against his side, the other brandishing his gun. "Get back here!"

They hightailed it out of there. A shot ricocheted through the rain, and a bullet whizzed by Sydney's head. She kicked her horse as rain pelted her face. "Hurry!"

CHAPTER 77

"We're too late!" Trey shouted over the pounding rain. His blood boiled as he combed the area.

Muddy hoofprints spread the soil, water gathering in the imprints. Empty beer cans littered a spot near a copse of larch trees about fifteen yards south of the cabin. Using a stick, he picked up a can and gave it to Chuck. "There might be useable DNA."

Chuck placed it in an evidence bag and headed toward his horse.

With a flashlight, Trey examined every inch of the area, including the cabin's door frame. Dark-colored splotches covered the dilapidated porch and smeared the door. It had to be blood. But whose was it? He stepped inside and swept the light beam around the tiny room. It landed on more blood spatter and scattered debris. He clenched his fists.

Chuck stepped up and rested a hand on his shoulder. "We'll find them."

Trey wouldn't sleep until they did. "You check the tracks outside?"

"Martin's on it."

Trey searched the rest of the ramshackle cabin. In the smaller of the two rooms, something crunched under his feet. The beam exposed a broken beer bottle and cut zip ties, a bloody shard next to them. It had to be the work of his clever wife. A fresh hope lightened his shoulders.

"Looks like Syd's handiwork," Chuck said.

"I know it is. Looks like she cut them loose in here. Which makes me think he may have left, then came back." But why? Then his mind shot to the empty beer cans by the larch trees. He might have only stepped out to drink and plan his next move. Sydney had the advantage with him drunk, his reflexes sluggish.

Chuck took out an evidence bag, collected the zip ties, and put them in his duster pocket.

"Got one set of hoofprints leading south," Martin said from the entryway. Water ran down his duster and pooled at his feet. "Looks like the rider is injured and sitting lopsided in the saddle. He's traveling slow. Those tracks are all over the place. Two other sets are heading west. Looks like they tore out in a hurry."

The men went back outside. Raindrops glimmered in Trey's flashlight beam. "Any sign of blood out here?"

The space between Martin's brows crinkled. "Should there be?"

"There's a lot on the floor, door, and porch," Chuck said. "Looks like Syd had a fight on her hands."

"The rain would have washed it away by now." Martin pushed the plastic-covered cowboy hat low on his head and wiped his eyes with his gloved hand. "She knows these mountains and valleys better than anyone. I'll bet the pair of tracks are Syd and Leena, and if they stay low and hug the base, they'll come out near Moses Meadows.

"I say we load up the horse trailer and drive there. It'll be quicker." Chuck sounded optimistic.

"I agree." Martin mounted his horse and headed down the way they'd come.

Trey and Chuck followed suit.

"I'll go after Cooper," Chuck said. "If he's hurt, he'll be easy to find."

"Follow the single tracks if you want. They seem to point to someone who's drunk and injured. I have a feeling Martin's right—the other two are my girls. Like he said, Syd knows this country, and it makes sense for her to head toward Moses Meadows."

"I'll stick with you," Martin said to Trey.

Chuck nodded. "Let me know if you find them."

"When we find them. Let's meet at the trailer. He can't be far. I have a feeling Sydney did more damage than we know." Trey hunkered down and kicked his horse into a lope.

CHAPTER 78

"How you holding up?" Sydney hollered against the pelting rain. She felt like a drowned cat. Their hooded pullovers did little to keep them dry.

"I'm fine."

She didn't sound like it. With the help of Sydney's flashlight, they headed up and around, over slick rocks and through shadowed brush and trees.

"Let Tumbleweed find his way." Her breath rolled out in puffs of mist. She hunkered down and prayed Creator would help them find their way off the mountain.

They came to a thin waterfall spilling into a creek. Thick brush lined the small deer trail. "We're too high. I missed the path. We have to turn around and backtrack a few yards," Sydney shouted over the torrent.

"I don't think I can do it. It's too slick. The trail's too steep."

"Yes, you can." Sydney took a deep breath, softened her tone. "Turn Tumbleweed around. Go slow and trust him. He's the most sure-footed horse on the ranch." At his age, Tumbleweed might struggle, but he'd take care of her.

One hand on the saddle horn, Leena pulled Tumbleweed's rein to her right. He backed up a couple of steps. "He won't turn."

"He's being stubborn. Kick with your inside leg."

"My what?" Fear and frustration lathered Leena's voice.

Of course she didn't know what that meant. Not being brought up in the saddle, horse talk must seem like Greek to her. "Kick him with your left leg when you turn. Keep him moving forward."

"I'll try."

"Do it, Leena!" Sydney yelled. She hated to raise her voice but knew her daughter needed it.

Leena reined and kicked and groaned until Tumbleweed spun around and plodded downhill. "He did it."

"Good job. I knew you could do it." Lord willing, the nudge would build her confidence.

Several yards down the mountain, Tumbleweed turned right. "This way?" Leena shouted over her shoulder.

"I think so. If it is, up ahead there should be a wide spot to your right."

"What if Cooper follows us?"

Sydney turned around to make sure no one trailed them. She shuddered. How far had the knife gone in? Did it puncture a vital organ? She could only hope so. "Not sure he can. The knife went in pretty deep."

"Eventually, he'll find us."

She hated Cooper. Hated what he'd done to her. But more than that, she hated what he was doing to their daughter. "We'll deal with that later. Right now, let's concentrate on getting home." The path widened, and Sydney urged her mare around Tumbleweed.

The narrow, slimy trail twisted through trees and brush. Branches smacked them in the face a time or two. Rain battering leaves and branches echoed through the woods. And pride surged through Sydney. Even in the dark, damp night Leena never complained. A good sign of a hardy, young woman—a Moomaw.

"What do you think he wants from us?"

"What I've learned is abusers want total control. It makes them crazy when they don't have it. With alcohol driving Cooper's wagon, he's not thinking clearly. I'm not sure he has been for a long time."

"I'm scared he's going to kill us. I don't want to go home. He knows where we live. Isn't Trey from Arizona? Can we go there for a while?"

With every plea, Sydney's chest clenched. She may have to give up the ranch to disappear. Protecting her daughter was her top priority. With Cooper on the loose, they weren't safe. "We'll figure it out when we get home."

Rain beat down on them harder and faster. They needed to find cover soon. Sydney could hardly see an inch in front of her. "I think there's an overhang around the bend. We'll stop there for a while."

Leena nodded, her teeth chattering.

Sydney shivered. Every hoofbeat sloshed through a stream of water down the trail, but finally, they came to the overhang. She dismounted. "I'll unsaddle the horses."

Once the animals were untacked, they used the saddles and warm pads to help shelter them. Hunkering under trees and the rock ledge, all they needed now was dry wood and a blazing fire. Too bad Sydney had nothing to start one with. Not after failing to restock her saddlebags after her last rat-infested excursion.

She held her daughter, rubbing her arms. "We'll get through this. Don't you worry, now. Us Moomaw women are fighters."

CHAPTER 79

Trey reined his horse to a halt. The water running off his cowboy hat made it hard to see much of anything. Not finding one sign of them, he cupped his hands and hollered for Sydney. His boots were soaked through and his toes were cold, but he didn't care. If his girls were out there, so was he. "You sure this is where they're supposed to come out?"

"Yes," Martin responded. His horse fidgeted, its ears pinned forward. "This is the spot. But in this storm, she probably found shelter. She knows better than to push a horse in these conditions. It gets slick out there. She's not about to put anyone in danger."

"The ground is good here where we are. Let's keep going. Maybe they're closer than we think."

"No," Martin swung his hand out to the side. "It's dark and dangerous. If they're holed up where I think she is, they're a ways out. They're safe, protected by an overhang. It's good shelter."

"By now they're soaked through and cold. Wearing hoodies. I'm sure they don't have warm enough clothes. No hats. No gloves. Hypothermia could set in." Trey urged his horse forward.

Martin kicked his palomino into a lope and blocked him. "I said no. Man has responsibility, not power. You're not thinking with a clear head. Let Creator speak to you. Your job is to listen to His wisdom. We won't make it far in this deluge. Now, come with me. We need to seek shelter and wait it out."

"You can hide out under a rock, old man. I'm going up." Trey tried to move around Martin. But he and his mount held him in place.

"Listen to—"

Something rattled in the brush behind him.

Trey spun his horse around and cocked his revolver with a sharp *crack*. "Who's there?" He urged his horse forward, squinting against the dark curtain of water. Branches waved. Was someone out there, or was it the wind? Could it be Sydney? For a short moment, a sliver of hope ran through him.

"Put the gun down, Trey," a man shouted from the trees. Soon after, Cooper stepped into view, riding Drifter. "You can't keep me from my girls. They belong to me."

Martin shined a light in Cooper's face, causing him to drop the reins and shade his eyes, exposing a pistol tucked in his waistband. Cooper's other hand gripped Lester Moomaw's shotgun. Blood mixed with water trickled down his battered face, and a dark blotch stained the side of his shirt.

Yep, looked like his wife had gotten the best of him. He felt a surge of pride. "Not anymore." Trey snorted. "You don't get it, do you? You can't have my family."

Cooper leveled the shotgun at Trey's chest as he coaxed his horse closer. "She's *not* your daughter," he said through clenched teeth, then waved the shotgun at Martin. "Get that light outta my face."

Trey clenched his fist "Maybe not by blood, but I'm willing to take care of her. Love her like she's my own. What have you done for her since you two met besides kidnap her? God help you if you laid a hand on either of them."

"What I do with my kid isn't your—"

"Sydney's my wife. Which makes them both my business."

"I will get my family back." Cooper spoke in a low, husky tone. "Nobody steals from me."

"They don't want you; can't you figure that out?" He fingered the revolver's trigger.

"Shut up." Cooper waved his firearm in the air. "The only reason she's with you is because you're a fancy, world-traveling photographer." Hate lathered his words. "Don't you get it? She's using you to save her beloved ranch. She doesn't love you."

"You don't know anything about her or the ranch." Trey had never met anyone so blinded by his own pride. "What will it take to get you out of our lives?"

"I don't ever plan on . . ." Cooper squinted. "Hey, where'd that Indian go?"

Trey kept his pistol aimed at him. He had to hold faith that Martin knew what he was doing. Seconds later, a blurry form sprang out of the pine trees beside Cooper.

"Drop the gun." Martin aimed his rifle at Cooper's head. He'd fixed the flashlight to the saddle horn with a strip of latigo and ground tied the horse. "It's over."

"No way—"

With Cooper's attention on Martin, Trey jumped off his horse and dragged Cooper to the ground. A shot fractured the whine of rain and wind. He wrestled the weapon out of Cooper's grasp, then straddled him, slamming his fist into Cooper's face. He belted him again. And again. For beating his wife. For kidnapping his daughter. Terrorizing his family. He bashed Cooper's lips, nose, eyes. Whatever his fists came into contact with, he didn't care.

"Enough!" Strong arms wrapped around him and yanked him off Cooper. "Enough, I said."

When Trey quit struggling, he pushed to his feet, breaths coming in heavy gasps. Martin stood next to him, lines creasing his forehead. "Get my lariat."

He wiped his mouth with the back of his bloody, swollen hand and unhooked the coiled rope from Martin's saddle. He and Martin secured both Cooper and Drifter to separate trees. Cooper's head hung chin to chest. Fresh blood ran down his broken face; his eyes swelled shut.

"He won't go anywhere. The rain has let up. Let's go get my girls."

Martin plunged his rifle into the scabbard and eased into the saddle. "We need to go slow."

Trey retrieved his flashlight from a puddle, then mounted. At the base of the trail, mud sucked at the horses' hooves. Two forms bobbed, coming toward him, horses snorting. "Sydney? Leena?"

The flashlight beams collided.

"Trey?" Relief filled Leena's voice.

Trey shined his flashlight on the trail. Cyan side-stepped as Sydney pulled her to a halt. She slid off and ran for him.

He jumped off his horse, encased her in his arms, and kissed her icy lips until they were both breathless, his fingers tangled in her drenched locks. She had never felt so good. After a long moment, he broke their bond and held her close. "Thank God you're safe."

"We got t-too cold." Sydney's teeth chattered as she talked. "I-I knew we couldn't s-stay. Leena n-needs to get somewhere w-warm, and fast."

Trey turned and held an arm out to his blue-lipped, red-nosed daughter. She slid off Tumbleweed and raced into his embrace. With both arms secure around his girls, he wasn't about to let them out of his sight. Not for a long time.

The rain had let up by the time Trey and the others met headlights on an old logging road south of Moses Meadows.

While Martin led Drifter, with a groaning Cooper slumped over him, Trey and Sydney bookended Leena. They met two sets of headlights and stopped. The horses' breaths spun in the beams.

Chuck jumped out of his tribal SUV and hurried to the group of riders. "You found him?" He took Drifter's reins.

"More like he found us." Martin eased out of the saddle.

Trey dismounted. "He's all yours."

Jim came around a rig pulling a horse trailer and handed Leena a steamy cup and a dry blanket. "Pam made you cocoa."

Trey handed Sydney one blanket and covered Leena with the other.

Chuck pulled Cooper off the horse, cuffed him, then read him his rights.

"I'm white," Cooper said, "you can't do a thing to me."

"You're an idiot." Chuck escorted him to his unit, then went back to the group.

Martin took Leena to Trey's truck and started the engine.

Standing in the beams of his headlights, Chuck took out his notebook and flipped to a blank page. "I'm glad you found him because the rain washed his tracks away. Anyhow, an Okanogan County trooper's on his way to get Cooper."

"You can't arrest him?" Trey asked.

"Nope, but I can detain him." Chuck turned to Sydney. "All right, tell me what happened." He took notes as she relayed every detail.

"You won't have to worry about him for a long time." Chuck closed his notebook.

"She won't have to worry about him ever again." Trey kissed her head. "I'm proud of you, honey."

CHAPTER 80

Saturday, September 23

From the landing of the southern staircase, Sydney shivered at the lodge's warm glow, moisture blurring her vision. She dabbed her eyes with a tissue. Free of migraines. Free of fear. And free of all her secrets. Ready to move forward in hope, rekindled faith, and a love that left her breathless.

Strings of white lights glimmered over the great room, and daisies and green-and-purple ribbon draped over the railings of both curved flights of steps and across the mantle. Below her, Pastor Jake stood in front of the fireplace. To his left, Trey beamed in his black Stetson and Western suit. His father, Beau Hardy, stood beside him, a look of pride on his face.

With a nod from the pastor, a friend of the family sang Blake Shelton's "God Gave Me You." On cue, Chad, Jim, and Rich escorted Trey's sister, Emmy, along with Pam and Leena down the steps over the gift shop and glided across a luminary-lined aisle.

June and Kimberly, giddy in their lilac-and-green dresses and white boots, sprinkled the steps and floor with daisy petals as they made their way to the bridesmaids.

Glenda turned to Sydney. "You look so beautiful. That vintage gown is perfect for you." With a quick hug, she said, "I've never been more proud to be your sister. I love you, honey."

"And I'm honored to be yours." She kissed her cheek. "I love you too."

Glenda took her hands. "Don't worry about the money. We'll work something out."

"Are you sure?" The offer released a clench in her chest.

Glenda nodded and gave her another light hug before taking Robert's arm and sashaying down the aisle in her green gown and beaded moccasins, holding a bouquet in various shades of purple.

Martin offered Sydney his elbow. "Creator gives us each a song. A woman's highest calling is to lead a man to open his heart. A man's highest calling is to protect his soulmate so she can walk the earth unharmed. I pray your song will unite you both with Grandfather." He kissed her hand. "Ready?"

Sydney smiled, admiring how striking he looked in his Pendleton vest and arrowhead bolo tie. "Thank you, Martin. For always being here for me. For your wisdom, and for loving me enough to be frank. For being by my side today." She nodded. "Ready." She lifted her gown, vintage cowboy boots taking the first stride toward the rest of her life.

With each calculated step, she took in the love radiating from her guests. Having Mandie, Nona, the hands, and Trey's family there to celebrate with them made her chest swell with bliss. She descended the steps, reflecting on how much God had blessed her.

Trey's jaw dropped and his eyes shimmered as they came around the arc of the staircase. A smile stretched across his face. He wiped an eye. *Oh . . . my.* Was the groom supposed to glow more than the bride? He'd never looked so handsome. Or sure of himself. Their eyes locked as she glided the last few feet to him. She kissed and released Martin, then entwined her fingers through Trey's, her heart picking up speed.

As Pastor Jake spoke about love and commitment, she thanked Creator for sending her a man who'd stuck with her and had been able to crack open her shell so she could trust again.

After they'd repeated their vows, Trey gave her a passionate kiss that left her winded. Then Martin sang a traditional wedding song while beating his hand drum. When the last soulful sound drifted from his lips, Glenda and Chuck laid a star quilt her auntie Marcie had made around Trey's and Sydney's shoulders and prayed a blessing over them.

When finished, she and Glenda hung the blanket on a rack. Trey summoned Sydney over to an odd-shaped, cloth-covered object in front of the gift shop.

Robert stepped into her path. "I'll do whatever it takes to keep this place going."

Sydney hugged him. "You better, Bobby. I'm countin' on you." She kissed his cheek and strode to her husband.

Trey waved Leena over, then addressed Sydney. "Why don't you unveil it?"

"What is it?" Sydney asked. What more could he give her?

"Your wedding gift from Leena and me."

Sydney's boots clicked the floor as she strode over to the covered item. The guests watched, their eyes holding anticipation. She pulled off the fabric cover and smiled at a long wooden sign hanging from a glossy seven-tined elk antler fixed to a brass easel.

"Seven Tine Guest Ranch, Sydney Hardy, Owner," Trey announced.

Everyone clapped and whooped.

Sydney inhaled a sharp breath. "Oh, my goodness, I love it. But . . ." She tapped her lips with her purple-painted nail. "There's something missing."

Trey peered at Leena, the corners of his mouth edging downward. "What?"

"Your and Leena's names."

Laughter danced around the room. Trey took her hand and twirled her around. "We can fix that, can't we, Leena?"

She giggled. "Yep."

Trey let go of Sydney and motioned to Robert, who handed him a guitar case with a big green bow on it. Leena's eyes grew wide. He handed her the case. "Welcome to the family, sweetheart."

Leena squealed and hugged them both, then took the case over to the couch by the big bay windows.

Trey held Sydney in his arms and swayed to the music. "All we have to do now is start from the bottom up. Your folks made this place theirs from humble beginnings, and now it's our turn to make it ours."

Beau Hardy cleared his throat, his wife, Vivienne, and two daughters by his side. All three were the images of runway models with sweet smiles and kind eyes. "Guess this is as good a time as any." He handed Trey an envelope. "Here are papers for one of our colts out of Very Smart Remedy. He should help start off your breeding business. I know he's not a Blue Valentine, but he's the best I've got." He tipped his hat to Sydney. "We can deliver him in the spring."

"I don't know what to say." Sydney pressed her hand to her chest. Her head spun with gratitude.

Vivienne hugged her. "Welcome to our family. Trey told us all about your hardships. If there is anything we can do . . ." She glanced at her husband with a look of compassion on her face, then turned back to Sydney. "Please let us know."

"That's incredibly kind of you. I will." Though no one could ever replace her parents, she looked forward to beginning her life with the Hardys.

Trey handed the papers back to his dad. "If you can hold on to these, I'd like to dance with my wife." He escorted her to the middle of the great room. "In the last few years, I've learned that every gift is a blessing from God. You, babe, are the greatest blessing in my life."

"I feel the same way about you." Her voice came out soft and tender.

He covered her lips with his. She slid an arm up his neck and pressed her body against his firm one.

The room cheered and heat tingled up her neck.

He kissed her again, lifted her up, and twirled her around. Hoots and hollers swirled through the lodge.

She threw back her head and giggled, then turned solemn as he set her down.

"What's wrong?"

"I didn't get you anything. I thought—"

He put a finger to her lips. "Your love is all I need."

She traced her finger down his smooth jaw. "That's all, huh? Nothing else?"

"Well, what did you have in mind?"

She nestled her face in his neck. "A little boy. Just like you," she whispered. She clung to him and her belief of new beginnings.

ACKNOWLEDGMENTS

A special thanks to Jennifer Uhlarik and the Iron Stream Fiction family for believing in this story of healing and second chances for battered women. To Linda Yezak, my editor, for stretching my limits and encouraging me to dig deep and help this story honor my niece who died at the hands of her abusive husband. Thanks to Susan Cornell, my copy editor, for making the pages shine. And thanks to Linda Glaz, my agent, for taking a chance on me.

There are so many people who helped make this story authentic. Thanks to Dave McClure for his insight on cattle ranching, taking me for a tour of his ranch in the Nespelem Valley, and reading through the manuscript to make sure it rang true; Dr. Charlie McCraigie, DVM, for her expertise in horse health care; Paul Bowden, chief of police, Coulee Dam PD; Charli Knight, Colville tribal attorney; Joel Boyd, prior tribal PD and Tribal Council; and Jon Simmons for helping me understand county and tribal law and the foster care system; Sherwin Womer, Colville tribal firefighter, for his help with structure fires; and John Guarisco, Realtor, for his assistance with real estate.

Debra Whiting Alexander and Linda Jacobs have blessed me with their feedback from initial reads. Thanks for your insight and willingness to help make this story touch hearts.

I'm incredibly grateful for my husband, Joe, who supports my writing dreams. He listens, answers questions, and cheers me on. God has richly blessed me with an incredible life partner. I love you, honey!

Most importantly, I want to thank God for inspiring me to write stories from the heart, for giving me the best writing community in Women Writing the West, and for giving me the means to write for Him.

DISCUSSION QUESTIONS

1. Why do you think it's easy for one lie to lead to another? Do you think it's ever acceptable to keep secrets?
2. What role can fear play in our lives?
3. Sometimes when we care about something so deeply, we do what it takes to nurture and keep it alive. At first, Sydney was not willing to sell the multigenerational guest ranch. But as time went on, she changed her mind. Why was she willing to let the Seven Tine go?
4. Have you ever loved someone so much you would protect them at all costs? How do you think Sydney felt when Cooper threatened Leena? How do you think Trey felt when Cooper abducted his family?
5. Sydney is afraid to trust and open herself up to Trey because of her past domestic violence experience. She pushes him away at times due to fear of being hurt again. What are signs of abuse? If you know someone you suspect is being abused, how can you help them?
6. Why do you think people turn to violence?
7. Most women are terrified to leave their abuser. Why do you think it's hard for them to leave their abusive relationships?
8. What are resources in your area to help victims of abuse?
9. What role do you think foster parenting can play in a child's life? Do you know any foster parents? What has been their experience?
10. What role does forgiveness play in our lives?
11. What is a source of hope for you?

A NOTE FROM THE AUTHOR

This book was extremely hard for me to write. It was inspired by the murder of my niece. In her early twenties, she married her abuser and within a few years he had beaten her to death.

I wanted to write a story not only to help me heal from the violent crime but to help women who are in a destructive relationship. Abuse, whether emotional, mental, physical, financial, sexual, or spiritual, is never love. Violence is selfish manipulation. It steals the victim's self-worth and isolates them from family and friends. It lies. Deceives. Betrays.

Friends, do you know how much Creator God loves and values you? I hope you'll take the time to discover how important you are to Him.

So let's talk about what love is.

Love is kind, tender, patient, truthful, respectful, selfless, and humble. Love uplifts and encourages. It never tears a person down.

I'd like to encourage you to recognize the difference of what love is and isn't and to seek help if you are in an abusive relationship.

https://www.thehotline.org/

OTHER BOOKS BY CARMEN PEONE

Contemporary
Girl Warrior

True to Heart Trilogy—Historical
Change of Heart
Heart of Courage
Heart of Passion

Gardner Sibling Trilogy—Historical
Delbert's Weir
Hannah's Journey
Lillian's Legacy

**For information on the author's young adult books and
curriculum and to connect with her,
see Carmen Peone's website:**
https://carmenpeone.com/books/curriculum-young-adult-
workbook-series/